"...fast-paced with thrilling action sequences and plenty of suspense..."

★ ★ ★ ★ ★

Literary Portals

"It was a perfect balance of serious and sweet— and to top it off, it delivers everything it hints at!"

★ ★ ★ ★ ★

Feather Tone Reviews

PRAISE FOR

UNIQUE

"...loving this book as much, if not more than, the first book."

★ ★ ★ ★ ★

Feather Tone Reviews

"It's non stop action, from the start till the end. I feel like I didn't even blink till the last page."

★ ★ ★ ★ ★

Diary of a Wannabe Writer

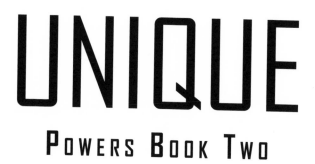

UNIQUE

POWERS BOOK TWO

STARR Z. DAVIES

PANGEA BOOKS

Starr @ Pangea Books
PangeaBooks.online
www.starrzdavies.com

Book Layout ©2020 Pangea Books

Cover Design by Fay Lane Graphics

Unique / Starr Z. Davies. -- 2nd ed.

1] Survival Fiction 2] Superheroes 3] Post-apocolyptic 4] Coming of Age

ISBN 978-0-578-62554-6

For my son, Grifynn, whose response to puzzling theories is an upbeat, "Maybe!" that would make Ugene proud.

UNIQUE | noun | u·nique | yoo-nēk : distinguishable from all others in its class, the only specimen of its kind, of a person with remarkable or extraordinary features.

Part One

"THE DIRECTORATE IS PROUD TO PARTNER WITH Paragon as it releases a groundbreaking vaccination, IVD Veritax. Elpis is still in danger. Regression remains a serious threat to our security. But with IVD Veritax, we can work toward eliminating that danger. The partnership will present the citizens of Elpis with opportunity as we have never seen before—a way to help boost the Powers of regressing citizens and take us toward a better, brighter future."

~ Directorate Chief Seaduss
4:45 p.m. – Two Days Ago

1

THIS ISN'T WHAT I WANTED. I WANTED TO DO THE RIGHT thing, to help people, but now I can't help but question just what the right thing is.

I've lied.

I've broken promises.

I've failed more people than I would like to count—though I could, and the number would be too many.

And for what?

This isn't freedom.

2

THE CLEAN, CRISP SCENT OF EARTH AND STONE FILLS
the small room I've been living in for what I can only assume to be
days. I haven't felt the warmth of the sun or watched the stars for so
long and I yearn for their comfort. Occasionally, I catch a whiff of
rotten eggs, but the smell is so fleeting and rare I'm not certain if it's
real.

Where am I? This is a prison. Did we even escape Paragon? Maybe
this is all part of the same simulation, giving us hope then isolating us
to see how we react.

Since waking up here, I've only spoken to two people. A woman
who told me through the door in a very reassuring tone that I would
be released soon. They simply had to make sure that everyone was
safe, and with so many people it could take a while. I asked her a
million other questions, but she didn't answer any of them. Instead,
she offered the same assurances that all would be revealed soon.

The second person is the guy who delivers the meals. But he
doesn't say any more than, "It won't be much longer." Sometimes, I
swear I can hear the sympathy in his voice. Am I imagining it?

The last thing I remember is that we escaped Paragon and I
followed the address Mom gave me to Lettuce Eat, where for nearly
two days Harvey gave us food and a place to rest while he arranged
our escort to safety. Those of us who remained—forty-two of us
out of more than one hundred—climbed into the back of a cold
transport truck on the second day. Harvey reassured us that we were
being taken to a safer location and that my mom would meet with me

soon.

But then I woke up here, in this cell. Alone.

Did he sell us out to Paragon?

Or maybe none of it actually happened.

I lay on my single bed, atop worn flannel sheets, and run my fingers along the smooth gray stone walls of the cell, carved out with Powered hands. The bed and a toilet are the only furnishings. The door is made of reinforced steel with a small window revealing a brightly lit stone hallway and a panel in the center of the door where the food comes in. More than once, I've tried forcing it open by pushing on it, or digging at the cracks until my fingers ache. It never budges.

Projecting in a small square on the wall, the Elpis News is the only station—a station Bianca's dad operates. The famous newscaster, Elpida Theus's, smooth, sand-colored face and perfectly styled golden hair is my primary source of contact with any form of life. Paragon has already rebuilt the destroyed lower levels of the tower to operational status, and they have called the "released" subjects to return. Not that anyone will. We are either locked in this place or too scared to risk returning.

"Daily operations are returning to normal," Elpida reports from the lobby of the building, which is still under construction.

Other reports, released by Directorate Chief Seaduss, remind the citizens that regression is a looming threat and that the eastern boroughs, particularly Pax, have seen a significant spike in crime and terrorist activity. Are the reports real? Can I trust that any of this is real?

It's exhausting, and these questions often put me to sleep.

When I sleep, I have nightmares about Dad, Bianca, and Celeste dying all over again. The other test subjects who once counted on me to get them to safety now crowd around me en masse, calling me a failure, a fraud, a worthless traitor. Of all the wounds I've sustained since arriving at Paragon, I have learned that words are the most cutting of all—and they take so much longer to heal.

My waking hours are plagued with worry about those who escaped with me and made it to Harvey's place. Where is everyone? Where am I? So many questions tumble through my head that I try making a list, but as the days blend together that list begins to muddle, and I have nothing on which to write my thoughts. I can't decide what's real anymore.

Why did my mom send me here? Where *is* here?

Not for the first time, I try to reach out with my mind and see if Madison is out there somewhere. Not that I can use Telepathy, but my hope is that, if she can sense me reaching out, she will find a way to connect.

And not for the first time, nothing comes back. All my life, I'd been isolated in a crowd of people and I couldn't imagine anything worse.

Now I can.

3

THE WHOOSH OF THE DOOR OPENING STIRS ME. I ROLL over on the bed just in time to see the door disappear into the wall. Fear makes my muscles tense, ready to act. Maybe, if I'm fast enough, I can get out of the room. But the man who walks through is huge, with wide shoulders and a neck thicker than my thighs. Clearly a Strongarm. Any hope of getting past him quickly evaporates.

"Ugene Powers?" he asks, his voice deep.

My fingers wrap around the edge of the bed, heart pounding. I nod.

"Follow me," he says. "And don't try to run. You won't get far."

An overwhelming need for human interaction pushes me to my feet, paired with the fear that he would leave, and the door would close again. I follow close to him—probably closer than he would like—as he escorts me down a set of metal steps to the next level.

He gazes at me from the corner of his eyes as we descend. "We don't mean you harm. All of this is just standard safety protocol."

Safety. What a joke. I've been locked in that room for days. I know exactly what he can do with his safety precaution.

"What's your name?" I ask, struggling to keep up with his faster strides. It's been a few days since I've done much more than pace the cell.

He doesn't answer. The guy is like a brick wall, but I really want him to engage somehow in conversation. No one has talked to me in days.

We stop at an arching stone doorway and he waves me in. Unlike the cell I've been in for the last few days, this room is far more comfortable. A worn-out, patchwork-repaired sofa rests against one wall, and beside it, a mismatched chair.

This is definitely not Paragon.

The only light in the room comes from the three lamps. One between the sofa and chair, one in a far corner, and one on the desk against the opposite corner. A woman with blonde hair pulled back in a severe ponytail perches on the edge of the desk, facing the room. We lock gazes, and something about her teases my memory.

"Do I know you?" I ask.

She shakes her head, making the straight tail wag. "Willow Barnes. I highly doubt we've met before. I would remember you, Ugene."

Not really sure what that means.

Willow hops off the desk and approaches, holding out her hand. The moment she moves I see the slender, older man sitting behind the desk, frowning at an old computer as he scrolls through the contents. His white coat is wrinkled. He can't be much older than my dad, but his sandy hair is peppered with silver.

The memory of Dad makes me freeze, chest clenching.

Willow takes her hand back. "Okay." Her gaze follows mine to the older man. "That's Doc. He looks after all of us."

"All of who? Who are you? Where are we?"

"Have a seat, Ugene," Willow says, motioning to the sofa.

It doesn't feel like a request, so I obey and move to sit on the sofa. It's a little lumpy, but still more comfortable than my bed. Willow perches on the edge of the chair, resting her forearms on her knees.

"You have a lot of questions, I'm sure," she says.

"Understatement of the year," I mumble, glancing again at the old Doc. Even *he* seems familiar.

"I want to explain a little bit about where you are before we get into your questions," Willow says, drawing my attention back to her. "We call this place The Shield."

I can't help but snort. Confinement has made my cynicism a touch sharp.

"It exists in a secure location outside of Elpis, away from the prying eyes of the Directorate," she continues as if nothing is out of the ordinary. "Doc and I make a point of collecting people the Directorate targets and offering them a safe space to live. When Harvey contacted us about your group, we jumped at the chance to help you."

"Wait, help? Is that what you call this?" I wave around the room, though it isn't the cell I'm used to.

"I understand why you would distrust us, Mr. Powers," she says calmly. "But I can assure you if we hadn't helped you would be back in Paragon already."

"It's Ugene, not Mr. Powers." Reminds me too much of my dad.

"Ugene." She nods. "My job, along with Chase, the man who escorted you, is to make sure everyone inside The Shield is protected. Doc oversees research and the medical team."

I flinch back when she says research. Willow notices.

"It isn't what you think," she reassures me. "Our research is more about what Paragon and the Directorate are up to, deciphering their plans. That sort of thing. We won't ever subject you to any form of testing and everything you do here is completely voluntary. Though we would love it if everyone found some way to pitch in to help The Shield operate more smoothly."

Voluntary. I want to believe her but being locked in a cell doesn't really leave me with a feeling of comfort.

"Why did you lock us all up? And how did we even get here?"

"I know the last thing you wanted was to be put into another cell, but we had no choice," Willow says. "We needed to assess each of you individually against the potential risk you could pose to the safety of the people living here. It's just how things are done. Everyone goes through the same process."

Somehow, none of this is reassuring.

"As far as how you arrived at The Shield, we took extra safety precautions with a group your size. To protect everyone here, we must make sure that new members don't know where we are located. So we used sleeping gas once you were all safely in the transport truck."

"Afraid one of us is a spy or something?" My words drip with sarcasm, and I'm not sure if I mean them to or not.

Willow's lips thin into a line, and she straightens.

My eyes widen. "You are."

"It wouldn't be the first time," she says, and I can hear the anger simmering in her voice. "And yes, we do have reason to believe that someone in your group is a spy from Paragon, working with the Directorate. I trust I can tell you this, based on what others have told me about you. They see you as their leader."

I grimace. I would like to say they can trust everyone who escaped, but honestly, I only know a handful of them.

"Why would a spy be sent here?" I ask.

"The Directorate has been hunting us down for years," Doc says. "We don't agree with most of their policies, which makes us a threat."

"So, we aren't in Elpis," I say, trying to piece some of this together. "But I thought we couldn't exist outside the city."

"That's what the Directorate would like you to believe," Doc says. "But as you can see, we're doing just fine."

Just another Directorate scare tactic. Figures. "Well, I don't see, actually," I say, feeling the heat of days of anger building. "I've been locked in a cell like a prisoner. Why should I believe you?"

Willow heaves a sigh and scrubs a hand over her face, gazing at Doc. He doesn't seem to notice, so she turns her attention back to me. The tension in her shoulders is obvious.

"We are sorry about the conditions," she finally says. "It doesn't usually take more than a day or two for intake, but there are so many of you, and not everyone has been…compliant."

I wince. "Don't say that word."

"What…compliant? Why?"

"If you had any idea what we've been through, what Paragon put us through during their trials, you'd understand."

"We do know what you've been through—*I* know what you've been through." Willow scratches at her arm, and I notice a small incision scar. "I was in there just like you. I would have died in there if it hadn't been for Doc." She shifts, raising her chin up as she does. "I've heard a lot about you. I know you are the one who led the others out of Paragon. We are prepared to release you to your quarters if you can answer a few questions for us."

Every part of me wants to resist. This feels an awful lot like being used again. Same problem, different devil. But do I really have a choice?

I nod.

"How did you escape?" Willow asks.

"If you talked to the others, you already know," I answer, but Willow crosses her arms and I wonder if the others did tell her anything. "Didn't anyone else explain it?"

"Sort of," Willow says. "Most of them couldn't really explain what happened. Just that they followed your lead. Impressive, since half of them couldn't even tell me your name, and the half who could, wouldn't tell me anything else about you."

I bite the inside of my cheek to keep from grinning. Good to know I'm not the only one who doesn't trust these people.

"So? How did you do it?"

"You don't need Powers to have brains," I say, quoting my old biology teacher, Mr. Springer.

Willow raises her brows impatiently.

I huff out a sigh. "We found a weak spot in the system. A window that allowed us to get out of the simulation into one of their PSECT rooms. From there it was just a matter of getting out of the building. We lost a lot of people to their guards on the way out."

"Do you know how we can access one of these PSECT rooms?"

I shake my head. "Not exactly. I could probably show you where it is on a map of the building, but…" Grief clenches my throat. "But Bianca was the one who accessed it."

Willow glances at Doc, who consults the computer, then shakes his head. Willow turns her attention back to me. "Where is she now?"

My jaw twitches and I struggle to pull the word to the surface. It comes out as a croak. "Dead."

"Are you sure?"

Is she serious? Anger burns through my veins, and every muscle in my body tenses almost painfully. I clench my hands into fists. My voice takes on a dangerous edge. "I held her in my arms when she took her last breath. So yeah. I'm sure."

"I'm sorry," Willow says, but the apology feels stale to me. "Do you know why Paragon was interested in you?"

My back stiffens. "Yes."

Willow doesn't say anything else. Her blue eyes pierce me, waiting for me to say more.

Will they use me as Paragon did? Why do they want to know? "I know exactly why Paragon is interested in me." I want to flee, but there's nowhere to go. I'm just as trapped as I was in Paragon. Instead, I pace the rug. "I'm…unique." God, I hate that word. "I have no Powers. None at all. And they used my test results and blood and spinal fluid as a base against other subjects so they could find a way to enhance Powers. They used other subjects; expendables they could inject with a serum that *killed* them."

Willow blocks my path. Is that excitement in her eyes? "Do you have proof of this?"

"Do you think I'm an idiot? I wouldn't have left without something. But it's encrypted."

Willow closes her eyes and actually smiles. When she opens them, her blues bore into my soul. "Where is it?"

I shake my head and step back. "Lock me back up. I'm not handing it over." Not that I could. Miller has it. Where is he? "I know what that information is worth, and I won't give it up. Paragon needs to be exposed."

"What do you think we're trying to do?" Willow asks. Her hand falls on my arm, but I jerk away. "Paragon is only a piece in a much larger puzzle. Ugene, the Protectorate is dedicated to exposing the truth and balancing things out in Elpis. Directorate Chief Seaduss has a plan, and we are trying to figure out what it is. Those in control need to be removed, and we need information like yours to make it a reality."

I *have* met this woman before. And I remember exactly where.

Career Day feels like so long ago, years. So much has happened since I stepped off the bus, but I definitely remember Willow being there. She was part of the group of protesters outside the Convention Center. She was the one who put that flyer in my hands. Maybe she's telling me the truth now. Maybe she does want to help, but after everything I've been through, I find it hard to trust anyone.

"Ugene, please." The tone she uses sounds patient, but her demeanor reflects the opposite. "Your information could help us link Paragon to the Directorate, and if we do that, we can tear down the entire broken system."

I cross my arms over my chest and stand as straight as I can.

Willow huffs, turning to Doc, hands on her hips.

I follow her gaze to him, and he's staring straight at me like he can see through me. Or into me. The penetrating gaze makes me uncomfortable. I lift my chin, even though he makes me want to squirm.

"Fine," Willow says, at last, drawing my attention back to her. She drops her hands to her sides and starts toward the door. "Let's get you to your quarters then. This way."

Once again, Doc's gaze draws me in, locked in place. When I break free, I have to sprint to catch up to Willow.

"You're a Telepath," I say when I match pace with her.

"Sort of," she says.

The big Somatic—Chase, I think she called him—follows us a few paces behind. Where Willow's steps are silent, Chase makes up for it with the loud thump of his boots against the smooth stone floor.

"What do you mean, sort of?" I ask as we descend a metal staircase.

"I mean sort of," she says tersely.

Willow stares at me, weighing me, sizing me up.

"So, what is the Protectorate, anyway?" I ask when we reach a floor marked out as Level VII. "I've never heard of it before."

"Well, you wouldn't have, would you?" Willow says. "The Directorate wouldn't want the citizens of Elpis knowing we exist. Plus, if we're doing our jobs right, you would only hear of us when you need us."

People in ordinary street clothes move along the halls with purpose as I follow Willow down a tunnel. I don't recognize anyone, but that doesn't mean any of them aren't from our group.

"So where were you when I needed you after Career Day?" I ask. "Where were you when the Directorate started kicking down doors and forcing people like Leo into Paragon's program?"

Willow's expression shifts from stoic to sad. The slope of her shoulders swings downward ever so slightly. When she speaks, her voice is more tender than it has been so far. "We did our best to fight the Proposition, and when it passed, we struggled to keep up with the speed of the Directorate. They mobilized the Department of Military Affairs faster than we anticipated." Willow shakes her head, and the ponytail whips behind her. Then she stops abruptly, staring at the ground. "We lost good people during the waves of arrests."

Chase rests a large hand on her narrow shoulder. I jump, forgetting that he still lumbers behind us. Willow looks up at him, forcing a smile, and her blue eyes shimmer with unshed tears.

I know that look. I've worn it myself before. She blames herself for failing them.

Willow blinks, and the tears disappear, her expression stoic once again. We resume the march as Willow guides the way through a steel door that leads into a rounded tunnel lined with rusting steel walls. Reinforcement rings support the weight of the walls around them. For some reason, this tunnel fills me with anxiety.

"What about my friends?" I ask, trying to ignore the knots forming in my stomach. "When will they be released? What about Enid?"

Willow grimaces and nods. "She hasn't left her quarters since her release. She refuses to say anything more until she sees you."

"And Miller?" I ask. Last time I saw him, he was barely conscious, suffering from a shot he took for me. "He was shot. Is he okay?"

Chase speaks behind us. "I remember him. The John Doe. He's in medical. Dr. Lydia has taken care of him."

"But is he okay?" I ask again. What if they scan him and find the drive? I can't give anything away. Not yet.

Willow stops and turns to me. "He will be okay, but his injuries are…serious."

"But it was just a shot," I say.

Willow rubs at her arm, uncertain. "Somehow, he lost his Power."

"Can I see him?"

Willow and Chase exchange unreadable glances, then Willow nods at me and turns up a tunnel. I rush to catch up on her heels. If that drive in his arm falls into the wrong hands, we could lose whatever leverage we might have.

4

THE SHIELD ISN'T QUITE THE MAZE OF CORRIDORS
like Paragon, but I still feel a little lost. Much like in Paragon, each
tunnel looks much like the other. Willow knows exactly where she's
going, and her steps are not in the least bit hesitant.

The stone tunnels have a very distinct smell like a combination
of dirt and metal, mingling with the occasional scent of orange oil.
Polished wooden planks cover the stone walls of the tunnels. Small
tripod lights sit in recesses atop the wooden walls, fanning across the
stone ceiling and filling the spaces with a comfortable light.

The whole atmosphere reminds me of those dank underground
lairs in superhero movies. Either the hero or the villain is stashed
away in an underground lair to help avoid detection by the outside
world. It allows access to some natural resources while offering a
natural stone barrier that most powers couldn't penetrate. Which is
the Protectorate—hero or villain? And do these walls offer that sort
of protection?

Every ten feet or so, another room branches off. Some have
polished wood doors, others steel. It's a curious place.

The Shield isn't empty of people, either. Occasionally, someone
will pass and nod politely or give Willow a status report: the water
filters are no longer backing up; a batch of crops failed overnight;
the kitchen flue system is clogged. Willow either says thanks or
directs them to someone else to handle the problem. Such mundane
problems.

A big red plus sign painted above a wide doorway reads:

MEDICAL.

The space spills into a massive chamber as we march through the doorway. Beds form rows all around the room, each with a privacy curtain—though most of them are open. Less than a handful of beds have occupants. How many of them are from our group? Would I recognize any of them if they were?

A woman with dark, cropped hair approaches Willow as we enter. She hands a glass tablet to Willow and I try to peek at it, but Willow moves it just enough to prevent me from peeking.

"Dr. Lydia, this is Ugene," Willow says as she reads the tablet. "He's here for the PTPD patient."

I frown. "What's PTPD?"

"In a minute," Dr. Lydia says, waving me off as her focus remains on Willow. "I have to press this again. I strongly suggest you pull Jayme from rotation. His condition is progressing."

"It's too late," Willow says with a sigh, handing the tablet back to Dr. Lydia. "He's already out on rotation. And I highly doubt we could keep him here if we wanted to anyway. You know him."

The conversation is somewhat fascinating and were I not so eager to see Miller I would care a little more. Still, they carry on as if I'm not right here.

"Does he know?" Dr. Lydia asks.

Willow's lips thin. "We will talk about this in a minute. Can you talk to Ugene about the PTPD patient?"

Dr. Lydia takes the tablet and tucks it under her arm, finally acknowledging me, albeit grudgingly. "You are his friend?"

"Miller? Yes." Despite betraying us to Paragon in exchange for information about Murphy, Miller admitted that he considers me a friend. Since he took that bullet for me during the escape, my anger about the betrayal has dissipated…mostly. "What's PTPD?"

"Post-Traumatic Powerloss Depression," Dr. Lydia says. The creases on her forehead wrinkle up, appearing out of place for someone who can't be much older than thirty. "He came in with a gunshot wound, but the shock his body underwent wasn't from a bullet. We've never seen anything quite like this, though we have seen people who lost their Power before. Most of those cases have been through injection or extreme stress. Was he injected with anything that you know of?"

I shake my head. How much should I tell them? "He jumped in front of that bullet for me. Then he fell to the floor and started seizing, thrashing. I thought he was dying. I…I think that whatever took his Powers was in that bullet."

"What?" Willow's eyes widen, her small frame tensing. She clutches her fists at her sides.

"Are you certain?" Dr. Lydia asks.

If these people are fighting against those bullets, they have a right to know. "Pretty certain. I mean, I can't imagine what else it would have been."

"Willow…" Dr. Lydia gives her a meaningful glance, and there is something I'm missing here.

"I need to contact the team," Willow says, then adds before darting out of the room, "I'll send someone to escort Ugene to his quarters."

"Where is Miller?" I ask. Despite my growing curiosity surrounding that whole situation, I am still here for a reason. "I want to see him."

"I'll take you to him, but you need to understand something first," Dr. Lydia says, now hugging the tablet against her chest. "Your friend isn't well. Miller's reaction to losing his Powers is no different from that of anyone else. Physically, his body is fine. He's healed. But his mind is sort of…incomplete. Splintered. No one handles it well."

I frown. "How often do people lose Powers around here?"

"Not very," she says, glancing over her shoulder momentarily, then lowers her voice. "They say that having their Powers removed is like having a piece of their soul ripped out like they're broken. The depression that these victims typically suffer is different from what we know. And thoughts of death are not uncommon, and often extreme. This Miller isn't the guy you knew. He will be more withdrawn, even in a crowd of people."

"He was always that way," I say, smirking and making a lame

attempt at humor to lighten the situation. It falls flat.

Dr. Lydia shakes her head. "No, Ugene. This will be worse. I usually recommend counseling for patients like this. He won't eat. The sooner we can get him back into everyday life, the sooner he will recover." Dr. Lydia places a warm, reassuring hand on my arm. "He can get through this, but he will need his friends."

I nod dumbly. What am I supposed to do for him? "If I can get him up, is he free to leave?"

"Yes, but he will have to be with someone at all times, and he will be kept under observation." Dr. Lydia offers a consoling smile. "This way."

I follow Dr. Lydia along the rows of beds to Miller's. The curtains are drawn back so he can easily be observed no matter where the doctor is in the medical bay. She leaves the two of us alone.

"Hey, man," I say when I reach the edge of the bed.

His eyes are open, staring at the ceiling. Seeing the weakened state of him, a sense of guilt turns my stomach. How could I suspect this guy is a spy? He doesn't even look like he's eaten in days. He either isn't the spy, or he's a really good method actor.

My voice generates no reaction in him. Does he blame me for what happened to him? Is he angry? I lick my dry lips and sit on the edge of his bed, careful of the IV going into his arm.

"Miller?" What can I possibly say? What do I hope to gain here? The bandage over the healed wound in his shoulder makes my throat tighten. "I heard what happened. I…" The whole situation puts me at a loss for words.

"Don't blame yourself," Miller says, his voice hoarse, emotionless.

I open my mouth but telling him he didn't need to jump in front of that bullet for me would only rub salt in the wound. He's like me now. Powerless. I fall into silence, staring at the monitor sharing his vitals. They all seem normal.

The two of us sit like this for a while, avoiding looking at each other. I know I should say something, but what? What could possibly make up for this?

Miller rolls on his side, his back to me. Steady breathing makes his side rise and fall. I wait for him to say something or to roll back over, but he doesn't budge.

"You still awake?" I ask.

"Only because you keep talking," Miller mumbles.

"I can't even begin to imagine what you're going through right now," I say. "But don't forget why you wanted out of Paragon in the first place. Do you think this is what Murphy would want you to do?"

He doesn't move. I find it hard to reconcile this lump with the Miller I know.

"Our purpose hasn't changed, Miller."

Still, he does nothing.

"Come on, man," I say in the most commanding voice I can muster. I cross my arms beside the bed. "Get up."

"Get lost."

"I'm not moving until you get out of this bed and come with me. I'll stay until you get so annoyed you leave the room just to escape me if that's what it takes."

Miller half-shrugs. I have no idea who this guy is. Miller is stubborn and strong and blunt to the point it's often painful. He isn't the guy that lies around in bed feeling sorry for himself.

"You still have it?" I ask.

"Yeah."

"Good." I noticeably relax. We still have an ace in the hole.

Miller flops his arm out toward me, staring in the other direction. "Take it."

I push his arm back over his body again. "Not now. Not here."

Maybe having it with him will give Miller a reason to stick around and not consider death too seriously, as Dr. Lydia warned.

Miller doesn't respond. He just lays with his back to me. What do I do, drag him out of the bed?

"Miller...talk to me. Please."

His breathing is shaky as he rolls on his back. Still, he refuses to look me in the eye. I can almost hear him swallow the lump in his throat. "Losing my Powers... It's the most painful thing I've ever experienced."

I have no idea what losing a Power is like. I never had one to lose. But the misery in Miller is clear. I hate seeing my friends suffer. I hate seeing *anyone* suffer.

Everything inside of me is in a vice grip. How could Paragon do this to anyone? I feel like I might be sick. My blood heats up just thinking about it.

"It hurt worse than all the tests. Worse than...than losing Murph. I wanted to die." Miller's voice quivers. "My insides were on fire and something inside of me was trying to rip out."

Anger boils hot inside of me, like a volcano ready to erupt, one prepared to burn Paragon to the ground.

Miller licks his dry lips, his voice strained so tight I can hear him fighting off tears as he continues. "The last thing I remember is the pain. Then I woke up here."

To my surprise, Miller breaks down and starts crying, smothering the grief by pressing his hands to his face. Seeing someone so tough break down like this makes my stomach twist and only adds fuel to the inferno burning in my veins. I do the only thing I can think to do. I lay a gentle but firm grip on his nearest shoulder and just hold it there as he struggles to collect himself. Dr. Lydia is right. Miller needs counseling.

I rub my free hand over my mess of hair like the action can shake answers free. The reality of this entire situation presses down on my shoulders. I have the drive, with the encrypted video files. But even if I could get them unlocked, what would I do with them against Paragon? Especially if Paragon is in the Directorate's pocket—or the other way around. I can't broadcast it because the Directorate has control of the media. I'm well aware of this because Bianca's dad is in charge of the network.

Miller is staring at me now, his tears quickly coming to heel. Is he looking for an explanation? No. Miller wouldn't just assume I know anything more than he does. He's waiting for me to say or do something clever.

"I'm sorry." It's the best I can offer. "If I knew how to reverse what they did to you, I would."

He nods. Miller knows me well enough to realize that it's true.

"Look." I pull my hand away from his shoulder. "I won't pretend to understand what you're going through, but this…" I wave a hand from his head to his feet. "This isn't you. The Miller I know wouldn't be able to stay still for this long. You wanted to bring all of Paragon down, but you can't do that from a bed. You wanted to find Murphy. He's alive out there somewhere, Miller. You said so yourself. You lost your Powers, but you can still find him—we can find him." I hold out a hand. "Time to get up."

Miller stares at my hand for so long I'm afraid he will refuse. But then he grasps my hand feebly. He still seems reluctant, but at least he's sitting up now. I pull him to his feet, but he's been bedridden for so long his face pales from the sudden movement. He stumbles a step to the side, catching himself on the edge of the bed, and I jump forward to help steady him.

Miller pulls the IV out of his arm and drops it on the bed. I slide his arm over my shoulder and help him toward the exit. Miller isn't out of the woods yet, but at least he is up. That's a start.

Dr. Lydia meets my gaze as we pass her at a bed, and she nods.

Dr. Cass will suffer for everything she's done. I don't know how yet, but I will stop her.

5

MILLER AND I STEP INTO THE HALLWAY AND NEARLY
collide with a girl our age I definitely don't recognize. Sho stops at her
side, and a smile splits his round face.

"Man am I relieved to see you," Sho says. "I tried Locating you
a couple times but didn't have much luck. Worried me a little, if I'm
being honest. But Lily reassured me that you were fine."

He doesn't need to explain for me to understand what he means
by Locate. Sho can use his Echolocation to find people who are close
to him. He did it in the first Survival test at Paragon.

"Lily?" I ask.

"Sorry." Sho nudges almost playfully at the girl beside him. "This
is Lily. She's been here for a couple months now."

Lily's smile splits her round, alabaster face, making the corners
of her eyes scrunch up. She holds out her hand. "I've heard quite a
bit about you from Sho. It's great to finally meet the man behind the
legend."

I scoff, "Legend. Clearly, he's been telling lies."

Lily's pretty, in a simple way. Her dark eyes have the same almond
shape as Sho's, and her black hair is thin, straight, and shiny. "Maybe,"
she teases.

I shake her hand, and the moment our hands touch her eyes
adopt a half-glazed look. Suddenly, she jerks her hand out of mine
and wipes it against her shirt. *What just happened?* It reminds me a little
of when Michael first touched me at Paragon, and it nearly sent him
into shock. *But now Michael is gone.* Forrest took him away and I can

only assume Michael was injected with an experimental serum. More than likely, he didn't survive.

"Sorry," she mutters, wiping tears from her eyes before they have a chance to fall. "Willow asked me to see you to your quarters."

"And I couldn't resist tagging along," Sho adds.

Miller grumbles something I can't quite decipher.

Lily leads the way through The Shield.

"Have you seen any of the others?" I ask as Miller and I follow the two of them.

"Sure. Boyd has taken a liking to the greenhouse. He spends most of his time there. Enid pops in for meals but not much else." Sho scrubs a hand through his spikey black hair. "Leo...well, he mostly keeps to himself."

I frown. Leo and Mo were best friends since year two of school, but Mo died during our escape. It can't have been easy for Leo to deal with losing his best friend. I know it isn't for me. Bianca and Celeste's deaths weigh heavy on me.

A group of children races past on their way out of the structure back into the main tunnels, laughing and squealing in delight.

"There was a girl from Rosie's group," Sho says. "She was out before me. We talked briefly, but she said something about being recruited for some top-secret mission. I haven't seen her since."

"When was that?" I ask, but it isn't the question my mind is stuck on. Top-secret missions... What is the Protectorate doing? Are they using us as fodder for their purposes?

Sho scratches at his week-old stubble. "Um, two days ago, I think?"

"The security process seems worse than it really is," Lily says. Her voice is just as small as she is. "I went through it. We all did."

The glare I shoot at her must be something bad because she shifts a little closer to Sho.

"It's really not bad here, Ugene," Sho says.

I can't help but wonder: Is he the spy? Making friends with someone in the Protectorate so quickly does make him appear suspicious.

"The people are nice," Sho says. "The food is better than I would have expected, and they don't make us throw ourselves into tests every day."

"No, instead they lock us in cells without any contact for days," I say tersely. "And then recruit us for top-secret missions that are who-knows how dangerous. It feels like a different sort of prison."

"This isn't a prison." Sho waves a hand around. "You're free to go wherever you want. Our rooms don't lock us in every night. No one is out to get anyone else. You can do whatever you want, whenever you want."

"Sounds peachy," Miller says, his tone weaker but reflecting my own feelings.

"When's the last time any of you were outside?" I ask.

Sho falls silent. Lily's lips compress as we enter a new tunnel.

I just nod. *As I expected. No one has been outside.*

Rectangular doorways appear in perfect symmetry along the new tunnel, each door roughly every ten feet. I peer through an open doorway as we pass, where a table and chairs wait with personal items, plates, and food.

"Where are we?" I ask.

"Willow says before Atmos destroyed the world, this was an old military base, abandoned even then," Lily says. "We transformed the space into living quarters. Or, at least, the founders of The Shield did."

The tunnel opens into a massive underground silo. Steel bridges crisscross from one side to the other; some lead to ascending and descending staircases. All along the walls, I see level after level of living quarters. People walk across the bridges much like anyone else would walk the streets in the city. This is just…life.

"And this place is safe?" I ask. "I mean, I thought these old places were bursting with radioactive contamination."

Lily smirks. "And where did you hear that?"

School history lessons sanctioned by the Directorate. Another lie.

Just how dangerous is the world outside Elpis? Is it dangerous at all?

And moreover, if a place like The Shield can exist, are there others out there as well, somewhere beyond the Deadlands in the world we all assumed was beyond repair?

Lily strides along the bridge lining the outer rim of the silo as she shows me to my new living quarters. We stop outside my new door.

"Get yourself cleaned up and settled," Lily says. "We left a map so you can find your way to the common room for food. The bag you had on you when we brought you in should be in your quarters."

Miller pulls away and lumbers into the quarters, but I linger outside the doorway.

"Wait. Lily, right? How long have you been here?"

"Two months." Lily stands taller, as if proud of this accomplishment.

"Yeah, get this," Sho interrupts, stuffing his hands into his denim pockets, "the Directorate isn't putting people who can't pay the Consumption Tax in prison like they claimed they would. Lily's parents paid her back tax, but when she started to fall behind again, the Directorate sent her out of Elpis with a pack of supplies and said, 'Good luck.'"

My back stiffens. "What?"

"Too many people in jail for back tax, they told me," Lily says. She glances around the silo. "A lot of people here were either hunted by the Directorate for Paragon's new research initiative or turned out of the city altogether. It's all very hush-hush. The public has no knowledge that any of this is happening. Best guess is that the Directorate made a promise to stop regression before Elpis buckles, but when they couldn't get a solution fast enough, they just started kicking people out. Mostly repeat offenders."

"So, what happens to the people they kick out?" I ask, but I already know the answer.

Lily leans forward like she's sharing juicy gossip. "The Protectorate scoops up people who are sent out of the city and brings them here for protection. They found me in a dried-up ravine in the Deadlands.

My supplies were gone, and I was in really rough shape. I would have died if the Protectorate hadn't saved me."

I find it hard to believe, hard to accept after the way we were treated upon arrival, but so many people here seem happy. Maybe this is just false hope that this place really could offer a solution.

"If you ask around, everyone will share their story. Most of us had a similar experience. Either the Directorate gave us a pack and said good luck or Paragon targeted us for research, and we were lucky enough to end up here instead. I've heard about what happens there. I know you've all had it far worse." Lily's voice takes on reverence as she meets my gaze. "Sho told me what happened in Paragon."

Who wouldn't be eager to work for the people who saved them from certain death? *Me.* If it makes me ungrateful, I don't care. I'm hardly ready to throw my faith at another group before I know what's really going on.

"What do they do on their missions?" I ask.

Lily shakes her head. "I really can't say. I assume some of the missions are rescue operations like when they found me. Other than that, I don't know anything more than you. Anyway, it's late. You should get rest. We will see you in the morning."

But the Protectorate has a purpose. Why are they recruiting our people for these missions? Just how dangerous are they? And what is this group up to? They can't just be happy living in a hole in the ground. Something more *must* be going on here.

6

THE FIRST THING I DO IN MY NEW LIVING QUARTERS is inspect the door. A thick steel frame encases the wide rectangular space. The door is currently open, and, as I examine it closer, I can see the steel door within it, which means there are controls somewhere.

Outside the door, a scanner pad is embedded in the wall. It's bigger than my hand, so I press my palm flat against it. The door slides out of the wall and closes. It's straight-up like something out of those old sci-fi movies, something I would expect to see on an old-school spaceship. A window on one of the doors lets me see into the living quarters.

I put my hand to the pad again and the door slides back open. If it's connected to my handprint or biosignature somehow, that means the Protectorate scanned me while I was unconscious, because it didn't happen when I was awake. The very idea makes me uneasy.

The quarters themselves are basic but functional. I step through to inspect them. Just inside the main doorway is another hand scanner with buttons above it. On closer examination, I notice the buttons lock the door and filter the window so no one can see inside. Everything in here is ancient tech that's been upgraded to suit the Protectorate's purposes, but how did they find this place?

To one side of the door, a bed is built into the steel frame of the wall with a couple of small shelves in the crevice and drawers under the bed. Miller dumped my dad's military bag on the floor beside the bed, where he currently lies with his back to me. Did the Protectorate inspect the contents of the bag? Did they take something? I have hardly had a chance to look through it myself, so I wouldn't know if something was missing.

The only furnishings besides the bed are shelves built into the walls, as well as built-in drawers for clothing storage, and a rusting metal table with two mismatched chairs. On the table, a couple of composition notebooks, just like the ones I used at Paragon. I step closer and see a pen and a map of The Shield on top of the notebooks. I only give the map a cursory glance before continuing my assessment of the room.

A door in the back wall has me curious, and I pull it open to find a toilet, sink, and narrow shower within the cramped space.

In the small mirror over the sink, a reflection of a young man with dark skin and angry eyes stares back at me. I hardly recognize myself. Scrubbing a hand over my mess of thickening hair and along the week-long growth of facial hair, I search for a razor or something else that will help me take care of the problem. A basic shaving kit with a Never-Cut blade and shaving cream sits on the shelf of the medicine cabinet hidden in the mirror. I set to work, starting with the facial hair, then moving on to my hair, using the scissors in the kit to trim the black curls on the top and the razor to smooth out the sides and back.

My reflection feels more like me, but the stench of my dirty clothes and unwashed body suddenly becomes overwhelming. I peel everything off and slide into the narrow shower.

Once I'm cleaned and dried, I go to the bag Mom packed me—Dad's old military bag that he used to pack when he had overnight duty on the other side of the city—and fish out clean clothes. But the bag has more than just clothes. Inside are new black running sneakers, protein bars, and a black lightweight jacket with flannel lining and a ribbed collar. My hand falls on something more solid than the clothes and other materials near the bottom of the bag, and I wrestle the contents aside to pull it out.

Celeste's book. *The Fabric of the Cosmos.* I remember it from her backpack when she handed it over to me in the final Survival test. What happened to the rest of her pack?

After dressing, I sit on the bed beside Miller and press my back against the cool, metal wall, opening the hardcover book. I'm not sure what I hope to get out of reading this, if anything. Maybe a chance to find some answers to our current problem. Maybe just a way to reconnect with Celeste. I miss her patient innocence so much it makes my chest hurt.

In the margins of page fifty-four, Celeste squeezed in her small messy handwriting. *Removing a single time slice changes the outcome of those slices to follow.* The pages explain the relativity of simultaneity, and how two different observers don't see a single event at the same time because of perspective. I'm not sure what Celeste's comment means.

I never had a brother or sister, and Celeste certainly felt like the closest thing to a sister I could ever imagine. I still have no idea what happened to her in that Paragon lobby. One moment she emitted a brilliant, devastating blast of cosmic power. The next moment she was just gone. No trace of her existence remained aside from the backpack I carried out of the building. Celeste gave us all the chance to escape as Paragon recovered from her cosmic ray.

Celeste had a way of speaking in riddles that I found fascinating. Once I got used to it, her words made sense to me, even if not to anyone else. The memory of those swirling colors in the night sky as she showed me what she saw in the stars slams against my chest. One thing Celeste told me again and again was that she could see Andromeda breaking free and that Cassiopeia would fall from her throne soon.

My understanding of ancient mythology is a little sketchy, but if memory serves me, Andromeda was the daughter of Cassiopeia and Cepheus. But Cassiopeia was vain and boasted of her own beauty. As punishment, Andromeda was chained up for a sea monster to abuse, but Perseus rescued her. Knowing Celeste, Cassiopeia is Dr. Cass, full of her own vain brilliance. But if that's the case, does that make me the chained-up Andromeda or Perseus?

Celeste also fell into a state of fear, repeating the words, *The chains have broken. He has risen. He comes.* But does that mean Andromeda has broken free and the monster is coming for her? Was she talking about me at all? I can't ignore the coincidence. Celeste was too prophetic for me to ignore her warning. But I still don't fully understand what it means.

I read her words in the book again. *Removing a single time slice changes the outcome of those slices to follow.*

The prophetic words make that ache in my chest even more pronounced, so I snap the book shut and set it on a shelf by the bed.

The metal wall leaves a chill in my skin through my t-shirt, and I pull on the jacket. One of the large pockets on the front is stiff, and I unzip it, pulling an envelope from within. My name stands out on the envelope in Dad's sharp handwriting. Tears blur my vision.

Miller snores softly, then grunts and shifts.

I don't have the strength to open the note right now, so I stuff the envelope back into the pocket and zip it shut.

The pain of remembering both Celeste and Dad exhausts me, so I lay as best I can in the small space beside Miller in my clothes and jacket.

I've wanted human contact for days. Now I've had it, and I'm still not happy.

I squeeze my eyes shut and try to sleep. Despite being utterly exhausted, I can't seem to fall asleep. But much like every other night when I try to fall asleep, memories haunt me. The way Enid stuck close to me the days following our escape as we waited for Harvey to arrange safe passage. The warmth of her presence makes me crave seeing her again, in turn overwhelming me with guilt for another girl who was never mine. Bianca.

Just thinking her name conjures an image of her on Career Day in her skirt and red shirt. The smile on her face when she moved for the woman on the tram. The way her heels accentuated her legs. The way she pulled me close and kissed me as she died. All the warmth and comfort of Enid dissolves replaced by the weight of Bianca's dying body in my arms. The memory of her weight grows heavier and heavier, pulling me down into sleep.

Then the nightmares come.

7

THE CAFETERIA IS MORE LIKE A COMMON ROOM. IT'S huge, with alcoves containing comfortable pillows on stone benches carved into the wall. Wooden tables matching the planks on the walls along entries rest in each alcove. It reminds me of a massive wine cellar with tables and chairs. Some tables with wicker chairs fill the center of the room, and along the longest wall, another stone bench covered in one long cushion and dozens of mismatched pillows. In another corner, a chess and checkers table. The light is much the same as any other room, but this is much more comfortable. More like home.

There are people here, too. Dozens of them. I can't identify most, though I do spot my friends sitting in one of the alcoves, along with Lily. Miller and I shuffle toward them with our trays.

"Ugene!" Enid cries out, rushing toward me. Her shining eyes lock onto mine.

Seeing Enid releases an unknown tension, and my steps feel lighter as I close the distance. All the fear and pain balled up in my stomach dissolves as she throws her arms around me the moment I set my food on the table. Enid collapses against me as I hug her back.

Warmth radiates from her small body, and the contact with another person I know and trust fills me with comfort. Maybe this will be okay. I pause to revel in the moment, but we don't have the luxury of standing around, comforting each other. These people may have released us, but I don't doubt someone is watching. Especially if they think one of us is a spy.

"I thought we were back at Paragon…that we didn't even…" Fear creases her smooth face, reminding me of the skittish way she reacted in that first test we had together in the dead rainforest. I completely understand her apprehension. "They said we're safe here."

"I know."

"Are we?"

I wondered the same myself. "We're safe," I say with more confidence than I feel.

Enid pulls in a breath and steps back, stiffening. A small group of natives gives our group a fleeting, curious look as they pass along toward another table. What are they thinking? Are they watching us for Willow? Enid notices as well and takes my hand, pulling me away from the crowd.

"I don't trust them," Enid says, keeping her voice low despite the closed door. "I mean, how do we know this is even real? What's saying this isn't a Paragon simulation?"

"I wondered that myself. But I feel like this is too much. All the people and everyday life moving around us. It's just…it's too intricate to be another simulation." *Isn't it?* I smile, hoping to convince her even though I'm not even close to believing it myself.

Enid frowns but nods in agreement. She glances at our hands then lets go, stuffing her own in her pockets, then says, "And the whole transportation thing…I find it hard to accept that it was a simulation. But Paragon has so much tech we don't even know about."

"What's the last thing you remember before waking up here?" I ask, sitting on one of the table chairs.

Enid glances around the common room anxiously and keeps her voice low. "We all crammed into the back of the truck at Lettuce Eat and it started rumbling down the road. I noticed people started falling asleep, and when I looked at you, you told me that something wasn't right."

I don't remember any of this. How can I have a conversation with her that I don't even remember?

"Then you pointed at the vent and we saw the gas pumping into the truck, but you were groggy already." Enid shifts, hugging her arms tight over her chest. "I tried to use my Power to stop it, but by then it was too late. There was too much in the back of the truck and just about everyone else was already out." Her eyes shimmer with tears. "I'm sorry. I tried. I really did."

I rest a hand on her shoulder, offering reassurance. "It isn't your fault. I don't think any of us could have stopped it."

Enid's gaze falls to my hand and she gives a small nod. "Why are we here, Ugene?"

I shake my head. No good answer comes to mind. "Because of my mom, I assume. I mean, she must have known when she gave me that address that Harvey would put us on that truck. And I have to believe she knew that truck would bring us here. Though I suppose that doesn't really answer the why."

I turn back toward our friends, then hesitate, glancing at her over my shoulder. "Did Willow say anything to you about a spy in our group?"

Enid shakes her head. "A spy for who? We don't have contact with many people."

I can trust Enid. I have trusted Enid. "Willow said they know one of us is a spy for either Paragon or the Directorate, and she was wondering if we would have any clues as to who."

Enid scowls. "Sounds like a ploy to cause division between us, if you ask me."

"Yeah." But I don't know that I agree. If the Protectorate is really after information, and the Directorate is after them, it would make sense to insert a spy, and using a group as big as ours, it would be easy to pull off.

"You believe her," Enid says.

I don't want to admit it to her, but I nod.

"Ugene, Paragon used the same tactics to keep us from banding together because they knew it would make us dangerous. Why would this group be any different?"

"I agree…to some extent. But think about it, Enid. If you wanted to find out where a group of underground resistance fighters was hiding, don't you think a group like ours would be the easiest way to do it? Dr. Cass knew we were trying to escape. She could have easily inserted someone into our massive group in case we succeeded."

"No." Enid's back stiffens. "Because she couldn't have known we would end up here."

"Why not?" I wave a hand around us. "Where else would we go? They knew that the Protectorate was somehow gathering up people with weak Powers. Our group is a huge, obvious target."

Enid resists at first, but I can see that she starts to accept my explanation. "So, what's our play here?"

"I'm not sure yet," I admit. My plan was to get us out, which I did. Beyond that, I have no idea. "But I'll figure it out."

Enid nods as if she already knew as much. Her faith in me is unwavering. I only hope I don't let her down.

We rejoin the others.

When I get back to the table, Madison is staring at Miller, anxiety twisting her forehead in knots. Miller picks at his pancakes carelessly, and I watch as he pulls one of them to pieces but doesn't eat a bite.

Unfiltered chatter makes this common room livelier than the one at Paragon ever was. People talk and laugh at their tables, say hi as they pass one another, and come and go freely.

The illusion of freedom offers some comfort as I finish my meal and sit back on the bench, watching.

At Paragon, everyone appeared rundown, often an inch from death. Few people talked, and no one just walked around the room to meet with different people. They came in, ate their meals, and left. But this place, it's almost…peaceful.

After everything I've been through and losing Dad, Bianca, Celeste, and Mo—along with so many others I didn't really know—I don't think peace is anything but fleeting. We may have escaped Paragon, but this is far from over. When I led these people out of Paragon, I started a fight we can't possibly win. Especially if the Directorate has a part, as Willow suggested.

How many more will I lose before the end? I glance around the table at my friends: Madison, Enid, Sho, Boyd, Leo, Miller...I can't handle losing any of them like I lost Bianca.

Bianca. Her last words to me weren't poetic. They didn't offer any sort of closure. She simply kissed me and told me to go. And I did. I left her body there on the floor of the Paragon lobby and fled. I'm not a leader or a legend. That makes me a coward, doesn't it?

And Celeste. I still don't understand what happened to her. One moment she was standing in the lobby with the few of us who remained. The next, she was bursting with blinding cosmic light, destroying everything in its path. Burning the Somatic Bianca had been fighting right out of his shoes as if he didn't exist. But when the light faded, Celeste was gone. As if *she* had never been. To what end? Did she burn herself up? Was she still there in Paragon somewhere? It feels more like a sacrifice on Celeste's part than any sort of salvation.

Did I actually help anyone by leading the escape from Paragon, or just lead a bunch of new people to an early death?

"Ugene?" Boyd's voice calls me back from my misery. "Y-you o-okay?"

I blink and focus on his face across the table behind a large stack of pancakes. Tears slip out and roll down my cheeks. I quickly brush them away and suck in a shuddering breath, smiling as a trickle of relief at seeing his face washes through me. "Yeah. Fine."

Why do I keep telling lies?

"Tears of j-joy, then?" Boyd asks, his deadpan tone making it obvious that he doesn't believe me. "C-c-come on. T-talk to us. After ev-everything we've been thr-through..."

"I'll be fine," I say. "It comes and goes. Not a big deal." Nothing would interest me less than talking about my feelings.

The Protectorate people drift out of the room. Miller snoozes beside me, alternately snoring softly and shifting restlessly in his seat. He's hardly eaten more than half a pancake.

Madison raises her brows impatiently at me, and I wonder why. Did I miss something?

What? I try sending the question out with my mind.

We need to talk about Miller, Madison says, watching him snooze. *I'm worried about what's going on in there. It's distracting.*

I know, I think. *It's a side effect of losing his Powers.*

No. Madison's lips compress. *It's inexplicable. His mind is both racing and completely empty at the same time. Like there are two different parts of him. One that's running like a hamster caught in a wheel, and the other that's just sort of…dead.*

He's going to be fine, I say, though I don't really feel as confident in my words as I should be. *Obviously, he isn't dead.*

But he wants to be. The despair on Madison's face makes me tense.

Is Miller really so bad off? It's my fault. He would still have his Powers if those security guards hadn't shot at me.

He needs help. Sooner than later. Madison adds the last with pressing emphasis.

I nod stiffly, glancing at Miller as he snoozes. I want to understand, but I don't. Not really. Being Powerless sucks, but it isn't the end of his life. I should be proof enough of that.

A Somatic I recognize from Paragon approaches with a blonde girl holding his hand, distracting me from the conversation with Madison. He was the one who carried Miller out of the building and saved him.

"Glad to see your face," the Somatic says to me as he reaches the table. Sadly, I don't even know his name.

"Noah was one of the first out," Sho offers.

Noah. I open my mouth to thank him for helping us when we escaped, but before I can say anything more, Willow marches into the room.

ONLY THOSE WHO ESCAPED PARAGON REMAIN IN THE common room. We all shuffle closer to Willow as conversations die down. Enid shifts toward me. Everyone has turned attention to Willow. The way that woman commands their attention makes my skin crawl.

"I know you have all been through a horrific ordeal, and you survived it by sticking together," Willow says. "I admire your determination and courage. What you've managed is no easy task. With that said, I understand why some of you are hesitant to trust us," she glances toward Enid and me for a second, "and I want to apologize for how long it took to get some of you through the intake process."

Enid and I both grunt, which catches Chase's attention beside Willow. Enid shrinks back, but I don't. He's a musclebound bully, just like any other. I've had enough of being intimidated by people like him.

"The Shield has a noble purpose," Willow continues. "We protect those the Directorate and Paragon have targeted. We rescue those the Directorate has turned out of Elpis under the guise of the Consumption Tax, people whom the Directorate believes are useless to the future of the city. We gather. We grow. And we fight back."

A few people in the gathering shift or nod, murmuring their agreement. Is she really inspiring them? Are they really falling for this? I don't like it. Something about the whole thing feels…off. I almost *want* to believe her.

Miller snorts loudly in his sleep and I elbow his side. He opens his eyes, staring at me through tired, empty blue irises. Hearing Willow's voice makes him sit a little more upright, but he still slouches low like he doesn't care. *He probably doesn't.*

"To do this, we work together, as a community," Willow says, causing the murmurs to fall silent. "We respect each other and our common purpose. Everyone is encouraged to find their own way to contribute to life in The Shield. And anyone who wants to help fight the Directorate and Paragon is welcome."

These people aren't soldiers. Even if they want to fight back, we don't have the collective strength to do it. Not against the Directorate. Fighting out of Paragon was one thing. What she is asking is something else completely. Willow's subtle manipulation to encourage voluntary recruitment will get some of these people in trouble. We came here to be safe.

I won't let Willow use these people.

"What exactly is this group doing to fight against the Directorate?" I ask, making sure I get the attention of not just Willow, but everyone in the room. They all followed me out of Paragon, so if they want me to lead, I will.

Willow turns on her heel and her ponytail swings like a pendulum behind her head. "Are you interested in joining the Protectorate, Ugene?"

"I'm interested in transparency," I say, crossing my arms. "We've been manipulated long enough."

Chase subtly moves his position halfway between Willow and me, just at the edge of our direct line of sight. The guy is a beast, and he could probably crush me without breaking a sweat, but he won't. He's nothing more than a dog obeying his master's commands.

"Says the man using information stolen from Paragon as a bargaining chip," Willow says.

Only a few of us knew about the drive, and Willow's announcement creates a stir of confusion and curiosity from the others. *No point in denying it.*

"You're right," I say. "We struggled to escape that nightmare. We fought side by side against the worst odds, far beyond anything you could imagine. We lost more than sixty percent of the people who started the journey with us. All to save ourselves and get that information out of Paragon. Why are we here, Willow?" I cross my arms.

"Because Paragon is looking for you," Willow says. "The only way you can be safely away from their grasp is here, underground with us. Because we all need each other to prove the Directorate is wrong."

I won't let Willow use us, or that drive, as a manipulation device to force a wedge between our group. "You want to know what's on that drive?" I ask, more for the benefit of the others than for Willow. "We have video evidence against Paragon. Proof that they have not only been conducting unethical experiments on test subjects but that some of those experiments have resulted in deaths they have covered up. And there's a chance we could have downloaded the formulas from those experiments, but the data is encrypted."

My announcement gains a wave of alarmed responses from yelps, gasps, and wide eyes to heads shaking in denial. Madison and Noah adopt expressions of horror. The blonde girl beside Noah clings to his arm. She now realizes what a few of us already knew. Any one of us could have been next in those experiments.

"That's why my friends and I worked so hard to save everyone," I say. The full steam of my confidence and anger propels me forward. "So, tell me something, Willow. Besides rescuing the helpless from the Deadlands, what are you doing to fight back? What secret missions are you running that would risk the lives of people who aren't strong enough to stand up against the Directorate? How are you any better than them?"

"Wars are won through action, not inaction," Willow says.

"We aren't soldiers. We won't fight a war for you," I say. "Enough people have died."

The tension in the room is thick.

I cock my head to the side at Willow's silence. Time to move in for the kill before she has a chance to recover. "Tell us honestly, Willow. If you didn't need one of us, would you turn us back in to Paragon?"

Willow's eyes shoot wide open. "What?"

I take a confident step forward. "You need something from us, but once you have it, if it kept the Directorate off your back, would you turn us back in to Paragon?"

"We don't give them people," Willow says, perching white-knuckled fists on her hips. "We save people from them. It would go against everything we have worked for to turn anyone over. *Everyone* is valuable to us. The Directorate has been seeking us out for years and hasn't found us yet. I don't expect that to change any time soon... Do you?"

"I will do everything within my meager Powerless power to protect every person that came out of that building with me," I say. "We lost enough already. No one else will die for your cause."

Willow stalks toward me, one cat-like step at a time, like a lioness hunting her prey. "What do you think is happening out there right now, Ugene? While you worry about Paragon and Dr. Cass, Directorate Chief Seaduss prepares something bigger. Who do you think pushed for the Consumption Tax that targets the more impoverished neighborhoods like Pax? Who do you think is ordering the DMA to double and triple sweeps of offenders? Do you even know what's going on in Pax? Mothers starve to death so their children can eat. Citizens turn to crime just to pay back-taxes or provide for their friends and family. The Directorate and Seaduss, they don't care. They get rich and take advantage of the weak. If you think this isn't a war, you have lived a sheltered life."

I grimace. No one breathes, as if the tension has drawn out all the oxygen. Everyone who escaped with me learned on the Metro that I grew up in Salas, one of the richest boroughs in the city. Does Willow know that? She must if she knows who my mom is. Every muscle in my body is coiled tight.

Enid must sense it, because she slips her hands around my bicep, giving it a reassuring squeeze.

Willow lets out a breath, and with it, her shoulders slump. "Ugene," she says in a softer tone. "I recognize everything you've been through, everything you've suffered. Truly, I do. And you've all made it out, against all odds. But there are still people suffering, and if we don't help them, no one will. It's the curse of the leader burdened with knowledge to bear the responsibility of using that knowledge to liberate others. *That* is what we do here."

Everyone is watching me, waiting to see how I respond. I look at each of them, weighing their expressions, measuring their reactions. Some of them sag, weighed down by everything. Others sit up straighter, and I already know they will be among the first to volunteer to help the Protectorate. Noah among them. Maybe he thinks that since he's a Strongarm he can make a difference.

"Show me," I say at last.

Miller groans.

Willow tilts her head to the side. "Show you?"

"I want to see Pax," I say, putting my shoulders back. "I want to walk the streets and see the people and witness all of this for myself."

"You just got here," Willow says, her palms up and gaze fixed on me.

"I've been here for days. I'm ready to see this truth for myself." I slip off the bench and step closer to Willow, lowering my voice. "These people follow me. If you want us to help you, then you need to convince me. Show me."

Willow sputters for a moment, and as she does, a few of the others rise in a show of solidarity. Did they hear what I said? Noah and his blonde female friend, Leo, Madison, Rosie, a guy I only vaguely recognize. Soon, ten of us stand together out of the forty-two gathered. With each who joins me, I fight off a satisfied grin threatening to stretch across my face. Instead, I do my best to stare her down, remaining as stoic as possible. I feel taller than I have in a long time.

Willow and Chase exchange looks, and again I wonder if they are communicating via Telepathy. Finally, Willow presses the heels of her palms into her eyes and releases an exaggerated sigh. "Fine. But it will take some time to arrange."

My heart races, but I don't yield any ground, afraid it might make Willow change her mind. "Fine."

Did she really just agree to take me to Pax, or was she just trying to shut me up? She agreed too easily. Maybe she is playing a game with me, but I don't understand the rules yet.

THE PROTECTORATE RELEASES OUR GROUP INTO THE general population. Everyone is welcome to move around The Shield freely. Willow encourages us to use our maps to explore and find a place to contribute. Enid hangs back with me as others filter out of the common room.

"Madison," I call as the girl heads toward the door.

Madison says something to another girl, then jogs up to me. "What is it?"

Paragon may have planted a spy in our group, I say, sending her a Telepathic message.

Madison's eyes widen and her jaw slackens as she glances from me to Enid and back again. *Are you sure?*

No. But I need you to try and read everyone who came with us, see what you can find out. I bite my lip before continuing. *And I need you to try and read the natives to this place, see if they are hiding something from us.*

Madison hesitates. *Ugene, there are people here who are stronger than me.*

I nod. *I understand. But I need you to try.*

I'll do what I can, she says.

Enid watches the two of us curiously, but my gaze shoots past both girls as someone approaches Willow, and the two dart out of the common room like there's a fire with Chase on Willow's heels as always.

I drop a hand on Enid's shoulder. "Get Miller to my quarters, will you? And make sure he isn't alone."

"Why, what—?" Enid turns after me, but I don't wait for her to finish before rushing out after Willow.

Keeping up with Willow and Chase while not letting anyone notice I'm following them is more difficult than I expected. The tunnels are so long that I have to wait for them to turn a corner before entering the tunnel in their wake. Then I rush down the tunnel to reach the next intersection before they disappear again, while simultaneously appearing *not* to rush and gather attention. More than once, I tuck my hands casually into the pockets of my jacket and try to act like I'm just wandering aimlessly as someone steps out from a room or enter the tunnel headed my way.

Unfortunately, this level of stealth means I can't hear Willow or Chase's conversation along the way. I'm too far behind to hear much more than distant voices carrying off the walls. I nearly lose them at one intersection, stepping out and checking both directions, then ducking out of sight when I spot them at the far end of the left junction talking to Doc. The tunnel is probably a good sixty feet long, and they speak in urgent whispers so I can't hear any of the exchange.

I hide around the corner, listening to make sure their voices continue as I fumble out my map. Where are we? The same level as the common room, but we turned down several intersections. I glance up from my study of the map to read the sign on the door next to me, then compare it to the map.

Willow, Doc, and Chase are outside Medical. What's going on there that would be so urgent?

Silence fills the tunnels. They stopped talking. I dare to peek out. The tunnel is empty. Did they enter Medical?

Just in case I run into one of them, I keep my map out as I round the corner, walking at a casual pace and keeping my eyes fixed on the map in my hand. If they catch me, I can try to claim I was just getting acquainted with The Shield's layout.

The closer I get to the medical bay, the commotion catches my attention from within. Before I go in to get a closer look, I peek around the corner to get a handle on where everyone is. Particularly Willow, Chase, and Doc.

A handful of people young and old in scrubs rush around the medical bay as Dr. Lydia barks out orders. Five of the beds are newly occupied and medical tools rest on steel trays colored with fresh blood. One of the patients—a guy I can't really see too well from my hiding place—begins seizing.

"Hold him down!" Dr. Lydia barks.

Chase appears beside the seizing patient and pins his shoulders to the table as Doc injects something in the patient's arm. A moment later, the seizing stops. He goes limp. But the twisting in my gut starts. That seizure reminded me of Miller thrashing on the Paragon floor after they shot him.

"I can't heal her," one of the women in scrubs calls out to Dr. Lydia.

"Someone go find that Rosie girl," Dr. Lydia barks. "Tell her if she doesn't come help, this girl will die."

I slip into the medical bay and hide behind one of the curtains. No one notices me enter in all the chaos. Just as I dip out of sight, someone in scrubs hands something to Willow and I strain to hear their conversation over the commotion from the doctors and nurses—or whatever they call themselves here. Another woman in clean scrubs runs out of the medical bay, presumably to find Rosie.

"Jayme said it might be damaged," Scrubs Guy tells Willow.

"Well hopefully something from it is salvageable or this mission was for nothing." Willow's voice is a combination of concern and irritation.

The smell of antiseptic, blood, and urine is overpowering. I struggle to keep from gagging and giving myself away. Swallowing bile, I close my eyes for a moment.

"Not completely for nothing," Scrubs Guy says to Willow.

"Is that—?"

"He says it is."

I peer out from behind the curtain just in time to see Willow tuck something under her shirt at the small of her back. I can't make out what it was.

Dr. Lydia's voice is closer to where I'm hiding, and I can't hear anything more of Willow's conversation over Dr. Lydia's admonishing tone. "Jayme, I told you to stop overexerting yourself. You push your Power too far."

"I had no choice, Lydia," the patient, presumably this Jayme person, says. His voice chafes at my memory. "The Directorate was on top of us. If I hadn't, she wouldn't have made it back here. None of us would have."

Where do I know that voice from?

"I'm putting you on the Reserve list," Dr. Lydia says.

Something like cloth rustles from the other side of the curtain. "Please. I can't stay here. I have to keep going out there."

"You're killing yourself."

"I know what I'm about." The familiar voice flashes me back to a memory from the final Survival test when we were trying to escape the simulated Paragon Tower. *I'll kill you all!* My heart jumps into my throat.

Caution aside, I step out from my hiding place so I can get a clear look at the guy. His red hair isn't a mess, and he sits up confidently on the edge of the cot, back straight, but there's no doubt in my mind.

"Murphy." The name is barely a whisper from my lips, and my feet shuffle toward the bed almost of their own accord. I could never forget the feral way he screamed and leaped at me in that office in the simulation.

My sudden appearance attracts attention.

"Ugene, what are you doing here?" Willow asks from across the medical bay.

I ignore her.

"You...you're Murphy," I say.

He looks at me like I'm crazy, head cocked slightly to the side, but there's no mistaking those green eyes, no longer wild with rage, but curious. He leans forward. "Who are you?"

"Miller...I..." It's him. It's really Murphy.

At the mention of Miller's name, Murphy's eyes widen, and he sinks back, staring at me. I realize he's waiting for me to say more.

"Ugene!" Willow marches over, but I don't care. Murphy, or Jayme, as Dr. Lydia called him, is the reason Miller betrayed us in Paragon. And here he is. Right in front of me.

I lick my lips, excited. "Okay, we were together at Paragon. I'm Ugene. Miller was my mentor."

Murphy's eyes narrow slightly. "Is he okay?" His gaze flits around the room. "Where is he?"

"He jumped in front of a bullet for me when we escaped."

Murphy sucks in a sharp breath and his shoulders slump.

"He's fine," Dr. Lydia says, making a few notes on the tablet. "Unlike you, if you don't quit overusing your Power."

Murphy waves her off.

"He's not fine," I say sharply. "The bullet had something in it that removed his Powers."

Willow steps in front of me, taking my arm and pulling me away from the bed toward the exit. "You don't need to be in here right now."

I resist, pulling back and shaking her off, which isn't easy. Her grip is oddly strong.

"Where is he?" Murphy asks again, slipping off the edge of the cot, towering several inches over me.

"Jayme, sit down." Dr. Lydia crosses her arms and cuts off his path. "You need to rest."

Murphy ignores her and easily sidesteps.

"My quarters," I say.

Murphy grabs a fleece-lined denim jacket off the cot and bolts toward the door before Dr. Lydia or Willow can stop him. I jog to catch up. Murphy exudes confidence as he makes long strides down the hallway, shoulders squared, and the jacket clenched tight in his fist. I can't help but admire his sudden determination.

"Who are you, then?" Murphy asks, turning left at a fork in the tunnel.

Wait. I thought I already told him. "As I said before, my name's

Ugene. Miller and I are...friends."

We take a sharp right and descend a set of stone steps. At the bottom, Murphy casts a sidelong, furtive glance at me. He's sizing me up, though I'm not sure why.

"So, you both came with that big Paragon group?" he asks.

"Yeah." He knew about the group already. How could he not have known about Miller?

Unless Willow didn't tell him. But why would she keep it from him?

Murphy's jaw clenches and the muscles in his neck become more distinguishable.

"He took a bullet for you, huh?" Murphy asks as we round a corner. He won't look at me for some reason. "Why?"

I open my mouth, but no explanation comes out. I don't really know why.

My lack of answers seems to irritate Murphy. He clenches his jacket tighter, making the muscles in his shoulders tense.

"I wasn't sure we would find you," I say. "Miller told me all about you, Murphy."

"Jayme."

"What?"

"It's Jayme. Not Murphy."

I frown. Why would he not be Murphy? Miller never called him Jayme. But then again, everyone else did. Willow. Dr. Lydia. Maybe Murphy was just for Miller, like a pet name or something.

Jayme casts that critical glare at me again, and I'm not sure why. "Then you two were... close?"

"Sure. We spent a lot of time together."

His pace slows gradually until he comes to a full stop, turning to face me. He looks almost hurt. "What does that mean?"

Oh. Now I get it. He thinks Miller and I are a thing.

"It's not like that at all," I say quickly, maybe too quickly. "We're just friends."

Jayme shrugs and turns forward to continue, his stride growing in length like he wants to lose me. Maybe he does.

"As I said, he talked about you all the time."

We enter the silo and I nod toward where my quarters are. Jayme's stride only slows slightly.

"Like what?" Jayme asks.

"That he loves you, for starters," I say, "and that he would walk through fire for you."

Jayme's expression softens. "He said that?"

"Well, not exactly in those words, but it was pretty clearly implied."

To say the least. Miller turned the rest of us in to Paragon just so he could get information about Jayme. If he hadn't chosen to stay with me in the lobby, if he hadn't taken that bullet for me, I'm not sure I would have the heart to forgive him.

Did the fact that Jayme is here play into Miller's decision to stay with me? If Miller *is* the spy, Paragon might have told him Jayme was here, which would motivate Miller to make a deal. He did it before. Maybe this is all part of Paragon's plan.

As I struggle with this line of thought, Jayme steps through the open door to my quarters. Should I follow?

Yes. I need to see how Miller reacts to seeing Jayme. I need to exonerate him.

Enid paces the doorway to my quarters, watching up the gangway. As soon as she sees me, her shoulders sag with relief. "What is going on?" she asks, glancing curiously at Jayme.

"Thanks for watching him," I say.

Miller sits upright on the edge of my bed, shoulders sloped downward with his hands stuffed deep in the pockets of his hoodie. He's staring at nothing. It's like nothing else exists but the wall.

Jayme freezes, the tension in his shoulder's sagging away as he takes in the state of Miller. I give Jayme a moment, but he just stands there. Biting my lip, I step forward just enough to see the tears welling in Jayme's eyes. Maybe I can act as a buffer here.

I give Jayme a pat on the shoulder and approach Miller, pulling a chair over from the table and taking the seat across from him so I fill his line of sight.

"Hey, Miller."

Nothing but a slow blink.

"Good news," I say, hoping he is actually listening. Miller's state is almost catatonic. "I found Murphy."

Miller blinks a few times, and his eyes begin to focus on me. He releases a breath that makes his entire body shake. "Here?"

I nod, offering him a reassuring smile. "Yes. Here."

No surprise breaks his blank expression, but Miller's voice cracks as he speaks. "He can't see me like this."

I bite my lip. "Well. Maybe pull yourself together a little bit then, because he's waiting by the door." I glance over at Jayme, waving him over.

Miller swallows a lump in his throat and slowly turns his head toward the door. Upon seeing Jayme, he sucks in a shuddering breath. "Murph…" Miller's never sounded so small or weak…or relieved.

Jayme shuffles closer, draping his jacket over the back of a chair as he passes. Miller rises, his limbs shaking as he steadies himself.

"Miller." Jayme's voice quivers, then a smile stretches across his face and he closes the distance in a few strides and pulls Miller into a tight hug.

Miller shakes, buries his face in Jayme's neck, and returns the hug.

I slip away from the two of them toward the door.

Miller pulls back and brushes red hair away from Jayme's face, his hand lingering tenderly. "I'm sorry."

Jayme runs his fingers through Miller's blond hair and leans their foreheads together.

Even if this means Miller *is* a spy for Paragon, I can't help feeling happy for the two of them. How far would I go if I could be with Bianca again?

Sadly, I'll never know.

10

ASSIMILATION INTO LIFE IN THE SHIELD PROVES EASIER for some than others. Many of my friends have found a place to contribute—the kitchen, janitorial room, laundry room, granary. The Shield exists like its own city underground with numerous opportunities.

I expected Miller to improve after reuniting with Jayme, but he seems to slip further with each day that passes. Madison has warned me more than once that Miller's mind is still broken in two. Sometimes his attitude is too sharp or too friendly, and other times he just doesn't respond to conversations at all. More often than not, I catch him staring at nothing, his eyes glazed over. He's become a husk of his former self, skin and bones and nothing more.

With each day that passes, Jayme casts more and more angry glances in my direction when Miller isn't looking—and sometimes when he is. The daggers in his eyes are deadly like he blames me for Miller's condition. And he's probably right to blame me. Miller never says anything about the growing tension between Jayme and me. Maybe he doesn't even notice.

The Shield is massive, so much bigger than I imagined. Exploring the tunnels and rooms is a monumental task, which Enid has volunteered to help me with. Much like I did in Paragon, I spend my days observing the people and activity, making notes in my notebooks each night. My interest is in snippets of conversations that leak through doorways. Mostly gossip about other people. People simply go about their daily life here.

Everyone wears ordinary clothes—jeans, T-shirts, hooded sweatshirts, and jackets. No tension fills the air around these people. No one dips their heads or shies away as our group approaches as they did at Paragon. They look up at me and smile. People are happy here, but I can't help but wonder how many of them suffer from PTPD like Miller. No one else appears in as rough of condition as Miller, though.

Today, I wander the halls with the map tucked safely in my jacket pocket, just in case. From the end of a corridor, a small group of people in desert camouflage uniforms heads my direction. Their gazes fall on me and the conversation stops. I peer over my shoulder as they round the corner and disappear, then stare straight ahead.

Quickly, I inspect my map, unfolding it so I can see what's behind the closed doors. Only one is unmarked. Folding the map back up, I glance up and down the hallway and shuffle toward the solid steel door. Beside the door, a hand scanner rests in the wall. I place my hand against it. A blue light scans my palm, then the activation light turns red. No sound emits from the device, but it's clear that whatever is behind this door is something I'm not allowed to see, which only makes me want to see it more. If Miller still had his Power, I could get him to pop the lock. Maybe I can find someone else to do it.

"What are you up to?" a voice asks, making me jump out of my skin and spin around to face Jayme.

I collect myself. "What's back there?" I stab my thumb over my shoulder at the door.

"When you're ready, Willow will show you."

"I'm ready right now."

Jayme's lip curls up into a sneer. "You expect trust from us, but the road goes both ways."

"You have access, don't you?"

Jayme crosses his arms and juts out his chin. "She trusts me."

"Aren't you special. Any chance you will open it for me?"

Jayme's indifferent expression is answer enough.

I roll my eyes and head back down the hallway.

Jayme grabs my arm, tugging me to a stop. "This isn't a game, Ugene. People die if we aren't careful."

I yank my arm free. "Got it."

Miller trusts him, and I want to as well, but Jayme clearly has some sort of dislike for me, which leaves me uneasy about trusting him.

Rubbing my arm, I return to my quarters to find Enid and Leo waiting at my table. The moment I step through the door, Enid jumps up and rushes over, taking my hand and pulling me toward the table.

"You need to see what we found today," she says, keeping her voice low. We are all very aware that someone could be listening.

I allow her to guide me to the table. Enid glances toward the door, but Leo is already moving to close it. She spreads out blueprints on the table, and I lean closer. In the bottom corner, thick, blocky letters read: Paragon Tower. The first sheet shows the tower in slices, level by level. Circles and X's in red marker identify out structural points in the tower. I flip to the next sheet, marked "Lower Level," and note the same red marks.

"Where did you get this? What is it?" I ask, turning my gaze up to Enid and Leo.

"I stole it from Willow's quarters," Enid says. "I was hoping you would understand it."

"You stole this from Willow?" I quickly roll it back up and shove it toward her. "Enid, you need to return this. She will notice it missing."

"What is it?" Enid asks, grabbing the rolled-up blueprints.

"I don't know, but we can't keep this. You shouldn't have taken it. If we get caught with it Willow will punish us for sure, and I have no idea what they do as punishment here."

Leo shifts anxiously and thrusts a set of sheets at me. I hesitate to take them this time.

"Where did you get it?" I ask.

Leo chews his lip. "Research. They're up to something. I don't comprehend it."

"Enid, take those back." I wave her toward the door. "I'll make some notes about it in my notebooks."

She nods, hustling toward the exit, but I take her hand and pull her to a stop. "Please, be careful. If you're caught with those…"

"I know. If I'm not back in thirty minutes, find me," she says, then squeezes my hand and leaves.

Leo nods at the papers in his hand. "I copied these myself. No one will miss them."

Maybe the Protectorate is planning to infiltrate Paragon Tower, and the marks are access points. I take the sheets from Leo and sink into the empty chair, reading the first page, filled with chemical formulas. None of it makes sense. I understand chemistry well enough, but some of these bonds are unlike anything I've seen before. One of them does make sense though. It's a chain that breaks the linking mechanism that creates Powers. Without that link, Powers won't work. But the rest I need time to decipher.

Leo clears his throat. "Anyway, I'm gonna go."

I wave a distracted hand at him as I review the next sheets. The two sheets both have a drawing of a DNA strand. I lean over the drawings, trying to glean some kind of information from them.

The differences between the two strands aren't obvious at first. Both have disconnected linking mechanisms in the chain that brings Powers together. But the longer I stare at them, the more I realize that there is one significant difference.

"This is amazing," I say.

Enid returns from her own mission and flops down on the bed facing me. Her dark brown eyes lock onto my own, shining. The intensity of her gaze traps me and makes the hair on my arms rise. Why is she staring at me like that? Time just sort of passes as we sit like this until the weight on my chest fills me with panic. I clear my throat and look away.

Enid licks her lips and ducks her head, but I can see the heat in her cheeks. "What's amazing?" she asks in a small voice.

"Assuming Leo's drawing skills can be trusted, one of these DNA chains is only broken."

"Meaning what?"

"Someone who lost their Power hasn't lost it completely." I lean close to the drawing. "The linking mechanism that makes the Power work isn't gone or misaligned. Just disconnected, like a power cord that just needs to be plugged in again."

"Can it be plugged back in?"

I chew my lip, scanning the entire drawing critically. "I don't know. But if I could get a hold of the actual sample, I could probably try to extract some kind of coding from the DNA that will help me address where and how this is disconnected. And if I can find that, I can find out how to reconnect it…maybe." If this is someone who lost their Power, then maybe this is Miller's DNA. It could be too much to hope for, but I haven't encountered anyone else who obviously lost theirs. Dr. Lydia said there were a few others who lost their Power as well, and there's a chance this could be theirs, but it makes sense that Miller, being the most recent person to lose their Power, would be investigated closest right now. "I need to get a hold of the real sample."

"Mm-hm," Enid says, pulling the blanket over her.

The other DNA strand, however, isn't as promising as the first. I've looked at this strand enough over the years to know exactly what I'm looking at. It's my sample. It must be. I've never seen another structure that appears like this one. The alignment is completely off.

I sink back in the chair, scrubbing a hand over my face, and open my mouth to explain all of this to Enid, but she's asleep, something that still eludes me. Not wanting to wake her, I step out onto the metal gangway.

"You're an idiot," Jayme says from behind me.

I jump out of my skin and spin to see him leaning against the railing not ten feet away. Miller slouches over the rail, staring straight down. He glances over his shoulder at me with a hint of amusement on his face, but it doesn't reach his eyes.

Jayme snickers, but I don't really know what's so funny.

"I'm a what now?" I ask.

"An idiot," Jayme says again.

Miller nods in agreement.

Jayme is laughing. I don't find it very funny.

"He doesn't get it," Miller says, rolling his back against the rail and leaning backward in a way that makes me uncomfortable. "Look at his face."

Jayme pushes off the rail. "She's obviously into you."

"Who?"

Miller scoffs. Jayme slaps a hand over his face. Their amusement is getting a bit old, fast, and I'm not in the mood.

"Enid," Miller says, waving a careless hand toward my quarters.

"What? That's…but she's…" I sputter like an idiot, proving their original point. Heat fills my cheeks. They must be wrong. We're just friends, close friends, and she's been there to comfort me through all of this, offering hugs, holding my hand.

But the way she looked at me…The hair on my arms raise again, and my heart hammers against my ribs as I stare at Enid sleeping in my bed.

Miller gives another halfhearted smile, and the way he points at me feels incredibly sarcastic. "There it is."

All at once, a chill rolls down my spine, and my hammering heart is seized in a fist of guilt. I step back toward my open door, shaking my head.

"Your door was open, dude," Jayme says. "Not sure why she was on your bed, but she sure wants to be there."

"Nothing happened," I say, stepping over the threshold.

"We respectfully disagree," Jayme says.

"It doesn't matter. Nothing happened and nothing will."

Jayme steps up to my doorway and leans against it, keeping his voice low enough that Enid won't hear, thank god. "Why not? Are you blind? She's strong, smart, pretty, and for some dumb reason, she's into you. Why wouldn't you make a move?"

I stop, my feet suddenly too heavy to lift, and an overwhelming ache presses down on my chest. "Bianca." I didn't think about her the whole time Enid was in my room. I should have.

Jayme casts a questioning glance at Miller, who sighs.

I stare at my shoes, willing my feet to move. Silence settles between us, filled only by other residents of The Shield returning to their own quarters. Shoes scuff the plate-metal floor, then Miller's hand falls on my shoulder. "Look, Bianca's gone. She's not coming back. Enid is here. Do you really think Bianca would want you to sit around lamenting what never was?"

I can't help it. Bianca was the center of my universe for so long. It doesn't just go away. I slide Miller's hand off my shoulder and wave him toward the door, then walk over to the scanner to close it.

Miller shrugs and moves back over the threshold, joining Jayme. "It's okay to move on. No one will judge you for it."

"*I* will," I say, as I activate the scanner and close the door, then hit the button to engage the lock.

I slip onto the bed beside Enid, careful not to bother her and far too aware of just how close she is to me here.

In the morning, I'm more refreshed than I have been in a long time. For the first time since I arrived at Paragon, my sleep was dreamless. Enid smiles at me as she steps out of the bathroom, a shy sort of smile that makes those hairs on my arms raise.

"I can't remember the last time I slept so well," she says, slipping her shoes back on.

I swing my legs over the bed and do the same. "It's been a while."

We head to breakfast together. There's no handholding or anything. In fact, the space between us feels awkward. Does she want me to hold her hand? Uncertainty keeps me from reaching out. As does the memory of Bianca.

11

THE PUZZLE CONTINUES NAGGING AT MY MIND, AND I keep the DNA structures in the pocket of my jacket as if having them close will reveal what I am missing. *What* am *I missing?*

The days blend together as I continue to try and figure out what the Protectorate is doing, and what that chemical bond Leo gave me is about. Enid comes to my room every night. Sometimes we talk until we fall asleep. Sometimes we don't say a word, instead taking comfort in each other's presence. Nothing ever happens. We are both just as awkward around each other as ever, and Enid keeps a friendly distance between us. Every morning, Enid and I discuss our plan for the day, where each of us will hunt for information. Every night after dinner, the two of us meet in either her quarters or mine to go over what we learned.

One afternoon, I sit at the table with Celeste's book, *The Fabric of the Cosmos*, and start reading. Most of the pages are littered with notes in the margins. Comments about how Newton's laws of motion are not entirely correct, *We are always everywhere*, and how the theory of relativity is almost correct. *Time is* not *linear.* Celeste took a lot of time reading, digesting, and picking apart the text. I can't help but wonder why.

At the end of one chapter, Celeste left a note on key points in the chapter.

Remember the stars.

Again, it feels like she is speaking to me, reminding me of the stars we used to watch in her room at Paragon.

The rest of my friends have fallen into daily habits, gotten comfortable with life in The Shield. Madison drifts from department to department, moving from one small cluster of Paragon defectors to another as she seeks out the spy. After weeks, we have only a handful of leads and all of them run to dead ends. I'm no closer to finding the spy now than I was when I started searching.

After breakfast, I head back to my quarters today to review my notebooks before heading to the upper levels to try and sneak into the lab and find out exactly what Leo says they are concocting up there. On the way, I pull out the sheet with the formula on it and read it for the thousandth time. The answer is there, tickling at my mind.

I place my hand to the pad and the door slides open.

Madison half-leans over the table, over my notebooks, appearing caught in the act of something as she stares at me. She's paralyzed by her own fear.

"What are you—?"

My head begins to swim and pressure builds in my temples until I'm quite certain I will be sick. My legs shake. A wave of dizziness slams against me. I've only felt this sort of sickness and pain once before when Terry tried to force his way into my mind. I stumble back a step, leaning against the doorframe for support. Madison fills my growing tunnel vision. Sweat beads on her forehead.

"Ugene, why can't I read you? Not even on the surface." Madison drops one of my notebooks and glides around the table toward me. "I can hear your thoughts when you share them with me, but otherwise there's nothing."

For some reason, no one can read me. Terry tried in Paragon, as did Dr. Cass's assistant, Hilde. I really don't have an answer for her, nor do I have the brainpower to sort it out right now.

"Madison…" Her name barely escapes my lips. All this time, I had the spy looking for the spy. No wonder she never found anything. Despite the pressure on my temples, I manage to scream, unable to form real words. Hopefully, it will call someone to my aid.

Madison crouches in front of me, snatching the formula out of my hand and reading it over. "What's this?"

I press my back against the wall, struggling against the intensity of her trying to force her way in. She waves the paper in my face.

"I need answers, Ugene. You don't understand what's at stake here if I fail."

"You okay in here?" Noah steps through the doorway, freezing when he sees Madison crouched in front of me.

Madison launches herself to her feet and rushes out the door, bumping Noah on the way. Her shoes pound on the metal gangway as she flees.

"Stop...her..."

Noah takes off after her. A moment later, the gangway rattles with a thunderous thump, and the pressure on my head disappears. Rosie steps into my quarters and crouches in front of me, pressing her hands to my temples. Her healing moves in swiftly without Madison's meddling, and the room rights itself again.

But as Rosie pulls away and I rub at my forehead, the ill sensation doesn't disappear with the other symptoms and I'm completely drained of energy.

"What happened?" Rosie asks, picking up my formula and holding it out to me.

"Madison's a spy," I say, then suck in a cool breath of stale air.

Rosie's face scrunches up. "For the Protectorate?"

She glances toward the door as Noah lugs a limp Madison back into the room.

"No. Paragon. Or the Directorate. I don't know for sure which she worked for."

Noah drops Madison on the ground in a careless way that makes me wince.

"I asked Madison to figure out who it was, not knowing it was her the whole time." I rub at my temples, then tuck the formula back into my jacket pocket.

Rosie offers me a weak smile, but her heart isn't in it. She and Madison were friendly, and I'm not sure how close they were. Did she know? "I'll get someone to collect her," she says, motioning toward Madison on the floor.

I nod stiffly.

Noah helps me off the ground and we sit together at the table. My gaze continues to drift back to Madison, a weight of sadness pressing down on my chest. I trusted her. Why do I keep trusting people only to have them betray me?

"Hey," I say, a feeble attempt at starting a conversation.

"Hey," Noah says back, casting a small smile.

"I wanted to say thanks." Well, that could be more awkward.

"For what?"

"Back at Paragon, when everyone else fled, you stayed to fight with us," I say. "You didn't have to. And I just wanted you to know I appreciate it."

Noah shrugs. "It was the right thing to do. Besides, what kind of Strongarm runs from a fight?" He grins.

"A smart one."

We both chuckle softly.

"In all seriousness," I say, leaning back and slumping down in the chair. "You still stuck with us. I don't know why, but I do think it's pretty awesome."

"I stayed that night for the same reason I'm going to Pax with you," Noah says. "I believe in you. We all do."

For a moment I stumble over my own thoughts. "What?"

"The way you stepped up and organized all of us when no one else could," he says, ticking off on his fingers as he continues. "The way you understood what was happening just about every step of the way. When we were trapped in the lobby after that sandstorm, you could have easily led all of us straight to the exit, but you waited. Where others would have abandoned the stragglers to the storm, you refused to leave anyone behind. Even people you didn't know. And right after losing your dad, you still rallied all of us together."

Everything he says feels like a lie. I led the group because they wanted me to. And any decent person wouldn't leave others behind.

Besides, I didn't lead everyone out. "We lost sixty percent of the people who left that valley. You call that victory?"

"You can't expect to enter battle without some casualties along the way," Noah says as if that excuses anything. "You need to stop looking at your failures and start looking at your victories. We see them. That's why we follow you."

"What if I told you we're going to lose?" My words hang heavy between us. Just because I got lucky a few times doesn't mean I will lead any of them to the life they deserve. I don't even know how to do that.

Madison stirs once as we wait for Rosie to retrieve help. I freeze, but Madison doesn't wake. However Noah knocked her out, it's effective.

I can't stop thinking about Madison as the spy. Was she a spy all along, before she introduced herself to me? She must have been because I didn't meet her until we were trying to escape. I needed a Telepath, and she stepped forward from the crowd. If she was the spy all along, did she purposely lead everyone into PSECT security hands on floor 189? Security was waiting, as were Dr. Cass, Forrest, and a handful of others. Was Madison responsible for walking everyone into the trap that cost Mo and seven others their lives? And if she has a way to communicate with Paragon or the Directorate somehow, what do they know about this place? Do they know about my mom and Harvey helping us escape recapture?

"There," Rosie says, leading Willow and Chase into my room, pointing at Madison on the ground.

Chase scoops Madison up and throws her over his shoulder.

Willow squares off in front of me, hands on her hips. She doesn't say anything at first. She just watches as Chase lumbers out with Madison. Noah follows close behind, asking what he can do to help the Protectorate. He's ready to fight. I'm not.

"Do you realize now why we keep our missions secret?" Willow asks. "The fewer people who know the details, the less the risk to our cause. Should you choose to fight with us and not against us, you will get the answers you're looking for."

I nod. What can I really say to argue at this point?

"Doc and I would like to talk to you in our office," Willow says. "You want to know who we are and what we do, but I think first you need to learn who *you* are." Willow's statement throws what little remains of my confidence in the trash.

What does she mean by that? I know who I am.

Part Two

"TO THOSE WHO WOULD OPPOSE THE DIRECTOR-ate, make no mistake: we will work tirelessly to preserve our way of life and protect the sanctity of our city and everything it was founded upon. By any means necessary."

~ Directorate Chief Seaduss
Today

12

MY MOOD IS SOUR AS I TRAIL INTO DOC'S OFFICE. WIL-low leans over Doc's shoulder as he shows her something on his computer. The screen is old tech with a black plastic casing on the back, so I can't see through it like with the more modern screens.

For a moment, neither of them acknowledges me, so I clear my throat and they both look up. Doc stares at me much as he has since the beginning, like a puzzle he has to solve.

"What are you going to do with Madison?"

Willow sighs. "For now, she will be held in a Power-dampening cell to ensure she can't communicate with anyone. We need to be sure she didn't leak information before we proceed, so she will be questioned." Willow cocks her head. "You know, she was caught more than once trying to read people. This doesn't come as a surprise. We were preparing to bring her in for questioning already."

"Some of that she was doing for me," I admit. "I asked her to learn more, but she never really had anything to report. Or maybe she just didn't want to share it with me."

"Why?" Willow asks.

"You have to understand, after everything we've been through, it's hard to trust anyone. Especially when we aren't even allowed to know what's really going on. I just wanted to know we weren't setting ourselves up for more trouble."

Willow raises her thin brows at me.

I wave dismissively. "Clearly, I missed the mark."

"I guess so."

I sink into the empty chair in front of Doc's desk. "Anyway, you wanted to talk to me."

Willow perches on the edge of the desk, hands folded on her thigh. "You told us before that Paragon wanted you because you are unique, that they used you as a base against other subjects so they could find a way to enhance Powers."

I nod.

"And did they ever discover your Power?" Willow asks.

I shift and fold my arms over my chest. Is this a trick question or a joke? Either way, I'm not in the mood. "Dr. Cass said they couldn't find any traces of any abilities. That my skills are in leading others to be stronger and in my intelligence, for whatever that's worth."

Willow snaps a glance at Doc, who sits back, rubbing at his graying beard as he watches me. Something about him feels familiar, but the way he stares makes me so uncomfortable I can't focus long enough to place him.

"You are unique, Ugene," Doc says. "Joyce was right about that. But she lied to you. You have what we call recessive genetic allele mutation."

An Allele mutation? This must be a joke. Now hardly seems like the time, and I have to stamp down a surge of irritation. I've studied myself over and over again, and I don't recall ever discovering something like this. Sure, I understand that recessive alleles can make me a carrier of certain genetic dispositions, but the mutation of the alleles is beyond my knowledge. Is that what makes me Powerless? I shake my head. It can't be true.

"It's okay to feel confused," Doc says, folding his hands over his slightly paunchy stomach and drumming his stubby thumbs together. "Typically, people with two recessive alleles act as a carrier, and when it comes to Powers, this usually means they have a dormant Power that hasn't surfaced."

Dormant Power? Is it possible? I sit up straighter in my chair. "So I do have a potential Power?"

Doc's expression saddens, offering absolutely no reassurance.

"Not exactly. Ugene, your alleles aren't matching pairs."

The news knocks the hope out of me, and I slump down. Why do people offer me hope just to rip it away again? If the alleles aren't paired, they aren't compatible. If they aren't compatible, I'll never have a Power.

"Sounds to me like Dr. Cass wasn't lying at all," I say bitterly.

"You misunderstand, Ugene," Willow says. Her blue eyes sparkle. Is she excited about this? The very notion disgusts me. "You don't have two, but dozens, all mismatched."

"But…but that's…"

"The next link in Power evolution," Doc says.

I rub my forehead, try to push away the headache forming.

"You see," Doc continues, "those alleles are mutated and missing the linking mechanisms that create Powers, which is why Powers aren't manifesting for you. It's like the links in a chain, and a piece of the link is missing, which creates a gap that prevents other links from connecting to it. But you can't just force the link closed or it changes the entirety of your DNA in ways that could be potentially catastrophic. Or deadly."

Didn't sound promising for me in the least.

"I have not finished decoding your genetic structure yet, but so far I have discovered more than twenty of those broken links. Twenty Powers that could potentially link together to become one dominant hybrid Superpower once that gap is closed."

"But not for me," I say as an eddy of disgust swirls my stomach. "I'm a carrier, right?"

"Unfortunately, yes." Doc heaves out a sigh. "However, given enough time, your DNA could be used to force us into that next step of evolution. Maybe not a Hybrid yet, but the knowledge and actual DNA could be used to strengthen the linking mechanism in others."

I blink. Taking all of this in is too much, and my mind can't make sense of everything.

Willow leans forward. "Dr. Cass could have used your biology to selectively offer those Superpowers to anyone."

Now I realize why Dr. Cass wanted me. She wanted to use me to create these selective Supers. All that blood they took. All those samples. Paragon still has those.

Wait, Doc has a sample to examine, but I never gave him one. I never had blood drawn or gave them anything to use to study me. "Where did you get a sample of my genetic structure?" I ask, unable to look up, still pressing my fingers to my temples.

"We took samples from everyone during the intake process," Willow says.

"Without permission," I say.

"It's standard security protocol," Willow says.

I glare at her, and I'm not sure if I look angry or scary or what, but she flinches back. Deception is deception. How can they not see they are making some of the same mistakes as Dr. Cass?

"We need to know who we are bringing into our home," Doc says.

Their home? Is that what they call this place? "That's funny because the people at Paragon said basically the same thing."

"We aren't them," Willow says. "Why do you keep fighting us on this?"

"Why? Because you still haven't given me a good reason to trust you."

"Ugene, we need you to work with us, not against us," Willow says. "If not for yourself, do it for the others. They follow you. They see you as their leader, but what you're doing is hurting them more than helping."

I rise, balling my hands into fists. "I never asked to be the leader. They put that on me."

"Did they?" Doc asks. "Worthy leaders often find leadership thrust on them, even when they don't want it. And look where that got all of you." Doc waves around the room. "You led them out of that place and into safety. Not everyone is a fighter like you. They wouldn't have survived without you."

"I'm not a fighter!" Why do people keep assuming I wanted any of this? All I wanted was a cure for Dad. Maybe even a Power. Now

I can't have either.

"Willow, will you please excuse us?" Doc says it so patiently that it even pacifies me.

Willow huffs as she marches toward the door, but she doesn't question his request. As soon as we are alone, Doc leans on his forearms so he can be closer to me.

"Let me ask you something, if I may." Doc pauses, waiting for me to nod. I do. "What are your plans for the future?"

The question takes me aback. "What do you mean?" I've not thought more than a few steps into the future since all of this began.

"I mean if the Directorate gets their way, and people with weak Powers have no true value to society, where does that leave you? What will you do if we fail and the Directorate carries out their plan?"

The question grates on me. My desire to be ordinary is what drove me to Paragon and set me on this course. If I truly can never have a Power, as Doc suggests, then according to Directorate laws there is no place for me. Which means my options are to die in the Deadlands or stay here and help the Protectorate. The weight of this reality makes me sink down on my chair.

Doc nods. "We aren't your enemy, Ugene. We want the same thing as you—a chance for everyone to have equal rights no matter their Power. This is what we fight for. But to succeed, we need information, security, and strong leaders." He sinks back in his chair, but never breaks his gaze from me. "Imagine the good that someone with your intelligence could do to our cause. Your people from Paragon follow you. They trust you. To them, you are their leader, their Ambassador."

There's that word again. But he's right. I've known it for a while now. Like it or not, those people follow me.

"If you can inspire such dedication from your friends, imagine what you could do for Elpis."

Silence falls as Doc lets his suggestion hang in the air like a guillotine. Finally, I sigh. "I'm not a fighter."

"Sure you are." Doc offers a kind smile. "You fought your way out of Paragon. You've fought us every step of the way to protect them.

You're doing it right now. How do you not see that? Until you let down your guard, you'll never trust us." Doc stands, waiting. I realize he's waiting for me to join him, so I rise as well. "Do you know what happened to the handful of people who decided to trust Dr. Cass's promise of safety and return home?"

More than anything I wish I could tell him no, but a sinking feeling in my gut says otherwise. All I can manage to get out is a number. "Twenty-three."

"What?"

"That's how many went home."

Doc nods as if he already knew that. "Paragon has swept most of them back up. We don't know what Paragon is doing with them, but I have no doubt they've already grilled each one for information about you."

And again, I have failed them. We fought so hard to escape that place, and of the sixty percent who made it, only thirty percent remain. We went from one hundred thirty-nine to forty-two. I can't think about this anymore. Not right now.

"Will you help us, Ugene? We sure could use someone like you on our team."

"I get to be the Ambassador for my people?"

Doc shakes his head. "My dear boy, you're thinking small again. You are far more important than that."

What does that mean? Aside from my genetics, I don't understand how I can be so important to this group.

"Are you ready to join our cause and help us create a better future for everyone, no matter what their Power?"

The line sounds an awful lot like what Dr. Cass asked me before I signed up at Paragon. But how can I argue with that? What choice do I really have? Either I help them and have a purpose, or I'm nothing. I nod.

"Good." Doc claps my shoulder in a very fatherly way and guides me toward the door.

As we step into the hall, an alarm on Willow's watch chimes

repeatedly. Doc's face falls.

"What is it?" he asks.

"Directorate announcement," Willow says.

The three of us enter a conference room, where Doc turns on the announcement.

Directorate Chief Seaduss's face fills the holoscreen, his strong jaw and angular facial features making me flinch. The way he stares at the camera makes it seem like he's staring straight at me, and it makes my skin crawl. I've never understood how a Somatic ended up in charge of the Directorate, but his face certainly is imposing, commanding.

"Citizens of Elpis," he begins, his voice just as strong and commanding as his presence. "I stand before you today with rousing news. When I took this office, I promised you that we would find a cure for regression. I have kept my promise."

Hope lifts my chest. Maybe this is it then. Maybe the entire fight, the unlawful experiments, will end.

The camera pulls back, revealing a clear plastic podium in front of him. At his shoulders, each member of the Directorate stands with their chins raised proudly—Director Collins and Shielding, Director Jordan, and four others whose names I can't recall. Dr. Cass waits at his side with her hands folded together, wearing the same pencil skirt and jacket she always does.

Seaduss continues, "Paragon has developed a vaccine that will slow the rate of regression in our citizens. The new vaccines are a breakthrough, but they will only work if all regressing citizens submit to them."

So far, his words seem logical enough, but I can't shake the sensation that something is off.

"Tomorrow morning, vaccinations will commence for all citizens with a Cass Scale rank below thirty, particularly those between the ages of sixteen and thirty. The Department of Military Affairs will set up vaccination stations first in Pax and Clement. We ask that citizens report to their local station for immediate vaccination."

I glance up at Willow and Doc, and both wear the same bearing of red-hot fury. I'm missing something important.

Directorate Chief Seaduss's voice pulls my attention back to the video clip. "It has been the Directorate's goal to ensure the safety and continuity of our way of life since the founding of our city. This vaccine offers us a chance to focus on improving the living standards in Pax and Clement, increase the quality of water supply and food in these impoverished boroughs, and make life better for all our citizens.

"However, a new danger looms, and it lives within our own borders. A group of dissenters continually evade us, and the Directorate has declared a state of emergency to pass a new proposition immediately."

And here it comes…

"Proposition 9 begins tomorrow," Seaduss continues. "Each citizen with outstanding debts under the Consumption Tax Law will have the opportunity to erase their debts in exchange for services to the Department of Military Affairs. Those who continue to actively work for the DMA will receive a ten percent increase in wages."

My hands start sweating and I glance at Willow again. Her jaw is twitching, she has it clamped so tight.

"All citizens with debts are required to report to their local DMA station before the end of this week for assessment. Those who are selected for service will be given a second booster to aid in the facilitation of the protection of Elpis.

"Together, we can oppose this dissension and begin eradicating regression from Elpis for good," Seaduss says, then the video stops.

For a moment, I'm too stunned to speak. The Directorate is turning regressing citizens into a military force. They are already viewed as expendables if Lily's story about being sent out is to be believed. This also means no one else will be sent into the arms of the Protectorate. They have cut us off at the source.

Us. Funny. That's the first time I lumped this group with my own.

I lick dry lips.

"Elpis is more dangerous now than ever before," Willow says. "You know it, too. It's written all over your face. And Pax is going to not only be crawling with DMA enforcing this new law, but they are bolstering their numbers using people we normally would target."

I nod. My mind is racing and it's hard to put everything into place, but one thought prevails. "Doesn't this make now the best time to recruit more people? We need to get to them before they do."

Willow raises an eyebrow. "*We?*"

Do I really mean we? Accepting that we should work together to save these people from whatever the Directorate has planned next is a big step, and I still don't know if I fully trust the Protectorate. But I told Doc I would help.

"We are all living here together," I say, hoping this explanation covers my tracks a little. "If the Directorate gets a large enough force, they will find us all living here and destroy what you've worked so hard to build. That effects my group as much as yours. All I want is to protect my people."

My people. I'm not sure I've actually referred to them as mine before, but I don't really know how else to define them. And they want me to lead. I suppose that makes them mine as much as the Protectorate is Willow's or Doc's.

"Does this mean we are working together?" Willow asks, crossing her arms.

"Is there another option?"

Doc chuckles, but I don't really know why. Willow smirks at him. "Okay then."

I cross my arms. "Tell me about the mission Jayme and all those others went on before when I found him in the medical bay. What were they after?"

"Information," Willow says.

"What kind of information?"

Willow gives me a blank stare.

Okay, so she isn't gonna tell me. I shake my head. "Good luck."

Doc nudges Willow and she fumbles with her words as I turn on my heel and head toward the door.

"Ugene!" Willow's sharp tone stops me in my tracks. "You're

right. We are out of time. We need to act quickly. *We* need to help those people the Directorate is targeting before it's too late."

I turn back at the door. "Then I guess we need to head to Pax."

Doc nods. "I'll see it done by the end of the day."

Seaduss gave the people one week. We have less than a week to stop the Directorate.

Willow's watch chimes again as I walk out. "Wait!" Willow calls as I step into the hall. "It's Miller."

13

THE PIT IN MY STOMACH EXPANDS QUICKLY AS I struggle to keep pace with Willow. People are wandering back from work, and they make way for Willow and me to rush through the increasingly crowded hallway. We rapidly descend a set of steps to another level and down a familiar tunnel, and my gut sinks further and further with each pounding step.

The two of us burst into the water treatment center side by side. My lungs burn a little from the exertion, but Willow doesn't stop. She turns and heads along the rows of massive water tanks, weaving easily from one aisle to the next. For a Psionic, she would make a great Somatic. I struggle to keep up.

The familiar thunder of the waterfall drowns out the hum of the water treatment system as we draw closer. Willow stops on a dime, but my feet skid on the damp stone and I pitch forward, flinging my arms out to catch my balance.

Miller sits on the safety railing in front of the chasm below, not bothering to hold on. One slip and he would plummet into the churning, deadly waters below. He slouches on the railing, precariously perched. The hood of his sweatshirt is drawn over his head.

"Get Jayme," I tell Willow, working hard at catching my breath. "I'll get him."

"Don't let him pull you in," she says.

"He's not going anywhere," I say confidently, though a flash of resentment rushes through me. Her priorities are out of order.

Willow nods tightly and slips away.

I inch closer, careful not to startle Miller into any sudden movements. I don't want to make him jump. After a few, careful inhales to get control of my breathing, I close the rest of the distance.

"Miller?" I call. "Been looking everywhere for you, man."

Miller doesn't move. He remains statue-still.

I manage to reach the railing and put my hands on the slick steel. *Keep it casual.* "Doesn't seem like a safe place to sit, but whatever. What are you doing here?"

Miller doesn't look at me, doesn't move or speak for a while. I wait patiently and am about to say something else, thinking maybe he forgot I'm here when he finally does speak. His voice barely reaches over the thunder of the waterfall in front of us crashing into the chasm far below. "I screwed up. Murph and I had a big fight. Big."

"About what?"

His response is hardly audible over the noise. "You."

Me? Why would they get into a fight about me? "It can't be that bad."

Miller shakes his head, and for a moment I'm afraid he will slip off the rail. My muscles tense, ready to grab him. Thankfully he doesn't budge. "I don't think I've ever said anything so ugly to someone else. I deserve everything he said to me." The emotion drains from his voice and it becomes completely hollow. "I don't know what I'm doing or why I even bother to try. I can't do a ruddy thing. I'm Powerless. Completely useless. And broken."

"We all are."

"No. I'm not me."

I would love to argue with him, tell him that he's wrong, but it's hard when I have admitted over and over to myself that he isn't himself. And right now, he certainly doesn't sound like Miller.

"You don't sound broken. You sound human. Why do you think you're useless?" I lean my forearms carefully on the railing, so I don't shake him or slip forward unexpectedly.

The new angle makes the desperation on his face more apparent. Miller has no intention of leaving this room. The reality and weight of his conscious decision presses down on my shoulders. He's given up.

Miller doesn't look in my direction. His entire body appears on the verge of giving out. I glance over the chasm at the churning force of water below. He won't survive the fall. Miller raises a hand and looks at it like a foreign object. And then he speaks.

"I can't live like this." Miller's voice is devoid of emotion. "I'm incomplete."

I can't understand exactly what he means. I never had Powers to lose in the first place. How horrible it must be, but if I can survive without Powers, Miller can, too. And I do know what it feels like to be incomplete, even if our situations are a little different.

"If you think losing Powers makes you useless, what does that say about me?" I ask.

"It's not the same."

"Maybe," I admit, watching the water thunder into the chasm below. "But we both have something no one else does."

Miller snorts and drops his arm, making him slip forward just a little bit on the rail. His attention finally turns to me instead of the promise of death below. "What's that?"

"When you're Powerless, you have to find other solutions to problems. Solutions that people who have Powers could never even think of because using Powers is the easy answer. We're wildcards, man."

Miller doesn't say anything, and his expression remains blank, but his eyes examine me, weighing my words. My offer.

"We aren't the same," Miller says, and the words hurt. "You're smart and resourceful because you've never had Powers. You adapted."

"So will you."

Miller shakes his head. "You don't know what it feels like to have a piece of yourself torn out, gone. I'm tired. Empty."

Miller turns his attention back to the churning abyss. Reality slams into my chest. My stomach drops again as I feel the railing shift forward just a touch. Miller pushes himself forward toward the water. Throwing myself against the railing, I lunge forward. My hands grasp Miller's arm, but we are both slick with mist. The grip slips to his wrist. Bracing my weight against the railing, praying it doesn't give out, I try pulling Miller up.

He doesn't grab my wrist.

I grunt, pulling, but Miller's weight is too much for me. My grip slips a touch. "No!"

"Let go."

"No!" I lean back, pushing my knees against the railing, struggling to pull him up, gritting my teeth. "I'm not...losing...you!"

The thunder of falling water dulls. I watch as the water itself falls slower, more deliberately. What is going on? That's not natural. Were I not entangled trying to keep Miller from certain death, I might be more intrigued. But all I can think is, *Please don't die.*

"Miller!" Jayme's scream comes from the edge of the water tanks, too far away to offer immediate assistance, and his feet slip on the stone as he tries to reach us.

"I can't..." I call back over my shoulder at Jayme.

He stops near one of the tanks and raises his hands toward the waterfall. Sweat beads on his face. My grip slips a touch more, snapping my full attention back to Miller.

"Come on, Miller," I growl, tugging him up. "Grab...hold!"

Air pressure shifts, thickening and making it harder to breathe.

Miller glances down at the chasm. The waterfall shifts on the far wall, moving horizontally toward us. My heart thuds against my ribs as I watch.

Then slick, clammy fingers clamp around my wrist. *Thank god!* Miller swings his other hand up, trying to catch my arm or hand or anything to give him purchase, but it's too slippery. With renewed hope, I lean back and pull, but my feet slip out from under me, dragging me under the railing.

A wave of water rises, shoving Miller and me toward solid ground. We slide under the railing across the stone floor. Water fills my nose and mouth. Then all at once, everything returns to normal. As I cough and gasp for air, clothes plastered against my skin. The roar of the waterfall as the water plummets back into the chasm fills my water-logged ears. Air pressure normalizes.

Pushing myself upright, I take stock, searching for Miller.

Three feet away, Miller lies face down on the ground, unmoving. I crawl toward him, clawing at the stone to pull myself along. When I reach his side, I sit upright and nudge Miller, who coughs and sputters up water, brushing wet blond hair away from his face. He's okay. I glance over at Jayme, kneeling near the tank. Blood trickles from Jayme's nose, and I recall Dr. Lydia warning him to stop pushing himself. What exactly are Jayme's limits? Did he go too far?

Beside me, Miller sucks in a shuddering breath, and he presses a shaking hand against his eyes.

"Don't do that again," I say, hoping it sounds humorous even though I don't feel any humor in me.

When Miller speaks, his voice is tight. "I'm sorry."

"And don't apologize," I say.

Jayme rises, hauling Miller up as well. The two pull each other into a tight hug and I step back.

I just nod, watching as Jayme pulls back an inch and grabs Miller's face in his hands. There's so much intensity in the way they look at each other and cling to each other, both just as soaked as me. It's so obvious how much they love each other. I look away to give them some privacy.

14

JAYME AND MILLER ARE TOGETHER, AND I HAVE A
feeling the two of them will be just fine. Willow and Rosie show up as
I leave the chamber, but I reassure them that things are under control
and the two of them just need some space.

When I reach the open door of my quarters, dripping and eager
to change into dry clothes, a collection of familiar faces greets me. All
my friends, except Miller, sit around the table or on my bed waiting
for me. I hesitate, and Enid jumps to her feet and rushes toward me.

"What happened?" she asks.

"Everything." I don't have the energy to provide details at the
moment.

"Have you heard?" she asks.

Everyone else is staring at me expectantly.

"What?" I ask, twisting water out of my shirt.

"About the DMA!" Noah says.

My face falls. Can't I just change? "Oh. Yeah. Just now."

The questions come in rapid succession.

"What does it mean?" Leo asks. He's perched on the edge of the
bed, gripping it tight.

"D-do they really h-have a c-cure?" Boyd asks from the table.

"I won't take it," Rosie says.

"What if they find us?" Sho asks.

"Are we fighting back?" Noah asks.

"What's our plan, then? What are we going to do?" Enid shifts
her feet anxiously.

"I'm working on it." Not completely a lie. But also not completely the truth. My head is reeling from the questions. "Just…" I hold up a hand and march across the room to my notebooks.

Noah vacates one of the chairs for me to sit. I sink into it as I flip open the notebook to a fresh page. My pen flies across the page as I write down everything I learned from the broadcast before any of it can drift away. I don't want to screw up any of the details. Noah peers over my shoulder and I slouch to obstruct his view as I finish. Then I sit back, frowning. Noah tries to see it again and I snap the notebook closed.

"You're awful quiet," Sho says from the edge of the bed beside Leo. "What's going through that head of yours?"

I lick my lips, unsure where to start.

"We will need to go up to Pax soon," I say. "I won't force anyone to come along, but the Directorate is forcing the Protectorate to act, and if we don't help then we may as well have escaped Paragon for nothing."

"How do you figure?" Leo asks, frowning.

I glance at the open door.

"The Directorate is beefing up the DMA's numbers, most likely to attack the Protectorate. Once they find this place, we will be right back where we started. Which means we need to stop the Directorate before they can gather too many people to their side."

Everyone nods, waiting for me to say more, but I don't really know what else to say.

Noah punches a fist into his other hand like he's ready to pound some heads. "Then we need to strike them now."

Bri—the blonde girl always clinging to Noah—sits up straighter as if she agrees.

"With what?" I shake my head. "We don't have any weapons to use against the DMA. The Protectorate doesn't have the information they need to expose the truth. And even the collective Powers of the people in The Shield won't be enough to fight back against the full force of the DMA."

"Well, we can't do nothing!" Enid says, crossing her arms. "So, what's your plan?"

I open my mouth, fumble for a moment, then sigh. "I don't have one this time."

"You're saying we just sit and take this?" Sho says, surging to his feet. "*No!*"

Again, I work my jaw for the right words.

"Ugene!" Enid snaps, pulling my attention back to the room. "What can we do? We can't just wait around."

I bite my lip. There has to be a way to be sure that no one here is a spy. "Okay…I have an idea, but it's completely crazy, and we will probably die."

"Better than waiting for Paragon to claim us again," Rosie says. "What's the idea?"

"We have to get the people of Elpis to revolt against the Directorate."

A stunned silence falls like a smothering blanket over the room. No one says a word. Noah, who was so eager to smash some skulls just a few moments ago, has taken a step back, arms hanging limp at his sides.

"But you…you said…" Enid fumbles to find the right words.

"That we can't hold against DMA forces. But if the Directorate falls, their plan falls with them, and we can't succeed unless everyone follows our lead."

Boyd trembles in his chair and starts rubbing his hands together to cover it up, but it doesn't fail my notice. He shakes his head just a little, and the fear in him makes his stutter worse. "I-I-I c-can-can't…"

"It's okay. I won't force anyone else to do this. But I am leaving. Tonight. Willow and Doc agreed we need to go to Pax."

Enid steps forward and takes my hand. "I told you. We finish this together or not at all. I'm with you no matter what."

"I would rather go down fighting than hiding," Noah says. "I'm in."

Sho clenches his jaw and nods in agreement as well, along with Lily.

One by one, they all agree to join me, with the exception of Boyd. The ease with which they accept one of my hairbrained, off the cuff ideas—particularly a clear suicide mission like this—makes my stomach twist in knots. Noah was right. They follow me with blind faith... *Right to their deaths.*

15

AT DINNER, DOC CAME TO OUR TABLE AND INFORMED me that they secured a line with Mom, who went underground for her own safety. With Dad dead and me on the run, I suppose it was only a matter of time before the Directorate came after her. I'm just glad she's found a safe place to hide.

Doc escorts me to the conference room, and we stop in front of a closed door. I take a moment to really study him. The sadness makes his aging face sag like the sorrow is pulling all the skin down. And those eyes, usually so critical of me, now appear soft and caring. Like a parent. In some ways, he reminds me of everything I wish my father could have been: soft, caring, imparting wisdom.

"Is Willow your daughter?" I ask.

Doc laughs. "No. Not by blood. But I do see her as a daughter." He opens the door, motioning me inside. "And she bears the burden of all the people in this place. It's a lot to carry on one's shoulders."

I can understand that. What horrors are those I've failed facing now?

"I have met Willow before," I say, facing Doc. "On Career Day she was there, handing out flyers. She invited me to some rally or something to fight Proposition 8.5."

Doc's shoulders sag. "Yes, well, it's probably best you weren't at the rally. The DMA stormed in and people died in the chaos, and the Directorate blamed it on us, called us radicals and convinced the people that we are trying to destroy everything. Willow blames herself." He cocks his head, examining me. "You two aren't so different, you know. Maybe that's why you butt heads."

"Maybe."

I step into the room, and Doc closes the door behind me to give me privacy. The light in the room comes from lamps in each corner. A round table with chairs waits in the center of the room. Above the table, a holograph flashes blue light. I settle into a chair. There are so many questions I have for Mom, and I'm not sure where to begin. I tap a button to turn off the blue light, and the box on the table announces, "Establishing connection now."

Mom's face lights the room in full color. It almost feels like she's actually in front of me. I wish more than anything she really was. Having her here would help lighten the burdens weighing me down.

"Ugene." She breathes out a sigh of relief. "I'm so glad you made it. I wanted to join you, but the Directorate is watching my every move. I can't get to The Shield without risking its exposure. Just establishing a secure enough connection to contact you has proven difficult. How are you?"

"I don't know." Just seeing her face brings tears of joy to my eyes. I would give anything for one of her hugs right now. "Where did you send me, Mom?"

"Oh, my Tough Guy. I'm sorry. There is so much your father and I didn't tell you. We tried to protect you from all of this, but the Proposition made it hard to keep you safe." She hesitates. "Did you find a letter from Dad?"

"I haven't read it."

"It's okay." She smiles, and I wish she would stroke my cheek like she always did when I was younger. "It's time for you to know the truth. I should have told you sooner. We just…we assumed we had more time." She shifts, making the holograph wobble. "Do you remember when we had to take you into the hospital when you got that infection in your foot seven years ago?"

I nod. "It was horrific. That was some of the worst healing." Not worse than Celeste healing my back during that first Survival test, after that fight with Derrek and Terry.

"They had to take blood samples to make sure it didn't spread before they could remove it all," Mom says. "But the samples went missing. Later, we learned that Joyce had taken the samples for her new project and that she had a secret meeting scheduled with Director Seaduss regarding some proposal, so your dad worked his way into the meeting. Dr. Finnias can tell you the details, but the short version is that the Directorate split."

What did she mean by that? How could I ask Dr. Finnias?

And just like that, it hits me. Doc is Dr. Finnias. He was the CEO of Paragon before Dr. Cass took over, deposed during the Directorate split. That's why I recognize him.

"Shortly after that," Mom continues, "Paragon released their research on the dangers of regression, and people started to panic and begged the Directorate to do something, but the Directorate Chief offered false reassurances. In a matter of weeks, he was found dead in his office—the Directorate blamed it on extremists—and Seaduss took his place."

I slump in the chair. "Wait, what does this have to do with me and those samples?"

"Ugene, you are unique. Those samples proved it. And they killed people to find you."

"But I don't understand. I thought it was fear of regression that caused the Directorate split."

Mom nods. "It was. Seaduss used Joyce to orchestrate the split." Mom rubs her brow and sighs. "Once the dust settled, he introduced Proposition 8.5 to the Directorate agenda. Now, he is pushing a new Proposition that will further his cause."

Proposition 8.5 passed after I went to Paragon, and it allowed the Directorate to force people into testing at Paragon. If I hadn't volunteered myself, the DMA would have knocked down the door to take me anyway.

"What is his cause?" I ask.

"I can't be sure, but it has something to do with the people in Pax." Mom sighs. "We wanted to get you to the Protectorate sooner, but it was too late."

"Because I ran away." Tension seeps into my voice, and my throat tightens. "I thought I had something to prove. I thought he resented me. He was so mean to me, Mom."

"He just didn't know how to react," she says. "Ugene, he loved you more than anything, and, for the last seven years of his life, he dedicated every moment to protecting you."

Is she serious? She calls that love? "Why are you defending him? He treated me like I was less than worthless. All I ever wanted was to prove to him that I wasn't. But the things he said to me, how he treated me every day…and you're defending him!"

Mom's expression shifts from tenderness to anger, the lines on her forehead deepening. "You have no idea what it was like for him. Don't you dare assume you comprehend what your father went through to protect you. It was never about him or me! It was you."

I open my mouth, but no words come out. All those times he screamed at me to try harder to fit in, insisted that I could make a Power manifest, wanted me to be ordinary. And all that time he must have known it would never happen. He *must* have. Tears roll down my cheeks, and I brush them away.

"The second he found out where you went," she continues, the anger slowly dissipating from her tone, "he set out to find a way to get into Paragon and get you out, no matter what." Her words choke off and she sniffles, then brushes away her own tears. Her voice thickens with grief, "We both knew he might not make it."

My head is swimming, trying to process all of this while battling the grief threatening to break free. I just can't understand why he would act the way he did toward me while doing everything he did for me. It doesn't make sense. "I lost them both," I say, but the voice that comes out doesn't sound like my own. "Dad and Bianca."

"I'm so sorry, Ugene." Mom's expression takes on gentle compassion that makes me feel like I'm home, even though I'm not. "I know how much you cared about her. And her poor parents. They haven't been the same since."

My chest clenches, like my heart is trying to implode. "It hurts. How do I deal with the hurt?"

"It's ok to grieve for them," Mom says. "But it's also important to remember that you are still alive, and they would want you to focus on living."

A loud knock makes me jump in my seat, but when I look around I'm still alone with the holograph. Mom glances over her shoulder, and her whole body tenses up. When she looks back at me, it's with urgency. Her words come out in a rush. "You are the future, Ugene. The Protectorate is prepared to defend you, but you need to trust them. They can help."

"You trust these people?" I ask, pressing my fingers against my eyelids to stop the tears.

"I do, and you should, too." Another knock, and I realize it's coming from her end. "You need them. And they need you. You are the one who can show the people that the Directorate is wrong. You are hope."

I lean closer like I can reach out and stop her from leaving. "I don't want this."

"I told you that you have the potential to save us all. That hasn't changed. If anything, I grow more certain of it by the day."

Leadership isn't something I ever asked for, and being in charge of the people I helped escape is one thing…being responsible for the future of the entire city makes me want to crawl back into my quarters and hide until all of this blows over. But both she and Doc seem to think this job has fallen on me. I can't let them down.

"I have to go," she whispers leaning closer.

"Will you come here?" I ask, reaching for her before realizing I can't actually touch her.

"I hope so."

Muffled voices come from somewhere around her.

"Read the letter, Ugene."

Before I have a chance to respond, the communication cuts out, leaving the room bathed in the soft blue glow of the inactive holograph. I rest my elbows on the table and bow my head into my hands. It's too much. The truth about my genetics and my father. The expectations on my shoulders. Death and murder. Hiding in my quarters feels like the perfect thing to do.

16

ANGER FILLS MY CHEST, PUMPS OUT THROUGH MY veins as I perch on the edge of my bed. Nothing makes sense anymore. The life I thought I knew was an illusion. Dad told me I used to have so much promise, that I was lazy like I could just *will* myself to be different. And I tried. I really did, but I would never be like everyone else. Dad had to have known that. So why did he push me so hard?

My nostrils flare. My grip on the edge of the bed tightens.

When Dr. Cass came to our house and I challenged Dad, he had been so adamant that I obey him. If I hadn't acted like a stubborn, ignorant child at that moment, if I hadn't been so sure I was right, he might still be alive. His disease might not have taken him. Whether he sacrificed himself for me or not, I failed him. I failed him in the worst possible way.

Why would my parents not just tell me the truth? All my muscles are coiled up tight, ready to spring.

Before Testing Day, Dad had distanced himself from me. After Testing Day, he'd alternated between devastating looks of disappointment and musclebound anger. Just remembering those fights makes the vein in my neck pulse.

When we fought, he would slam things around, tense his muscles, and talk to me like a soldier. While he never actually struck me, I have no doubt that there were several occasions where he would have loved nothing more than knocking some sense into me. My breaths come in sharply over bared teeth.

Was it all an act? If he loved me so much, why did he always pick fights with me?

I slam my fist against the mattress.

Has anyone ever told me the truth?

I scream loud and long, not caring who might hear, and grab the nearest object, hurling it across the room. My fist connects with the metal wall, sending a jolt of pain up into my shoulder.

I scream until my throat hurts. Until my breath runs out. Until the rage binds everything inside so rigidly that I have to hunch over, coiled tight until there's nothing left. No anger, no strength, no breath.

I sink to my knees and cry. The rage is gone, replaced by utter devastation. Why am I here, in this place? What am I supposed to do?

I'm proud of you, Ugene. His final words come back to me, and I start to shake on my knees.

There's nothing to be proud of.

I should have protected you from this.

But it was my own stubborn will to prove I was right that cost Dad his life.

You're stronger than I ever was.

But I'm not. I'm not even half as strong as Dad.

I'm proud of you…

It can't be for nothing.

I brush the tears from my eyes. Celeste's book is open upside down on the floor, the pages bent, and the corner dented from where it hit the wall. Shaking, I push off the floor and move toward the book, numbness creeping through my body. I pick it up, and as I smooth out the pages the blood on my knuckles stands out in sharp red contrast to the white pages.

The book fell open to chapter five, "The Frozen River." At the top of the page, Celeste's handwriting catches my attention. I sniffle and brush away the last of the tears.

A man who hides behind The Shield is safe. A man who raises The Shield is the Hero.

It feels oddly like she's speaking to me, like maybe she knew I would throw the book and it would land open on this page. When we rode the metro away from Paragon, I suspected that Celeste's prophecy about the fall of Cassiopeia could be directly related to Dr. Cass. But if that's the case, could The Shield in this quote literally mean this place? Maybe this is Celeste's way of telling me I can't just live here quietly, but that I need to fight, just like everyone else wants me to do.

"I could use your crazy brain, Celeste," I say, my voice strained. "I don't know what to do."

Before closing the book, I flip to the first page and unfold it. Again, Celeste's handwriting in large letters stands out on the title page. *If you wonder where you need to be, it's exactly where you are.*

I suck in a breath. *Did* she know this would all happen? I brush my fingers over the ink indents of her penned hand, then close the cover and set the book on the table.

"Ugene? I heard you scream. Are you okay?" Enid calls through the closed door.

I don't want to be alone anymore. I don't want to hide anymore. I don't want to lie anymore.

"No," I call back, moving toward the pad to scan my palm and open the door. My eyes still burn from the tears, and I wipe at my face once more as the door slides open, just to be sure the tears are all gone.

I must look like some sort of mess because the second Enid sees me, she offers a sad smile. "Your hand!" Enid holds my hand tenderly in hers, examining the wounds, then pulls a handkerchief from her pocket and wraps it around my knuckles. "What's wrong?"

"Dad…" I can't get any more out. The words are just sort of… lost.

"Oh, Ugene." She pulls me into a hug.

I hug her back, alleviated by her presence. With Enid here, I feel comfortable letting go of the grief. She makes me feel less alone.

When I pull away, my fingers fumble at the zipper on my jacket where Dad's letter remains. I sink down on the edge of the bed, then pull out the letter, turning the envelope between my fingers.

"What's that?" Enid asks as she joins me.

"A letter from Dad."

She stares at the envelope. "Why haven't you opened it?"

"I couldn't bring myself to do it."

"You…you want to open it now?"

I glance over at her. "I can't do this alone."

Enid slips her fingers through mine and gives my hand a squeeze. "I'm not going anywhere."

I nod, and with my fumbling free hand, I manage to get the envelope open and slide out the paper tucked inside. Enid shifts closer, offering her support with a rub on my back. I pull in a breath, then let it out slowly and unfold the paper, reading to myself.

Ugene,

Understanding emotions has never been a strong point for me. Your mom calls it my kryptonite, whatever that means. Even now, I'm not sure I'm getting my point across. So I guess I'll just come out and say it.

I've never been a good parent. I never knew how to be a parent at all. I've made so many mistakes and had no idea how to fix them, so I used the only tool I understood, my Power. That was a mistake. One I will regret well into the next life.

I should have told you sooner about how special you are. I should have accepted it or embraced it or something instead of using force to try and make you something you're not. Maybe if I had, things would have turned out different. I just wanted you to fit in because it would keep you safe. But you were never meant to fit in. And you were right. I can't understand what you've been through. I've never been in that position. It's easy to use Powers to show everyone how strong you are, but it's harder to do that without Powers, which makes you stronger than anyone I know.

You do have superpowers though. You're smart, strong, confident, all in ways none of us ever will be. You're unique. That's why you will succeed where the rest of us have failed because your strength is their weakness. You will find everything you need at the coordinates below. I have no doubt you'll understand it better than me.

I'm proud of you. Always have been.

Dad

I don't bother with the coordinates at the moment. One word jumps out at me.

Proud? I never had that impression, and the word is full of so many conflicting emotions. Love, loss, sadness, happiness…and fear. He really thinks I'm strong enough for this. Did he honestly believe I could do anything against Paragon or the Directorate?

My quarters suddenly feel small, like the walls are closing in. I suck in a few breaths and close my eyes.

"Ugene?" Enid's voice is filtered through a torrent of my inner emotional aggression, a perfect storm of all the feelings I have ever felt for Dad and all the pressure placed on my utterly incapable shoulders.

I start pacing like I can force the energy out through my feet and into the floor. As Enid approaches, I thrust the letter out to her, but she doesn't look at the page right away. Her gaze is fixed on me, brows drawn tight together as she chews her lower lip. I just shake my head, no idea what to say, so she turns her attention to the page, reading as I pace.

"Wait," Enid says as she finishes, her gaze snapping to me. "What did he leave behind for you to use? Where do these coordinates take us?"

I throw my hands up in the air. "I don't know. Does it matter?"

Enid tucks her hair behind her ears, sets the letter down on the table, and approaches me. "Ugene, stop." She takes one of my hands, and my feet lose steam, planting into the floor. "Stop. It's okay to be upset or confused."

"I spent years of my life convinced he was ashamed of me." My shoulders slump, all the energy has drained out through my feet into the floor.

"He didn't know how to maneuver around this," Enid says as she steps in front of me. "His letter makes that pretty clear. Ugene, not everyone can express themselves appropriately. Some people really struggle with emotional connections." She folds her hands, picking at her nails. "I may not have known him, but I can understand that. It doesn't make it right, but it at least looks like he was sorry for his mistakes."

Was she saying that she had the same problem? I shake my head. "That's not true. You've never been afraid to speak your mind."

"Speaking your mind isn't the same as knowing how to connect with people. Did he ever have trouble speaking his mind?"

My heart pounds against my ribs. "No," I breathe.

Enid shifts her feet, and her enchanting dark eyes pull me in and hold me. Straight black hair frames her light face, and a small smattering of freckles bridges her nose from one cheek to the other. Enid isn't just pretty, she's…alluring.

Bianca was alluring. The rogue thought makes my heart stall. What am I doing?

The moment our hands touch, energy shoots up my arm then through my entire body. The hairs on my arms and neck stand straight. I try to find words, but nothing comes. My mind is a jumble. I miss Bianca, but I need Enid. Am I a terrible person for being attracted to anyone else so soon? Or is it okay to move on?

The warmth radiating from Enid makes me inch closer.

Maybe Miller was right. Maybe it's okay. Nothing ever really happened between me and Bianca. But Enid…she is here. Am I holding on too tightly to something that never would have been?

I struggle to gather the courage to kiss Enid, leaning slowly closer, and awkwardly. She doesn't pull away. I wish she would pull away because that would make things easier but she tilts her head back so our gazes stay tethered.

A knock startles both of us and we pull apart so quickly we stumble away from each other and throw down our hands as if ashamed of what almost happened.

The door slides open, revealing Willow on the other side, looking from Enid to me and back again.

"Sorry to interrupt...whatever this was...but we are leaving in a couple hours," Willow says. "Be in Doc's office in one hour for briefing."

Relief at the interruption washes over me followed immediately by guilt for feeling relieved in the first place.

Enid and I glance at each other, awkward energy vibrating between us.

17

BEFORE HEADING TO DOC'S OFFICE, I MAKE SURE I have Dad's letter tucked in one of the pockets of my jacket—this is my chance to find it—and add the DNA diagrams and formula to another pocket with a pen. Sadly, I can't bring along Celeste's book or my notebooks without my old bag, lost somewhere in Paragon during the escape.

Enid goes to collect a few things as I review my notes and refresh my memory on what I've learned since arriving at The Shield. On the way out the door to meet with Enid and gather the others, I put a hand over the cover of Celeste's book.

"I'll do my best to raise the shield," I say as if she can hear me.

When I reach the gangway, Enid has already gathered the others, those who were eager to join me in the fight against the Directorate and Paragon. I'm still unsure how the Protectorate will fit into all of this, but for now, I need them as allies.

Noah claps a hand on my shoulder as he follows along toward Doc's office and our eyes meet briefly. He doesn't have to speak. The look we exchange says it all. They follow me because they believe in me. I only hope I don't let any of them down.

Our group reaches Doc's office before Willow or Doc. There are seven of us in total—Sho, Leo, Rosie, Noah, Bri, Enid, and me. The second we step through the door, Lily rushes toward Sho and takes his hands, pulling him away with urgency.

"Please don't go," she says to him in the corner of the room.

I watch the two as everyone else gets comfortable.

Sho's brows pull together. "Ugene needs my help."

"It isn't safe," Lily says, her tone thick with anxiety. "People die on these missions. If the DMA doesn't get them, the dangers of Pax do. I'm begging you. Stay."

Sho shifts his grip on Lily's hands, cupping them as he pulls her closer to his chest. "I can't sit here and do nothing. I don't expect you to understand, but this is something I need to do. I'll be fine." He tucks her dark hair behind an ear. "I'll be back."

I duck my head, a little ashamed for eavesdropping on this intimate moment.

Lily pulls away and shakes her head, then her entire body stiffens as she draws herself to her full height. "Then I'm going, too."

"You don't have to—"

"I won't stay here worrying about what's happening to you." Lily shakes her head firmly. "If you're going, so am I. Get it?"

Sho smiles so sweetly at her that I feel like I'm invading their space. When I look away, Enid is staring at me with her big, beautiful eyes. But Lily's urgency has seeped into my bones. What is she afraid of, exactly? How bad could it be?

A male voice booms down the hallway. "You can't do this!"

I rush to the door. Enid and Noah stop beside me in the doorway.

Miller halts dead in his tracks in the hall and turns. His shoulders slope downward dangerously, and his hands ball into fists at his side. His words are razor sharp. "Don't you dare tell me what I can and can't do."

Jayme slumps as he lumbers toward Miller. "I just don't think this mission is a good idea in your condition. You're unstable."

I dip back into the office, but not before noticing the way Miller's fingers flex and twitch at his side. If he had his Powers, he would have thrown them at Jayme for sure.

"Don't look at me like that," Jayme says. "You know what I mean. It isn't safe."

"I'm going." Miller's words are so final that even I know there's no point in arguing.

But Jayme is right. Miller isn't himself, and if Lily and Jayme are both so convinced we will be in danger, Miller could be a liability in his condition.

Miller storms into the office, and I jog a step to catch his stride.

"Maybe he's right," I say. "You haven't been the same without your Powers."

Miller drops into the armchair, slumping down as he glares at me. "You, of all people, should know better than to say that."

I flinch but have no argument.

Jayme kneels in front of the chair, reaching for Miller's hands. Miller snatches them back and shoves them into the pocket of his hoodie. His jaw sets with determination, and when I try to catch his attention, he ignores me. Jayme glares at me as if this is all my fault while I make my way to the sofa and sit on the arm beside Noah.

"Is this everyone?" Willow asks as she strolls in with Chase on her heels.

"I think so," I say, not sure who she's really asking.

Willow doesn't respond. She slides a holograph projector onto the coffee table, activating it with a touch. A 3D image of Pax lights up in front of us. I lean closer, examining the narrow streets and cramped buildings.

"We are taking a transport truck to this location," Willow says, pointing to a red building in the blue holograph, "using the night to cover our movements. We will stay in the adjacent building overnight until it's safe to move around in the morning. Under no circumstances are any of you to leave that building during the night. Pax will have DMA troops patrolling the streets, and the people who roam the streets of Pax at night are dangerous. If you step out that door, you're likely to get killed or captured. Either way, we can't help you."

Even though she speaks generally, Willow's eyes lock onto me.

"Our primary objective is to meet with our head operatives in Pax so they can begin gathering those at the greatest risk to fall into the Directorate's hands. We need to cut them off at the source before they can recruit too many citizens into their ranks. Before the meeting, we will stop at a clinic here," she continues, pointing to one of many narrow buildings a few blocks from our starting point, "where a supply of medicine is waiting for pickup. Our meeting with the operatives is scheduled for noon at this location." Willow points out another narrow building. Her attention turns to our group, gauging each of our reactions. "Whatever you do, *don't* attract attention to yourself. The Directorate's always watching for suspicious groups or gatherings. Which is why we will split up into groups of three. You *must* stick with your group. If you get separated, we can't guarantee you will make it back to The Shield."

This news draws a few uneasy movements. Lily reaches over and grasps Sho's hand tightly in her own. Bri straightens, shifting her body a little closer to Noah. I just stare at the holographic map, struggling to stuff down my growing anxiety while simultaneously wondering where in that mess of buildings the package my dad left behind could be.

As much as I want to be paired with Enid and Sho—his Echolocation will be handy to find the coordinates—I also know that Willow won't let it happen. In fact, I know what Willow is going to say before the words come out of her mouth.

"I want two of you to every one of us, so we can be sure you are protected," Willow says. "I don't care how you pair up, as long as there are only two of you."

Maybe I can get Jayme to be my escort, then. But, judging by the shade he's throwing my way, I don't think he wants to.

"Ugene is with me," Willow says, waiting for me to challenge her, but I don't see the point. I doubt anything I say will change her mind.

Jayme sits upright, resting his arms on his knees. "Miller and I were hoping he could group with us."

The proclamation sends a jolt of surprise through me.

"I don't care," Willow says. "If I had my way, he wouldn't be going at all."

"I'm sorry," I say, mimicking Jayme's posture. "But how is your mind-bendy Power, whatever it is, going to protect me better than his

Natural Energy?"

Chase chuckles, a deep rumble that makes my skin crawl.

Willow cocks her head, amused as she crosses her arms over her chest. "I think you of all people would appreciate that Powers aren't the only way to protect yourself."

"Yeah," Jayme says, "she may not be Somatic, but she can crush *you* in a fight."

The jab at my expense isn't lost on me, but I don't react.

"When we finish," Willow continues, "a team will stow us in the back of a couple armored DMA shuttles, which will take us to the extraction point, where our vehicle will be waiting to bring us back here."

Willow reaches toward Chase, who produces a military-issued vest. "You will each get a vest for emergency use only. It contains two smoke bombs, a stun gun, zip-cuffs, a switchblade, a flashlight, and a cyanide pill, just in case. I can't stress this enough. If you use weapons while we are in the city, the DMA will be on us in a matter of minutes. In fact, don't use anything in this vest unless you are confronted by the DMA."

What is the cyanide pill for? I don't want to think about a situation where it might be useful.

Enid presses her back against the sofa near me, arms folded tight over her chest. I glance at my friends, and all of them have the same anxiety written all over. We are about to try and take on the Directorate, and the last thing we need is the DMA's attention.

"Code words?" Jayme asks as if he is used to this sort of briefing.

"Turnip and tulip." Willow straps on the vest. "Let's go."

She and Chase lead us out of the office and up the stairs to the top level of The Shield.

Should we let Miller have the weapons in that vest knowing he's struggling with suicidal tendencies? I watch his slumped back as he walks alongside Jayme, his hands stuffed into the pockets of his jeans. Everything about his body language makes me nervous. Jayme glares over his shoulder at me, and I quickly avert my gaze. What's his problem?

Instead of focusing on them, I turn my attention to our trek to the upper level of The Shield. We follow Willow to the end of the long hall of cells and around the corner until we come face-to-face with the steel door I tried to open about a week ago. Willow places her hand on the scanner. A moment later, the lock releases and the door hisses open.

The hangar on the other side of the door stinks of fuel and rubber. I cover my nose and mouth. Concrete floors are coated in dirt and sand from the massive tires on the vehicles. Every one of these vehicles is ancient—old military jeeps and trucks and cargo vans rusting along the edges. Someone tried to cover the rust with camouflage paint, but it didn't really work. Three camo trucks with sharp edges and flat sides sit closest to the blast doors leading out of the hangar.

Only a few people are on duty. Along one wall, an observation room overlooks the hangar through glass windows. Two people sit in there, watching old computer monitors. The Protectorate has gone through a lot of trouble to find tech they can use, and it must have cost someone a lot of Power to get this stuff up and running.

My friends are just as awed as I am by all this ancient crap the Protectorate has running as we follow Willow and Chase in wide-eyed disbelief.

Doc hovers near the edge of one of the angular trucks with a tablet. Six people climb in the front cab of the truck—Willow, Chase, Leo, Rosie, Lily, and Sho. The rest climb into the bed of the truck, three on each bench facing each other with a canvas canopy over the back. Vest are distributed as we pile in.

Before I climb in with them, Doc calls for my attention. I pause, wondering what he could want at this moment, trying to keep my nerves steady.

"Remember, we are after the same thing," Doc says. "I feel as you feel, and I would like to see as many people survive this as possible."

I swallow a lump in my throat and nod.

"Think big," he says, then lets go of my arm.

For a moment I stand there, searching his aging eyes for more wisdom, but he just nods and turns away.

I sit across from Miller. Enid settles on one side of me with Noah on the other. Bri sits directly across from Noah, with Jayme on Miller's other side. The engine starts, much quieter than I expected for such a big truck.

Enid leans toward me and whispers in my ear, "How will we get out to find the package?"

I just shrug. We will probably have to sneak off during the night, get the stash, and get back before anyone wakes.

The truck rolls through the blast doors and down a long tunnel, the only source of light being its headlights through the dark space. It's hardly the most comfortable ride, but it is incredibly smooth. And at least we are conscious this time around, unlike when the Protectorate brought us in.

Jayme continues to glare at me as he leans back and stretches his arm across the bench behind Miller. What is his problem?

18

NERVOUS TENSION FILLS THE TRUCK. AS SOON AS THE truck leaves the tunnel, Bri starts fidgeting with her vest. Soon after, Jayme leans forward, his leg bouncing as he strains to stare out the front windshield. Willow continually glances in the rearview mirror, and I'm not sure if she's looking at us or watching for trouble. Chase keeps his focus so firmly on the road that I'm not sure he would notice anything else unless it hit him in the head.

The canvas cover we are crouched beneath has no windows and, at the angle I'm sitting, I can't see out the narrow front window. Everything is faded light and drab colors indistinguishable as anything. The smoothness of the ride doesn't give many clues as to what conditions we are driving over either.

Enid reaches over and takes my hand, giving it a squeeze, and I can feel her shaking ever so slightly. The only person who doesn't seem to care what sort of danger we might be riding into is Miller, with his hood drawn and his body slumped down. No one else speaks. Knees bounce. Hands fidget. Bodies shift. But no one speaks.

When the truck pulls into a large garage and Chase turns off the engine, Jayme adjusts the straps on his vest, then pulls his jacket on over it. The rest of us quickly follow his lead, putting on our vests and checking straps to make sure it's secure as Willow and Chase hop out of the cab. The doors slam shut with a finality that makes both Bri and Enid jump in their seats. A moment later, Chase opens the zipped flap on the back and lowers the tailgate. Willow stands beside him.

"We are heading through the first door on the right at the top of the stairs," Willows says as we pile out. "There is a connection from the window to the next building, where we are staying for the night. Follow Jayme. He knows the way."

I stretch cramped muscles from being slumped over as I walk down the ramp connected to the tailgate. As I do, I also take in the dark space of the garage. Even in the dark, I can tell this place is abandoned. Dirt and debris cover the floor. The stench of mildew is stifling. A stack of old rotting pallets leans against one wall. Graffiti colors another wall—a burning earth, words and phrases that imply the end of the world and hopelessness. Some of it I can't really make out. Windows covered in layers of grime are so high up on the wall that I can't see out. High above, the beams supporting the structure are rusting out. We can't be in Elpis yet. This place is so clearly a remnant of life before the War and Purge.

Jayme leads us through a wide doorway out of the docking room and into the main warehouse. It shares the same lack of charm as the docking room. We climb a broken set of concrete stairs. Along the edge of the stairs lies thick, packed-in layers of lime mortar shaken free from the wall. The others use the rusted railing as they climb, but it looks unstable. If we slipped, that rail might just snap off the wall. It wobbles unsteadily as we climb, and I hold my breath, hearing only the pounding of my heart and the scratch of the railing brackets against the wall.

The group turns through the first door on the right, and Jayme leads us to what must've been office space. Now it's a graveyard of a world that no longer exists, all dust, dirt, and broken furniture.

A plank bridges the broken window to the adjacent building. Willow explained on the ride that we have to move buildings because there isn't a secure place to sleep in the warehouse garage. Now, one by one, we walk the plank.

It's only a couple feet, close enough to reach out and lean on the opposite building for support. I don't trust the stability of the structure, though, and hesitate at the edge of the plank.

"Get a move on, Ugene," Jayme says. The way he says my name

reminds me of Jimmy the Idiot—my high school bully—calling me Pewgene.

Clenching my jaw, I step onto the plank and hold my breath as I cross. The one floor down to the ground feels like a long way, and I stiffen up in fear. Sadly, I'm also afraid that Jayme will move the plank on me, but Willow would probably kill him if he harmed me. Still, even after everything I've been through, I maintain a healthy fear of people who dislike me.

In a matter of seconds, I'm safely on the other side, exhaling and sagging against the wall. I close my eyes and take a moment to get control of my nerves.

This room is large enough to hold all of us comfortably for the night. Near the front of the building, dirty windows hide us from prying eyes. The floor is surprisingly clean, maybe from recent use or someone sweeping it. Willow pulls open a metal cabinet door and the creak shatters the silence.

"Sleeping bags are in here," Willow says. "Set yourself up for the night. In the morning, we put them back. Keep your conversations to a minimum. We don't need people hearing us out in the street."

People? There's no way we are in Elpis. This place is a relic!

I move toward the windows and peer out at an angle. It's hard to see through the dirt, especially when it's already dark outside. I squint and lean closer, almost pressing the side of my face to the edge of the window to see through a sliver of non-grimy glass.

Across the street, red brick buildings with cracked or crumbling facades butt up against one another. Windows are boarded or covered by bars. Cracked and broken concrete steps lead from the narrow sidewalk to decrepit porches. Tin roofs on rotting wooden posts cover the porches. No lights are on in the houses. One porch hosts a group of guys who lean against the metal railing, which looks ready to snap under their weight. They watch the street and talk amongst each other.

Only a few people move along the cracked road, their gazes averted from the group on the porch, steps hastening as they cross to our side of the street to pass. No other vehicles are on the road. Most people in this part of town can't afford it, and transit doesn't run at this time of night anymore because of the rise in crime. How did they not notice our vehicle? The engine was quiet, but surely driving past them would have gotten attention. *Unless we entered from a back alley.*

If no one lives outside of Elpis—with the exception of the people in The Shield who have established their own ecosystem—that can only mean we are actually in Pax. Yet all these buildings are uncared for, bordering on abandoned.

A patrol of men and women in dark DMA uniforms approach the porch. I lean closer to try and listen, but the rustling sounds of movement and hushed conversations in the room make it impossible to hear anything. The troopers say something to the men on the porch, and the men respond with stiff postures and rude gestures. One of the guys strolls down the porch steps, cocky in the way he moves. He gets in a trooper's face and says something.

A second later, the trooper has him pinned to the ground as another presses the guy's palm against a scanning device. Zip-cuffs are fastened around the guy's wrists, and he is dragged down the street. His friends rush off the porch after him, and a fight breaks out. A fight the DMA quickly wins as they pull weapons and shoot something at each of the men. Soon, all of them are carted off toward the end of the block. I can't see that far.

I avert my gaze and catch Willow watching me as she sets up her sleeping bag. I expect her to act smug, but even in the dim light, I can see the sadness on her face.

Enid approaches, offering me a sleeping bag. "Hey. You okay?"

I shake my head not really knowing how to put this gut-gnawing feeling of remorse into words.

Willow has moved on, reviewing something on a handheld device and shaking her hair out of her ponytail.

"So, we expect to sneak off," Enid says, keeping her voice low, "but if we are forced into a group with Willow, how are we going to find what your dad left behind?"

I unroll the sleeping bag and lay it out beside her. "We pretend to sleep until the others are out. Then you, me, and Sho head off to retrieve the stash and get back as quickly as we can."

"Sho?" Enid casts a glance over her shoulder at him as he sets up beside Lily.

"I need his Echolocation unless you know where we're going."

"Okay, but Willow was just talking to the Protectorate people about watches," Enid says, hugging her sleeping bag and glancing over at Willow.

It certainly makes this more of a challenge. My gaze drifts to Jayme, sitting on his sleeping bag, watching Miller slide his own bag up to his ears with his back to the room. Jayme grimaces, and his attention snaps fiercely to me. He wanted me in his group, and the anger he throws my way makes me wonder if maybe I should be concerned about my safety around him. He wouldn't hurt me, would he?

"I have an idea." I nod at Enid's sleeping bag. "Get yourself in that thing. We need everyone to think we are sleeping."

I do have an idea. A very bad one.

THE ADRENALINE PUMPING THROUGH MY BODY MAKES it impossible to sleep. I lie with my back to the room until soft snores and steady breathing make it clear most of the group is asleep. Lily takes the first watch with Sho keeping her company, and I wait patiently, running through everything I learned at The Shield, seeking clues as to how we can take down the Directorate. No answers reveal themselves.

Enid snoozes beside me, curled up in a tight ball in her own sleeping bag. Until we are ready to go, she should sleep.

In the middle of the night, during Willow's watch, a concussive rumble rattles the windows. I jump, and a few of the others stir as well.

Willow leans close to the wall beside the window and peers out through the crack in the grime.

Arguing filters up to us from the street, but I can't make out what's being said. Someone is angry. That much is clear. A bang shakes silt from the ceiling and Lily coughs. Willow tenses, motioning for everyone to stay quiet as she keeps an eye on the street. Another bang, followed by a wave of heat, then the wailing of a fire siren.

Enid sits up. "I can put it out," she whispers to Willow.

Willow shakes her head sternly, holding a finger to her lips.

Shouts of anger turn to frantic cries for help. The fire siren deafens my eardrums, and I, like several others, press my hands against my ears to drown out the noise. It takes nearly an hour for the emergency services to show up. By that time, our group is waiting to see if we will have to flee. A fire has burned up one of the houses and spread to the two neighbors. The response time of the fire services is abysmal. When they do show, Willow motions for us to go to sleep again. Everything is under control.

I need Willow to think I'm asleep, so I settle back down and close my eyes.

Enid shifts closer in her bag.

No one falls asleep for a while.

Jayme takes third watch. Once I'm convinced Willow is asleep, I roll over and assess the room. I need to talk to Jayme, but more importantly, I need his help. Hopefully, he isn't truly out to get me, or I'm in serious trouble.

Careful not to stir Enid, I slide out of my sleeping bag and pick careful steps around everyone between Jayme and me. Miller scowls in his sleep at Jayme's side.

"Get back to sleep," Jayme whispers, glowering and crossing his arms.

"I can't," I say. "Not with the fires and noise that keep coming outside."

Jayme acknowledges the comment with a half nod in the dim light but won't look me in the eyes.

"Besides," I say, crouching in front of him, "I'm curious to figure out why you've been so irritated with me."

Chase snorts in his sleep and rolls over with a thump. Jayme and I both glance his way briefly.

When I look back, the corner of Jayme's mouth curls up into a half sneer and he shakes his head, keeping his voice down. "And he said you were brilliant."

I glance over to Miller. "So, his compliment made you angry?"

"No." Jayme barks, then his lips thin and he sits up straighter, raising his chin, forcing himself to lower his voice. "The fact that he took a bullet for you—lost his Powers for you—and now is suffering because of you. That makes me angry. The fact that he insisted on coming on this mission with you when he shouldn't be out of The Shield yet. That makes me angry." His voice grows little by little with each proclamation, then he rises.

I stand as well, shrinking back at the way he towers over me.

Jayme continues, growling as he struggles to keep his voice down and not wake the others. "The fact that, despite all the shit you've put him through, he still doesn't talk about much of anything but supporting *you*. That makes me angry. And the fact that he continues to put his life at risk to protect you. That…" He clenches his jaw and shakes his head, to furious with me to finish.

His logic is somewhat reasonable. I would be lying if I didn't admit to blaming myself sometimes. But it isn't just that. Jayme is jealous of my friendship with Miller.

"Do you think something is going on with us?" I ask. "Because there isn't."

"Yeah, sure there isn't."

"Look," I say, leaning in close to keep my voice down. "Miller betrayed all of us to Paragon when we were preparing to escape. Do you know why? It wasn't because of me."

Jayme flinches, and some of the lines of anger smooth out of his face. *Guess he doesn't know everything.*

"When I told him to run with the others, do you know what he said?" I aim a finger at his chest. "That *you* wouldn't forgive him if he abandoned me."

Jayme glances around the room then leans closer. "If he did such horrible things, then why do you keep hanging around him?"

"Because he deserves it." I flick my gaze to Miller to make sure he is still asleep. "Sure, he did some dumb things before, but he's also sacrificed so much for everyone—more than we can ever repay. I stick around because he's been there for me when I've needed him, and he deserves the same in return from me."

Jayme leans back against the wall, crossing his arms and clenching his jaw. "Fine. If there's nothing going on between you, then just let him go."

"As long as he is suffering, I will stay by him…but only as his friend." Frustrated, I scrub a hand over my face. "Look, I came over here because I need your help."

"That's rich."

"Trust me, if anyone else could help instead, I would ask them."

Jayme isn't fazed by the comment.

I pull out the letter from my dad and point at the coordinates at the bottom of the page. "I need to get here, but I don't know where it is, yet."

Jayme grimaces and snatches the letter out of my hand. I only intended for him to read what I pointed out, but his eyes scan the page as he reads the whole thing. When he finishes, Jayme thrusts the letter against my chest. "So?"

"My dad was DMA General Powers," I say as if that should explain it.

Jayme gets the picture now, raising his brows. "Your dad is general."

I take the letter and smooth the page out again.

"Was," I correct. "He died helping us escape Paragon, presumably right after he wrote that letter."

"And what do you expect to find?"

Miller stirs and Jayme tenses, watching Miller for a moment.

"I don't know. But Dad wouldn't have gone through all this trouble if it wasn't important. It could be the key to taking down the Directorate and Paragon."

"Then we need to tell Willow."

I should have expected that reaction. I huff out a breath. "I can't."

"I can." Jayme starts toward Willow, but Miller grabs his ankle to stop him, propping himself up. "Miller, let go."

"No. If Ugene can't tell Willow, there's a good reason. And that means you can't tell her either."

Jayme growls and crosses his arms, giving me a look that should destroy me. "I told you, there's a way things need to be done or people get killed. You might think you're something special, but you aren't. Ugene, you're no better than anyone else."

"No." Miller blocks Jayme's path to Willow. "But he's smarter."

By this time, Enid has realized I'm not beside her and she now approaches. "Are we going?"

"You don't even know where it is," Jayme says, growing more irritated as Enid joins us.

"No, but he will." I nod toward Sho, sleeping with his arm around Lily.

Jayme looms over me, his jaw so tight I'm surprised I can't hear his teeth cracking against each other. Panic seizes my chest. Would he hurt me in front of Miller?

He growls, "You're going whether I agree or not." He says it like a statement of fact.

And he's right. I nod.

"We don't have long," he snaps under his breath, snatching his jacket off the floor.

"Long until what?" I ask.

Jayme glances at the rest of the sleeping party. "Next watch starts in about an hour, which doesn't leave us much time to find this thing and get back here."

I start picking my way through the slumbering bodies behind Miller and Enid, but Jayme grabs my arm in a painful vice grip and leans close. His blue eyes flash dangerously as he stares down at me.

"No funny business," he hisses. "I've been warned that you don't like following rules. But out here if we aren't careful, we will either die, or worse, end up in the Directorate's hands. This trip goes against my better judgment. Only me and Enid have useful fighting Powers to protect us. So, this package better be worth the risk."

"I hope so." I lower my gaze to his grip and then flick them back to his still crazed eyes. "Now, can we go?"

After one last snarl, he releases me and heads for the door. Enid is already quietly waking Sho to fill him in, and in moments we are all gathered to go, leaving the rest of the group behind for now.

20

JAYME ASSUMES THE HEAD POSITION AS HE LEADS US into the hallway. No one else argues the fact because none of us have been here before. But Jayme has been on missions for the Protectorate in Pax before. He knows his way around. He instructs us to stick close to the wall and keep our steps as quiet as possible. Every scrape of a shoe on the dirty floor makes me flinch. Every sound echoes off the walls.

I can hardly see Sho walking in front of me in the darkened hallway. Enid is close at my back, her fist closing around my jacket.

"The rail is stable," Jayme whispers back to us. "Hold it and step down carefully. Nine steps down, follow the wall around the landing, then nine more to the ground floor."

Sho sneezes, and Jayme hushes all of us.

I hold my breath, waiting for something terrible to happen, but not sure what that might be. Willow catching us, maybe? With my heart pounding, I continue down, counting the steps and shuffling along the landing to the next flight.

When we reach the bottom, I see the exit—a large, rectangular window above the double doors is boarded up. An eerie yellow light from the street slips through the cracks around the doors, which also have boards over them. The dim light doesn't offer a good view of the room. This was once a commercial building, now abandoned.

The rattle of a chain echoes off the walls, and I hold my breath again, watching the stairs. But again, nothing comes.

Jayme opens a gap in one of the doors, motioning for us to hold, then he slips outside. Enid nudges closer to me.

"Sho, what can you make of this?" I ask, waving him over as we wait for Jayme to return.

Sho takes the letter I offer and squints at the page in the darkened room. "This is where we are going?"

I nod. "Do you know where it is?"

Sho raises his head, turning in a slow circle and stops, facing a certain direction—I can't tell which way it is from inside this building.

"That way." He nods forward.

"Jayme told me we need to stick to the shadows and keep quiet if this is going to work," Enid says.

I nod. "He doesn't like me much."

"Give him some time," Sho says. "I don't think any of us liked you at first."

"Thanks," I say, then chuckle a little, wary of making too much noise.

Miller hovers near the door, waiting for Jayme's return. He pulls his hood tight against his mess of blond hair. Judging by the way he shifts anxiously and peers through the gap in the doorway, someone might think Jayme's been gone forever. But after only a few seconds, Jayme slips back in and motions for us to follow.

This is the part of town I've been cautioned to avoid since I was a child. Dad worked out here a lot, but he never let me come along. I watched the news though and heard him complain to Mom about crime here. Pax is the worst, most impoverished part of town. People live here when they have nowhere else to go. And now it seems the Directorate is determined to drive the poor even out of this neighborhood.

Cool night air caresses my face, bringing with it the stench of rotten food and refuse. Trash piles up on the side of the street, enhancing the pungent aroma. The plumbing system in Pax is clearly far from adequately operational. It's a wonder this place isn't a breeding ground for disease. *Maybe it is.* How would I know? I've spent my life sheltered from the truth in the richest neighborhood in all of Elpis.

I zip my jacket and glance at Enid in her oversized sweatshirt as she folds her hands into the sleeves.

The borough was named Pax during the founding of Elpis in honor of the symbol of peace it represented. Walking the dimly lit streets, Pax feels anything but peaceful. Yellow streetlights and the glow of the moon are the only illuminations against the dangers lurking in the shadows.

The slums in Pax are some of the worst in all of Elpis. While the city was founded with Powers, it's hard to believe looking at the state of the buildings in Pax. Wooden structures were erected as the city expanded to accommodate the growing population.

At night, it's hard to tell which buildings have been abandoned and which are occupied. All of them have the same boarded or shuttered windows and darkness within. The roads are paved but full of potholes unfilled because vehicles don't travel the streets anymore, and DMA shuttles don't need a smooth road to travel.

Shouts from an alley a block away make me jump, but it isn't directed at us.

Jayme keeps us close to the buildings, moving from shadow to shadow. Sometimes I feel eyes on me and glance into the depths of the darkened alleys. Even the smallest noise makes us leap and hurry our steps. We walk in a tight mass, occupying as little space as possible.

No one speaks. Silence is our friend.

The homes in Pax are in a pitiful state. The little homes sit so close together only a narrow path offers access to even smaller backyards. Most of the homes are one story, with a few two-story homes mixed in. Aside from barred or boarded windows, the foundations are cracked, and one corner sinks deeper into the ground. Collapsed porches are rigged with metal posts scavenged from abandoned buildings. Some of the homes with sloped roofs have boards nailed in over the shingles.

Aside from hearing a few shouts or laughs from a distance, no one else walks the streets. The complete absence of people instills a deep sense of urgency in me. I know thousands of people live in Pax.

Where is everyone hiding? And why? Downtown, people would still be moving around. It would be spread out, a person here, another there over a few blocks. But we manage to make it three blocks without seeing another soul.

Jayme pulls us up against one of the houses as Sho uses his Echolocation Power to try and find the right coordinates. The soft hum of an approaching engine pushes all of us into an alley as we hold our breath. A few seconds later, a DMA shuttle crawls past, making sweeps with its spotlight. Who will they find at this time? Who are they looking for? *Is it us?*

Sho nods Jayme to the right, and motions around a corner nearby.

Jayme is the first to slip around and immediately ushers us back as stone arrows hammer against the side of the DMA shuttle. A trooper jumps out, boots thumping on the broken pavement, and points toward the assailant. We watch from the shadows as a stone arrow glances off the uniform and the trooper lifts a hand, twists his wrist, and the assailant yelps in pain, yanked toward him. The trooper never touches the man as he uses his Power to levitate the assailant into the back of the shuttle.

Just as he's about to pull himself back into the vehicle, he pauses and turns abruptly in our direction. All of us jump backward and press our backs to the brick wall of the apartment building. I hold my breath, listening closely for the thump of approaching boots. After a minute, we all let out a sigh of relief as the shuttle disappears down another street.

Jayme steps out and looks both ways, hesitating as he looks back the way we came as if debating whether or not we should go onward. *Please don't turn back now.* Finally, he turns in the direction Sho indicated and we stick as tight to the apartment building as we can.

Along the next street, the homes look more like houses and less like businesses or apartment buildings butted against each other. There's a little yard space on either side and a couple of feet of dead grass in front of the porch on each house. Jayme leads us halfway up the block, glances up and down the street, then motions for us to crouch as we hustle across and through one of the narrow spaces between houses.

Both houses have barred windows, and no light emits from within. Either no one lives there—which I sincerely hope—or no one is awake.

The backyard is a narrow space as well, maybe ten feet deep and only slightly wider than the house itself. Jayme takes a knee in the brittle grass and motions to Sho. Everyone gathers around.

Jayme pulls a small tablet from his pocket, and a moment later a holograph of Pax appears with a dot blinking exactly where we crouch.

"We're here," Jayme whispers, pointing at a dot. "Best guess is that this is the block the coordinates lead to. Was there anything else that might hint where exactly this stash is?"

I glance at Enid and we both shake our heads. "I don't think he wanted to give away too much. Sho, now that we're closer, can you pinpoint it?"

Sho chews at the inside of his cheek, staring at the map. Is he using his Power? As he moves his hand over the map, I glance at Miller. The rest of us are crouched around the map, but he lingers at the edge of our little circle, staring off into the distance with his hands stuffed into his pockets. Why did he insist on coming along when he clearly has no interest in anything that's going on?

"I think," Sho says.

Jayme, Sho, and I rise as Jayme shuts down the map and tucks the tablet away.

I offer Enid a hand to help her up.

"Lead the way," Jayme says.

21

AFTER HOPPING A COUPLE OF SHORT CHAIN-LINK fences, Sho guides the group through another backyard, where I nearly trip into an old firepit. Enid grabs my arm for balance, pulling me along. Sho climbs the back steps to one of the houses. The mask of darkness provides us with cover as we huddle in a mass.

"I'll clear the house, then you follow me in," Jayme says.

Sho shakes his head. "No one is in there. Just a couple rats." His Echolocation allows him to detect life. Sho used the trick to find me in that first Survival Test in Paragon.

One of the hinges on the screen door is broken, making the screen slant and strain the metal of the lower hinge. I expect the rusted hinges to grind, but Sho pulls it open without a sound. The wooden door behind it is closed tight.

"It's locked," Sho says when the handle won't turn.

Jayme nudges him out of the way and wraps his hand around the metal doorknob. After a few seconds, a click resounds inside the door, and Jayme turns the knob. Miller made Jayme out to be weak when he told me about Jayme in that second Survival Test—the torture he sustained and how frail he was near the end of his time there. So far, that hasn't been my take. Maybe it was something Paragon was doing to him that made him weaker.

I'm the last one through the door, and I close it behind us and lock it. Maybe the door was locked because of Dad. Was there a key I should have found in that bag?

The inside of the house isn't in any better shape than the outside.

Furniture left behind, aged through disuse. Sun-bleached curtains with rods broken off the walls. Layers of grime on the linoleum. We make our way through the back kitchen toward the living room at the front of the house.

"It's too dark," Enid whispers, and I can hear the tinge of eeriness in her voice.

Miller halts beside me and pulls his hands from his pockets. The tips of his fingers bridge together as he instinctively attempts using his Power, then he lets out a frustrated grunt and his arms slap against his sides. Getting used to not having it anymore can't be easy.

My hand falls on his shoulder. "It's okay. We're fine." I fish out the flashlight from a vest pocket.

Miller scowls and pulls away, moving toward a bookshelf with the shelves fallen and no books in sight. From the corner of my eye, I can see Jayme glaring at me, but I don't engage.

"Ugene, why don't you take someone to search upstairs," Jayme says.

Enid joins me as I approach the bottom step and gaze up. The staircase is enclosed and dark, but I have just enough light from the streetlights outside to see the warped and cracking wood. There's no way those steps can hold my weight.

"It's not up there," I say, stepping back.

Jayme places himself subconsciously—or maybe consciously—between Miller and me, and the way he looks at me makes my skin crawl. "How do you know?"

"Because Dad was Somatic, and Somatics are naturally denser than the rest of us," I say. "And there's no way he would have risked walking up those stairs. They look ready to break under even my weight."

Sho moves toward a doorway on the opposite wall, brandishing his own flashlight. "I'll check the dining room. Any idea what we're looking for?"

I don't really have an answer for that. "Not exactly. A package of some sort. It could be small or just a stack of papers. He didn't say. But he wouldn't leave it out in the open."

Jayme gives a sharp nod. "Why don't you and Enid check the

kitchen? Miller and I will search the living room."

Taking orders from Jayme doesn't settle well with me, but I'm in no mood to start a fight. We don't have a lot of time. I nod, and Enid follows me into the kitchen, and we both turn on our flashlights.

Like the rest of the house, the kitchen is in serious need of attention. Some of the cupboard doors hang from hinges. Other cupboard doors are missing like they were stripped away and taken to another house. Linoleum peels up in the corners of the room. A table and chairs lie at angles against the far wall, and dirty, crusted-over rags lay abandoned on the counter and floor. The space doesn't exactly smell fresh either. It reeks of rot.

Enid moves toward the cupboard under the sink and gags, covering her mouth and nose with her sleeve. "Oh my God. It smells like something died in the pipes."

Enid grips the flashlight between her teeth and covers her nose to block the pungent smell without hindering the light.

The two of us move methodically through the room, starting with the cupboards. Opening a few proves to be a mistake. They either stink of decaying vermin and rotting wood or are coated in cobwebs. The time it takes to create webs that thick convinces me that whatever we're looking for isn't in those spaces. They've been untouched for too long.

Enid sits on the floor in front of the sink, the doors spread wide as she presses against the bottom shelf for a hidden compartment. A rat scurries out from under the cabinet and Enid instinctively uses her Power to toss it across the room into the wall with a small yelp.

"Sorry," she mumbles.

Muffled voices begin raising from the living room, followed by a thump and crash like something shattered. The noise scares the crap out of me, violating the working silence.

"Stop," Jayme says. "Please."

Enid and I exchange a glance, then I move to the doorway between the kitchen and living room.

Miller hunches in front of a broken mirror hanging on the wall near the stairs. His hands are balled in fists at his side, blood dripping from one.

I move toward Miller to help, but Jayme pushes at my shoulder as he steps in. It isn't a hard shove, but it's clear this is one of those places where he doesn't think I belong—or he doesn't want me involved.

"Hey!" Enid says, hustling forward.

I shake my head at her, grabbing her hand. "It's okay."

"Is it?" Jayme snaps, glaring at me as he lifts Miller's fist to look at it. Miller just stays there, his entire posture indicating utter defeat. "It would be nice if you knew what we were looking for here."

I don't respond. Hopefully, Jayme will get over this and realize he's overreacting about this whole thing.

With no desire to go back into the kitchen, Enid and I join Sho in the dining room. He has a number of trinkets laid out over the table, examining each of them.

"Everything okay in there?" he asks, turning a ceramic penguin over in his hand. "I wish Lily was here with us."

"No," Enid says, picking up a snow globe off the table. "Everything is not okay."

I wave her off. "It's fine. Jayme has it under control."

A scuff against the pavement outside fixes me in place. Sho and Enid must hear it, too, because they both gaze toward the street. Not that we can see anything but the wall. After a moment, no more sound emits and we resume our search.

I step toward the table to examine the items Sho has found, and a floorboard creaks under my weight. I step back and experimentally bounce my weight on it again. The board creaks. Frowning, I kneel beside the board and pull out my switchblade from the vest. It provides leverage to loosen the board, which pops up easily. Another board pries loose as well, revealing a hidden compartment in the floorboards. And inside, a bundle wrapped in fresh red fabric.

"What is it?" Enid asks.

"I think…this might be it." I put away the switchblade, remove the bundle, and turn it over in my hands. The fabric is soft cotton. Excitement forces a fresh wave of adrenaline through my veins. My gaze shoots up to Enid. "It has to be this."

Enid opens her mouth to respond, but nothing comes out. Her entire body suddenly becomes rigid, frozen in place with her eyes wide. A spike of fear rushes through me.

"Enid?" I step toward her as the snow globe slips from her fingers and breaks on the floor. The base pops off the bottom. Glass shatters. The liquid inside spills out on the wood floor.

I rush in front of her, placing my hands on her arms so she doesn't fall over. "Enid, what's wrong?" *Was the globe coated in poison?* That doesn't make sense, though. Why would someone put poison on it? The only alternative is that someone is somehow using a Power on her. But no one knows we are here.

Enid doesn't budge.

Sho hustles around the table to her side.

Jayme runs in, pulling Miller along with him. "What is all the—"

After laying eyes on Enid, Jayme's irritation vanishes. *He knows what's going on!* Jayme presses Miller toward us and lays his hand against the open wooden doorframe—one hand on either side.

The sudden leap to action makes me uneasy. I draw Miller away from the doorway toward where we gather at the edge of the table. "What—?"

Jayme shushes me.

Leaning his weight against the wood, Jayme bows his head. The wood of the frame grows across the gap from both sides like spreading tree roots as he uses his Transformation Power. The wood slowly stitches the open doorway closed.

A hard thump against the front door makes all of us jump—except Enid. We all extinguish our flashlights, putting them away.

Another thump and crash. The door breaks in. Someone else is here. Who is it? Are they looking for us?

Only a narrow gap remains, just wide enough to see the light shining in the living room. Panic turns my adrenaline into high gear.

The last gap in the doorway becomes concealed in a knot of roots as a shot fires at us. Jayme releases the now mangled door frame and stumbles back.

Did they shoot him? I rip the jacket away and search for a wound, praying I don't find one. What if those are Power-removing bullets?

"Who is it?" I ask as Jayme tries to swat my hands away.

Blood drips from his nose, reminding me of Dr. Lydia's warning. Overuse of his Power is dangerous to his health.

"We have to go," Jayme gasps.

A thump hammers against the root-wood barricade Jayme created.

Miller nudges me aside and brushes his hands over Jayme's chest and torso. They come away with blood.

Jayme shakes his head. "It's just a scratch. We need to move now."

Miller and I hesitate. If he's been shot—

"Go!" Jayme growls, pushing both of us away.

Thump!

Everyone launches into action. Everyone except Enid. As the others move toward the boarded-up window on the side of the house, I try to figure out what's going on with her. A tear slips out of each of her eyes.

Thump!

"Ugene!" Sho calls as Jayme and Miller pry the board off the window.

No. I left Dad. I left Bianca. I won't leave Enid.

"Go!" I call back, stuffing the cloth-wrapped bundle into the lining of my jacket and zipping it tight.

Thump!

Several Powers could immobilize her. Telekinesis. Powerful Telepathy. Cellular Manipulation. I don't have time to puzzle out which one to help her. Right now, we need to get out.

"Don't worry," I say, trying to offer her some reassurance.

"Don't be an idiot," Miller snaps as the board pops off the window and Sho slips through the gap.

"I'm not leaving her here."

Thump. The root-wood barrier cracks. A shot fires at it, and I instinctively duck. Jayme rolls his weight through the window.

Miller remains at the window, staring at me. His expression is unreadable.

"Miller!" Jayme hisses from outside.

Ignoring Jayme's call, Miller joins me beside Enid and says, "Grab her arms."

Thump! Crack!

I slip my arms under hers and lean her weight back against me as Miller bends down, his movements almost robotic, and lifts her legs. Thankfully, Enid's condition doesn't make her body stiff. It only immobilizes her muscles. Her body goes limp in our arms. *Not Telekinesis, then.*

We carry her toward the window.

Thump. Crack!

Sho and Jayme wait impatiently outside. Miller and I lift her and slide her out the window legs first. Sho scurries to catch Enid's legs. Miller squeezes through around her and jumps to the ground, then raises his arms to take the burden from me.

Thump. Crack!

The root-wood barrier blasts open. Wood shrapnel flies into the dining room. I cover my head with my arms and jump from the window. Hopefully, once we get Enid far enough from whoever is doing this to her, she will be able to move freely again.

Jayme leads the group away from the house, sticking close to the other houses for cover. Miller and I each slide an arm under Enid's and drag her along with us.

"Where to?" I whisper. Whether he likes me or not, I have nothing against him.

Jayme nods between two houses. "We need to get out of sight."

Sho focuses his Power ahead of us, then motions for us to go. He leads the way, followed by Miller and I holding Enid, with Jayme at the rear of the group. We scurry around the corner of the house into the backyard, to a screened porch. The screens are partly ripped. Sho rushes up the steps and eases the screen door open, holding it for the rest of us to slip inside.

Enid seems to be regaining some of her senses enough to sit with her back to the wall, head below the trim around the screens like the rest of us.

Sho holds a finger to his lips and all of us freeze, holding our breath.

Boots crunch the dead grass outside in the backyard. Not one set, but several. Maybe three?

I shoot a glance at Enid, but she just gazes at me in wide-eyed fear, hugging herself. I look from one of my companions to the next. Sho is balled up low and tight, out of sight, with powerful concentration creasing his face. Miller huddles close to Jayme, trying to look at the wound, but Jayme seems fine. *Maybe the bullet just grazed him.*

"Anything?" a deep male voice says.

Silence.

I run my fingers over the pockets of the vest, wondering if this is the right time to use one of the pieces of tactical gear. Maybe the smoke bomb.

Jayme closes his eyes and presses his head against the half-wall of the porch.

"Are there animals nearby?" Deep Voice asks his partners. "It's keeping me from detecting their blood. Can you pinpoint them?"

Blood... A Bloodhound? I haven't heard of many people with that skill—it's exclusive to highly-ranked Hematology Power. If a Bloodhound is on our trail, we are in far more trouble than I first suspected.

Enid raises her hand over her knee and closes her own eyes, focusing her Environment Creation Power elsewhere. I can't tell what she's doing, but the flick of her wrist away from us makes it clear she's trying to throw off the scent they are using to track us. Maybe she created the smell. *It reeks of stinkweed.*

"They aren't far, but I can't seem to pinpoint them," another, more familiar male voice says.

I would know that voice anywhere.

Terry the Telepath.

Terry threatened me in Paragon, nearly made my brain explode with his Telepathic Powers. In the final Survival Test, he tried to kill me before Bianca laid him out. We left him on the ground in the simulation as we escaped. He didn't—to my knowledge, anyway. What happened to him after we left? His Telepathic Power could have frozen Enid, but if so, he has learned some new tricks. I have no doubt where those tricks came from.

But how could Terry not pinpoint us? His Telepathy should easily find my friends, even if he can't detect me.

"Okay," Deep Voice says. "We will sweep each property. Are you sure it was him?"

"I would recognize that weasel anywhere," Terry says.

"Then we need to call this in."

Crap!

Their steps recede, and I ease up over the porch window's trim, peering through the ripped screen. They are gone, but it won't be long before they find us.

"How long do we have?" I ask Jayme. He's our Pax and DMA veteran.

Jayme shakes his head. "Not long. If they're DMA, this place will be crawling with troopers soon."

"Can we make it back to the others?" I ask.

"Not if they're starting sweeps. They'll spot us for sure."

So, we're trapped. If we stay, we're caught. If we flee, we're caught.

"I'm not going back there," Enid says with a wave of fervent anger that sends a chill down my spine. Those are the first words she's spoken since she dropped the snow globe.

None of us want to go back. We need a plan. A way out. They will sweep the neighborhood, which means we need to figure out which house they will search last.

"We aren't going back," I say confidently, moving toward the screen door. "Follow me."

"Where are you going?" Jayme asks, rushing up to my side.

"To the last place they will look for us." It isn't a great plan, but it's a start.

22

AN OMINOUS WEIGHT PRESSES IN ON US FROM THE shadows along the street and darkened windows. We do our best to seem small and move fast, zigzagging between houses, but it's hard to shake the sensation that someone is watching.

The hum of a DMA shuttle approaches from the distance. Backup is almost here. I glance across the street to an apartment building. If we hurry, we might be able to get back to the rest of our group before the DMA backup arrives. Jayme doubted, but I can't help holding onto hope.

As we round a corner, a squad of DMA troopers climb the front stairs of a house. We duck back and change course. The squad blocks our path across the street, our path back to the rest of the group.

We huddle close to the side of the house where the attack was first launched, and I peer toward the street. The squad is still there on that porch. We can't cross.

I signal toward the open window of the house. Jayme grimaces then pulls himself up through the window. Once he's inside, he pulls up the others. I follow at the end, and he yanks me roughly through. I tumble to the floorboards and something skitters across the wooden floor.

Biting down a nasty comment, I brush myself off and join the others in the dining room. All of us hunker down with our backs pressed to the outside wall near the window, facing the remnants of the root-wood barricade.

Silence hangs over us as if even the smallest whisper will draw the

DMA straight to us. We can't stay here forever but hiding in the house we started in should buy some time to plan a way back to the group.

Miller kneels in front of Jayme, trying to move the vest to get a better look at his wound, but Jayme keeps swatting his hands away. The vests are bulletproof, so there's a good chance the bullet grazed his side.

Enid sits so close to me against the wall that I can feel the warmth of her body. My fingers itch to pull out the bundle and inspect it, but leaving it tightly bound together is probably best for now in case we need to run again. I don't want to risk dropping anything.

A way out. We need a way out.

The hum of DMA shuttles grows closer. Multiple shuttles.

It's me. Terry knew it was me and they are sending all of these troopers in to get me. But that also means I can use myself as leverage to get the others out of danger.

Outside, troopers exchange reports on the status of the sweeps, but without Parabolic Hearing, none of us can hear exactly what they are saying.

At Paragon, Terry was given an injection of some sort of serum. I saw the video myself, saved it to the drive that Miller still possesses. Is his new Power a side-effect of that serum, or did they develop something else? Jayme seems to think Terry and the others are part of the DMA, but if that's true, then Paragon is delivering their successful test subject experiments to grow the DMA's force. Why is Paragon working so closely with the DMA? What will they gain from this partnership?

I rub at my forehead as if trying to coax out the answers. Jayme inches closer to the only open window in the room, peering out into the street.

For years, Paragon has touted its research into ending regression. Those videos I saw didn't seem to have anything to do with regression therapies though. Paragon did something that pumped an influx of Power through the subjects. Some of them died as a result. Jade. Vicki.

But Terry didn't.

So, what has changed?

Dr. Cass could have used your biology to selectively offer those Superpowers to anyone. Willow's warning felt a bit stale before, but now…

Did Dr. Cass give Superpowers to Terry? I shudder at the thought.

"He's making that epiphany face," Sho whispers, pointing at me.

The sound of his voice pulls me from my thoughts. I look at Jayme and Miller near the window, but instead of watching the street they're both staring at me.

"Out with it, genius," Miller says.

A woman screams to be released. "I didn't do anything! I pay my taxes!"

I join them at the window and peer over to see a family huddled in the street as troopers storm the house. Another squad knocks down the door to the house beside it. The DMA doesn't care that it's late at night. They storm into houses both abandoned and inhabited. *Searching for me. We need to get the heck out of here.*

Shuttles can hover over the houses, so if we try and sneak out the back door, they may still catch us. If we try to run across the street, we will surely be spotted. One way or another, we need to take the risk. We can't sit here forever.

But we can use our Powers to escape. It wouldn't be inconspicuous if Enid used that fog I once saw her create in the Survival Test at Paragon. A wall of fog will at least provide us with cover. Sho can use his Echolocation to detract from our exact location so the DMA can't use Powers to pinpoint us.

But when I open my mouth to speak, a familiar voice calls to me from outside. One that sends an initial bolt of shock through me.

"Ugene!" Forrest's voice echoes off the houses along the nearly empty street. I haven't seen him since he ordered his sister's death during the Paragon escape. Just the sound of his voice makes my blood burn with rage. "We know you're still here. Come out and no one will get hurt."

A lump swells in my throat and my stomach drops. How did he get here so fast? Is he part of this partnership between the Directorate and Paragon? Which side is he working for?

Enid grabs my arm in quivering hands.

Miller scowls at me and shakes his head in warning.

"I'll give you one minute to show your face," Forrest calls, "Citizens, harboring a fugitive will result in immediate expulsion from the city, but you will get one free pass. Right now."

This is what Willow feared. Paragon wants me back. This is why Willow didn't want me coming to the city. I close my eyes and take a deep breath to calm my nerves.

Directly in front of me, two tiny trees that were once inside the snow globe Enid broke now lies on the floor with branches broken. Scattered around the trees are small bits of pink confetti meant to be petals of the cherry blossom tree. It's just like the one I gave to Mom for Mother's Day when I was eight.

Scrambling forward, I pick up the base of the snow globe, still intact. The front of the base has a quote about the change that comes with the petals of the blossom. I turn it over. On the bottom, scratched in with a knife, is my name and the year.

I don't believe it.

I dig in the pockets of the vest and find a switchblade, then slide the blade between the base and its bottom to work them apart as carefully as possible. Everyone else starts crowding around, watching me pry this thing open. It finally pops off, and we panic for a moment, imagining the sound to be much louder than it was. I pull out a square of paper and unfold it. A small data drive falls out. Sho picks it up as I read the brief note Dad left with it.

DMA Action Plan: Purification Project

"What is it?" Jayme asks, leaning toward the drive.

I hold the note to him and all four crowd around to read it.

"What's the Purification Project?" Enid asks, but the anxious tone in her hushed voice reveals she suspects the same as the rest of us.

Paragon and the DMA aren't planning on curing regression. They are working some kind of a purge. Maybe just like the government did to people with Powers during the Change.

"So be it!" Forrest calls from the street. "Search all the houses. I don't care who lives there. I want him unharmed."

We're out of time.

23

IT'S ONLY A MATTER OF TIME BEFORE THE DMA FINDS us huddled in this house. We're surrounded. We can either fight our way out or I can turn myself in while they escape. *Or I can pretend to turn myself in as we fight our way free.*

"How fast can you run?" I ask Sho, slipping out of my jacket, where the bundle we found in the floorboards and the new hard drive are zipped up safely.

"Pretty fast. But I don't like this."

I hand over the jacket. "Enid will provide cover. You run as fast as you can and get my jacket to Willow. Everything is in there. Get help."

Miller snaps out of a trance. "No." He moves into the broken doorway, then stabs a finger at my chest. "I know what you're thinking, and it's a terrible idea."

Why does he always have to fight me? I step toward him. "We don't have a choice. Enid can use fog as cover. I'll distract them. You all escape across the street. Sho runs for help. It's the only way you all get out of here."

"And you give that prick exactly what he wants," Miller hisses.

"We don't have time to argue."

Jayme inches toward us and takes Miller's arm. "He's right. We get across the street and we can regroup and rescue him."

"No." Enid shakes her head.

"Please, Enid. I need your help. Use your fog to cover your tracks. I'll distract Forrest and the DMA. You can regroup with Jayme to get me out," I press on with more confidence than I feel. "This will work."

Miller appears ready to voice his strong distaste for this plan, but he bites his tongue and leaves with the others as I turn away and move toward the front door. I wait until the others are all out of the line of sight before stepping out.

Three massive black military-grade shuttles barricade each end of the block. Forrest waits beside one of the shuttles in street clothes, a bullet-proof vest over his polo shirt. He watches as nearly two dozen men and women in DMA tactical gear fan out to search each house.

If this doesn't work, we're all in serious trouble. I clear my throat and call out, "Forrest! I'm right here."

Forrest scans the houses, searching me out.

I step forward and the wooden step of the front porch creaks beneath me. In seconds, DMA troopers surround the porch on all three sides with weapons aimed at me. I raise my hands so they don't think I have a trick up my sleeve or a weapon or Power to use against them.

"Where are the others?" Forrest asks as he strides toward the porch.

"Others?"

"Don't play coy, Ugene." Forrest stops behind the backline of troopers surrounding me like he actually thinks I'll stand a chance against such a force. "I know you well enough."

"You wanted me. Here I am."

Two of the troopers inch up the steps. They begin a search by stripping off my vest. I don't resist.

"No. I said no one would get hurt." Forrest turns his attention to one of the troopers, and my stomach drops out at his next words. "Continue the search. If they resist, shoot. Try not to kill them. If you can help it." The last was more of an afterthought.

The troopers around the porch break off into small groups as the two with me take my arms and twist them behind my back. The force sends a jolt of pain through my shoulder. One of the troopers pushes me forward down the porch steps toward Forrest.

"Didn't realize you were part of the DMA," I say as nonchalantly as I can manage. Whatever happens next, I won't give Forrest the gratification of seeing how anxious I am. I can only hope the others will regroup and come to my rescue soon enough. "Research get boring without me around to prod?"

Forrest walks alongside me as the troopers escort me to one of the shuttles. "I'm actually a little disappointed in you. I thought you would want to stop regression, get a Power."

I scoff. "Come on, we both know that's not what this is about. Regression is nothing more than an excuse. I think genocide is a better word."

"You don't comprehend."

"No, but I'm starting to." I turn to face him at the back door of the shuttle. "Was Bianca's death really worth all of this? How do you look your parents in the face?"

Forrest grins in a manner I can only describe as evil.

Rage burns in my chest. Does he think her death is a joke? I sneer, and my voice fills with predatory hunger, "You should have restrained me."

I lunge at Forrest, wrapping my fingers around his throat and digging my nails in, growling. Hate boils in my veins and I squeeze tighter as he claws at my hands. One of the troopers grabs my shirt and attempts hauling me back, but all he does is pull the collar of my t-shirt tight against my throat. I gag, cough, my eyes water, but I don't let go. Not when I can watch with satisfaction as Forrest's face grows red. Not when I can feel him struggling to breathe, clawing and beating at my hands and arms feebly.

Pressure on my head pulses as Forrest attempts to stop me with his Divinic Power. A noble effort. A pointless effort. Never in my life have I hated someone so much. I want to squeeze until he can't breathe, until his eyes pop from his head, until the whole thing just pops off like the zit he is, an unwanted blemish on the skin of humanity.

Sudden, sharp pain twists at my temples. I try to fight it off, but it feels like my head is getting pinched in a vice. I grind my teeth and try to fight through it, but the pressure is overwhelming, forcing me to let go of Forrest and press my palms to my temples. It has little effect.

"Don't kill him!" Forrest rasps, rubbing at his throat.

The pain lessens, turning to a dull throb that disorients me. Not enough to prevent me from seeing the blood I managed to draw from Forrest's neck with my nails.

I take a moment to gasp for air and recover, then lunge forward again.

Strong hands grasp my wrists and hold my arms tight behind my back.

"Load him in the shuttle," Forrest says.

As I'm pushed toward the back of the shuttle, the road beneath our feet begins to quake. It isn't a massive quake, just enough to throw us both off course. My captor releases me as he stumbles. I grasp the edge of the shuttle for balance, then push off the back and run. A wall of fog rolls up the street toward me.

Enid!

My friends had a chance to regroup! I bought enough time. I just hope all of them managed to escape the DMA earlier.

I tuck my arms tighter to my sides and pump my legs, putting all the steam I can muster into running into the fog. It's still half a block away, crawling toward me.

"Don't shoot him!" Forrest yells from behind.

Each step feels slow despite my speed, like trying to run through molasses in a nightmare.

A set of boots pound against the pavement behind me, but I don't dare look back. With the ground quaking, I can't afford to take my eyes off the road ahead. The fog rolls closer. Did Enid escape then? What about the others? Did everyone scatter?

The boots are closing the gap. It's a Somatic giving chase. It has to be. Even if I reach the fog in time, whoever this is will be right on my heels, able to catch me. I need to get off the street.

To the left, an apartment building sits mostly dark, its corner encased in fog. Only a few lights are on in windows, but no one looks out. I veer toward the door, and in seconds I'm at it, yanking the rusted metal frame open. But it doesn't immediately shut when I let go. My pursuer is only steps behind.

The inside is an old apartment building foyer. Minimal light stretches inside from long thin windows. No lobby lights are on, probably because of the extra cost of running them. The light from the windows is just enough to see the weak, worn-out wooden steps going up. They might hold my weight, but Somatics are naturally denser. My pursuer may be too heavy. I turn and run to the stairs, launching my light body up as quick as I can, two steps at a time. The stairs protest, creaking and cracking against my weight.

One of the stairs snaps behind me, and my pursuer yelps.

I glance over my shoulder as I round the top of the steps, but it's too dark to get a good look. I'm being chased by a female, judging by the momentary glance at the shadowy form, but I don't pause to learn more. I need a place to hide until she passes so I can slip back out. This may be my only opportunity to lose her. She may be able to catch me in a footrace, but not if she can't find me.

Another quake throws me off balance, and I stumble into the wall. Dust rains down from the ceiling. This whole building might collapse if that quaking doesn't stop.

I run along the narrow hallway, feeling my way in the dark, testing doors along the way. All locked. I need a place to hide before she reaches the top of the steps. I can hear her weight and the stairs protests increase threefold. With nowhere else to go, I grab one of the handles, turn, and throw my weight against it. The door pops open and I slip inside, easing it shut behind me.

The apartment is dark. Too dark to get my bearings, and I can't risk pulling out my flashlight. I inch deeper, feeling along the wall for a closet door or bathroom, even a cupboard to hide in. Before I can find a place, the door shatters off the hinges into the apartment. My pursuer crashes into me so hard the force puts both of us through the cracked tile floor.

Somehow, she rolls our bodies midair so she takes most of the impact. Still, my ears ring and my whole body pulses with pain. Dust clogs my throat, and I cough, pushing off her, scrambling to my feet. Each cough feels like a punch in the ribs. Her hand clamps down on my arm, and through the stench of mildew, the familiar scent of citrus shampoo mingles with musky body odor.

My chest seizes. "Bianca…"

24

MY PULSE IS RACING. BIANCA CAN PROBABLY FEEL IT pumping against her firm grip. I squint into the fading darkness, and the coppery color of her eyes almost seems to glow. The only hints of light come from the window covered by musty curtains. But she's so close to me that I can just see her features. The shape of her face and slope of her nose.

Bianca is *alive*? But I held her in my arms as she died! My gut churns in a torrent of confused emotions. The ache in my ribs becomes more acute as my chest tightens.

"Don't resist," she says. Her voice chases away any doubt.

It's actually her.

"You are in DMA custody. If you resist—"

"Bianca, it's me."

"—I will be required to use force."

The darkness. She can't see me. "Stop. It's me… It's Ugene!"

Bianca doesn't relent her grip on my arm. "Put your hands behind your back," she says as if she hadn't even heard my words. "Resisting is pointless."

What is wrong with her? I do as she says, if for no other reason than to buy a few seconds to collect my thoughts. Bianca is alive. How? Sometimes I can still feel her blood coating my hands and arms, making my shirt stick to my chest.

Bianca waits patiently as I turn slowly, moving my free arm behind me. She holds tight to my other arm but allows me enough freedom to move it. The way Bianca acts reminds me of someone, and it takes a second in my flustered state to recall his name.

Derrek—the Strongarm test subject from Paragon. He wasn't in control of himself in that final fight in the Paragon lobby, just as we escaped. Could they be doing the same to Bianca?

Maybe I can snap her out of it.

As she nudges me forward, my words pour out. "Bianca, it's Ugene. We grew up together. I lived right across the street. We were friends. We played in the rain and built mud castles. Your brother, Forrest, broke your arm and blamed it on me."

Bianca's boots stop scuffing the ground behind me, and I risk turning around. She faces me statue-still, and I can't tell what she's thinking or feeling. Still, I hold my breath and pray that something I said reached her.

I take a bold step closer. "At Paragon, you fought beside me, helped all of us escape. They shot you and I carried your body. Just before you died, you told me to go and kissed me. God, please, remember me. Remember something."

The two of us linger in front of the window, and the light is just bright enough here to see her more clearly. Her lips are compressed and forehead pinched. Her shoulders draw tight and her muscles tense. Bianca struggles with something. *I struck a cord!*

I shudder, and pain throbs at my ribs, forcing me to take shallow breaths. Clutching at my side, I reach an unsteady hand toward her.

Bianca's hand shoots out and snatches my wrist, twisting it away from my body. I cry out as the sudden movement makes my ribs burn and my shoulder pulses. Every breath is like another punch in the ribs.

"Don't touch me," she says, and I notice for the first time that her voice sounds vacant.

"What did they do to you?"

A thump against the outside wall makes her jump into action. Bianca twists my arm around behind my back and places me between her and the window like a shield. I try to move out of the way, but she's so much stronger. Resisting only makes the pain worse.

My pulse drums in my ears as I struggle to hear what's going on outside. *Who is out there?* Bianca isn't the only person trying to capture me. Is this her DMA backup? Did Sho and the others reach Willow?

Silence settles over us. Her warm breath rolls across my neck as we wait, unmoving. After a minute, her body never relaxes, but Bianca loosens her grip on my arm enough for me to pull away from her and the window. *Something else caught her attention.*

Then everything happens at once.

Glass shatters. A musclebound body barrels through the window into Bianca. I'm shoved back by the force of the collision and stumble into a corner, knocking the air from my lungs. The two tumble across the floor.

A scream tries to escape as burning agony in my chest makes it hard to breathe, but no sound comes out. Gasping for short breaths, I lean against the wall and collect the strength to help her.

Bianca and the other Somatic throw punches at each other, each one sounding as vicious as a car wreck as it connects. In a flash of light from the window, I recognize Chase's bald head as he winds up then launches an uppercut into Bianca's jaw, his thick arms rippling with muscles. She flies into the opposite wall, cracking the plaster and leaving a Bianca-sized indentation. But she doesn't slow. Bianca pushes off the wall like the blow was nothing, launching her body with incredible speed and force into Chase. They slam into the outer wall of the room and break through the brick exterior, tumbling out of sight into the alley.

It takes everything I can muster to suck in air, but I manage to get up and follow them. Should I try and intervene? If Bianca wins, I could end up back in Paragon. But I can't stand by and allow someone to hurt her again. *What do I do?*

Gingerly, I step through the hole in the wall, wincing at the searing agony in my chest, puffing out short breaths. The fall must have broken at least one of my ribs. Rosie and Lily rush to my side the moment I step through.

"Ugene!" Rosie calls.

"My ribs…I broke my…" I lean against the wall, yearning to step into the fight even knowing I'll be no good to either help Bianca or shut down Chase.

"Don't move," Rosie says, pulling up my t-shirt.

I don't protest but can't help jumping as Bianca picks up Chase and throws him into the brick wall, embedding him in the stonework.

Rosie's Healing Hands are less than pleasant, like she's actually grabbing my ribs and popping them back into place. Every muscle in my body seizes. I clamp down my jaw and growl a guttural scream.

When she finishes, Rosie stabs a finger in my face. "Don't you dare leave us behind again."

Before I can respond, Noah bursts into the alleyway, shoulder-checking Bianca off Chase and sending her flying sideways. I push away from the wall, but Bianca tucks and rolls as she hits the ground.

Noah yanks Chase out of the wall. Chase stumbles, stunned. In the growing light of early dawn, the damage Bianca did to Chase is obvious. One arm hangs limply at his side. Blood seeps from several wounds on his arms as well as through the fabric of his shirt. His face swells around one eye. He falls sideways into Noah, who grabs his arm and rights him. *This isn't Bianca. She wouldn't do this. She couldn't do this.*

By the time Chase and Noah are steady, Bianca has vaulted back to her feet and launches at both men. While her black DMA uniform is torn in places, she doesn't show any signs of injury. And Christ is she ripped! The muscles in her arms are far more defined. Her skin-tight pants show off the chiseled shape of her legs. This isn't Bianca. It's like a Super Bianca.

Rosie grabs my arm, pulling me toward the mouth of the alley. "Let's go before the rest of the DMA finds us."

I can't leave Bianca. Not again. She may not be the same person at the moment, but I have to believe the girl I know is still in there somewhere. *What will happen to her if we leave her behind?*

Bianca takes down both Noah and Chase—one with each arm.

Willow charges into the alley. Chase grabs one of Bianca's arms and Noah grabs the other. What are they doing to her?

Rosie's healing did its work, and cool morning air burns in my lungs as I rush toward the three of them.

"Stop!" I call out.

"Get Ugene out of here!" Willow snaps. She jumps and lands on Bianca's back with cat-like grace, grabbing Bianca's head.

Rosie gives my arm a more urgent tug toward the mouth of the alley. Lily pushes on my back.

"I can't." I pull away from Rosie, repeating with more fire, "I can't leave her again."

I rush toward them as Willow focuses on Bianca, who struggles more feebly each second. Bianca's body slumps. I skid to a stop, chest heaving with anxious breaths. "What did you do to her?"

"*Her?*" Willow jumps off. "Look at these two! She did that. All on her own."

Noah sits up and touches the back of his head. His hand comes away with blood.

"We gotta…" Chase wheezes, squeezing his one good eye shut and clutching his chest with his good hand. "Gotta go."

Willow nods in agreement. "But you won't get far without healing."

Rosie is already rushing to their sides, tending to Chase first. Rosie's hands shake, and her skin seems paler, but her Healing Hands do their job on Chase.

Noah waves her off. "I'm good for now. We need to move."

"We can't leave her here," I say.

Willow's brows shoot up her forehead as she helps Chase to his feet. "Why not?"

Because I already left her behind once. "You obviously can subdue her, and we might be able to get information from her. Bianca has value to our cause."

"She's one of them," Willow says. "They travel in squads, and hers will come after her soon. And I guarantee they can track her. She can't come with us. It will put all of The Shield at risk."

The echoes of tactical units calling out orders to each other emanate from inside the building. The DMA will be here in moments.

I left her once before. I can't do it again.

Willow is right. I know it, but compassion overrides logic and I clench my hands into fists. "There has to be a chance she is still in there somewhere. I won't leave her in their hands."

The rest of our group enters the mouth of the alley, and my friends freeze, staring at Bianca's prone form. Jayme grumbles something, then moves to the hole in the wall and uses his Power to close the gap and buy us time. His face is scary pale, and his eyes are bloodshot. Enid freezes in place, looking from me to Bianca, and back again, trying to sort out what's going on and how this is possible. Then she turns on her heel and leaves the alley.

"She helped save us at Paragon," I plead, looking from one of my friends to the next. "This is our chance to save her."

Leo shifts, glancing at Sho. Rosie chews her lip, staring at Willow with a sense of admiration that makes me uncomfortable. Bri's forehead wrinkles as she enters the alley. For a second I think she's moving to help me, but she walks up to the brick wall instead. Even Noah won't meet my gaze. Miller slumps and pulls his hood tighter around his face. *They would leave her.*

"Jayme, what would you do if they wanted you to leave Miller behind?" I say in a rush. If anyone can understand, it has to be him.

Jayme glances from Miller to me to Bianca's prone form. He scrubs a hand over his exhausted face and heaves out a sigh.

"He's right. She might be useful to us."

"Get us to a safe place and I can disable her tracking," Bri says, placing her hand against the brick wall of the building the DMA now searches.

Willow scowls at Jayme. "We don't have time for this. Chase, get her. We will sort this out once we put distance between us and the DMA."

Bri turns to face Willow from beside the brick wall of the building. "I scrambled their signal, but it won't last for too long. We have about a minute to get away."

Chase grumbles and hauls Bianca over his shoulder.

Jayme and Willow lead the group out of the alleyway. Enid waits petulantly with her back against the wall. The second she sees me walking beside Chase, with Bianca in tow, Enid joins Jayme at the front of the group as Willow falls to the back.

The sun begins to rise, breaking over the houses and apartment buildings. Throngs of people begin filling the streets, hustling along with their heads down as they rush off to work. DMA troopers are stationed at each corner, but we melt into the crowd of people, spacing out just enough to still see each other without appearing to all walk together. Chase shifts Bianca and he and Noah share the weight so it looks like she's walking with us.

A DMA trooper stationed along the side of the street watches the crowd. We keep our heads down like everyone else. I pray she doesn't notice us. When she steps off the curb, my breath catches.

"You!" The trooper approaches Enid near the front.

I tense, ready spring into action.

But the trooper grabs a young man three feet from Enid and pulls him out of the crowd. Simultaneously, I feel terrible and relieved.

Most of my attention sticks on Bianca, minus the few glances I make toward Enid. Where before she'd clung tightly to my side, now she is about as far from me as she could be. She's upset, and rightfully so, but she will understand. Enid is smart and reasonable. I can convince her this is the best course of action…right after I convince Willow.

We don't stay in the open for too long. Jayme leads us to another alley three blocks away. Just as Willow slips into the alley at the rear of the group, a shuttle hums to life, speeding down the road. Did they catch sight of us?

The jack-booted march of DMA troopers thumps along the street. They won't stop looking now that they know I'm here.

"Citizens," a male voice announces from a megaphone somewhere in the street. "A group of rebels walks your streets. Report any sightings of unusual activities to the tented stations posted at the corners. Your safety is our priority."

That can't be good.

The announcement repeats on a loop as Jayme stops at the back door to one of the buildings along the alley. Everyone else presses against the wall.

"We have to get off the streets," she says just loudly enough for all of us to hear. "Then we can find a safehouse to wait for extraction. Our mission is shot." While her comment sounds like an assessment of the situation, the way Willow glares at me makes it clear she is far from pleased.

I risked the mission for the information Dad left behind, and to help Bianca, but I'm convinced that this will play out in our favor. How, I don't yet know. But it will. *It has to.*

Jayme opens the backdoor, and he and Sho enter to make sure the space is clear. Every second of delay could be a potential chance for the DMA to track Bianca's location. We all wait in the alley for their return, listening to the announcement repeat. I pray no one spots us hiding in the alley. Would these people turn us in to the DMA?

Jayme and Sho announce that the building is clear and we all slip inside.

I have either given us a deadly weapon or doomed us all.

25

THE NARROW SHOP WE CURRENTLY OCCUPY IS MAYBE twenty feet wide at most. We entered through a backroom containing empty metal shelves, mistaking a tiny bathroom for a closet. I follow Chase into the front of the shop, turning sideways to slip past Willow when she tries to cut me off in the doorway.

"Ugene." Willow grabs my arm. "She endangers us every second we stay with her."

I stop and turn to her, though I give her no indication she can change my mind. "She sacrificed herself for the rest of us. The least we can do is try to save her this time." I flick my gaze between her grasping hand and her eyes.

Willow drops her grip, though I know I haven't heard the end of it.

The front of the shop has a few old barber chairs and mirrors covered in years of dust and grime. The stations are bare of haircutting tools, though wrappings and empty food cans litter the floor. Shutters cover the windows with a few of the slats broken. This place closed shop a long time ago, and people have used it to squat in. The dust in the air makes someone sneeze as we kick it up.

Chase thumps Bianca down in the middle of the floor and glares down at her.

Leo and Bri kneel beside Bianca and start seeking out the tracking device.

I hover nearby. *Bianca is alive.* The memory of her dead weight in my arms grows into a fresh, painful wound.

But she was alive.

The whole time.

The Paragon crew crowds around Bianca.

"How is she here?" Rosie whispers, as if Bianca will hear.

"She died, right?" Sho says, matching Rosie's hushed tones. "I mean, that's what Ugene and Enid said."

Enid. She is the only one missing from among my friends.

I scan the barbershop and find her sitting on one of the chairs in the back corner of the room staring into the dirty mirror with her back to the rest of us. I can't see her face clearly. I was ready to give up on Bianca, to move on. Where does this leave us? Not that there is an us for either Bianca and me or Enid and me.

Bianca stirs, waking up, and Willow hustles to Bianca's head. In seconds, she has worked her Power again. *What* is *her power?* Bianca returns to a state of unconsciousness. Back at Paragon, Trina knocked out Forrest with her Hematology Powers, and it took a toll on Forrest, exhausted him. Is Willow doing the same?

I step forward. "What are you doing to her?"

"Relax, she'll be fine," Willow says. "Which is more than I can say for the rest of us."

The looped announcement continues outside. "…Your safety is our priority."

I just wanted the information Dad left behind. I didn't mean for all of this. I never could have anticipated the DMA showing up so quickly, or Terry or Bianca working for them. And I'm well aware that I have put our group at risk, but Bri said she could disable the tracking.

I swallow the lump swelling in my throat.

"Bri, Leo, have you found anything?" Willow asks.

"Almost," they say in unison.

Sho and Lily are perched at the edge of a window together watching the street through shutters.

"Lily," I say, hoping for a distraction. "I don't think you've ever mentioned your Power."

She leans against the wall as she turns away from the window to look at me. "I'm a Psychometrist."

I blink. Lily can trace the history of something through touch. It makes sense. When she touched me back in The Shield, she jerked back. *Can she read people through touch, too?*

"You were pretty fantastic to observe at Paragon," Sho says. "Like you could see how the game played out."

"Yeah, you were," Leo agrees, sitting back on his heels.

I harrumph, glance at Bianca, then move to the shuttered window near Lily to peer out at the street. I didn't do anything special at Paragon. I just put the puzzle pieces together and found our way out.

For the moment, I try to block everything else out. I need to focus to understand what's going on in the Directorate and in Pax—to comprehend how Bianca is alive.

The streets aren't quiet anymore. DMA troopers move up and down the road in droves, questioning citizens who look like they would rather be anywhere else. Pax is well known for violence and crime. It's that one part of Elpis I've always been warned to stay away from. But Dad must've known I would find my way here. He hid those items in that house, after all. And the way these citizens are dressed. A lot of the clothes are pretty tattered. This borough isn't violent, it's impoverished. The only violence I've witnessed was caused by DMA presence.

Why haven't DMA Telepaths found us yet? I wonder, watching as a woman picks up a boy—her son presumably—and clutches him close to her chest as she hustles past one of the troopers, keeping her head down. A rotting apple falls out of her bag as she sweeps him up, and she hesitates, staring at the fruit, then gives up on it and moves along. She just abandoned her food on the ground to get away from the DMA.

"Our building has a perception filter on it," Willow says, stopping beside me with her arms crossed. "I can't hold it for too long, but it will keep Telepaths away from us for now."

Did she just read my mind? I can't make heads or tails of what Willow can do, and for some reason, she won't tell.

I press the side of my face against the window frame so I can see to the corner where a canvas tent has been hastily constructed. Troopers corral a handful of people into a line, sometimes holding them by the sleeve of their shirt and shoving them forward.

A young man who can't be much older than me bolts out of the tent, panic written all over his expression. He stumbles, almost running on all fours in an attempt to escape. Without hesitation, one of the troopers raises his gun and shoots. The bang of the gun makes everyone on the street duck for cover.

"No." I press a hand against the pane.

Two troopers grab the boy and haul him to his feet. His body is slumped, head hanging as they drag him toward a shuttle. He isn't dead. His chest still rises and falls. *Where are they taking him?* But I have my suspicions. Either Paragon or to do whatever the DMA wants to do to these regressing citizens.

A young woman runs out into the street after them. "Gerry! Stop!" She grabs one of the troopers and he shrugs her off as others surround her, pointing their guns in her face, forcing her to her knees.

"What is going on out there?" I barely breathe out the words. Something has to be done. What if they find us?

"Ugene, you need to calm down," Willow says, putting a hand on my back as I press my hands against my head.

My tightly coiled muscles relax, and I back away from the window, sinking into one of the vacant barber chairs. Rosie, Noah, and Sho have crowded the window to see what's going on.

"I warned you about attracting DMA attention," Willow says. "The Directorate has been pinching people with weak Powers into a vice grip, squeezing some out. Pax gets the worst of it."

I shake my head. How can the Directorate do this? They don't have the right to steal away the chance at a good life from anyone. "Someone needs to stop this."

"What do you think we've been trying to do?" Willow asks.

I take a breath to steady myself. Things are starting to click into place like the picture is becoming clear. Consumption Taxation hurts people with weaker Powers, and Proposition 8.5 forces those people to undergo further testing. But the testing isn't for a regression cure.

Willow's voice breaks through my thoughts. "Ugene, if you would just—"

"Let me think!" I lean forward in the chair.

"That's his thinking face," Enid says flatly from across the barbershop. "Give him a minute."

Doc and Willow were certain that Dr. Cass would find a way to create Superpowers if she had me in her possession. But even though she lost me—and probably needs me back for more samples—she doesn't need me to get things started if she's already figured it out. And if Doc has learned about what my DNA has to offer, then Dr. Cass certainly has.

"Found it," Leo says, "but it isn't good. The tracking is in her head. Can we do anything about that?"

Implanting tracking in the brain makes it nearly impossible to remove without causing serious damage. But nearly impossible *isn't* impossible.

"I can deactivate it for now," Bri says. "But my Power won't keep it off forever. She needs the tracker removed."

"Do it," Willow says.

Bri places her hands against Bianca's head and closes her eyes.

"If she comes to, we will have a hard time containing her," Chase says. "That girl is scary strong. I've never fought anything like it before. And nothing seemed to slow her down."

Stronger...

Terry had stronger Powers last night. Different Powers.

Purification Project. The DMA is pinching out the weak or recruiting them into service with the promise of a booster, with Paragon's help. *And my DNA.* Creating Superpowers. Making some people stronger. People like—*Bianca...*

"She's enhanced," I say.

Willow turns to me, cocking her head to the side. "What?"

"You said Dr. Cass just needed the right samples to create a sort of super-serum, right?" I start pacing again, unsure of when I stood from the stool.

"Here he goes," Enid says, leaning back in her chair with her arms crossed.

"Dr. Cass had them already. Not much, but they took samples weekly while I was there. Some of it was probably used up in testing—which is on the videos we saw before with Jade and Vicki and…Terry." Has Terry been Super all this time? I shake my head. "Anyway. They push down the weak, then force them into Paragon's testing so they have bodies to find out how effective their serum is. And it fails. A lot. But then it doesn't. Now they have the formula to create more Supers and use the Tax and Proposition as excuses to force people to join the DMA."

Willow perks up. "Okay, but to what end? This force can't just be to sniff out our resistance. Directorate Chief Seaduss is very meticulous. Getting rid of us is probably just a small part of a much larger plan."

I stop, turning to face her. "I was hoping you could fill in that part. Maybe this is their way to stop regression like he promised he would do when he took office."

"And he hasn't." Willow nods.

"Right. Instead, he turns the weak into expendable supersoldiers to find the Protectorate, secure the rampant crime in these boroughs, and dispose of those who pose a threat. It ensures their control with an iron fist, and if it works, no one else will ever stand up to them. Why would they?"

"But they would need you to do it," Willow says.

"Would they? Sure, having me might make the job easier, add a sense of security to their plan, but Dr. Cass doesn't need me to replicate DNA artificially. She has a whole building full of labs and scientists to do it for her."

The two of us just stare at each other, and I can see her processing everything I've just dumped out.

"Where does he get this stuff?" Jayme asks.

Willow gapes at me. "He might be right."

"Not to make matters worse, but they have a Bloodhound," I say. "A guy. I didn't get a look at him, but he has a deep voice."

Willow freezes. Chase shoots his attention my way. Jayme stiffens as he leans against one of the stations behind Miller's chair.

"Are you sure?" Willow asks.

"Not completely, but judging by what he said, pretty much." I take in the three of them and notice Lily has gone significantly pale. "We've gotten this far."

"Bloodhounds never lose their prey," Willow says. "Do I even want to know who he was tracking?"

I shrug. "Could have been any of us." *But judging by his conversation, he was after me.*

"We can't stay here. We have to move," Chase says.

"Are you done, Bri?" Willow asks, moving with urgency toward Bri still working on Bianca's tracker.

"Done," Bri says.

"Good." Willow finally tears herself away and catches Chase's attention. "We need to move now. The Bloodhound is probably already closing in on us. I can block Telepaths, but I can't block that."

Chase nods then moves to pick up Bianca.

Willow taps a message on her watch, then grabs Chase's arm. "Miller and Leo can carry her together. We need all our fighters ready."

"Down?" Chase asks.

Willow nods. "Down."

I frown and begin to ask what that means, but Willow already ushers all of us through the back door and into the alley, where Chase easily hefts off a manhole cover.

Then, it becomes clear.

Down.

26

MILLER AND SHO CLIMB INTO THE SEWER FIRST, followed closely by Jayme. In less than a minute, only five of us remain above ground. Chase pulls out a set of clips with a long, thin cable from a pocket in his vest, getting assistance from Willow and Enid to strap in Bianca so they can lower her down.

I make my way along the wall of the building toward the mouth of the alley. Using a dumpster for cover, I peek out at the street. I know Willow wants us to get back to The Shield, but the image of that trooper shooting that young man haunts me.

From here, it's much easier to see the canvas tent set up on the corner. A DMA shuttle waits idly beside the tent.

The line of people outside the tent spans generations, from infants in their mother's or father's arms to elderly people who struggle to stay upright as they wait. One of the old men reaches for a trooper as he passes, pleading with him. I can't hear what he says, but the trooper stops, looks the man over, and pulls out a handheld body scanner. The old man shrinks back and stumbles into the woman in line behind him, but there is no escape.

A blue beam emits from the scanner as the trooper presses the old man's hand against it. In seconds, the old man is yanked from the line and thrust toward the shuttle. He tries to pull away but is too weak against the trooper. The old man practically falls into the back of the shuttle. The trooper gives him a shove and slams the door in the old man's face.

Everyone else in line instantly turns their attention to their feet, waiting for their turn to be deemed worthy of a DMA uniform. No one moves to help. No one rises up against the dozens of DMA troopers patrolling the street. These people just accept there is no other option. *They're beaten down.*

My fingers search the front of my vest before realizing Forrest took it away. I wish I could disrupt the line, throw in a smoke bomb, stop the abuse of power. Again, I find myself helplessly watching the horror unfold.

Willow joins me, drawing my attention back to the alley. Only she and Chase remain. Everyone else is below.

"We have to help them," I whisper, hoping she can hear the urgency in my voice.

"We are helping them."

"No. Now. Not later."

The announcement continues, attracting my focus onto the street.

A girl about ten years old walks away from the tent on the opposite side of the street with her father's hand gripping hers tightly. Her gaze turns toward the alley and locks on to me. She doesn't say anything or tug on her dad's hand, but simply watches as he pulls her along with him, trying to get out of the street.

"You!" A DMA trooper stops them, blocking their path.

I fear what comes next. "Willow." My hand falls on her arm. "Please. Do something."

The father resists as the trooper grabs his arm and pulls him toward the tent. The girl screams and cries as her father is ripped away from her hands. He calls out to her, reaching desperately as he is forced away. Tears roll down her cheeks.

"Run!" the father yells.

But she's frozen in place as her father is dragged away to the tent. I can't watch it anymore.

Before Willow can stop me, I pull one of the smoke bombs from her vest and slip my finger through the pin. It's enough to cause a distraction and maybe some of these people can escape. Maybe that father can flee with his daughter.

Willow grabs my wrist. "How good is your aim?"

I shrug. I've never had to find out before.

"You're rubbing off on me." Willow takes the smoke bomb from me as she releases another from her vest. "Join the others now. Don't wait. Just go."

I gulp and shake my head, but it's too late. Willow has pulled a pin and launched one toward the tent with a throw that would impress an adept Somatic.

One of the troopers turns our way, and I immediately recognize his face. Panic rises in my throat. Jimmy the Idiot—my old high school bully and nemesis—is in the DMA. Does he see me?

Willow launches another smoke bomb as I take off to the open manhole then hustle down as the bomb goes off in the street. Screams give away the chaos that surely has broken out above.

My shoes splash in the water lining the bottom of the sewage pipe.

Jimmy. Is he enhanced like Bianca? I thought he would be working in a lab. The sound of his deep voice taunting me as he used his Hematology Power on me to watch me squirm floods my mind. The intensity of the pain. The dizziness. *The deep voice… No.*

Jimmy is the Bloodhound.

Can this nightmare get any worse?

"Ugene, you okay?" Noah asks, putting a hand on my shoulder.

I lean forward, hands on my knees, sucking in breaths that taste like sewage, and shake my head.

Rosie rushes over, sloshing water around our feet, and puts her hand on my chest. "He isn't injured."

"Jimmy," I say.

"What?" Enid scrunches her face, glancing at the others.

I look up at Leo. "Jimmy Richmond. He's DMA."

Leo pales. He probably knows Jimmy almost as well as I do. "We need to move," he says.

I nod.

"What's the big deal?" Jayme asks, waving us along the sewer.

"Jimmy Richmond was a douchebag in high school," Leo explains as he shifts Bianca's arm over his shoulder and Miller does the same to support her weight. "Nothing good can come of him being DMA."

I follow the three of them, watching Bianca's boots trail along in the water behind her. "It's worse," I say. "I think he's the Bloodhound."

"Where are Willow and Chase?" Jayme asks.

"Coming," I say. "She said not to wait."

"Forgive me if I don't believe you," Jayme says, turning back to the manhole and gazing up through the opening.

Miller reaches out and grabs Jayme's arm, yanking him back and nearly dropping Bianca. "He wouldn't lie."

Jayme scowls and jerks his arm away, then glares at me. "Fine. Noah and Sho take the lead. Sho, use your Echolocation to find this exit." He pulls off his watch and hands it over. "Enid, you take rearguard with me. Everyone else in the center."

Everyone scrambles into position. I move toward the back, but Jayme shoves me forward.

"No. Middle of the pack. Now."

I do as Jayme commands.

The thunderous rumble of Power use above vibrates off the concrete walls around us. I cover my ears as we round a corner. My socks are soaked, and my feet slip in my shoes as the fabric squishes and shifts with each step. The stench of sewage seems stronger than before, and I struggle to avoid gagging on it.

A splash and crash echo from the tunnel we just vacated. Even over the sloshing of our own feet in the shallow waters, I can hear at least one other person approaching the rear of the group. *Please don't be Jimmy.*

I glance over my shoulder. Enid and Jayme are progressing slower, walking backward with their hands ready to attack. Except we can't afford hesitation. Not if Jimmy is following.

"Turnip!" the familiar voice calls from around the corner.

Jayme drops his hands and his shoulders sag. "Tulip," he says, giving the second codeword.

Enid also lets her hands fall, turning to face me. Our eyes meet and she freezes, then drops her gaze and steps around me, giving wide berth.

Chase and Willow come around the corner. Willow clutches her side, her arm slung over Chase's shoulder. They run toward us as swiftly as they can.

"Close it!" Chase commands Jayme as they pass him.

Jayme plants his feet and the walls of the tunnel start to vibrate and hum, then the intersection inches closed. I watch in awe. It's far more impressive watching the concrete grow together than the root-wood barricade had been. This opening is significantly larger.

Jayme begins to shake as all his energy channels into this impressive use of Power. Enid turns to the closing gap and attempts to help close it faster.

"Ugene, move!" Willow snaps.

Even injured, Willow doesn't mess around. She grasps my t-shirt and spins me with her free hand, forcing me onward.

Enid and Jayme rush to catch up with us, and we manage to navigate the tunnels with Sho using his Echolocation to lead the way. Rosie falls back to heal Willow's bullet wound.

The cold from the water slowly seeps into my bones the longer we walk. I shiver. Everyone does, but our focus is on escape. I clench my jaw to keep my teeth from chattering, wishing I had my jacket back from Sho.

A few times, I step back to try and talk to Enid, but she ignores me, hastening her step or falling further back each time. I do my best not to fuss over Bianca. Miller and Leo start sagging under her weight, and Noah offers to take over. I jump forward to help. Bianca's much heavier than she looks, because of her muscle mass.

Even though the tunnel was closed off, I can't shake the sensation that Jimmy is on our heels, glancing over my shoulder repeatedly.

But we are alone down here. Isolated from the world.

§

We have walked for at least a mile, allowing Sho to guide our group along.

"It's here," Sho says, pointing up at a manhole cover.

"You're sure?" Willow asks.

Sho nods, and Noah doesn't need further encouragement to start climbing. He easily hefts the cover and slides it out of the way. Chase and Sho follow, then Chase sends down the thin cable and clip. Jayme fastens it around Bianca, and Chase hoists her body up. I watch as her long black hair waves in the air. Miller starts climbing under her, keeping her steady so she doesn't hit the walls of the passage.

I climb out, followed by Jayme and Enid. Chase slides the cover back into place.

We've moved into the business section of Pax, all brick and stonework buildings with old, rusting roofs and broken solar panels. Windows of the shops are covered by posters reading *Sale!* and *Deep Discounts!*—among other things. Bodegas and second-hand clothing stores. A shoe emporium with a gigantic *Going out of business!* sign in the window. Lights are on, but only a few people walk the street. Many of them look like they could use a set of new clothes from the second-hand store. They all avoid our group, casting wayward glances when they think we won't notice.

At the end of the road, a DMA shuttle waits idly beside an empty canvas DMA tent. I hesitate, then step back. Everyone else follows Willow onward. Do they not see the shuttle or the tent?

"That's our ride," Jayme says, nudging me forward. "Get a move on, Ugene."

Right. Our ride. Willow said we would be in a DMA shuttle before we started this mission.

Willow speaks briefly to the driver, who wears a DMA uniform, and the shuttle door opens. Chase guides everyone inside and helps hoist Bianca up into the back. Willow climbs in and checks on Bianca.

I reach for the rail to pull myself up and in, and the air suddenly thins. The shuttle and the street under my feet tilt to the left. I stumble, catching my balance on the edge of the shuttle. My body feels heavy.

Too heavy to move on my own. I try to call Chase for help, but all I can do is gulp for air. These sensations are all too familiar.

A deep male voice raises from up the street, but I can't focus immediately on it. "Leave him and you can go."

Chase grabs my shirt and yanks me into the shuttle. I catch a glimpse of the figure down the road. My vision narrows on his arrogant smile and swaggering attitude.

Jimmy found us.

"A few more seconds of this and his brain is toast," Jimmy says, stepping toward the shuttle with slow, cocky strides. "We only need the body."

"Go," Noah says to Chase.

"Noah," I gasp, but I'm not sure if anyone heard me.

"You can't expect to enter battle without some casualties," Noah says, then spins around and rushes at Jimmy, barreling into him. They tumble to the ground. Noah lands on top. He wraps his hands around Jimmy's neck and squeezes. As the doors slam shut, the connection between me and Jimmy is lost. I gasp for air, rub my throat. The engine of the shuttle hums with life and the shuttle bursts up the road as my vision rights itself.

Clawing my way toward the doors, I plead for them to stop, but they either don't hear me or don't want to. I pull myself up on the door, peering through the darkened window at the diminishing forms, watching in disgust.

Jimmy destroys Noah in one of the most horrific displays of Power I've ever witnessed.

Blood streams out of Noah's pores, forming a swirling red cloud as Noah screams. The muscular Somatic body withers. Silence follows as we round the corner and they both disappear from view.

Gasping for air once more, horrified, I scramble backward as far from the door as I can manage, pressing my back to the wall behind the pilot's cab.

Jimmy has become what I always believed him to be.

A monster.

27

OCCASIONALLY, SNIFFLES RISE FROM IN THE GROUP. Otherwise, silence settles over the group as we ride away from danger, with the exception of the hum of the shuttle's engine. I can't blame the tears. Jimmy may not have a hold of me anymore, but I still find it hard to breathe. Everything has shattered.

How can the Directorate allow this sort of thing to happen? They are supposed to protect the people, the city. Their sole job is to fight for our survival.

But this isn't survival. Willow was right. This is war.

How can things be so blissfully wonderful on one side of the city and so horribly wrong on the other? How can the DMA justify tearing a father away from his child or shooting a young man in the street?

Why do these people allow it to continue?

As we ride toward the edge of the city, I stare out the darkened window. On the horizon, Paragon Tower twists into the sky, shrouded in clouds. Once a thing of beauty, majesty, and promise, the building now represents as a perverse symbol of everything that has gone wrong.

My thoughts begin to tire me. When was the last time I slept? I lean my head against the unforgiving metal wall of the shuttle and close my eyes.

"Word just came in," the pilot says from the front cab, jarring me back awake. "Exits are closed."

"Take us to the safehouse on Portland," Willow says.

The hum of the engine and sway of the cab lull me to sleep.

Soon, I dream of parents being torn away from children. Innocents getting shot in the street. The DMA bombing the Shield, killing everyone within. Jimmy bloodletting those I care about while I'm helpless to stop him. And Noah, blaming me and asking me why I allowed any of this to happen.

The shuttle stops and the engine cuts out. I rub my eyes. Several of the others are already gone from the cab. Enid hops out as I sit up straighter. I call to her and get no response. Just a tension in her back as she disappears around the corner of the shuttle. She either doesn't hear me or she's ignoring me.

Chase slides Bianca out and throws her over his shoulder like a sack of flour.

I follow right behind. Once out of the vehicle, it takes a moment to get my bearings. We're in a closed house garage. The others have already ventured inside the house. I scramble to follow Chase through the dingy kitchen and up the stairs to the second floor as he drops her down on the bed. A puff of dust flies up and I wave my hand to get it away from my face.

"Secure her," Willow says from over my shoulder.

Chase pulls out a braided nylon rope from a wooden chest in the corner, then binds Bianca's wrists together and tethers her to the bedposts. It won't hold her if she wants to break free.

"Wait, let me talk to her," I say.

"We have more important things to deal with right now," Willow says. "And you reek. There's a supply closet at the end of the hall. Get fresh clothes and a shower."

Can I trust these people to care for her? Willow didn't even want to bring Bianca along. I open my mouth to disagree—getting information from Bianca is the whole reason they agreed to bring her along—but my stench wafts in. It's a horrid mingling of body odor and sewage, which convinces me Willow may have a point.

Before leaving, I glance back as Chase begins a similar wrap around Bianca's legs and ankles. They brought her along, knowing it could bring the DMA right to us. I'm just thankful for that much.

I venture to the closet at the end of the hall, rummaging through the shelves of supplies. So many interesting items line the shelf in a surprisingly organized fashion. Some are innocent enough. Towels, clothes, a defibrillator and emergency medical kit. Other items are more aggressive. Smoke bombs. Guns. Knives. I fish out a set of clean jeans and a t-shirt in my size, then grab a towel.

Just how safe are we in this safehouse?

28

BIANCA'S ALIVE. AS I SHOWER, THE REALITY OF THOSE two words sinks in. The sense of joy I expected doesn't settle over me. No fluttering stomach or racing excitement. No tingles of heat. Instead, my relief mingles with a sudden coldness and a massive knot growing in the pit of my stomach, tightness in my chest, and an overall sense of a weight pressing down on me.

She's alive. That's a good thing…right?

I press my forehead against the shower wall and warm water rolls down my back. When I close my eyes, all I can see is Bianca's dead body on the ground as the ceiling falls around her. Something doesn't add up. How did Paragon rescue her from the collapse when I couldn't? She was in my arms, and I couldn't make it out with her. They were nowhere in sight. How could they have retrieved her after I left the building? There's just no way.

But she's alive.

I turn the shower off, wiping the water from my face before drying off. The only way to solve this is to talk to her.

The smell of food drifts up the stairs, and my stomach moans. Before I talk to Bianca, I need to eat.

I don't even make it to the stairs when I'm distracted by sobbing coming from one of the open bedroom doors. I stop at the doorway.

Bri sits on the edge of the bed with her face buried in her hands. Enid sits with her, offering hugs and backrubs.

Only one reason I can think of for this grief comes to mind. *Noah.* Bri has been attached to his side since we arrived at The Shield.

Now he's gone. Guilt wrenches at my gut and I blink back my own tears.

For a moment, I can't move from the doorway. Does she hate me or blame me for Noah's death? *I do.*

Enid notices me but doesn't wipe the tears in her own eyes as she rubs Bri's back. It's the first time she has looked at me since the alley when Bianca reappeared.

I want to go into the room, sit with them, try to help Bri, but the guilt presses down on my body. Noah's death is my fault, as is her grief. Nothing I say or do can change what's happened. I hang my head, stuff my hands into my pockets, and manage to shuffle my feet along the hallway and down the stairs.

Leo, Rosie, Lily, and Sho sit in all four chairs around the small table in the kitchen, poking at the food on their plates. My jacket hangs over the back of Sho's chair, and I quickly retrieve it and slip it on. Mac and cheese isn't much of a meal, but I grab a plate, then I lean against the counter near the living room doorway.

The living room houses several occupants. Willow, Chase, the shuttle pilot, and three others, only one of which I recognize. *Harvey.* These must be the operatives Willow wanted to meet with before.

"I've never seen so much DMA enforcement out at once," Harvey says, his deep voice carrying easily to me in the kitchen. "Seaduss isn't wasting time."

Willow nods. Her back is to me and she leans over the coffee table, but I can't see what they are looking at. My view is obstructed by the sofa and bodies.

"How many do each of you think you can gather?" Willow asks. "We have to get as many people out of the city as we can before the DMA forces them into service. Lord only knows what happens to these people once the Directorate and Paragon get their hands on them. I think it's highly likely that whatever they are injecting in these people turns them into mindless drones."

Another man shakes his head, staring at whatever is on the coffee table. "I think this plan is too risky. Besides, even if we get some people out, we can't help them all."

"He's right," Harvey says. "That many people will be impossible to transport without more DMA shuttles."

So, their plan is to try and shuttle DMA targets out of the city to The Shield before they are forced into service. It seems reasonable, but Harvey has a point. There are so many.

"Do you have a better idea?" Willow asks, gazing at each of them for answers.

"Each shuttle fits what, fifteen DMA troops?" the third man says. "We can probably double it if we really pack people in, but even if we steal more shuttles—which is unlikely now—we don't have enough people to pilot them."

"We take what we can," Willow says, "families first, and able fighters."

"And the rest?" Harvey asks.

Willow crosses her arms, her back stiffening. "We pray."

Silence falls in the living room as the weight of her implication settles on the gathering. I look at my friends for advice, but they are in the middle of a conversation about Noah. A small memorial of their own. Miller just pokes at his food, eyes glazed over.

I step into the living room. "It's too late to evacuate."

Everyone spins to face me. Harvey's face breaks into a grin. Chase hovers over Willow from behind like a protective shroud.

"We have no choice," Willow says.

Doc's message to me just before we left for Pax rings in my head. *I would like to see as many people survive this as possible.*

"We always have a choice." I take another bold step toward them. "I'm guessing you have what, maybe four shuttles? Five at most. Even if you can cram thirty people in each *and* manage to make a second trip, it doesn't put a dent in the number of people who need evacuation."

"This isn't your concern, Ugene." Willow's expression hardens. "You've done enough."

Harvey steps forward. "Wait. I want to hear what he has to say."

Think big. I cast a grateful glance his way. "The Directorate is causing division because they know if we rally together, they won't stand a chance. It's the same fault we exposed when we escaped Paragon. What you need to do is get everyone to unify at once to fight back."

"That sort of planning takes time and quite a bit of coordination," one of the operatives says.

"No, it doesn't. It just needs a spark to light the fire."

"And what would that spark be?" another operative asks, bushy brows narrowing into one thick line.

"Information."

He barks out a laugh. Willow just shakes her head. "If we had what we needed, don't you think we would have done this already?"

"Hear me out. Half this city turns a blind eye to what's happening in Pax. The other half is completely clueless. We just have to convince them—"

"With what? The drive you won't give us?"

"I will."

Willow shakes her head. "I'm done playing your games, Ugene." She leans over the coffee table and touches something, then picks up a tablet and hands it to Chase. "You've done more damage to our cause in a single night than you can possibly imagine. We do things the way we do for a reason. It protects everyone. Your impulsive schemes end in disaster."

"I'm telling you; this will work—"

"I want him and his friends sent back to The Shield tonight," Willow says.

No! Going back to The Shield is a step backward. If the Protectorate wants to win this war, they need to stay on the front lines and stop falling back into hiding. *I* need to stay in Elpis.

Doc asked me what I would do if the Protectorate failed and the Directorate carried out their plan and I had nothing to offer society. *If you can inspire such dedication from your friends, imagine what you could do for Elpis. Think big.*

I need to stay here. It's what Doc would want me to do. It's what Celeste would want me to do. Arguing with Willow further will probably end with me bound beside Bianca, so I clench my jaw shut and storm out of the room and up the stairs. *Let her think she's won.*

29

THE THIRD BEDROOM IS SMALL, WITH ROOM FOR little more than a bunk bed. I drop down on the lower bunk and unzip the lining of the jacket, pulling out the bundle. Information is power, but just what did Dad leave behind?

The twine wrapped around the fabric is knotted tight. I struggle with it, unable to get the knots free. Dad's Somatic strength bound it too securely together. I pull a switchblade I stole from the supply closet and start sawing at the twine. It snaps. I carefully unfold the red fabric on the bed beside me and inspect the contents. The cloth holding it all together is my old Memorial High T-shirt.

On top of the shirt, folders stuffed with pages of research notes, papers, and correspondence between Dr. Cass and Directorate Chief Seaduss. I thumb through the pages, but everything is out of order. Pages of reports date back more than six years about the radioactivity levels both in and outside of Elpis. Some of the data is redacted with handwritten numbers corresponding to each blacked-out line. Dad spent years gathering this information, stealing or memorizing the numbers to make note of later.

The first report dates back just over seven years ago. The radioactive levels are unlivable but not as high as the Directorate led us to believe. Even more shocking is the most recent report, dated a few months ago, right before Proposition 8.5 passed. The numbers are almost livable. At this rate, the world around Elpis should be survivable in just a few years. Which makes the Directorate's argument that regression will end life as we know it a lie. But why bother lying about it? What does the Directorate have to gain by fostering this fear of regression? It will end life as we know it, but it won't be the end of life.

Among the papers, a report addressed to Directorate Chief Seaduss from Dr. Cass catches my attention. A formula with a quick note at the bottom: *Power-removing serum success and weaponized, as requested.* The date on the report is during my stay at Paragon.

My stomach churns, but not just because Paragon created this weapon for the Directorate. I unzip my pocket and pull out the formula Leo gave me, spreading it out beside Paragon's.

They're identical.

Willow is reproducing Power-removing bullets.

After seeing how losing his Power effected Miller, the use of Power-removing bullets in all-out warfare would be catastrophic. If I don't stop this war, the fight will get out of control very quickly, and anyone who survives the bullet will seek death anyway.

Hundreds—maybe thousands—will die no matter who wins.

One report remains bound together. A big red stamp covers the title page: *Macrophage Stimulation Study.*

REJECTED.

Beneath the stamp is a handwritten note in sloppy writing. It takes a moment to decipher.

This report creates a problem with the Purification Project. We cannot allow this to get out. Bury it and delete the records.

I run my fingers over the red PD logo at the top of the paper. Paragon wrote this and gave it to Directorate Chief Seaduss before printing. Remembering the note that accompanied the drive Dad left for me, my curiosity is piqued. What is the Purification Project and what does this research have to do with it?

I flip to the first page and skim. A lot of the language is technical jargon, but I've spent the last few years reading so many of these papers that understanding is second nature.

From what I gather, Paragon discovered that macrophages—cells that help fight infections—can either excite or cause harm to the ability to heal wounds, raise or lower the immune system, or trigger a reaction in the cell that makes Powers overreact.

And, most importantly, the macrophages will work to heal the "wound" of weak or lost Powers.

Miller! I suck in a breath and flip to the conclusion. The answer makes me jump up and rummage through my pockets for the diagrams of the DNA structure I suspect belongs to Miller. I spread the diagram out beside the research paper. After tracing multiple paths across the paper, a thought rises.

Excitement pumps through my veins.

I could do it…with the right tools and calculations, I could jumpstart his Powers.

Dad spent years gathering buried research from Paragon, but he never understood all the technical jargon. He didn't realize how all the pieces connected. He just knew something was not right and gathered it up for me—his scientific-minded, puzzle-loving son—to figure out later.

God, I love you, Dad.

Everyone is downstairs, and I sneak to the supply closet, rummaging through the contents. I saw something in here that will prove useful. Pushing aside a stack of towels, I uncover it.

The defibrillator.

With the handheld machine, I rush back to the room and close the door. When Leo first gave me that diagram of Miller's DNA back at The Shield, I could tell his Power was disconnected sort of like a device that's been unplugged. Miller's very genetic structure acts like the magnets and copper wire used to generate electricity. They only need a jumpstart to get the power flowing again. With the numbers Paragon supplied in that report. Still…the amount of energy needed for that jumpstart would be dangerous, even if he still had his Powers. One wrong calculation in the joules and timing and Miller could die.

I pull a pen from the pocket of my jacket and start calculating the necessary length of time the connection needs to continue based on the maximum joules permissible in the device. Once I have the number, I use the switchblade to pry the device open and try to switch the relay over to continuous. Just giving a jolt won't be enough. The energy needs to be constant. I make notes on the drawing of Miller's DNA structure based on the information in the research document and my calculations. Slowly, I gather the pieces of the puzzle and begin finding their place.

I jump to my feet, stuffing Miller's DNA structure into my pocket and scooping up the rest of the papers as the door opens and Lily enters with Sho.

"Sorry," Sho says, backing away from the door.

I hold up a hand. "Wait."

They pause, giving me a quizzical look.

"Lily, you can read stuff, right? Like, the history of something?"

She cocks her head, clinging to Sho's arm. "The history of it, yeah."

"What about people?"

They both frown.

I move closer and lower my voice in case someone else is within earshot. "Could you read Bianca?"

"Why can't you just ask her what you want to know?" Sho asks.

I peek out into the hallway and glance both ways. "Because I don't think she will remember much, and I need to know what happened to her."

Lily takes a step back. "I won't touch her."

"Why?"

"Because..." She glances at Sho as if seeking help, then slumps. "Because she scares me, okay?"

I grin. "She scares me, too. But we need to know. *I* need to know."

"Know what?" Enid asks, joining us from the stairwell.

"What happened to Bianca," Sho says.

Enid scowls and crosses her arms. "She's a puppet, that's what."

"Bianca may hold the key to everything," I say, reaching for Enid.

She steps back. She's probably going to hate me for this. "You said we finish this together or not at all. No matter what."

Anger flashes in her eyes.

"It's important, Enid," I say. "To everyone… I need your help. Please."

Lily shifts uncomfortably, glancing from Enid to me and back again.

Enid sighs. "If I know you, you'll do whatever you want no matter what I say or do. Let's get it over with." Enid turns on her heel and heads toward Bianca's room.

And she's right. I would. Because it needs to be done.

30

BIANCA SLEEPS ON THE BED, A PEACEFUL LOOK ON her face. The bindings around her legs and arms won't stop her if Bianca somehow breaks through Willow's power and decides she wants to escape.

Lily and Sho both linger by the door, ready to run. Enid steps in with me.

"Can I help you?" Jayme asks, resting all four legs of his chair on the floor again.

Miller lays on the floor by the chair, snoozing.

Willow probably assigned Jayme to keep watch over Bianca. I should have expected this.

"I just want to talk to her, see what we can learn," I say. "And hopefully find out if the girl we knew is still in there."

Jayme places himself between Bianca and me, crossing his arms. Again, he towers over me. "Did you get permission from Willow?"

"Did she tell you I would need it or just ask you to keep an eye on her?" Jayme doesn't answer, so I press on, "If it were Miller in her place, you would do anything to help."

Jayme considers this, staring at Miller on the floor, then nods and steps aside. "Just don't untie her."

I hold in a laugh. Those ties are pointless.

When I move toward the bed, Enid grabs my arm and pulls me back.

"I don't trust her, Ugene. What if she hurts you?"

"She won't." I sound more confident than I feel. "Paragon wants me alive, and if Bianca is conditioned to follow their orders, she won't do anything. She could hurt me, but Rosie is here if something really bad happens."

Enid scowls. "At least let me put a protective barrier around her."

It seems unnecessary, but I nod. Enid raises her hands and her focus turns completely to Bianca. Once Enid is done, I edge toward the bed.

"Don't let anyone else interrupt," I say.

"I'm not leaving," Enid says.

"I know."

Sho takes up position in the doorway, using his Echolocation to warn us if anyone approaches.

"How do I wake her from whatever Willow did?" I ask Jayme.

He pulls a packet from his vest and offers it to me. I take it. *Smelling salts.*

I break the pack and hold it under Bianca's nose. It takes a minute to work. Her eyelids snap open, and the instant she sees me she lunges toward me but the bindings on her hands and ankles hold…for now. The bed creaks and cracks.

"Relax, Bianca." I keep my voice calm and even. "It's okay. I won't hurt you."

Bianca's gaze darts around me at the others. Her muscles tense. One good tug and she's free.

"They won't hurt you either," I say, hoping it offers some reassurance. "Bianca. Look at me, not them."

Her gaze flicks up to me. The tension in her muscles remains, but she nods in understanding.

I reach for the bindings at her wrists as a show of faith, though part of me is terrified she will lash out the moment her hands are free.

"Ugene…don't!" Enid says.

"It's okay, right?" I smile sincerely at Bianca.

Bianca stares at me with a completely indecipherable look as I untie her wrists. The moment her hands are free, Bianca reaches out for my arm, but a barrier pulses with a hum against her hand.

"I told you," Enid mumbles.

I ignore her, keeping Bianca's eyes locked on me. I used to get lost in those copper eyes. Now, they shine hard and cold. She rubs at her wrists, an indication that she does feel some of what happens to her.

That's promising.

For more than a week I asked myself what I would say if I had a chance to talk to her again. I ran through the scenario a million times. Now that she's actually here, none of it comes to me. Her death feels like forever ago, and also like yesterday.

"I can't untie your legs," I say, moving to give her a little more slack to at least sit up. "I hope you understand."

Bianca sits up, pressing her back into the wall. Nothing about the way she stares at me indicates that she has any idea who I am. It makes my heart clench. Her sharp copper eyes take me in like she's studying how to take me down.

"Do you know me?" I ask, hoping to coax some sort of response out of her.

Bianca's eyes narrow. "I do."

"I mean, do you know me as anything more than the person you're seeking to capture?" Slowly, I reach for her hand. "Do you remember…us?"

Bianca pulls away. "Don't touch me."

"Sorry." I ease my hand back, deflating. "I just…I need to know how badly they've hurt you."

"Ugene Powers," she says, wrapping her arms around her knees, drawing them to her chest. The way she says my name sounds foreign like she's stating memorized facts.

"No, to you I've always been just Ugene."

Her brows are knitted together and her head cocks to the side.

Please remember me.

Bianca pulls in her bottom lip and chews on it like she used to do when she was trying really hard to remember something. "I died. That's what you said back in that building. That at Paragon, I helped you escape, and they shot me. But you tried to carry me out of the building."

Again, a ray of hope peeks through. "Yes." I shift, pulling my knee up over the bed and turning more directly to face her. "Do you remember any of it?"

"Why would I kiss you?"

My cheeks burn. "I...well...what?"

"You also said I kissed you. Why would I do that?"

She doesn't remember it. I try to find an explanation that she might comprehend. *Because you cared about me. Because I care about you.* Nothing seems like the right answer.

I feel Enid's glare boring through me and into Bianca.

Bianca grimaces and presses her back against the wall again. She has accepted that I either don't know or maybe she thinks I made it up. I didn't. "Why would I help you?" she asks.

"We were friends before all of this."

Bianca stares blankly.

"I realize that it's hard to believe," I say, doing my best not to push too hard. "But, just for a moment, would you at least be willing to consider there is more to us than what the Directorate has told you?"

"Like what?"

"Well, like we actually grew up in the same neighborhood, across the street in Salas, on Cante Road. We rode the tram to school every day, and more often than not I was late, and you had to pull me onboard. Your parents—Nick and Gloria Pond—favored your brother and it drove you mad. And they used to have game nights with my parents until Forrest broke your arm and blamed it on me and they forbid you to be friends with me."

Bianca pulls in her bottom lip and chews on it again. Subconsciously, she cradles the arm Forrest broke. *It's working. I'm getting through to her.*

"I can go on and on, Bianca. About your childhood. Your likes and dislikes. Our...our kiss." I don't have to look behind me to know Enid's face burns red hot.

Bianca shakes her head, though not very hard.

"Think about it, Bianca. How is it possible I would know

everything about you if we didn't know one another?"

"You…probably have telepathy or something." But Bianca stumbles over her words.

I chuckled, softly. "We both know that I have no Powers, even if you don't remember our childhood." Paragon would have shared everything about me—minus our history.

"Fine. Then someone in your crew can read minds." She glares around, confident in her new line of logic. "You stole my memories."

"The memories I have of us were not stolen." I lean forward. "The memories I have were a gift, one that you gave to me over the years we spent together."

She glowers, unblinking. After a moment, she huffs out and says, "All right, then. We knew one another. So what? Doesn't change the fact that you're a wanted criminal conspiring with wanted criminals."

"The only crime we have committed is saving people from the Directorate killing them," I say. "Do you know what they have done to people with weaker Powers? Bianca, they send them into the Deadlands to die."

The robotic determination to carry out her orders has dissolved, replaced by uncertainty as Bianca takes in each of my friends. While she still doesn't resemble the girl I remember, I can see a piece of Bianca returning. Memories can be taken away, but the heart remains. Bianca always had a big heart for others.

"But people with regressing Powers are threatening the balance we need," Bianca says, glancing at each of us indecisively. "And you are leading the way. If we don't restore balance, regression will destroy us."

Hearing the words come from her mouth breaks my heart. They have pumped their lies into her, somehow convincing her they are the truth.

"The people I'm with here are regressing, yes," I continue, seeing that crack of hope breaking through, "but they also save lives. They want equality for everyone, fairness. Is that really such a bad thing?" I shift closer, wanting desperately for her to agree with me—needing her to agree. "I want to help you, Bianca. More than anything. But these people want answers that I can't give them. Please." I dare to look up, meeting her calculating stare. "What *do* you remember?"

Bianca's lips part and she breathes out in a measured breath. "My mission."

"And what's that?"

Bianca hesitates, and for a moment I'm afraid she won't tell me anything.

"To enforce Proposition 9, secure the city, find the dissenters, and bring you in to the DMA for questioning in connection with a bombing at Paragon."

"Bombing?" Enid says. I share her confusion.

Bianca begins reciting her orders, "Ugene Powers: DMA Primary Target Number One. Paragon Diagnostics property. Detain but do not kill."

Property? The word makes me flinch. My heart hammers against my ribs.

"Do you still feel that's necessary?" I ask, then hold my breath waiting for her answer.

Bianca pulls her hair over her shoulder, biting her bottom lip. "I'm not sure of anything."

Not the answer I was hoping for, but better than a yes. "Do you remember dying?"

"No. But there are gaps in my memory."

I motion Lily forward. Bianca tenses as Lily inches closer. "This is my friend, Lily. She won't hurt you. I promise. She can help fill in those gaps in your memory, but she needs to touch you to do it."

Bianca looks Lily up and down, then gives a tight nod.

I move out of the way as Lily sits beside Bianca. It's clear she would rather be anywhere else. Lily's hand trembles as she reaches for Bianca.

Bianca swats Lily away and stabs a finger in her direction in warning. "Stay away from my head. You guys used that against me already. I won't fall for it again."

"This isn't the same thing," I say. "She just wants to use her

Psychometry to read your history, if she can. No one here will knock you out again."

Bianca doesn't believe me, but clearly, she knows that she's in no position to argue. After another huff, she thrusts a hand toward Lily.

Lily swallows hard and edges closer, gingerly accepting Bianca's hand, then Lily sinks into a trance-like state. Several long moments pass. I pace the floor. Lily pales the longer she holds the connection, and tears roll down her cheeks as her face scrunches in twisted agony.

"That's enough," Sho says from the doorway. "Stop her now."

But I hesitate a moment longer to buy more time. We need all the information Lily can read from Bianca.

"Ugene, enough." Sho stomps toward us.

I place a hand on Lily's shoulder, breaking her trance.

Lily drops Bianca's hand, sucking in deep breaths as she tumbles back into my arms. Jayme rushes in to help and we ease Lily down in his chair near the door. Miller wakes and sits upright against the wall, watching with a muted interest.

Sho drops to a knee beside Lily. "Are you okay?"

"What did you read?" I ask.

Sho shoots me a filthy glare.

Lily's gaze locks on Bianca, eyes wide open in fear.

"Lily!" I snap my fingers in front of her. It seems to work. She turns her terrified gaze to me. "What did you read?"

Bianca waits on the bed, gripping the mattress so tightly that the mattress crunches in her fists.

"We have to...they have to..." Lily struggles to form complete sentences, and my typical patience dissolves with each stumbled word.

"What is it?" I press.

"Calm down," Sho warns me.

"Paragon," Lily says. "They experimented on her. They pumped her with epinephrine over and over after healing her wounds. There were so many different injections I couldn't distinguish what they all did. And..." Lily buries her face in her hands.

Sho rubs her back, whispering reassurances, but we need answers.

"And what, Lily?" I ask.

"They killed her," Lily says through her hands.

I shake my head. "What do you mean?"

Lily sucks in a shuddering breath and her reddened eyes meet my insistent gaze. "She came back fighting the first time, so they killed her again. Then they used someone with Telepathic Powers to infiltrate her mind and selectively wipe her memories and insert new ones."

A Psionic did this to her? How is that even possible?

"When she came back again," Lily continues, "they injected something in her. IVD Veritax."

My blood runs cold. The memory of the information I read on Forrest's tablet surges back. The ad, with its bold red letters. *IVD Veritax: Why be ordinary, when you can be extraordinary?*

I glance over at Bianca, my heart sinking. This isn't the same girl I knew. This is someone else. The Bianca I knew would be up and ready to help us. She would have already told us everything she knew, everything she remembered, and given us as much of an inside track on this whole catastrophe as she could. She would have taken my hand and offered reassurances.

This girl did none of that. And I can't help but wonder if she ever would be that way again. I don't want a Bianca who doesn't know me. I don't want to rebuild a lifetime of memories.

I sink down on the edge of the bed with Bianca. "Do you remember your family, Bianca?"

"Forrest is the Paragon liaison in the DMA," she says.

That's good to know. "And your parents?"

"The radicals killed my parents, so I joined the DMA to help them fight back."

I scrub my hands over my face to avoid showing my disbelieving amusement. They've completely brainwashed her. No one here attacked her family, and Forrest wouldn't allow anything to happen to his parents...would he? And just what did Forrest tell them about what happened to Bianca? Mom mentioned that they haven't been the same since her death.

Her parents! Bianca's dad runs the news network. If I can get her to him, prove to her they are alive, reunite the family, maybe he will help broadcast the information. Ignite the spark.

It's not much of a plan, but it's a start. "Your parents are alive."

I reach toward her but give her the option to reach back and take my hand.

Bianca hesitates, staring at my hand. "I've been to their house on Dysart Lane. A different family lives there now."

Maybe I'm wrong. Could they really be dead? Did the Directorate kill them to cover their tracks? "Did you say Dysart Lane?"

Bianca nods.

I almost laugh. *Paragon changed her parent's address in her memories to protect their lie!* "No. They have always lived on Cante Road, right across from my parents. I can prove it if you let me."

Bianca chews her lip again, then her hand shifts, inching closer.

Her fingers wrap around mine. It doesn't send sparks through me like it used to, as Enid does. Again, I wonder what we are to each other, what we ever were. I loved Bianca, and for years I crushed hard on her. But now, as I hold her hand, I realize that maybe I felt that way because she was my friend.

Bianca's grip tightens on my hand. "I want to see them."

"We will," I say ignoring Enid's radiating anger. Now isn't the time. "Soon. Tonight. But first I need to tie you back up, or Willow will be suspicious." I glance over my shoulder, shooting a warning look at Jayme.

He's too stunned by everything he's learned to respond. *Please don't say anything.*

"I also need you to promise me you won't leave this room or start a fight with anyone," I tell Bianca. "I'll come for you."

Bianca nods.

Enid makes a noise of disgust and I can hear her steps recede down the hallway. I want to follow, but at the moment there's something else I need to attend to before it's too late.

I turn to face Miller. "We need to talk."

31

TIME IS RUNNING OUT. WHILE I DON'T KNOW EXACTLY what the Purification Project is, I do know that the Directorate is about to set the wheels in motion—if they haven't already. After my outburst in the living room, Willow will send my friends and me back to The Shield as soon as she can. Before that happens, I need to slip away from her—or convince the others not to follow Willow's orders. We outnumber her. Sho and Lily are the only two I'm uncertain of. Miller will follow me if I can really fix him, and Jayme will follow Miller, hating me all the way. There's a good chance Jayme will rat me out, but I need their help getting that information to Mr. Pond, to make sure that the people realize the danger they are truly in.

I shift my feet, uncertain how to broach the subject of potentially giving Miller his Power back. *I hope he doesn't hate me for this.*

Sho escorts Lily out of the bedroom, leaving me alone with Miller, Jayme, and Bianca.

"I read some of the stuff my dad left in that bundle," I say.

Jayme and Miller stare at me expectantly.

"I…have a theory."

"On what?" Miller asks, his brows drawn together.

Jayme is tense. I'm quite certain he will tell me to jump off a building when I explain.

"A way we could get your Powers back," I say, fumbling the sheet of paper out of my pocket.

Miller appears skeptical as I unfold the paper and show it to him.

"Your ability was directly linked to electricity, so that makes this sort of unique to your situation."

Miller takes the paper, and Jayme looks over his arm at it. Neither gives any indication they recognize what it means.

"When the Protectorate took us in, they took samples from all of us. I managed to get a hold of yours and analyze it. Your Powers are still there. It's sort of like…like the connection was just unplugged." Miller appears both intrigued and uncertain. No. Untrusting. *Just say it.* "All it needs is a jumpstart. Like a battery. But first, we need the drive so we don't risk damaging the data."

Jayme frowns. "What do you mean by jumpstart?"

"Finally," Miller says. "I was thinking you would never ask. Do you have a knife?"

"Did you just ask for a knife?" Jayme tosses up both hands.

Giving a suicidal Miller a knife of any kind is not the best plan, but I need that drive out of his arm. I pull out the switchblade I found in the supply closet earlier and hold it out in my palm.

Miller snatches it, and as he flips it open, Jayme's eyes widen. "What are you doing?"

Rosie's healing made the mark from his original incision nearly unnoticeable. Miller doesn't hesitate to slice into it—or maybe he doesn't care about cutting himself open. He barely even flinches as he carves deep into his arm, wincing only a little and using the point of the blade to carefully dig out the drive. Perhaps losing his Power has dulled his senses somehow so he can't fully feel what must be excruciating pain.

Jayme fumbles over his words. He reaches out for the blade but hesitates. Stopping Miller at this point would probably do more harm than good and Jayme is smart enough to know it. Bianca shifts on the bed, craning her neck to see what Miller is doing.

The whole thing is incredibly gross, and I wish I could look at anything else, but my eyes are glued. I can't lose that drive.

Jayme finally grabs Miller's wrist and pulls it away carefully. "Stop. What are you doing?"

"Getting this." Miller holds the blood-covered drive between his fingers.

"How long has that been there?" Jayme asks, dumbfounded.

"Since we left Paragon," Miller says.

I reach for the pillow, which Bianca hands to me, and pull the pillowcase off, tearing off a strip of cloth to wipe the drive clean, careful not to damage it. "Thanks."

"And you never told me." Jayme takes the pillowcase and tears off a couple more strips of cloth, thrusting the bloody knife at me. "Why?"

"It wasn't mine."

Jayme shoots me a dirty look. I do my best to ignore him as I clean off the switchblade. He doesn't hate me nearly as much as he soon will. As the two argue, I slip out of the room to grab the defibrillator. By the time I return, Jayme is wrapping the wound, jaw clenched in frustration, muttering that they will have Rosie heal it soon. Bianca sits with her back against the wall, watching with intense curiosity.

"Are you ready to jumpstart your Power?" I ask, biting my lip and avoiding Jayme's deadly glare.

"Yes." Miller takes in the device in my hands and comprehension clicks in his widening eyes. "What is that for?"

"I've reviewed the research from Paragon, and I've looked at your DNA extensively. I've done all the calculations several times to make sure I got it right. This will work." Or *should* work but telling Miller that will ensure he doesn't agree.

"Go to hell, Ugene!" Jayme snaps.

I ignore him.

"Miller, I'm talking about getting your Power back." I'm not sure he can handle the coming fight against the Directorate without his Power. I'm not sure *we* can. Miller's ability to manipulate electronics and wield lightning is a needed skill going forward. "If you want your Powers back, this is the only way."

Miller holds the strip of cloth against his bleeding arm, gaping at the defibrillator. "There has to be another way. Those things are meant to jumpstart hearts, not Powers."

"You told me you were broken. I'm telling you that you're right, but this can fix it. The defibrillator's electric current will give your Power the surge it needs to restart. You can't really expect to fight the Directorate in your condition. You need to be ready."

"Ready for what?" Jayme asks, arms crossed. He takes a step between Miller and me.

I glance at him. "The Directorate is ready to launch its Purification Project. If we don't want to stand by while the Directorate forces thousands into the DMA's arms—and potentially to their deaths—we have to stop them now. The time for falling back to regroup has passed. We need to act."

Miller begins pacing the floor.

"Miller, we need you at full strength." I don't flinch when he glares at me. While he's bigger and probably stronger, Bianca taught me a thing or two about fighting back at Paragon. Besides, I can't back down now.

Bianca continues watching the exchange with growing interest, silent in her observations.

"Do you have any idea how much it hurt losing my Powers?" Miller hisses. It's the sincerest reaction I've heard from him since he lost his Powers. "What do you think it'll be like having them jumpstarted like this? No." He shakes his head adamantly.

I swallow thickly.

Jayme shifts feet, regarding me for a moment, then steps in front of Miller, putting a hand on Miller's chest. "Stop. I can't handle the pacing."

"I can't help it. There must be another way."

Jayme flicks his gaze to me momentarily. "Look, I have no love for this guy, but you are the one who called him brilliant. You convinced me that he could fix things if he had the right information. You said if anyone could figure out what to do to stop the Directorate, it's him. Are you now saying none of that is true?"

Miller opens his mouth, then snaps it shut and pulls his good hand through his blond hair. Blood seeps through the pillowcase bandage.

"No. But this…" He waves at the defibrillator in my hands.

"I have your back, no matter what." Jayme takes Miller's hand, and their eyes meet. Miller's expression breaks from anger to fear. "You told me to trust him," Jayme says. "Do *you* trust him?"

Miller's shoulders slump. "Yes."

"And anyway," Jayme says with a smile, "if he kills you, there'll be nothing stopping me from ripping him apart, limb by limb."

The comment, while seemingly made in jest, is a clear warning shot across my bow.

Miller's body shakes, and he swallows hard before stepping away from Jayme, staring at me as he sets his jaw and presses one hand over the cloth on the other arm. His free hand tightens into a fist.

"It'll be easier for you if you lie on the floor," I say softly, pointing at the worn-out rug.

Miller lowers himself down until he lays flat. I kneel beside him and power up the defibrillator, then pull up his shirt to attach the power strips to his chest. Miller's muscles are tense and twitching as I prepare him. The machine beeps a warning that Miller's heart rhythm is slightly elevated but not in need of assistance. I ignore the warning. It isn't his heart we are worried about—though I should be. Hitting him with this many joules when his heart works fine is seriously dangerous. If his Power doesn't jumpstart, his heart could kill him.

"On one." I hold my finger over the button to activate the device. To keep it running through the bypass I connected earlier, I have to hold down the button. "Three…two…one."

Miller tenses every muscle in his body the moment I activate the current. I hold my finger down on the button, forcing myself to watch as he convulses, letting out a jolted scream. Tears roll down his temples. Tension knots my chest and throat. Jayme steps forward to help him, or maybe to pull me back.

"Don't," Bianca calls to Jayme. "It won't work if you stop it now."

Surprisingly, Jayme freezes.

I did the calculations repeatedly. Now, I just need to hold the button and count the seconds it takes to give him the right electric jolt to ensure the disconnected links in his Power DNA have a chance to fully reconnect. One missed connection could make this all pointless.

Miller's screams turn to half sobs, then whimpers the longer I hold the button. His body begins to sag with exhaustion despite the arch in his back.

"You're killing him!" Jayme screams.

Five more seconds…

Willow and Chase reach the doorway with everyone else on their heels. "What—?"

Four…

Jayme strides toward me. "Enough, Ugene!"

Three…

"Ugene, are you mad?" Willow darts through the narrow doorway, sprinting toward me.

Two.

Tears roll down my cheeks. Willow's hand clamps down on my shoulder.

One.

I release the button as Willow yanks me backward. The current stops. I stumble over my own feet.

Willow rips the power strips from Miller's chest. Jayme shoves me into the wall so hard my vision blurs on contact.

Everyone else crowds around the doorway, watching with horrified expressions.

"You went too far!" Jayme is venomous with anger, and rightfully so. It takes three people to pull Jayme back, and he still struggles wildly against their grip, ready to tear me apart.

But I don't fight back. I'm stunned, staring at Miller's unmoving body, willing him to get up.

Rosie falls to her knees beside Miller, pressing her fingers to his wrist to check his pulse. The color drains from her face.

Jayme crumbles into hysterics.

"What did you do?" Willow barks, rounding on me.

I'm numb.

Come on, Miller. I can't move. I'm nailed in place, dazed into deadlock.

"He tried giving him his Power back," Bianca says in my stunned defense.

"And who gave him the idea it was possible?" Willow snaps, glaring at Bianca.

Bianca glares back at her. "All his idea."

Rosie begins working her Power. The longer she performs her healing, the more her body shakes.

My knees give out and I sink to the floor. *I miscalculated. I killed my best friend.*

Jayme continues to struggle against the three sets of arms holding him. Chase places himself between Jayme and me. I want them to let go. I want him to punish me. I deserve it.

"Get Jayme out of here," Willow snaps at the others. "This is exactly why I can't trust your decisions, Ugene!"

A rough, loud gasp breaks through Jayme's manic anguish, bringing silence to the chaos of the small room. No one breathes. Even Jayme stills.

And we all look to Miller…and his rising chest.

My breath comes back in a massive wave. I break into frantic laughter. *He's alive!*

Jayme shrugs off the stunned hands holding him and skids to his knees in front of Miller, brushing shaggy blond locks out of Miller's eyes.

Miller continues coughing and shaking, but he's breathing.

Bianca tosses a blanket toward them and Jayme drapes it over Miller.

All I can do is sit there and laugh with relief.

After a moment, I manage to get enough control to crawl over to them.

Jayme shoots me a deadly glare. "Go away, you—"

"It's fine," Miller croaks. He rolls on his side and Jayme helps him sit upright against the far wall.

"What happened?" Willow demands.

Miller lifts his hand toward me, pointing as I sit on my knees in front of him. All the hairs on my body prickle and rise. Then a jolt of electricity rips out of me, crackling along the floor. I grind my teeth against the burning pain and shoot him a dirty look, but I had it coming. I laugh.

"You got it back," I say, breathlessly. "How much?"

Miller focuses, and his gaze goes distant. Not just through me, but beyond me. Lily, Sho, and Leo yelp. Some of the lights pop and go out in the hallway.

"How…?" Willow gapes at me with a newfound sense of awe. For the first time, someone is looking at me as if I have a Power. But it wasn't a Power. It was science.

Everyone gawks at Miller, and he rises with a newfound level of confidence and grins at me like he used to grin before he lost his Power.

"I saw the sample the Protectorate took from Miller," I explain to Willow. "His Power wasn't gone. Just disconnected. Since it's related to energy, I learned how to reconnect it using energy. It won't work for everyone."

Willow plants a fist on her hip. "Where did you get the sample from?"

Leo licks his lips and raises a nervous hand. "I gave it to him."

A few of the others offer me a congratulatory pat on the shoulder or arm as they all crowd into the room, around Miller. Willow has launched herself into a tirade about trust and appropriate use of information, and how she expects a full explanation on how exactly I helped Miller get his Power back once we return to The Shield. I agree, but with no intention of ever returning to The Shield. If she only knew what I haven't shared with her yet.

With everyone's attention now on Miller and what just happened, I caught a glimpse of movement, watching as Enid slips out of the room.

32

WHILE THE OTHERS DISCUSS MILLER'S RECOVERY AND offer congratulations, I manage to make excuses and leave, searching for Enid. Since Bianca's return, we haven't really had a chance to talk. I need to make sure she isn't angry. I need to make sure she knows how I feel. *How* do *I feel?*

The DMA shuttle takes up most of the garage. Light from the setting sun filters through the heavily curtained window, casting a muddy brown light in the space.

"Enid?" I take the single step down from the doorway and peer around the edge of the shuttle.

She quickly wipes her hands on her pants and clears her throat before turning to face me. "Yeah."

The last thing I want is to make her cry.

"Are you okay?" A terrible start and dumb question.

Enid raises an eyebrow. "Seriously?"

I rub my neck. "Sorry. I know Bianca coming back from the dead has...complicated things," I say, unsure where else to start. Somehow, I need to find the right words to fix this.

"I don't know what you're talking about." She crosses her arms and juts out a hip. Enid is doing what she did at Paragon—blocking out what's happened between the two of us as if it never happened.

I sigh. "Please don't do that. I would like to think I know you, and that I'm not that stupid." I step closer and reach for her.

Enid steps back and raises her chin.

I offer a sheepish smile. "Okay, maybe I am that stupid."

I hold my hand out and wait. Enid considers it for a long time. Maybe she doesn't see this…whatever this is…the same way I do. I drop my hand.

"What am I supposed to think?" she asks. "You've hardly said a word to me since Bianca's miraculous return." Enid shakes her head and slouches. "I get it, okay? I was never your first choice. Better that we both accept that now and move on."

My heart sinks. For years, I was infatuated with Bianca, the girl next door, the girl I could never have. While Bianca may be back, the girl I knew is gone. But Enid is still here. She's been here since the start, following me, trusting me…believing in me. And I was so blinded by Bianca's presence—so eager to gain her attention—that I never noticed Enid doing the same thing to me.

I do still love Bianca. Erasing her memories doesn't erase my own, but in almost every sense, she's gone. She's changed. Or maybe I have. The way I feel around Enid is different. I wanted Bianca and losing her left a hole in my heart. I *need* Enid in a way I've never needed anyone else before. Losing her would be like losing air. I can't survive without it—and I can't survive without Enid.

"What are you staring at?" Enid asks tersely, cocking her head to the side and regarding me like I've lost my mind.

"Enid…I…" Words once again fail me. I have no idea what to say to her, how to organize my thoughts or express them to her. "Nothing has changed."

Enid blinks and flinches back. "You don't seriously believe that."

"Okay, one thing has changed."

"Ugene, I know how you feel about her, but she isn't the girl you knew. For all you know, taking her to see her parents could be walking right into a Directorate trap."

"I know, but that's…that's not what I'm talking about. I'm talking about us." Why is it I can break down a DNA chain, but I can't figure out how to talk to girls? It can't really be that much more complicated.

"Us?" Enid's tone is dubious. "I'm not stupid, so don't treat me like I am. There is no us. There never was. Let's be adults about this and just…move on." Her words are laced with bitterness.

My heart sinks into the pit of my stomach, and not in a good way. "No. I don't think you're stupid. I think you're brilliant. And Bianca's back, but—"

"But what, Ugene? Are you going to tell me that you suddenly don't feel that way about her anymore? That you want *me*?" The emphasis she places on the last word is incredulous like she would be the last choice anyone would make.

But she isn't.

"Yes." The word falls out of my mouth.

Enid freezes, blinking at me. "What?"

I step closer, taking her hand.

She doesn't withdraw.

"I do want you. More than anything else. More than any*one* else." I pull her small body against me.

Our gazes tether.

I slide my arm around her waist, and she tenses in my arms. My hand slides up, cupping her cheek in my palm. For once, I'm not sweating. I'm not nervous. It isn't just a spark of electricity running through me, but longing, like I've been waiting for this moment. As I lean closer, Enid's hand glides along my arm, leaving a trail of warmth in its wake before her fingers wrap around my forearm. She pops up on her toes and a rush of exhilaration surges through me as our lips meet. It's soft, intoxicating. Nothing else exists. The last thing I want is for this kiss to end.

When Enid breaks away, her hands still cling to me. I press my forehead to hers.

Her lips part as she prepares a protest, but I kiss her again, hoping it will cast away her doubts.

"I want *you*," I say the moment our lips part, then kiss her cheek.

Enid nuzzles into my neck and it gives me shivers. Really good shivers! My fingers slide into her silky black hair, and I kiss her temple.

"Can we just stay right here all night?" Enid says against my skin.

The weight of reality presses down on my shoulders and, not for the first time, I wish I could just hide from all the troubles coming our way. "I wish."

Enid pulls back just enough to gaze into my eyes.

The intensity and longing from her make me immediately regret my words. I can't help but grin. "Well, maybe a little longer."

The garage is pitch black when my eyes open. Enid and I had stretched out together in the back of the DMA shuttle, enjoying as much alone time as we could steal before Willow tries to send us back to The Shield—or before I make my stand against Willow.

I don't want to wake Enid, but it's nighttime, which means our time is running out.

"Enid." I nudge her awake.

Enid nuzzles against my chest and mumbles, then turns her eyes up to mine and places a kiss against my lips.

"It's time," I say as soon as the kiss breaks and before either of us can do it again.

Enid grumbles but sits up. My body abruptly feels very cold without her. What if this was it? What if we don't see each other after tonight? *This will work. It has to.*

The two of us head back into the house, where Miller and Jayme are sitting close together at the kitchen table. I hesitate when they look up, expecting to get more of Jayme's anger despite healing Miller's broken Power. Jayme doesn't move, though.

"Welcome back," Miller says, grinning at us. "We wondered where you disappeared off to. Found you making cozy in the garage."

Enid's face turns bright red.

"Relax, we're all adults here," Miller says. He sounds more like himself now.

Jayme rises and I take an unconscious step backward as he closes the distance between us.

"I owe you an apology," Jayme says. "I'm not sure why you both are so close, but I'm glad you are."

"You don't owe me anything," I say, waving off his apology. "I don't know if I would have survived Paragon without him, and I don't know if he would have survived without the hope of seeing you again."

"He…" Jayme bites his lip, stuffing his hands into his jacket pockets. "He's everything to me. I didn't even know who I was until I met him. When Paragon took me in for that last experiment, I thought that was it, and all I cared about was that I would never see him again. They threw me out when the experiment failed. Like garbage. Thought I was dead until Chase found me in the Deadlands in a pit with…" Jayme stops and presses his thumbs against his eyelids. "…With other bodies."

My stomach twists. Enid's hand tightens in mine. They literally threw him into a pit of bodies?

Jayme shakes as he pulls his hand away from his face, tucking them into his armpits. His eyes are reddened. "I went back to that pit so many times, scared of finding him in it."

Anger brews in my stomach. How many others suffered as he did…or worse?

"Then he shows up with you, and it seems like you're all he talks about," Jayme says. "After all that fear and misery, I found him again only to worry I'd lost him anyway. But you brought him back to me. Three times."

I glance at Miller, who nods once, then looks back at Jayme.

Enid nudges me, and I follow her gaze to the clock. It's only eight, but I have no idea what time Willow plans to get us out of here.

"I have an idea," I say.

33

THE IDEA IS SIMPLE ENOUGH. TAKE BIANCA TO HER parents, pray they don't turn me in and convince her father to help me share the truth about what the Directorate and Paragon are up to with the entire city. The best way to slow or stop the Directorate is to get information to the masses before it's too late. I explain that Mr. Pond is in charge of the network, and maybe he can either broadcast the news for me or help me connect with Elpida Theus, the famous newscaster.

"Ugene, she's been missing for at least two weeks," Jayme says.

"Missing? Why?"

Jayme glances toward the kitchen doorway, then leans over the table as if sharing a secret. "We shared information with her about what really happened at Paragon the night you guys escaped. As far as we knew, she was launching a secret investigation, but we never heard from her again. The Directorate blamed her disappearance on us. It probably was partly our fault for sending her down such a dangerous path, but Willow and Doc are convinced Elpida was too close to getting to the truth so the Directorate silenced her."

The implication is clear in the way he says it. Elpida is probably in one of those body pits Jayme mentioned earlier.

"Then I will have to convince Mr. Pond." It's not what I wanted, but it's the best option I have. "If I can share the truth with the city, the Directorates' grip on the city will evaporate. But to get him on our side, I need to take Bianca to him and Willow will never go for it. She's angry with me and I'm pretty sure she doesn't trust me."

"Willow wants to get everyone back to The Shield soon," Jayme says. "Especially you."

"I know. But I can't go. I don't think any of us should. We can't afford to retreat anymore. The Directorate is taking action now, and Willow intends to save only a handful of the people who need Protectorate help. We need bodies here in the city, fighting back, not retreating. Which brings me to my next point." I hold my breath, expecting an argument. Instead, Jayme stares at me expectantly. I let out a breath. "I need to go alone."

"Like hell," Jayme says at the same time Miller says, "Over my dead body", and Enid says, "Excuse me?"

I raise a hand to quiet their protests. "I realize the risks involved, but the more people we have with us when we leave Pax, the more suspect we will look. Besides, Mr. Pond knows who I am. He doesn't know any of you. Imagine a group of extremists showing up in your home unannounced."

"Ugene, that guy has been broadcasting your face everywhere," Jayme says. "There's no way you will make it to the other side of town without being noticed."

"I don't need to get across town," I say. "I just need to get to the metro."

"Even if you do make it to his house, Pond is in the Directorate's pocket," Jayme says. "He won't turn against them. It could ruin him and his family."

"His family is already falling into ruins. Besides, I know him. Mr. Pond is a decent man. He might be in their pocket, but if the truth strikes close to home he might reconsider." *Probably.* "Especially once he finds out what they did to his daughter."

"Might?" Jayme snorts. "And let's say he does know what happened to his daughter—"

"He doesn't," I say confidently, recalling how Mom said they took the news of Bianca's death hard.

"Fine," Jayme waves off the protest. "He still knows his son works for Paragon, and he can't possibly be ignorant of what his son does there. You're asking him to choose between his two children."

"If we can't get to the network, there's no way we can make this city aware of what's really going on," I say.

"Ugene, you can't go alone," Enid says, shaking her head adamantly.

"I won't be alone. Bianca will be with me."

Miller snorts.

Enid slaps her palms against the table in defeat. "She could be a spy. We have no idea if we can trust her or not."

"I know. I realize the risk, but we don't have a choice." How can they not recognize that?

Enid shifts impatiently in her seat. "We *do*! Don't go alone with her!"

Miller tilts his head to look at Jayme, whose brows are drawing tighter and tighter. I turn in my chair and put a hand over Enid's. "You told me that I saved those people from Paragon. Willow and Doc keep telling me that I'm looking at the small fish instead of a much bigger one in the pond. It's time for me to do for this city what I did for the test subjects." Not that I'm sure how to do it yet.

The argument effectively silences Enid. I look at all three of them, my friends, afraid that Jayme is right and I'm walking them all to their doom. "I started this fight. Now it's time to finish it."

Miller rubs his chin, processing my plan and shaking his head.

"I need you all here," I admit. "For several reasons. First, Willow will try to stop me. I need you all to keep her attention so Bianca and I can slip away before Willow locks us up and sends us back to The Shield. Second, once I do make the broadcast, the Directorate will send DMA troopers out in full force to try and push their agenda ahead before we can stop them. That means Pax will need your full attention and support. Send word to The Shield to rally as many people as you can to back you up. Third, I think Willow is up to something."

"She's in charge of the Protectorate," Jayme says. "Of course she's up to something."

I shake my head. "This is different. When she was meeting with the operatives before I walked in, they were talking about something that seemed pretty sketchy. Plus, Enid found schematics of Paragon with strange marks on them. It can't be a coincidence. Please. I just want you guys to stick close and keep an eye on her."

Miller's mouth curves up in the corner at the mention of Enid finding something so secret. Jayme, though, doesn't seem nearly as amused.

"Last time I helped you on a covert mission someone died," Jayme says.

The reminder of Noah makes me grimace.

"Noah once told me that you can't expect to enter battle without some casualties along the way," I say. "I hate that we've lost people and I can't guarantee we won't lose anymore. But unless we stop the Directorate now, many others will continue suffering. And they'll eventually find us anyhow. This is what Doc would want me to do. He told me that I needed to think bigger when I talked about leading my people from Paragon. This is what he was talking about. I'm thinking bigger. Better to—"

"Ugene!" Willow storms into the room with the reports Dad left clutched in her raised hand. "What is this?" She slaps them down on the table.

I try to scoop them up, but Willow swats me away.

"We were looking for you earlier," she says, glancing at Enid briefly, "and found this in one of the rooms. Sho says this is what you were after last night."

I open my mouth, but Willow barrels over me, clearly not expecting any real answers.

"How long have you known about this?"

"Long enough," I say. "But I didn't know what it was until today."

"So, you just conveniently slip off when we visit Pax to retrieve exactly what we need to take down the Directorate for good?" She leans forward, pressing her knuckles into the table. "When were you going to tell me?"

"When were you going to tell everyone about the Powerless

bullets you're manufacturing?" I ask.

Miller's eyes widen. "What?" His limbs close in tighter to his body. Willow clenches her jaw. "I'm not—"

"—I found the formula," I say. She can't have a chance to lie and convince everyone else she's right. Because she's not. "Leo saw your people concocting it in the lab at The Shield. You know, people often underestimate me because I don't have a Power, but you don't need Powers to have brains."

"We need those bullets to protect ourselves against the DMA," Willow says, trying to sound calm and logical, but the tightness in her features gives her away.

Miller shakes his head as he rises, crossing his arms. His angry gaze fixes on Willow. "You can't use those."

"Who do you think you are to tell us what we can and can't do?" Willow rounds on him with a challenging glint in her eyes.

Miller's voice comes out as a growl. "Why don't we shoot you with one and then you can tell me what you think of using them?"

Chase hovers at Willow's shoulder, daring Miller to try.

"I know what those things feel like." Miller doesn't back down. His posture challenges both of them to try anything. And he has no reason to fear any of them. "Most of the DMA troopers are from Pax, people who signed up because they didn't have a choice. They don't deserve it any more than any of the other people you've rescued from the Directorate. You fight the Directorate and Paragon because you say that what they are doing is inhumane. Use those bullets, and you're no better than they are."

I smother a smirk behind my hand. It feels good to not be the only person challenging Willow, but even better to see the Miller I remember.

"We can't fight the Supers without those bullets," Willow says, forcibly relaxing her shoulders and using a compellingly calm tone. "Without them, without the same firepower, we'd be wiped out in seconds."

My own shoulders begin to relax, and the nerves building in my stomach slowly dissipate. Just like they did in the barbershop. *That's her Power. Willow is an Empath.* With that sort of Power, she can not only feel what others feel but help them calm down—or inspire others to follow.

Is that what Willow did? Is that how she started The Shield? Did she use her Power to get others to follow her? So why did everyone else trust her except me?

"You mean fight people like Bianca, who've been brainwashed by Paragon?" I ask. "We don't even know what it will do to the Supers. It nearly killed Miller. It could kill them." How do I fight against an Empath's grip on others?

Willow's expression turns cold. "To win this war, that's a risk we are willing to take." Her words slam against my chest.

I shake my head. Jimmy has always been a monster, but Terry wasn't—not completely—and Bianca certainly wasn't. If there are others, they could be like Bianca. Whether those bullets remove Powers or kill, it doesn't matter to me. Using them is wrong.

"She might be right," Jayme says, his shoulder sagging.

"What?" I round on him, then shoot a challenging look at Miller. How can he say nothing right now?

Miller just shrugs. "Maybe."

I clench my jaw, anger burning in my veins. "Tell them what you're doing."

Willow crosses her arms. "What are you talking about?"

"Your Power."

Willow doesn't budge.

"Willow isn't who you think."

Before I can explain, Sho runs into the room, grabbing the doorframe to keep from losing his balance as he skids to a stop. "They're—"

Sho's words are swallowed as a massive blast shakes the ground.

Enid throws a shield around the two of us as she pulls me down. The safehouse explodes around us.

34

I COUGH AND SLOWLY BLINK, DAZED. RINGING IN MY ears drowns out all other sounds, making me wince. Warm tiles press against my cheek. Where am I? My muscles ache as I push myself more upright and try to see through the haze of smoke and dust swirling around me.

"Enid? Enid!"

My voice is muffled by the ringing, but the sound begins to weaken.

Black boots thump down on the cracked tile, chunks of broken plaster, and splintered wood, landing directly in front of me. Before I can look up, a strong hand pushes me down against the floor. Someone is punched, followed by a braking bone and scream of pain. I dare to peer up as a DMA body sails overhead and crashes through the only remaining wall, rolling across the grass in a heap.

A hand grabs my jacket collar and yanks me to my feet. Surprisingly, I haven't suffered any serious injuries thanks to Enid's shield, but the sudden motion still sends agony through my limbs and back.

Bianca drops me on my feet. "You said my parents are alive. Prove it. We need to go now." She pulls me closer and whispers in my ear, "Play along."

Erratic panic tangles my ability to think clearly. *Enid*. My gaze flicks around on the floor to see her just a couple of feet from where I fell, unmoving under the rubble. Fear seizes my chest, and I jerk against Bianca's grip, but she's much stronger.

"I have the suspect," Bianca announces as she pulls me over

the rubble toward the street at the front of the house. "Thanks for coming to get me."

My heart hammers hard against my ribs. She told me to play along, but can I trust her or has she been toying with me this whole time?

"We didn't come for *you*." The familiar hint of disgust in Terry's voice makes me freeze, all the muscles in my body tense. "You allowed them to capture you."

"Allowed?" Bianca roughly shoves me to my knees on the pavement in the street and I can feel the scratches through my jeans. "They used some sort of Power on my mind and knocked me out."

My heart leaps into my throat. What can I believe anymore? Should I play along or is she manipulating me? I survey the rubble of the safehouse. Only the back wall and one corner remain. The rest of the house collapsed in the blast. Some of the rubble begins shifting. *Someone survived!* I can't have been the only one. Did Enid's Power shield anyone else?

A few feet away, Bri scrubs her hands together anxiously and stares at the destruction. Her gaze flits to mine and quickly dips away so her hair blocks her face, but not before I see the shame flushing her cheeks.

Terry grunts at Bianca then marches in front of Bri, his boots thumping on the pavement. Every step makes my breath shorter.

"I did what you asked." Bri's voice quivers. "I reactivated her tracking, and you said I would be let go."

Bri, no! The stab of betrayal plunges deep in my chest.

Bianca snorts and rolls her eyes.

Terry's teeth bare in a vicious grin. "Did you really think the Directorate would forgive you for siding with the radicals?"

Bri shrieks and jumps at Terry with her nails, scratching his face. Terry stumbles back in alarm. Bri's voice is hysterical, repeating the same words over and over. "You promised."

Bianca glances at me, and Jimmy hops out of the DMA shuttle, raises a hand like he's grasping something invisible.

Bri's voice chokes off. Her eyes pop. Her feet lift off the ground.

I struggle to try and get my feet under me, but Bianca presses a hand against my shoulder to force me down.

Terry turns his back on Bri and Jimmy, moving toward the rubble to seek out survivors.

Bri's mouth opens in a silent scream. Blood leaks from her pores and swirls in a cloud around her as her body shrivels then goes limp. Jimmy flicks his wrist aside, and Bri's body slides across the pavement as the blood bathes the street.

Sickness rises in my stomach. I gag, then fall forward on my hands and knees as dinner comes back up.

Bri reactivated Bianca's tracker. Why? I blink back tears. *Noah.* It must have been. Enid sat in that room with her and consoled her, then Bri disappeared. When I fixed Miller, Bri was the only one missing from our group. Did Bri leave to find the DMA and make a deal? But she sided with the same people who killed Noah. It doesn't make sense.

Booted feet step in front of me, and I look up, wiping my mouth on my jacket. Jimmy looms over me. Fury burns in my veins. Logic slips away. If I thought I hated Forrest before, it was nothing compared to the rage now consuming me. I surge to my feet to charge him but can't even take a step before intense pressure pushes down on me. I stumble, lose my balance, and fall on my side. Gravel digs into the fabric of my jacket.

"You've really become full of yourself in the past few months," Jimmy says.

I try to push myself to my knees, but a vice-like grip on my head makes it difficult to gather enough strength, and I fall forward again. It's impossible to catch my breath. I flop on the ground.

Jimmy crouches beside me. "Time to face the facts. You're too pathetic and weak to survive. You were never meant for this world."

"That's enough, Jimmy," Bianca snaps, pushing her way between us. "They want him alive."

Jimmy raises himself to his full height and squares off against Bianca. "They didn't say unharmed."

All the cells in my body feel like they are ready to be ripped out, and I flip onto my back, gasping for breath. The force of his Power lifts me off the ground, and my feet dangle inches from the pavement.

Jimmy's arm quivers and the whites of his eyes turn redder and redder as the blood vessels in his eyes thicken.

I can't speak. My skin turns cold, clammy. Blood trickles from my nose, and my skin feels like thousands of tiny hot needles are pricking it from underneath, trying to break outward.

"I do owe you one debt of gratitude, though," Jimmy says, flexing a hand. The sensation of hot needles intensifies. "Thanks to you, I'm more powerful than just about everyone else in this city. Who knew *you* could make me stronger?"

Instead of fighting him, I close my eyes. If this is the end, I won't stare at his face as I die.

"Jimmy, that's enough!" Bianca shoves him back, but it doesn't stop him from pulling me apart.

I gasp for breath.

"I said *enough!*" Bianca punches Jimmy in the jaw so hard something cracks and his eyes water. She leaps at him.

Someone screams my name. *Enid…*

Through the pain, I'm only vaguely aware of something landing nearby. Another DMA shuttle, maybe full of troopers. The struggle between Bianca and Jimmy has distracted him enough to release the pressure, but I just lie there on the street gasping for breath.

Two of the troopers grab me and drag me toward the shuttle as the blood pumps hot back through my veins. I scratch at their gloved hands but am still too weak from Jimmy's attack to fight back and escape. I can't let them catch me. Not yet. Not until I've had a chance to show the city the truth.

A body crashes into one of the troopers, breaking his grip on my arm. Chase rolls over the trooper on the ground and rips off his helmet, tossing it at the second trooper, who drops his grip on me to block the blow. Before the helmet strikes, Chase is already throwing punches into the first trooper's jaw. I grab the second trooper's ankle and sweep his feet out from under him.

As he falls, a gunshot fires and the second trooper falls to the ground, writhing in pain and seizing as Miller did on the floor of Paragon.

I push myself upright and stare at Willow with wide eyes as she turns the gun on another trooper. *No!* She's using the Power-removing bullets. She fires again.

"Willow, stop!" I struggle to rise.

The moment I get my feet under me, Enid calls my name and a loud *thump!* echoes off the houses along the street. Instinctively, I duck and seek out the source and see Bianca push away from the wall of a DMA shuttle, running toward me. I spin to see Jimmy charging in my direction from the other side.

"Ugene, down!" Willow yells.

I duck, not thinking twice, and Willow fires a shot at Jimmy. It slices his uniform but he doesn't slow. He throws his Power at Willow, forcing her to the ground. The gun falls from her hands. He grabs my collar and yanks me off my feet and into the DMA shuttle.

A bright light flashes, temporarily blinding me, followed by the stench of burning flesh. Something heavy falls on top of me and I blink hard as my eyes adjust to the dim evening light. Jimmy's body drapes over my legs with a gaping hole burned through his chest. A wound caused by lightning. *Miller...*

I yelp and push Jimmy off, scrambling away toward the door, but the door slides shut as the pilot secured in the front cab lifts off the ground.

"No!" I throw myself at the door, but it's too late, leaving me to peer through the darkened window at the scene below as we lift into the air.

Miller crouches beside Jayme, who's gripping his broken leg among the safehouse rubble. All of Miller's focus is on me—or possibly the shuttle. Rosie kneels at Jayme's other side, healing his wounds.

Terry struggles to hold his own against Bianca and Chase, but they are too strong for him. While his Telepathic Power is clearly slowing them down, it doesn't help him overpower their superior strength.

Chase struggles to stay on his knee as he holds Terry's leg to pin him down. Bianca throws punches that should have knocked Terry out cold.

One of the troopers grabs Willow in a stranglehold. Willow kicks her legs up and uses the momentum to pull the trooper down and flip him over her shoulder. Then Willow punches the trooper's neck, leaving the man gasping as Willow turns and swings a leg out to take out another approaching trooper.

Sho and Lily fight back to back, using whatever debris they can get their hands on to fight off attacks. In hand-to-hand combat, their Powers are useless. I try the door handle, hoping to free it and jump out. Enid will catch me with her air to break the fall. I just need to get the door open.

Enid keeps her body low, using debris as cover as she creates small tornadoes of wind that kick up debris and lob the shards and pipes at troopers to hold them back. Her attack punctures one and throws two other troopers into the wall of an adjacent house. Another trooper rises from the backyard, stumbles a step, then rushes Enid.

I bang my fists against the glass, calling out a warning pointlessly, watching helplessly as the trooper stuns her in the back with a dart that materialized out of his bare hand. Enid crumples to the ground in a heap as I scream her name.

A ball of blue lightning the size of a soccer ball flies at the shuttle, and I stumble back, throwing myself into one of the rubber-coated seats and strapping in as I lift my feet off the pressed-metal floor. The entire shuttle flickers with light as the lightning strikes, then it tumbles from the sky. I pull my legs to my chest and wrap my arms around them, making myself as small as possible. My stomach drops out.

The shuttle slams into an apartment building and rolls. We tumble back toward the earth. Momentum yanks me in several directions so hard I can't control my limbs. Jimmy's body smashes into a locked cage separating the front of the shuttle from the back. The pilot curses, punching at buttons until his helmet hits the side wall, knocking him unconscious. My own head snaps to the side, sending spikes of needles along my neck and shoulders. Finally, the motion stops. The shuttle comes to a rest on its side, leaving me strapped into the seat, hanging sideways, too stunned to move.

Boots thump on the metal frame above me. Someone growls out a battle cry. Metal screeches against metal as the bolts and pins holding the shuttle door in place bend and scratch against the frame. Bianca rips the door off, tossing it with a roar back toward the street, then she jumps into the shuttle. The second her boots hit the wall, now serving as a floor, she seeks out other troopers before approaching me.

My neck and limbs ache from the crash. Bianca grabs the harness holding me in, snapping it off the seat with a mighty yank. I fall into the side of the shuttle.

Bianca reaches for me. "Are you okay?"

I take her hand, shaking. "I think so."

Miller's voice calls from outside the shuttle. "Ugene?"

"He's okay," Bianca calls back, then pulls me up. "Let's get out of here before more reinforcements show up."

I nod stiffly and hobble toward the open shuttle door above. Bianca jumps up and hauls herself through the opening, then reaches down. I wrap my hand around her wrist, and I can feel the insanely strong muscles coil up just before she hauls me easily through the opening. As I fall back onto the side of the upended shuttle, the ache from the impact in my side reminds me of when Bianca used to haul me onto the self-driving tram before school.

Enid limps over pulling away from Rosie's healing hands in her haste to get to me. I draw away from Bianca and throw my arms around Enid, gathering her up and holding her close to me. Enid presses her whole body against mine, arms clinging to me and fingers digging into my back.

Bianca's boots retreat. I turn my full attention on Enid, away from the carnage. Her eyes are a nice distraction.

Blood trickles from a small cut on Enid's forehead. Her clothes and face are covered in dirt and her hair is a rumpled mess. But she's alive. *Thank god, she's alive.*

"I saw you fall and I…" I slide one hand along her cheek, cradling her face.

"I'm okay." She kisses my cheek. "Are you hurt?" Enid draws back a little, examining me.

I shake my head. I am hurt, but not seriously.

My attention shifts to the house. None of the DMA troopers remain. For a moment, we can breathe.

The door Bianca ripped off the shuttle struck down three DMA troops when she tossed it aside. Two others are dead from further wounds. The remaining five seem to be unconscious, but Willow makes rounds over each, laying her hands on their heads, presumably to knock them out longer like she did Bianca.

Chase and Bianca dig through the wreckage for survivors, but to my count, only Leo remains unaccounted for. Lily clings to Sho, her arm cradled against her chest. Miller and Jayme survey the situation. Rosie moves slowly from one person to the next, healing wounds. Even from a distance, I can see how badly her body is shaking. The healing is taking too much of a toll on her.

The shuttle crashed into a nearby apartment complex. The residents file out to escape the fire lapping up the side of the building.

I slide my hand into Enid's and pull her toward the building. "Can you put out the fire?"

"I can try." Enid raises her hands and sweat beads her forehead as she focuses her energy on the burning building.

As she does this, I climb onto the shuttle, calling the growing crowd to attention. "Please, for your safety move away from the building."

The residents listen, but they also shuffle closer to me asking questions about what happened and where they can go. They have nowhere else to stay.

"Why did this happen?" one woman asks, holding her shaking child against her chest.

I glance back at the others, still busy with the fallout. Enid has created a wind funnel to pull the flames up and out of the building toward the sky.

"The Directorate sent super soldiers into Pax to attack while we slept," I say. "They blew up our house, killed at least one of our friends, and injured several more just to protect themselves from the truth we now know."

"What truth is that?" another resident asks.

"That we are stronger united than divided." I wave a hand at my friends. "Most of these people want nothing more than the same freedom the Directorate affords itself. Most of us have little to no Power to speak of, but together, we are a real danger to them because we want equality for everyone. Take this night to tell everyone you know, the Protectorate is here, and united we will make the necessary change."

Bianca rushes to the edge of the shuttle, waving me down.

The hum of more DMA shuttles approaches. Several of them.

"Go, before the DMA comes back," I tell the residents. "And tell your friends the Protectorate is here."

The crowd disperses, rushing away from the building Enid has just extinguished. I hop down off the shuttle as Willow storms over.

"What are you doing?" she growls.

"Sparking the flame," I say, then walk away.

"We need to move," Bianca says, leaning close and eyeing Willow.

"We need to kill that tracking device the Directorate put in you for good," I say. "Bri somehow reactivated it while you were asleep. She claimed it was impossible to remove, but I'm not sure I trust her judgment anymore."

Sho finishes rummaging through what remains of the kitchen, collecting stray papers from my dad's bundle. Some burned up or blew away to another yard. Some were lost in the explosion. But most of what my dad left behind ended up pinned under debris. He rushes over to me and holds out the stack of papers he managed to gather. I still have the drives in my jacket, and I grab the papers, tucking them back into the lining of the jacket and zipping it shut.

The first DMA shuttle rounds the corner.

"Cover them!" I bark at the others, pointing toward the road.

Enid sticks to my side, and I nudge her toward the street. She knows this is where we part ways and her pleading gaze lingers on me. "It's too soon," she says.

"I need you to help them. Keep Willow from losing control. And don't trust anything she tells you. She's using everyone. I don't know what she will do once she finds out what I'm up to. Please." I take Enid's hand and kiss it. "It's time. Meet me at Harvey's place."

Enid's forehead creases, but she nods and places a quick kiss on my cheek before jogging toward Lily, Willow, and Chase. As Enid readies her Power against the new wave of DMA troopers, she turns around one last time and our eyes meet. This is it. It's time for me to go, and if all goes according to my plan, I may never see her again. But as long as she survives, it will be worthwhile.

Troopers spill out of the DMA shuttle, and the thunder of battle breaks out in the street once more. Gunfire and Powers combat against each other, making the ground quiver.

Miller approaches with Jayme, supporting Jayme as he limps along. The healing worked enough to close the wound and allow Jayme to move, but clearly, Rosie's healing isn't what it should be.

"I can kill the tracker," Miller says.

"Rosie, Bianca will need immediate healing," I say, moving to join the group. *And hopefully, Rosie has the strength to manage it.*

Miller reaches for Bianca's head, and she easily dodges, shoving him to the ground.

I jump forward. "Bianca, let him do this, we don't have time!" Her fierce coppery eyes turn to me. "Please. It will hurt like hell, but the DMA will find you, find *us*, no matter where we go." I put extra emphasis on the *no matter where*. I don't want Willow to know, assuming she's listening.

Bianca nods but the tension remains, keeping her muscles taut. Miller glares at her as he puts his hand on the back of her head where Leo mentioned yesterday that the tracking was located. Miller's hand starts pulsing with electric light, but it's so focused and controlled, more so than when he fried the nanos in our blood at Paragon. He couldn't manage that task alone and needed Celeste's help. Now he appeared to have no trouble at all on his own.

Miller hovers over Bianca and she lets out a shriek that makes me jump out of my skin. Blood trickles from her nose and the corner of her mouth. Her muscles flex, and I hold my breath, afraid she will take a swing at Miller. Then her body goes limp and Miller catches her before she hits the ground, easing her down. Rosie kneels at Bianca's side, her hands unsteady. I can't see what Rosie is doing, but I can tell that it takes several attempts before she successfully works her Power. I kneel beside Rosie, watching.

Bianca reaches out and snatches the collar of my shirt. Rosie leaps back. I jump, but Bianca's fierce gaze isn't meant for me. I know exactly what she wants. To see her parents. And so do I.

"Now." Her single word confirms my suspicion. Bianca releases with a force that makes me stumble back.

A house beside us explodes from the strength of a DMA trooper's Power. Screams emanate from inside. Startled, I turn toward the sound as the dust settles and see them staggering out of the house in a daze, carrying a child of about ten who hangs limply in his dad's arms. *This has to stop!*

"Go!" Jayme calls. "You're right. That information needs to get out. Willow won't agree, but we can't get out of Pax now. I'll deal with Willow. But you won't have long, Ugene."

I nod. "Try to protect these houses and the people inside."

Jayme waves us off as he and Miller rush off together toward the front line where the others battle four full squads of DMA men and women. Bianca and I take off in the opposite direction of the battle before anyone has a chance to see us.

As we disappear into a backyard, I glance back at the others. Four DMA shuttles block either side of the street. Enid casts a wild flurry of gale-like winds at one of the shuttles. It rolls on its side, pinning some of the troopers beneath it.

"Ugene!" Bianca hisses at me, grabbing my arm and yanking me around one of the houses.

But not everyone is accounted for. Leo is still missing.

35

I HAVE NO IDEA WHERE WE ARE. THIS SIDE OF ELPIS is a total mystery to me, having never ventured so far from Salas before. At first, Bianca and I just run away from the sound of battle, but Bianca is so much faster than me. I can't keep up with her speed for more than a few steps before she pulls ahead. She stops at the corner with her back pressed to a house with misshapen siding and an impatient look plastered on her face.

"Do you know where you're going?" I ask, resting my hands on my knees as I try to catch my breath. Running a block normally wouldn't leave me so winded, but trying to keep up with her is like trying to keep up with the metro as it charges along the tracks. "I can't keep running like this. I'm not a Super Somatic like you."

"I'm just trying to put distance between us and them," Bianca says. "We can worry about direction later."

"Unless we're going the wrong way."

Her lips compress in irritation—something I'm not used to seeing displayed so freely on her face. Bianca didn't irritate so quickly. She had more patience than most Somatics or most people in general. Not anymore. Yes, Bianca is certainly different.

I scrub a weary hand against my neck. "Just give me a second."

Bianca seems ready to argue, but instead, her gaze flicks around, searching for signs of trouble. I feel sorry for whoever tries to pick a fight with us.

I look to the sky with the hope that constellations will show me the right way to go, but the city lights make the stars hard to see. Instead,

I spin in place, peering over the taller apartment buildings and seek out the skyscrapers of downtown. I have to step into the street to get a clear enough view over some of the apartment buildings of the towers. Paragon looms in the distance.

"People are watching us," Bianca announces. "We need to keep moving."

Headlights from an intersecting street grow as a vehicle approaches us. The hum of the engine makes my skin crawl.

Bianca grabs my arm—not my hand like Enid would—and starts toward the mouth of the alley. We duck out of sight just as a DMA shuttle glides through the intersection on patrol.

My breath catches.

"I hope the others don't try to make a stand," I say. "The DMA will overwhelm them soon enough."

"They can hold their own," Bianca says curtly. "But we need to hurry before the streets are crawling with DMA shuttles."

I nod, and the two of us run back into the street. Bianca slows just enough for me to keep pace with her and guide the way.

Paragon Tower spikes out through surrounding buildings like a twisting rotten tooth in the distance. Celeste's cosmic ray decimated the first five floors of the building, but the integrity of the support structure wasn't compromised, and Paragon easily repaired the damage.

Going through downtown would be a serious mistake, but if we take the metro from the southern borough near Pax—since it doesn't run through the poorest part of the city—we can switch tracks underground, hopefully undetected, until we get to Lettuce Eat where Harvey will hopefully help us reach Bianca's house. He was open to my ideas earlier during the meeting with Willow. I can only hope he still is.

Bianca jogs so I can keep pace with her, but after a mile, I'm spent. Cold night air burns my throat and lungs as I suck in deep breaths.

"We need to stop running," I wheeze. "The two of us running through the streets like this has to look suspicious, especially with you in that." I wave a hand at her DMA uniform.

Bianca nods.

A few vehicles drive along the street sporadically, meaning we're nearly out of the worst part of town. No one in the slums can afford a car. We must be closer to downtown than I expected.

Bianca turns up one of the streets, keeping downtown ever to our right as we walk. A sense of urgency presses down on me from above. I glance at the sky—not that I expect to see anything.

But I do.

A set of bright stars form a line in the sky—the only stars I can see anywhere.

I stumble over my own feet in alarm. Bianca reaches out and grabs me for balance without allowing us to slow our steps.

Those weren't there before, were they?

The first star pulses with life then shifts to a dull glow as the next in line does the same, moving from our position toward the southwest.

Stars don't act like that. What are those lights?

Bianca and I continue due west, and the further along the street we walk, the brighter the lights pulse. But they don't grow larger, as I would expect light to do. They remain firmly in place like stars would, but the lights continue pulsing brighter and brighter.

What are they, really?

As Bianca and I step out of the intersection, I spy a DMA shuttle parked at the side of the intersecting street and grab her arm to pull her back into the alley.

Bianca doesn't hesitate to slip into the shadows, pressing against the wall before peering out. Then she turns her attention to me. "There are only two guys. I can take them."

I shake my head. "If we attack, even if you get to them before they alert others, the DMA will figure out where we are when those guys don't check-in. We can't leave a trace."

Bianca huffs. "Then what do we do? If we cross the street, they'll spot us."

I look up at the strange lights again. The first in the line glows steadily for a moment as if indicating a point of direction, then the line of motion begins again, guiding us southwest as it did before. Logic tells me to keep moving in the direction we are headed, but my instincts want to follow the lights. I need to know where they are leading. Did it warn us of the DMA shuttle? Bianca was right about one thing. We can't cross the street, and we can't backtrack too far. Time isn't our friend tonight.

We need to follow the lights.

I nudge Bianca's arm. "This way."

We follow the direction indicated by the mysterious lights for nearly two miles. A few times, I change course abruptly when the lights do, and Bianca protests, insisting that we go straight. Yet every time we don't follow the lights, we end up backtracking to avoid potential DMA confrontation.

At first, I think I'm crazy following some lights in the sky, but by the third near-encounter with the DMA, I can't ignore the instinct telling me the lights are keeping us safe from detection.

Near the end of the second mile, Bianca spots the entrance to the underground metro and grins, slapping me on the shoulder with more gusto than I think she intended. I wince and rub my shoulder as the two of us jog toward the steps.

Once we enter the metro, the lights in the sky won't be able to guide me anymore, and a sense of dread fills my gut. I hesitate at the top as that dread keeps me from descending. I glance once more at the lights and notice that they now pulse furiously away from the station. My heart jumps into my throat.

Bianca takes the first couple of steps in bounds, then stops when she realizes I'm not following. "Let's go. We're almost there."

I shake my head.

Bianca climbs back up the steps, glaring at me. "You said we should go this way."

"Something isn't right."

I glance up again, and the lights all blink like crazy away from the station.

Bianca looks up. "What are you looking at?"

But she either doesn't notice the lights—though I don't know how she can miss them—or she doesn't recognize the significance. I'm not sure *I* do.

Then the lights go out.

My stomach drops.

Logic screams at me to go get on the metro and ride it to our destination. Instinct screams at me to run away from this station as quickly as possible. So far, those lights have been our guide, protecting us from DMA detection. Now the lights want me to go anywhere else but down. I peer into the darkness of the station below.

My feet carry me away before I even make the decision that it's time to go.

Bianca quickly catches up. "What is wrong with you?"

"The lights went out."

"What?"

I wish I could explain why going into that station is a bad idea, why I trust those mysterious lights more than my own logic at the moment, but running has made me winded.

I follow the direction they were blinking before they disappeared, away from the station. Once we reach the next block and disappear around the corner, the thump of dozens of heavily booted feet fills the silence of the night. The sound comes from the direction of the station.

Good thing I'm trusting my gut…and whatever is guiding me.

Bianca hears the boots, too, and her steps hasten.

Neither of us speaks until we are three blocks away, out of trouble for the moment. Exhaustion makes my limbs ache and my lungs are burning as we approach a tram stop. I collapse on a tram-stop bench, leaning back to catch my breath.

Bianca sinks down beside me. "Do you care to explain how you knew they were coming?"

If I tell Bianca the truth, she will think I'm crazy. *Maybe I am.* Who follows directions from the sky? I'm also not sure I can fully trust her.

Enid's voice rings in my head, warning me that Bianca could be playing along to walk me into a trap. I can't ignore the logic in her argument. The less Bianca knows, the better.

"I just…had a feeling."

"A feeling," she says flatly.

"It's gotten me this far."

Bianca doesn't seem convinced, but the evidence makes it clear to me and that's all that matters at the moment.

A self-driving tram approaches from the east and I turn, examining the route map on the tram stop wall. A grin spreads across my face. Again, my faith in the lights in the sky has been restored.

This line will take us right into the heart of Salas.

"We are taking the tram instead," I announce.

It isn't very late. Just short of ten at night, but the tram is fairly empty. It's one of the last rides of the night. A few people give Bianca in her DMA uniform a curious look as we climb on board, but they all quickly avert their gazes. Because of her uniform, no one takes a second look at me.

Just to be safe, I keep the hood of my jacket over my head and try to keep my face obscured from sight. Despite this concealment, I feel exposed in the bright white lights of the self-driving tram.

Bianca and I take seats in the back. The tram heads out of the southern borough into Salas. The nearest stop to our old neighborhood is about a quarter-mile walk.

We keep silent. A conversation will draw attention. The silence between us leaves me too much time to think about the others… about Enid.

Up until this moment, I've been too preoccupied with escaping

DMA notice to think about them. Now, it's all I can think about.

What if the DMA overwhelmed them?

What if Enid died in the fight?

The thought leaves me devastated, forcing me to lean over my knees and take a few deep breaths with my hands laced behind my head.

She has to be alive. Enid is a survivor. A fighter.

After everything she's endured, I can't allow myself to believe Enid wouldn't survive again.

Will Willow listen to reason? Will she bring in more people to help fight off the DMA? My hope is that once word gets out about the truth, once we can get the people to rise up against the Directorate, that the new recruits from Pax will turn on the DMA.

The tram pulls up to a stop, and Bianca stands. "This is ours," she says quietly as if afraid someone might hear. Not that they wouldn't notice us getting off.

I follow her off the tram and survey the street.

The difference between Salas and Pax isn't simply jarring—it's revolting. Here, people live in large houses, well-maintained with nicely kept lawns, not condemned buildings on the verge of collapse. The smell of flowers and freshly cut grass fills the air instead of the stench of trash and sewage.

How can people be content to live like this when others survive in squalor?

I was one of these people.

The thought makes me loathe my former self. Maybe, like me, they don't realize how bad things really are in Pax. Or maybe the Directorate has convinced them that they really will fix things.

Bianca knows where she's going now. Still, I glance at the sky.

Nothing.

The two of us try to look like we belong on these streets—at one time we did—but her uniform and my soot-covered clothes don't really say "this is our neighborhood."

Residents linger outside even at this hour, which must be just past ten. They pull weeds from front yard gardens or talk to their neighbors. Their conversations are so mundane and oblivious to the horrors I've witnessed tonight that I want to scream at them, open their eyes to the truth. *Patience. I will do it soon enough.*

Salas is a completely different atmosphere to what I've grown used to, and I struggle to find comfort in my old stomping grounds.

Some of the residents glance at us, but no one says anything. Maybe they can't see who I am, but they can see her clearly. How many of these people knew Bianca before? Were they told the same lie—that she died? The more people the Directorate lied to about her fate, the more likely their lies would come undone.

"We need to take the alleys," I whisper after two blocks.

Bianca nods, and when we don't see anyone else around, the two of us disappear into the shadows of the alleyway.

Unlike the alleys in Pax, these are meant as mini roads for the residents, and the alleys all lead to garages—all of which have vehicles in them, unlike any other borough.

"I need you to make me a promise," I say, keeping my voice low in case anyone is in their backyard.

Bianca glances at me but doesn't respond.

"No more killing. Not the DMA recruits, at least. Some of them had no other choice but to join. They don't deserve death."

Bianca grimaces. She's Somatic. Her Power is in her strength, and I'm getting the feeling that it includes killing as a result. But it isn't right. And it isn't Bianca.

"Please?" I really need her to say yes.

Bianca sighs. "I will...try."

"Promise?"

"I promise. Unless I'm left with no other choice."

I nod. I suppose it's the best I can hope for under the circumstances.

After a few blocks, the scent of sarsaparilla reaches for me like a familiar caress. The houses on our street are in far better condition than I remember. Maybe it's the shock of seeing the way that others lived in Pax that makes these houses seem too elegant, too bold. The scent of the gardens in a few of the sprawling lawns doesn't calm my nerves like it used to. Still, the aroma is familiar. Like home.

Bianca's steps slow, then halt completely once her former backyard comes into view.

The lights are on inside, like many of the houses in Salas—another distinct difference between here and Pax.

I reach for her hand to offer support, but she pulls away and strides forward. I quickly follow, wondering how we will break the ice. Maybe a "hey look, your daughter isn't dead, and your son is an evil dick."

Bianca's hand trembles as she reaches for the knob on the back door. I don't think I've ever seen her tremble. It's the first real sign that she isn't as much of a programmed robot as she seems.

"We could knock," I offer, keeping my voice low.

Bianca shakes her head. This is home. Knocking doesn't seem right. "You had better be right, Powers."

I flinch at the dangerous edge in her tone. Even now, on the back doorstep, she doubts me.

With a surge of confidence, she turns the knob, and as I follow her through the back door, I glance once more at the sky to discover a single light pulsing brilliantly.

Is that a warning or validation?

36

THE HOLOVISION ADDS THE ONLY SOUND TO THE house as we enter through the kitchen, and a sense of dread gives me a shiver. A dim glow over the kitchen sink is the only source of light in the room as we step inside and close the door. Bianca's hand slides over the clean granite countertop as she moves toward the light in the living room. There's a sense of intimacy in her touch.

I follow Bianca toward the front of the house. This place is familiar to me, like a second home. I spent a lot of my childhood playing here as much as in my own home. It should make me comfortable, at ease, but instead, the house does the opposite.

Mr. Pond never much cared for me, the boy across the street who was far too interested in his daughter—later to become that Powerless boy who had no worth. Mrs. Pond had been fond of me though. If only she were the one running the network. Instead, I will have to beg for help from the guy who would rather see me disappear from his daughter's life. I can only hope that the spark of true investigative journalism still burns within his heart and mind. That desire for the truth will be critical to me swaying him to help.

But if he thinks Bianca is dead, what does he think of me? Does he blame me? Paragon can't have released much information about what happened. Maybe they don't even realize Bianca died helping me.

One can hope.

Bianca freezes in the broad living room doorway, staring at her parents with wide eyes. Sensing the motion, Mrs. Pond turns her head away from the television and lets out a squawk as she clutches at Mr. Pond's arm while he furiously sends messages to someone on his phone. He follows her frozen gaze to the two of us in the kitchen entryway, and his own eyes pop.

No one notices me at first. Not that they should. They obviously thought their daughter was dead, judging by the sudden paleness of their faces and frozen shock. Yet here Bianca stands, alive and well.

"Bianca?" Mr. Pond's brows pull together, and he eases his wife's hand off his arm to rise.

Bianca's voice cracks. "Dad?" The lines on her forehead tighten together, a genetic trait she shares with her father, and her arms fall like lead to her sides. "Mom?"

Mr. Pond breaks from his trance and rushes across the room, sweeping her into his arms in one of the fiercest hugs I've ever seen. In moments, Mrs. Pond joins them, and the three just cling to each other crying tears of joy and disbelief.

I step back to give them a little more space, carefully inching toward the window and peering cautiously out into the street. The black vehicles almost blend into the darkness. Almost.

Across the street, my house is dark. Mom went underground at least a week ago, and even though I know she isn't there, the urge to go across the street and confirm she isn't there tugs at my feet.

I glance back at Bianca's family, and my stomach twists in knots. I want that kind of reunion, but I wouldn't get it. Mom isn't there.

The television is tuned to the news, as it usually is in this house, reporting on the radical attacks in Pax. The spin is focused on how the radicals attacked a DMA transport vehicle, murdering all the troopers inside, proceeding to destroy several houses, killing residents as they fought off DMA reinforcements before escaping. *They escaped!*

The media spin is never truthful, but the Directorate wouldn't want to report a fake escape of the very people they want to capture if it weren't true. If anyone was detained in the fight, or even killed, the Directorate would want it reported for everyone to see, like saying "look at our success."

"The death toll continues to climb," the reporter says—not Elpida, further confirming what Jayme said about her earlier tonight. "And the DMA is calling for anyone who has information to report it immediately."

My friends won the battle, but the war isn't over. I glance back at Bianca.

Mrs. Pond kisses Bianca's forehead, holding her daughter's face in her shaking hands.

"My girl…" Mrs. Pond's voice trails off.

Bianca quivers as her dad slides his arm around her shoulders.

"How…?" he asks. "Forrest told us you died. He…" Mr. Pond seems unable to finish, unable or unwilling to put the pieces together.

"He told me the same about you," Bianca says, her voice thick with a mixture of joy and anger.

Mr. Pond shakes his head, utterly confused. "But why?"

Mrs. Pond looks up as if seeing me in the room for the first time, then takes a step back. "What is he doing here?"

It stings. She was the one I expected a little support from.

Mr. Pond looks me over, frowning. "Gloria, get my phone."

Mrs. Pond takes half a step toward the couch, where he left the phone, but Bianca grabs her arm. "Please, Mom. Don't. I wouldn't be here if it wasn't for Ugene."

Mr. Pond glares at me. "What do you want?"

I take a desperate step toward him, thankful that the shades are closed for the night. "Please, sir, we need your help."

"Why would we help a radical terrorist?" he asks, puffing up his chest.

"Wait, why do you think I'm a radical terrorist?"

"Because of the crimes you've committed," he continues, a snarl turning up his lip. "They say you are responsible for what happened at Paragon, and you are now leading a group of radicals against Elpis and may be behind this attack tonight. Anyone who helps you will be sent out of the city."

"Dad," Bianca says. "I'm not sure that's true."

Mr. Pond flinches.

"He risked everything to bring me here and prove the DMA lied to me…that *Forrest* lied to me."

"Forrest knew?" Mr. Pond's face screws up in anger.

A spark of hope alights in my chest and I take a cautious step toward him. "You know something is going on, that the reports the Directorate and DMA are feeding you aren't completely true, but you can't prove it."

His mustache quivers with indignation…but he hesitates.

"Families are torn apart," I continue, hoping I'm getting through to him. "I've seen it with my own eyes just this morning. People go missing with no explanation—like Elpida. What happened to her, Mr. Pond?"

His gaze darts to Mrs. Pond, and they share a knowing glance. It happens too quickly. I almost miss it.

"You comprehend more than you're letting on," I say, "even if you can't be certain how much of it is true. You were there during the transition when the former Directorate Chief mysteriously died and Seaduss took office. As all of these changes happened and new laws passed, you were given information that deep down you knew was at least partially false. If you are even the least bit suspicious, even the slightest bit curious about what happened to Elpida, don't you think others are as well? And you have the power to bring the truth to light."

Mrs. Pond joins her husband, taking his arm and casting an imploring gaze at him.

Mr. Pond stares into his wife's eyes, then shakes his head and turns his attention back to me. "Even if I wanted to, we can't help you." He waves at the television. "If we don't report you, the Directorate will order our arrests."

"Do you think I don't realize what I'm asking of you?" I adopt as casual and non-confrontational a pose as I can while displaying the urgency at the same time. "None of this is easy. But it's right. We've all acted like sheep, blindly following the herd and leaning on our Powers in lieu of knowledge. But knowledge is what could save us."

Mr. Pond goes still, raising his chin as he considers, and his gaze flits around the room as if uncertain where he should look.

"Daddy, Ugene helped me." Bianca takes her dad's hand. "Now we need to help him." She nods to me. "Show him, Ugene."

I swallow, reaching for the zipper of the jacket lining. What if this is a mistake? What if I hand all of this information over to him and he turns it in along with me?

"Ugene," Bianca says with urgency.

I pull out the papers. "This is why they are after me."

Mr. Pond doesn't move toward me at first. His lips compress, and he stares at me for so long I fear he may not even give me a chance. Then I realize he isn't staring at me. He's Reading my aura. Mr. Pond is a Divinic Aurologist, but unlike how Celeste could read people's futures through auras, Mr. Pond can sense emotional reactions and trauma—and on rare occasions, he can read moral alignments. He's trying to gauge whether or not I speak the truth. Thankfully, I have no reason to lie.

Finally, with a huff of irritation, he strides toward me and snatches the papers so fiercely it makes me flinch. As he lowers his head, he takes a moment to cast a challenging gaze at me. I swallow and rub my arm.

Lowering his glasses from the top of his head, Mr. Pond flips through the pages. His scrunched-up, angry face shifts. His jaw goes a touch slack. Then his copper eyes—so much like Bianca's—dart up to me. "Where did you get this?"

"Dad left it for me."

"And what am I supposed to do with this?"

"I need you to share it," I say, hope blooming in my chest. "People need to know the truth about what's going on in the Directorate."

Mr. Pond's brows shoot up. "You want me to report on this? If all of this is true, and they are trying to cover their tracks, the DMA will break down our door and kill us, then spend the next week spinning the report to make us look like we were part of the radicals all along!" He shoves the papers back at me. "No. I won't risk my family."

I step with urgency toward him. "Sir, I don't think you understand this fully."

"No, boy, I don't think *you* do. I can't use reports like this to try and discredit them. Reports like those can be fabricated, and if there is no other evidence of their existence elsewhere, as some of those scribbled notes suggest, then it makes that claim so much easier. It's unusable on its own."

"That's not all I have," I say quickly, fumbling in the jacket for the drive from Miller and holding it out between us. "This is from Paragon. It shows the experiments they are performing on test subjects. Deadly experiments. Formulas, project notes, test readings. It's all there. Most of the data is encrypted, so I can't unlock it."

Mr. Pond grimaces and takes the drive. "Just like that, huh? You're just handing it over."

"Yes."

"Why?"

I glance at Bianca. "Because I trust Bianca, and she trusts you."

He takes a moment to regard that drive, turning it in his fingers. "Encryption isn't an issue. I have someone I trust with a Power that should be able to crack it."

"You should know, though, that…" I shift, glancing over his shoulder at Mrs. Pond. Releasing those videos will destroy their family. "The researcher performing the experiments…it's Forrest."

Mrs. Pond sucks in a breath, covering her mouth with her hand.

I feel terrible, but they deserve to know the truth before we move forward. "And it isn't easy to watch."

Mr. Pond's expression shifts to anger. "You are telling me you bring one child back to us only to rip the other one away?"

"I'm sorry."

Bianca pulls away from her parents and moves to my side. "I trust Ugene, Dad."

"Of course you do." He turns away and starts pacing the living room. "You've always trusted him. Even when he led you into trouble, you trusted him. But this…Bianca, this will tear our family apart and put all of us in grave danger."

"I don't know him," Bianca says, which draws confused looks from both her parents. "He says I do, that we grew up together, but I only met him a day ago. Still, he is the only person who has been honest with me, and who trusted me when—by all rights—he shouldn't have. I owe him the same."

"They did something to her, sir," I say. "Experiments. I'm not sure the extent of it, but Paragon somehow selectively erased some of her memories—her time in PSECT at Paragon, me—and implanted some false memories, like your deaths."

Mrs. Pond takes her husband's hand.

"Experiments?" he says, looking at Bianca.

"I died," Bianca nods. "And Paragon did something to bring me back. They also somehow enhanced my Power to make me their super soldier."

"We have to do something," Mrs. Pond says. "She's our daughter, Nick."

"And what about Forrest?" he asks, clearly torn between his love for his children and what is right. "He's our son."

Mrs. Pond opens her mouth, but nothing comes out.

"It's possible Paragon has somehow corrupted Forrest," I say, though I don't really believe it. The idea could give them some sense of hope for their son. It's a terrible thing to ask parents to choose between their children, but what Forrest is doing is wrong. It needs to be stopped, even if he is being used.

"Please." I dare to step closer. "All I'm asking for is five minutes of airtime to share the truth and deliver evidence."

He shakes his head.

"Sir, the Directorate is using the Consumption Tax to force people into these experiments. I also suspect they are injecting something into those they select for DMA service. Something to brainwash them, like they brainwashed Bianca. Directorate Chief Seaduss is making a power move to purify the population. And if the people don't join willingly, he is using the DMA—with numbers bolstered by those same people he wants gone—to carry out his plan. If we want to stop them, we need to make sure everyone knows the truth. Letting me speak to them is the best way to do that."

My hands slip into the pockets of my jacket, and my fingers brush against the second drive—the one Dad left.

Giving Mr. Pond everything is a huge risk. I don't have copies of any of this data. But he is my best chance at using the numbers of the population against the Directorate like we used numbers at Paragon to overwhelm security.

I press my lips together and pull out the second drive, holding it toward him.

"What's this?" he asks, hesitantly taking it from me.

"Plans for the DMA Purification Project." It's hard letting go as he grabs it from my fingers. "It was with the stuff my dad left."

Mr. Pond turns the drives in his hands, scowling. He is trying to put the pieces together, clearly deep in thought.

I shift my feet as I wait, wondering if he will agree or not. The longer he thinks, the more thoroughly my hopes are dashed.

Mr. Pond is in a terrible position. I can only hope that his desire for the truth and that doing the right thing will motivate him.

"Ugene, a word…alone." Mr. Pond walks into the kitchen, expecting me to follow.

I stuff both hands deep into my jacket pockets, glancing at Bianca and Mrs. Pond before hanging my head and trailing him.

Mr. Pond waits on the other side of the island, both drives lying on the papers on the countertop. But his gaze is fixed sternly on me. *This can't be good.*

"It's time you learn that nothing in life is free." He leans forward, his hands flat against the granite. "So, here's what I'm offering you. No negotiations."

My stomach twists, but I nod.

"I will give you five minutes. My team will meet you at the broadcast location. After it's done, you leave. If you delay in the slightest, you will put everyone at risk. Even with someone using their Power to scramble our location, the DMA will close in on the block quickly. Is that clear?"

Again, I nod, trying my best not to freak out that he's going to give me the broadcast.

"Good. But I'm not finished. In exchange for those five minutes, you agree to stay away from my daughter, as well as my entire family. I won't have her pulled further into this. Especially if I am already faced with losing my son."

Bianca can make her own decisions. I open my mouth to protest.

Mr. Pond raises a threatening finger toward me. "No negotiating. You will leave her out from this point forward."

There's no way Bianca will agree to this.

However, if it's her choice, then I'm technically not breaking the agreement. *Think big.* I need to do this, and I'm certain this is what Doc implied when he told me to think big.

"Deal." I hold my hand out to shake.

His grip is firm and unrelenting.

"Good." He pulls out a business card and scribbles on the back of it, then hands it to me. "Meet me at that address in one hour. Not a minute sooner."

I flip the card between my fingers and read the address. It's at the edge of downtown, not an easy place to reach when the entire DMA force is searching for me. All I can do is hope that the battle in Pax has drawn most of the forces away.

"Go." The single word is not a request.

"Can I at least say goodbye to Bianca?"

"No. She might follow."

Well, he probably has that part right.

Mr. Pond walks to the back door and opens it. I glance toward the living room as I prepare to leave, but Bianca isn't in my line of sight.

With a sigh, I step outside and he closes the door in my face.

37

GETTING TO THE EAST SIDE OF DOWNTOWN PROVES easier than I imagined. With my hood drawn up, I take the metro. Only a handful of other travelers occupy the metro car, but no one sits anywhere around me. The whole way, I keep my head down and avoid eye contact with anyone else. It's late. Most people are already home.

When I reach the address, I'm a few minutes early. It's nearly 11:00 P.M., so I keep my promise and hide in the shadows of the alley across the street. It's a narrow space between two tri-story brick buildings.

The location isn't what I expected. I figured Mr. Pond would send me to one of the satellite stations for the network. Maybe that was too obvious for the DMA.

Instead, I find myself watching the activity around a small health clinic. An Elpis News Network van pulls up in front of the clinic, and a team of four people unload the camera and broadcast equipment into the building. Mr. Pond steps out of the van, scanning the street.

I shrink back into the shadows. His instructions were clear. I don't intend to piss him off before I get a chance to talk.

Not that I have any idea what to say. The reality of what I'm about to do sinks in my gut and my shoulders curl downward. I've never been good at public speaking. In high school, I often stumbled over my words, conscious of how my classmates were mocking me. What I am about to do is a whole new level of pressure. I'm not just reporting on something for school. Somehow, I have to convince the entire city that it's time to stand together against the Directorate. My fingers go cold.

Come on, Ugene. You got this. There's no other choice. If only I had more time to really think this through and create an irrefutable argument.

Once they finish unloading, the van drives away, disappearing around the corner at the end of the block.

I check for anyone watching from windows or vehicles coming up the street. It's quiet, so I slip across.

Mr. Pond holds the door open for me, then locks it behind us.

A surge of fear pulses through me.

His crew could be anyone. They could be undercover DMA agents. And now I'm locked in with them. *If they are DMA, I would already be under arrest.*

Mr. Pond leads me toward the back of the clinic to an office with blank eggshell walls that could be anywhere in the city.

The crew sets up the equipment across from a desk. A young woman only a few years older than me has a laptop open in her lap, clicking through something I can't see. Another guy hooks up the cables and checks connections for the camera while his coworker connects the pole to the boom mic.

Mr. Pond steps in front of me like a wall between myself and his team. "Do you know what you've given us? Do you know what is on those drives?"

"One of them."

He shakes his head, and I notice fear in his eyes. True, unfiltered fear. I've never seen Mr. Pond nervous before. He's always so confident.

"We read the DMA plan on the way over, and saw the videos…" He shivers. "They're horrible."

I know exactly how he feels. Is that what I looked like when I first saw them—sick with terror?

His upper lip stiffens. "The vaccine they're giving the regressing population, this IVD Veritax, it's a sham. The damn thing only has an eight percent success rate."

Eight? "And the other ninety-two…"

He doesn't need to answer. I already know. I've seen what happens. The image of Vicki's body convulsing on that lab table stokes the flames of my anger.

"Ready," laptop girl says.

Mr. Pond waves me toward the desk chair.

Anxiety knots in my stomach.

My body quivers as I step around the desk and ease into the chair, hoping no one else notices my fear. My heart is racing so fast I have to remind myself to breathe. My sweaty palms grease the arms of the chair and I ease myself down.

"Is it loaded?" Mr. Pond asks laptop girl.

She nods.

"Connection?" he asks the fourth team member.

"Citywide on your mark, Mr. Pond."

He nods, then turns his attention to me, crossing his arms. "Five minutes."

I nod stiffly, hoping no one can see how badly I'm shaking. What am I supposed to say? My friends follow me because they believe in me—that's what Noah said right before Jimmy murdered him. Somehow, I have to make the rest of the city feel the same. Doc seemed to think I was capable. So did Mom.

A holoclock appears in glowing blue light above Mr. Pond's watch, with 5:00 frozen in time.

I close my eyes and take a deep breath to calm my nerves. How do I convince an entire city to revolt against the government?

"Now," Mr. Pond says.

I open my eyes to see the cable guy counting down from five with his fingers, then the red light on the camera comes on and the clock begins counting down.

My stomach twists in knots.

Now or never.

"Hi. Um, for anyone who doesn't know, my name is Ugene Powers." The announcement makes the cameraman cast an anxious glance at Mr. Pond, though I'm certain he must recognize me if he works for the network. Jayme said my face has been all over the news lately.

I focus on each word, on keeping my voice steady. If they hear it quiver, they will know how scared I am, and they may not listen further. I need to fake confidence as best I can to convince them that every word is sincere.

"The Directorate has said a lot about the Protectorate radicals, and about me. That I am a tyrant, a liar, an extremist determined to destroy this city. But I'm here to tell you the truth. The Directorate has lied to you."

I rest my forearms on the edge of the desk and clasp my hands together, palms slick with sweat. Can they see me shaking?

The clock ticks the seconds away.

"I grew up in Salas as the Powerless son of General Powers. I trusted the Directorate just like you, believing in the goodwill of Paragon just like you. I entered a top-secret biological experiment at Paragon that was supposed to help me gain Powers. Instead, I watched them kill several of my friends—and my father—in the name of science. The rest of us barely escaped with our lives."

The revelation about Dad—and that I have no Power—sends a ripple of shocked expressions through the handful of people gathered in the small office. I can only hope it has the same effect on those at home.

Mr. Pond doesn't flinch, though I can see a hint of alarm when I mention my dad's death. Paragon and the Directorate probably covered it up.

And they will cover up more deaths if we don't stop them.

"The Protectorate took in my friends and me, gave us shelter, and showed us the truth. We don't need powers to survive. We need cooperation and intelligence. The Protectorate doesn't just believe this. They *live* by it, outside the limits of this city. The Directorate and Paragon have fed you the fear of regression, toting their propaganda that we can't survive without Powers. But we can."

I pause, giving that statement a moment to settle in before moving on. My gaze fixes on the clock.

3:19 remains.

"The Directorate is using your fear to pass laws that allow them to force the weak into lines a block long to wait for Paragon's newest *cure*, knowing full-well that ninety-two percent of those injected will perish. The choice isn't really a choice. Join the DMA or die."

Laptop girl's jaw is set, angry. She has seen what I uncovered on those drives, and her irritation is written all over her face. I need *everyone* to be outraged, so I push on.

"Today, I saw a man no younger than sixty tackled to the pavement before being hauled into a DMA shuttle. A girl, no more than five, cried for her daddy as the DMA dragged him off for injection. A man roughly my age attempted escaping a DMA tent only to be shot in the street as his girlfriend begged for his release."

To my own surprise, laptop girl strikes a key, and a video begins playing, presumably feeding through the entire network. Footage of DMA attacks on citizens, of the lines into the tents, of a child crying for mommy. I have no idea where Mr. Pond found these videos, but the emotional charge in each gives credence to my words.

"None of these people did anything wrong. Their only crime was obeying the law and fighting for their lives. The Directorate wants you to believe that being Powerless means weakness, when the truth is, being *afraid* of losing our Power is what makes us weak."

Sell it.

I lean toward the camera, putting more weight on the edge of the desk while attempting to push the urgency of the situation. My gaze flicks to the clock again.

2:03.

"But we are not weak. I call on all of you to take a stand with us, to show the Directorate and Paragon that our Powers can be combined into a source of strength. *This* is how we survive. United."

The boom guy's hands tighten on the mic. The cameraman's nostrils flare. Even Mr. Pond raises his chin and gives a small nod.

"This battle will not be won with a few of the strong holding against the tide of tyranny, but with fists raised in unity to build an indestructible wall against the tide, forcing it away from our shores. Let's stand together and show the Directorate that *all* lives matter. That we will not back down. We will not hide."

The cameraman nods in agreement.

My nerves begin dissolving in the wake of pure determination. I need the people to feel as strongly as I do, and the words tumble from my lips with newfound conviction as I fix my resolute gaze on the camera.

"To those of you who believe this fight is not yours, I ask you this: Have any of your loved ones gone missing or mysteriously died? I'm not asking you to believe my words as truth. I'm asking you to believe your eyes and see what's right in front of you."

Tears shimmer at the edges of laptop girl's eyes, her hands clenched into fists on the arms of her chair.

0:31.

I press on, "No matter what you choose to do, I will continue forward with confidence that my path will lead to liberation for everyone. Tomorrow, we fight for that right outside the Administration Building. I vow never to stop until Elpis achieves freedom. I fight for equality. I fight for balance. And I hope I survive to see it become a reality. But if I don't see another sunset in exchange for that freedom, I welcome my fate. For you."

With that, the time on the countdown clock expires.

The office is frozen, utterly motionless. The camera light turns off as the live feed cuts out. The crew remains statue-still as I take a moment to collect myself, then push away from the desk and head for the door. Even Mr. Pond only manages to stare as I open the office door.

"Start my call to action," Mr. Pond says as I step into the hallway. "And loop it through the van."

Though I'm curious about what his call to action is, I leave them behind.

My five minutes are up.

38

MIDNIGHT APPROACHES, AND I NEED TO REACH LETTUCE
Eat, where my friends—and Enid—should be waiting. With each step
I take toward the mouth of the alley, the reality of this entire situation
presses down on me harder. I just called on the entire city to start a
revolution. But what if no one shows up? What if I end up standing
alone at sunrise?

Stop focusing on the what-ifs.

The city is terribly quiet. No soft hum of engines or stray people
headed home for the night. My heart is racing as I reach the end of the
alley and peer out around the corner. I need to get to Harvey's place,
but it feels so far away. And now everyone knows my face for certain
if they didn't before. There's no way I can make it there unnoticed.

I step out of the alley and head east. The hairs on my neck and
arms rise. I pull my jacket tighter around me, keeping my head down
and hood up.

A rustle from one of the apartment buildings makes me jump,
and I spin around to see a woman about Mom's age peering out the
window at me. Our eyes meet, and for a moment I'm frozen in place.

She brushes a hand over her cheeks, wiping away tears. Then
something even stranger happens.

She holds her fist aloft in a sign of solidarity.

Without thinking, I return the woman's gesture.

She pulls closed the sash over her window and I continue down
the street. *What just happened?*

I stick to the shadows as much as I can, and my thoughts continue drifting to Enid, Bianca, and the rest of my friends. Did they see the broadcast? Are they safe?

Within just a few blocks it becomes apparent I'm terribly exposed. That woman is only the first of more than a dozen to catch my attention and raise their fist in solidarity. For weeks, I've been hiding in the shadows, afraid of Paragon or the Directorate finding me. After that speech, I finally understand my place.

The people need to see me. *Maybe I should be noticed.*

Now that the truth has come out, the Directorate and Paragon can't come at me directly without making my case for me. And with all these people watching the streets, a sense of confidence, of peace, settles over me. I lower the hood and pull my hands from my pockets. Let them see me. Let everyone see me.

Even if the Directorate arrests me right now, I am convinced that I am exactly where I need to be.

A man who hides behind The Shield is safe. A man who raises The Shield is the Hero. Celeste told me that people are defined by how they rise and inspire. Did she know, even then, that this would be my path?

With confident strides, I move along the sidewalks toward Lettuce Eat. The blinds are closed in most of the homes, but nearly every building I pass has someone in the window watching me walk the street at midnight. Each of them raises a fist and I acknowledge them with a nod of appreciation.

For several blocks, the hum of a vehicle's engine follows at a distance. The Directorate or Paragon, most likely. If they arrest me with people watching from their windows, they are only adding fuel to my fire.

After about a mile walking out in the open, under the streetlights, an unmarked vehicle cuts me off, narrowly missing me as I cross the street. I jump back and try to see inside, but the windows are darkened.

That can't be good. Paragon had vehicles like this one.

Glancing upward, I see several people watching from apartment windows. One girl holds up her phone, recording the events. Steeling my resolve, I hold firm on the sidewalk as the rear window rolls down.

Reaching Lettuce Eat was never going to be my final stop. Enid didn't know it, but somewhere deep down, I did.

To cut off the head of the gorgon, I have to enter the gorgon's den.

A muffled shot emits from the window. Warmth spreads through my shoulder and out into the rest of my body. I stumble, then fall to the pavement. Growing darkness swallows the streetlights as I'm lifted off the ground.

Part Three

"THE CITY OF ELPIS HAS REACHED A CROSSROADS. While Paragon and the Directorate work together to build a better, stronger future for all, radical leader, Ugene Powers, in his jealousy, would oppose us, hijacking our network to spread his message of hate. He attacked your city and filled your heads with lies. He planted the seeds of doubt—a doubt which could destroy what remains of humanity. A doubt which could destroy everything we have built and everything we continue to work for. My fellow survivors, I implore you. Do not let him win."

~ Directorate Chief Seaduss
Live

39

BRILLIANT GREEN EYES SHINE FROM SUNKEN, SLEEP-deprived sockets, peering at me with curious innocence. *Celeste.*

I spring upright to find myself in a Paragon dorm room. Everything smells lemony clean, like home. Dozens of lights on the building across the street give the otherwise dark dorm room an eerie glow. A bookcase is stuffed into the corner, but only one book rests on the shelf. *The Fabric of the Cosmos.*

Celeste sits back on her heels, head cocked to the side like a curious bird. She doesn't say anything.

I rise, my head spinning. This is a dream. It must be a dream.

"What's going on?" I ask.

Celeste motions toward the window.

Suddenly, all the lights in the city go out, and the sky becomes a swirling mass of stunning shades of blue and purple and black. The motion of color propelling around the stars is hypnotizing. It's the same sky she showed me in her room the night we met.

The stars themselves begin to move. Some fall down away from one constellation, others grow larger, brighter as if moving closer. Then all the stars shift, surrounding the broken constellation, creating a cage around it.

No. Not a cage.

A shield.

The stars in the shield begin spinning in a circle, around and around and around the broken constellation, closing in on all sides. A grouping of new stars rides in, and the resemblance to a man on horseback is almost uncanny. The shield breaks, the fallen stars gather together in his arms, then everything stops.

All the swirling colors.

All the pulsing stars.

Everything is still. Peaceful.

I press my hand to the cold window, my breath leaving puffs of condensation on the glass, and trace out the new constellation, creating a point on the brightest star. I step back and look at the image.

It's a map of downtown! The brightest star is right where the steps of the Administration Building would be, and the broken constellation is Paragon Tower. Surrounding them, thousands of stars fill the street around both locations.

I spin around to see if Celeste will tell me anything more, but the room is empty. On the edge of the bed, the book sits open to page seventy-one. At the bottom of the page is Celeste's note on the diagram above it. I read this before but didn't really understand what she meant. *To change the fabric, one must reach out and affect the true point.*

It still doesn't make much sense. Changing the fabric could be about changing how this city works, but what is the true point and how does one reach out for it? I'm still missing something. Celeste once told me books required finesse to bring out the right meaning. I assumed she spoke metaphorically about telepathy. Could it be possible that she was speaking of this book?

I turn back to the window as the condensation fades away, leaving a faint, smudged trail of the map. And the single brightest star in the center of it all.

Remember the stars.

That must be the true point.

But what is it?

"…*Ugene*…" A muffled voice calls to me. The room shifts like it's made of smoke and darkness surrounds me. Then something new coalesces around me.

Lemon cleaner. Cramped space. No light. Adrenaline pumps

through me, and at the sound of shoes scuffing the floor, I shift back in the dark, feeling the wall press against my back.

Mom will never find me here.

Where did that thought come from? It takes a moment to realize it was my own and not someone else.

Am I home?

No. I can't be at home.

"Ugene…" The familiar sing-song voice of Mom on the hunt filters through a crack in the door.

This isn't real.

It's a dream.

A memory.

I'm eleven, hiding in the front closet while Mom seeks me out. She tries to use her Telepathy to find me. I try my best to keep her from succeeding. But she will.

She always does.

I grin, pulling my knees to my chest to occupy a smaller space as her footsteps creak on the floorboards.

The doorbell rings. Mom's steps hesitate just outside the door to my perfect hiding place, then move toward the front door.

Dad's voice is muffled from the front entryway where he greets Mom. Whatever he is saying, he doesn't want to be heard. A moment later, Mom heads back toward the office again, toward me, as she continues her search.

The front door opens.

Mom continues to seek for me, but I strain to hear who is at the door. Maybe it's Bianca. She said she might stop over when they got back from lunch.

The voices at the front door are muted, and I steady my breathing to hear.

A man and a woman. One is Dad. The other is definitely not Bianca.

Curious, I inch closer to the door and press my ear to the crack to hear their conversation, aware that Mom might find me now.

"…future…You knew…coming, Gavin," the woman says. It's still hard to be sure if I hear the words right.

"Not of…" Dad says. "…development…don't…still time…"

She responds, but I can't hear her.

The door to my hiding spot flies open, and I jump back. Mom catches my hand, grinning, then puts a finger to her lips.

"Now we will both hide and see if Dad can find us," Mom says quietly, glancing over her shoulder out of the office. The entryway is just around the corner. "But we can't make it easy."

The two of us squeeze into the narrow space at the back of Dad's office closet, behind a false wall from a time before the war, before Elpis, and huddle down. Mom brushes her hands over my head. For a moment, her touch leaves me dizzy, makes my head feel heavy and stuffed with cotton, but the sensation quickly goes away.

The voices from outside are impossible to hear.

And the two of us cower there in the false wall, waiting for Dad's turn to seek. But Dad has never joined our game before.

40

COLD PRESSES AGAINST MY CHEEK AND MY EYES DRIFT open to find my head resting against a tabletop. I ease upright, but when I pull my arms back, something bites into my wrists. Restraints. Zip-cuffs bind my wrists together with an extra tie to connect me to a post on the tabletop. My senses jump into high alert as my pulse quickens.

No sounds emanate from the hallway. I close my eyes and focus, only to be greeted by deafening silence broken by the hammering of my own heart.

Whether it was Paragon or the Directorate, I'm not sure, but they must have tranquilized me and brought me here. Even if this is what I had expected, terror at being locked in this place without my friends to help me escape seizes me in a vice-like grip. My pulse thunders in my ears.

I cautiously reorient to my surroundings, my eyes darting around the room. Plain, off-white walls, smooth stone ceiling and matching floor. The chair beneath me is cold even through my clothes, sending a shiver up my spine as I consider just how completely I am stuck in the seat.

A handful of chairs line either side of the table in front of me. No windows reveal the world outside. A single door is closed across from me, and it's probably Power-reinforced to prevent anyone from getting in or out...or prevent any sound from escaping the room. Even if I manage to find a way to get out of the restraints, I won't be able to open the door.

I'm trapped.

I had hoped to end up in the gorgon's den, but now I'm not sure how to escape it and find Dr. Cass or Directorate Chief Seaduss.

The door beeps, and Forrest enters, wheeling a machine with the PD logo on the side into the room. *What is that for?*

"Ugene, I didn't expect to see you awake yet." Forrest's casual tone fills me with rage, and my chest heaves with angry breaths.

Forrest continues working with calm confidence, checking the tubing on the machine to ensure proper connection. He extracts an intravenous needle, holding it in one hand as he withdraws a different needle out of his pocket. "Keep still, please."

I drag my arms away from his as much as I possibly can, but the restraints prevent me from truly escaping. Forrest uncaps the second needle and approaches me.

I kick out. My foot connects with his shin and he yelps, stumbling back a step. But he recovers too quickly, and before I can kick again, he jabs the needle in my left bicep.

Warmth spreads out from the end of the needle with a slight tingle, then my arm goes limp. My heartbeat slows, but I can't be sure if that's Forrest using his Power on me or the drug he just injected. The leg on my left side feels like dead weight. I try to move away, but half of my body refuses. Forrest easily grabs my limp arm and secures the intravenous needle in place.

"What are you doing?" I ask, staring at the needle as he attaches the tube, then taps on the machine.

In seconds, blood pumps from my veins, through the tube, and into the machine. Forrest then connects a heart rate monitor to me, and he checks the numbers as it flickers to life. His lips compress. "You're angry with me. But not nearly as angry as I am with you. You told my parents, turned them against me, and put my sister in jeopardy."

What are they doing to Bianca? Did something happen to her parents? Maybe the Directorate acted against them after my broadcast.

"After your little stunt," Forrest continues, "my dad sent out a call to everyone to share their own evidence on social media where the Directorate can't stop them from spreading the truth. Photos and videos have poured in. Someone even posted a video of my team taking you off the street. Your insolence could cost this entire city the future it deserves."

The call to action… That must have been what Mr. Pond was talking about when I left.

"No smart comments for me now, huh?" Forrest asks. For the first time, I can hear real, simmering anger in his voice. Forrest has always been cool and collected, even in the face of adversity. This anger is new. "I knew you were trouble, even as a kid. A cocky little know-it-all who thought he had all the right answers. But you don't. You have no idea what you've done."

I close my eyes and tilt my head toward the ceiling. Blood loss is starting to make me light-headed, but only when I move.

"I don't understand what you were thinking," Forrest snaps. "We were making real progress at Paragon. Now everything is at risk. It's like you're trying to destroy the last of humanity."

Forrest checks the machine once more, then heads for the door, where a quick bioscan hums before opening it. Before he leaves, he glances back at me. "Dr. Cass and Directorate Chief Seaduss will be along to talk to you. I suggest you cooperate."

Then the door closes, and the lock clicks into place behind him.

This is it. No one knows where I am. Paragon could keep me like this forever, as long as they balance how much blood they are taking to avoid sending my body into shock. The fact that I'm not in a bed gives me hope that they won't keep me forever.

Hope is swiftly dashed when I realize Paragon may take what they need and dispose of me afterward. Like they tried to do to Jayme.

Why did I think capture would be to my benefit?

Terror presses on my chest as the walls of the room seem to close in around me. The injection that numbed half my body wears off, turning that half of my body into a mass of pins and needles. Flecks of black dot my vision. I can't regulate my frenzied breathing and begin thrashing awkwardly against the chair. Each yank and twist is less controlled than the last until the little energy in me drains away. I settle back with a whimper.

If I can't get out of here, they will have everything they need.

The door beeps.

41

DR. CASS STROLLS INTO THE ROOM AND SITS AT THE table to my left, glancing at the transfusion machine before giving a satisfied nod. As always, she is dressed immaculately like an upstanding corporate executive. She folds her hands in her lap.

Hilde is in the corner—as always, close at hand—with that tablet she carries like a child. Cradling it.

A bulk of a man with broad shoulders and unnaturally huge muscles ducks into the room. His cold gaze locks on me, making the room much frostier.

I would recognize that face anywhere: Directorate Chief Seaduss.

"This is him?" Seaduss asks, resting his fists against the tabletop as he leans forward to examine me. The table creaks under his weight. "He doesn't look like much."

"He's liquid gold," Dr. Cass says, but despite the cool tone, her eyes dart anxiously at Seaduss. "Ugene, I have to say you surprise me. When I first brought you into my program, I was under the impression you were interested in the science behind Powers. I expected great things from you; real interest in changing the world." She's like my mother when she lectures me, starting first with how disappointed she is. But this woman is nowhere close to being my mother. "Imagine my disappointment when you left just when we were on the verge of a breakthrough."

Left? She made it sound like I ran away from home instead of fleeing a deadly research program. "You said it yourself. Wisdom is a moral duty," I say, throwing her own words back at her from an old interview. "I have an obligation to share it."

Dr. Cass flinches, but her voice is steady, with a hint of sincere hurt. It's almost convincing. "Do you know how special you are, Ugene?" Her face lights up with happiness. Real, pure happiness. It sickens me. "You are everything I hoped for and more."

Escape. I must be able to escape somehow. *Think, Ugene. Think!*

My hands are restrained, but my legs aren't. What can I do with them?

"Alas, no real progress can come without its setbacks." Dr. Cass sighs, again, casting a cautious glance at Seaduss so quickly I nearly miss it. "And we've had our share."

Seaduss straightens, crossing his massive arms over his thick chest, and Dr. Cass stiffens. *She's afraid of him.*

Seaduss's fancy suit doesn't fool me anymore. Not after discovering what they've been doing.

I need out of here somehow. I think I read something about breaking restraints like this over the knee. But they have to be tight, and I can't do it with the extra tie locking me to the table. Somehow, I need to trick them into releasing me from the table.

"You are extremely troublesome," Seaduss says. "That broadcast has created quite a stir. However, when your little revolution dies, people will return to life as they know it because it's comfortable. Easy. They will forget you."

What kind of stir did I create? I can only hope it's one that leads to change. Or at the very least a chance to escape. Forrest mentioned the videos and photos, but just how much of a difference are they making?

Seaduss casts a menacing smile at me, and my stomach twists. Dr. Cass averts her gaze to the machine as if it needs monitoring.

"Your friends are going to die fighting this battle for you," he says.

"They know the risks," I say. I can't let him intimidate me, even if the idea of my friends dying scares the crap out of me. They do know the risks, but I don't want them taking those risks.

Hilde observes from the other side of the room, staring at me intensely, face set in deep concentration. Now that I recognize her using her Power, I know what she's trying to do, but it won't work. She won't read me. She can't.

Mom put up a wall on my mind. That's what she did in the false wall when I was eleven. I never felt her Power like that before, or since. It explained why Madison and Terry couldn't read me, why Hilde struggled so hard to break in back at Paragon during our final escape. It also explains why Willow's influence on my mind isn't as strong as it is on others.

Mom was preparing me for this like she knew this day would come.

Seaduss prowls toward my chair, sitting on the edge of the table in front of me. It groans in protest.

I press my back deeper into the chair.

The way he examines the tube drawing my blood makes me uneasy, and when he turns those icy eyes on me, any hint of his humanity is gone. "Do you know what happens to dogs who bite their owners, Ugene?"

I don't answer.

Seaduss's thick lips thin in a tight line. "They are put down. For the safety of everyone. Radicals are like rabid dogs. We need to find them all and put every last one down…for the safety of everyone in this city."

I raise my chin in defiance. "Safety of everyone, or just a select few?"

Seaduss stiffens but is quickly distracted by Hilde as she approaches Dr. Cass and shows her something on the tablet.

I cock my head to try and get a closer look.

Dr. Cass politely pushes her chair back to excuse herself, but no matter how much she tries to act calm, the fear in her eyes gives her away and she can't meet Seaduss's pressing gaze.

"What is it?" Seaduss barks.

"A security breach at Paragon Tower. I'll deal with it."

So I'm not in Paragon Tower.

The Protectorate had some sort of schematic for the building, and I have a bad feeling now that their intentions are more malicious than Willow would ever admit. On the other hand, they might be searching for me. Seaduss boasted that my friends would die. Are they walking right into a trap?

Seaduss grabs Dr. Cass in a tense grip. She winces, but he doesn't relent. "This is your fault. If you can't take care of the mess you've made, then I have no further need for you."

Dr. Cass's face turns ashen, and her elbows pull tighter against her body. Her gaze is frozen on his. "I will." Despite all the signs indicating otherwise, she sounds confident.

Willow was right. Doc was right. If even Dr. Cass is afraid of Seaduss, then he is the real threat. I assumed Dr. Cass was the big fish, but she's just one of his pawns.

Seaduss releases roughly and Dr. Cass stumbles a step away. To her credit, she doesn't rush to the door as I would. Instead, she smooths out her suit, raises her chin, and strolls out the door proudly. Hilde shoots a deadly glare at Seaduss as she follows Dr. Cass, but his attention is already back on me.

"It must be nice to remain ignorant of your own blame in all of this," I say.

I'm seeing stars before I even feel the sharp, pulsing pain in my jaw. I didn't even see him move.

"Do you have any idea the shitstorm you've created, Ugene?" he asks, folding his arms once more. I swallow and shrink down under his gaze. "You have no idea what kind of danger we all face without proper order."

"Enlighten me," I say, and despite a desperate attempt to sound in control, my voice quivers. I squirm in my chair, prepared for another backhand.

Seaduss's smirk is more like a snarl, baring sharp white teeth— or maybe they just seem sharp to me. "Without laws, without order, people with Powers descend into chaos. They use their Powers on each other, and civilization falls apart. Only through a balance of

Power, using our tools for a greater good, can we remain safe. But an epidemic has spread through this city. People with regressing Powers turn to lawlessness, threatening the balance we so desperately need. In the last ten years, incidents of theft, abuse, and murder have more than doubled, and in every case, it was someone with regression acting out against others. We needed a solution before those infected spread regression and destroy what remains of our great city."

Infected? Is that really how Seaduss sees people with regression, as victims of some sort of disease?

"But you've put them in positions where they had nowhere else to turn," I say. "Poverty forced their hand. They had to steal to eat. And when they continued to fail, they turned to anger. It's easy to lose control and make poor decisions when you have no hope."

"You are right, but only partly, because your judgment is skewed by youth." Seaduss strides around the table, pulling out a chair across from me and sinking down into it. The chair squeals as he settles in. "It *is* easy to lose control when you have no hope, which is why I've chosen this path."

I frown. He can't really believe that what he's doing gives them hope? He's allowing regressed citizens to be stripped of their Power, or forcing them into service—and who knows what happens once he gets his hands on them. My thoughts wander to Bianca.

"You see, with Paragon's help, we strip them of that hopelessness and give them a new purpose." Seaduss folds his hands together over the tabletop. "Now, those same people who were the worst offenders are given a chance at redemption. A team of DMA and Paragon employees take each of the regressing citizens and tests them to see if they are fit for service."

"By injecting them with a brainwashing serum," I say, then hold my breath and watch his reaction. I can't be sure I'm right, but the evidence is there.

Seaduss grimaces. "That's a poor choice of words."

"But it only has a narrow margin of success," I say, sitting up straighter. "So what happens to the unsuccessful tests?"

Seaduss's glare is so utterly cold that it freezes me. He isn't answering, but he doesn't need to.

"You kill them." My voice cracks. "How many have you killed already?"

"Such sympathy," Seaduss says, shaking his head. "Those failures would have turned to further crime, and who knows how many lives we have saved by taking theirs. Order must be restored."

That's what Bianca said, back at the safehouse. Order must be restored. But this isn't order.

The fact that he won't give me a number tells me that it's more than he can count. Or maybe that he doesn't care enough to count. Either way, I find it extremely disturbing. "So, you kill them to protect countless others. How does that not make you more of a danger?"

"Any great leader throughout history has learned that to restore order, some sacrifices must be made." He waves a dismissive hand. His words are dangerously close to what both Noah and Willow have said. "In another ten years, when regression is a memory and crime is nearly obsolete, people will forget how we came to that point. They will only be happy we arrived."

I crinkle my nose in disgust. "You think you're a hero. So, is this what the Purification Project is? Brainwashing regression away and creating a so-called perfect society?"

Seaduss blinks, probably wondering how I learned about the project. "You certainly have been busy, and again, you use a gross oversimplification. We can't brainwash regression away. Instead, with Paragon's help, we will create a pure line of children in the future, children who won't have to worry about losing their Powers, or not having one at all. I would think that you, of all people, would be thrilled at that prospect."

I've grown quite tired of people believing I would do anything to be ordinary. There was a time I might have made poor choices, but a line exists, and this clearly crosses it.

Back in Pax, I assumed the dots all connected to one conclusion, absolute control. I assumed the Directorate wanted to force out everyone with weaker Powers to make more space for those with stronger Powers—which they are doing by forcing people into service or death. But if expansion into the Deadlands isn't the problem, as the very existence of The Shield has proven, then control isn't the only answer. Seaduss is talking about pure bloodlines. Selective eugenics.

A true Purification Project.

But something else still doesn't make sense.

"I've read the reports about radioactivity in the Deadlands," I say. "And something changed three years ago. The calculations shifted dramatically and the projection for how long it would be to live safely without Powers swayed in our favor. We don't need Powers to survive anymore. So why would you try to purify our bloodlines if it doesn't matter?"

Seaduss laughs. "You aren't listening, Ugene." The speed with which he approaches forces me back reflexively into my chair. After turning off the machine and removing the needle from my arm, Seaduss pulls out a switchblade and cuts the tie holding my wrists to the table, then drags me to my feet. "Come see for yourself."

The room tilts from the sudden motion. I've lost too much blood. Maybe only ten minutes or so connected to the machine, and possibly only a single pint of donation, but still enough. The drug Forrest injected has mostly worn off, with the exception of a strange mixture of cold pain and numbness in my foot.

Seaduss pulls me into a wide hallway, and I glance around, leaning against him for support. The walls are covered in eggshell paint with matching half pillars pressed against them. Black marble tiles flecked with gold cover the floor. It only takes a moment before I recognize this place.

I'm in the Administration Building.

42

SEADUSS CALLS AN ELEVATOR AND WE RIDE UP TO THE top floor. His grip on my arm will likely leave a bruise, but there's no way I can shake him free and I highly doubt he will let go. The doors slide open, and we are met with a flurry of activity. More than a dozen administrative aides flit from one office to the next. DMA officers mill around a command room as we pass, nodding respectfully at Seaduss or scowling at me.

Those with eyes on me stiffen or jump a few steps back like I have a contagious disease. *Do they think I'm infectious?* Jaws slacken and most people stop mid-stride.

My notoriety is known even here, it appears.

The hush inside the building allows the noise outside to filter through. A mass of voices rising in chaotic protests. Seaduss hauls me toward the sound, through massive wooden doors into his office, a notably large space. On one side of the room, plush black chairs with wooden legs face each other with a coffee table between. On the other, a wide, tall fireplace is surrounded by a sofa and chairs, much like a living room in some mansion.

Several other Directorate members are in the room, speaking hurried instructions to their aides, who move around sharing information. Forrest nods as one of the Directors speaks to him, his angry gaze falling on me. The Directorate is in full-swing deterrence.

"Out!" Seaduss barks the command over all other voices, and everyone scrambles to obey. "Pond!"

Forrest halts in the doorway. His shoulders immediately tighten.

Seaduss scares everyone, but he's just a man. What could he possibly be capable of that would make them all jump like this?

"Here!"

Forrest takes a step backward before turning and approaching, his chin tucked against his chest.

Seaduss shoves me onto a sofa. "I want to know what's happening at Paragon," Seaduss says.

While the two are engaged in conversation, I concentrate on tightening the zip-tie cuffs until they bite into my wrists. If I want to break them, I need them to be much tighter.

Forrest nods, clutching his tablet tight against his chest. "Last I heard, a group of radicals infiltrated the building on the lower levels, but I haven't heard anything back from Dr. Cass yet."

Seaduss grinds his jaw. "Get her on the phone now. You don't go anywhere until you have something useful to report." He stabs a finger at the sofa beside me.

Forrest shoots a look of disgust at me, but he doesn't argue with his superior and sinks down, making sure to leave plenty of space between us. As much as all present company disgusts me, I can't help but feel a sense of satisfaction rising in my chest at the way Seaduss makes Forrest cower. At least he knows what it feels like.

"Boy, come." Seaduss starts toward the French doors on the far side of the room beside his desk, stopping once he realizes I'm not following. "Now."

I sigh, casually slipping off the sofa. While my insides may be churning in a mass of sickening nerves, I refuse to give either of these two the satisfaction of knowing just how much they scare me.

The second Seaduss opens the doors, the noise from the street turns from a muffled din to a roar. I edge toward the sandstone balustrade, placing my sweating palms against the cool stone and leaning forward to get a better look at the chaos below.

Hundreds of people fill the square outside the Administration Building, spilling into the street and around corners. While I can't make out what anyone is saying—it's all just a roar of noise—the overall protest is clearly directed at those in this building. At the Directorate itself.

Blockading the Administration Building, DMA troopers make perfect lines, three rows deep, surrounding the building on all sides, but the crowd has pushed them back from the square. Over the cacophony of voices, one announcement loops repeatedly.

"Citizens, for your own safety, please return to your homes or we will be forced to take further action."

But no one cares. They press on, hundreds—thousands—of bodies shout in protest. The first row of troopers hold blast shields up to protect against occasional projectiles thrown from the crowd—bricks seem like a popular choice, along with other objects. The second row points guns at the crowd, but no one fires. The final row holds, but occasionally the crowd is thrust back by a gust of air. The protests are about as peaceful as they can be so far. All it will take is a spark to ignite them.

"This is what happens when people believe they can use their Powers however they choose," Seaduss says, folding his hands into his pockets as he steps up beside me. "Perhaps you are right, and we are removing some of their freedoms, but the end result is worthwhile. Prosperity. Security. To affect significant change, you have to be willing to take significant chances."

I shake my head. "Your security is false. When you lose freedom, what do you have left? That is what we fight for. Our freedom. It saddens me that you don't recognize that."

Seaduss stares blankly at me. He doesn't understand. He genuinely believes what he is doing is the only way. *He's deluded.*

"Why are you willing to risk your future for this cause, Ugene?" Seaduss looks out at the crowd. "You know how this will end for you."

I do know. Doc made it clear to me when we spoke in his office. My future doesn't exist in Seaduss's vision. I wasn't sure if Doc was right at the time, but now I know for certain. When I lowered my hood in the streets last night, I knew either he or Dr. Cass would come after me and I was happy to let them think they won. Because that would bring me here. Exactly where I need to be.

I gather myself up proudly, edging closer to the balustrade while turning to face Seaduss. "Even when light breaks through the darkness, darkness fights back," I say, quoting Celeste.

People among the crowd point up at the balcony where we stand. The roar of the crowd slowly shifts. Fists raise in solidarity toward us. I'm exactly where I need to be. Exactly where I wanted Seaduss to bring me. The chaotic noise transforms into a thunderous chant.

Unity! Unity! Unity!

The words bring goosebumps to my skin, and I square my shoulders. "If Powers are so important, if we can't make this city a base for equality, then what is my future anyway?" I raise a closed fist toward the crowd with my wrists still tightly bound together.

Seaduss yanks my arm down, which only enrages the crowd.

"I am neither the problem nor the cure," I say, emboldened by the mob. "I am simply the voice of the people, the face of their fight. And we've reached a tipping point. There's no going back. You brought me here, where they can see me. Things will only escalate from here, Director. And there is only one way this ends, whether I live to see it or not."

A vein in Seaduss's neck pulses as he clenches his jaw. The muscles in his shoulders and arms tense and flex. I can't be sure just how strong he is, but I have no doubt he could crush me with a single blow. In fact, I'm fairly certain he's considering it.

I grin, stepping closer as all the tension that's bound my muscles up tight melts away. My breathing evens out, more relaxed. Seaduss has played right into my hand.

He can't harm me here, in front of this crowd. Not now that they see me. Not now that their voices are raised in unity against him. Doing anything to me will seal his fate. He knows it. His gaze darts out over the crowd as red flushes his neck and face.

"It's over, Director."

His nostrils flare and he bares his teeth as he returns his rage-filled eyes to me. "You've forced my hand. Do it."

I cock my head to the side. Who is he talking to?

A crack thunders in the courtyard below. I rush forward and lean over the balustrade, watching in dread as the ground opens, revealing a deep, dark chasm beneath the mob. Screams break up the chanting. Dozens of people are swallowed into a pit of darkness. The ground closes back around them. I blanch, recoiling and turning my back to the horrific display of Powers.

Just like that, all those people are buried alive. My stomach rolls.

"End this and spare them," Seaduss says with dangerous confidence that borders on insanity.

"I can't. It's out of my hands now."

Something so powerful can't be done by one person. It would take a team. Swallowing down the disgust churning my gut, I force myself to face the ghastly scene. My quivering hands grip the balustrade in fear as the third line of DMA troopers raises their hands in unison.

But the people fight back. In seconds, everything has turned to pure chaos. Fireballs fly in both directions. Tear gas is tossed into the crowd, only to be volleyed back by a vacuous tornado of wind. Power-fueled attacks lob back and forth, rending gaps in the concrete, burning people alive on both sides of the line. DMA troopers fire their guns at the crowd, and dozens of people along the front lines fall to the ground, replaced by others. And then the seizures start, rendering the victims helpless, stripping them of their Powers—and possibly, killing them. The protest descends into battle. I couldn't end this if I wanted to.

All those people are in that courtyard because of me. Because of my broadcast. All those deaths are on my hands.

No, not my hands. This is all him. I turn on Seaduss. I dive at his waist, hoping to throw him off balance.

And at that moment, the whole building quakes.

43

BOTH SEADUSS AND I ROLL ACROSS THE BALCONY. MY head strikes the sandstone floor, and a white-hot pain shoots through my head. It takes a moment to remember where I am.

Seaduss rolls to his side, easily getting back to his feet. Before he can attack, I raise my hands over my head, pulling the zip-cuffs tight so they bite into my wrists, tensing my muscles with all the strength I can summon. With one mighty yank down, I jerk my wrists outward as I strike them against my knee. The ties snap, freeing my hands.

A breathless laugh escapes me, and I jump to my feet, running toward the office. Seaduss's massive hand clamps down on the collar of my shirt and hauls me backward off my feet, tossing me like a bean bag.

Seaduss stalks toward me, a sinister smile on his face.

"The tower!" Forrest yells, running out onto the balcony with us as I hit the balustrade.

Seaduss freezes at Forrest's shout, staring at the skyline.

Rubbing the aching pain in my shoulders, I twist around and peer through the stone balustrade.

Plumes of smoke and dust boil upward in a massive cloud around Paragon Tower, obscuring all but the top third from sight. The cloud moves outward through the buildings, rolling along the streets of downtown Elpis like a sandstorm, consuming everything in its path and shrouding all from sight.

People in the streets scramble toward shelter, forgetting the battle. The DMA troops also break formation and rush back into the building with citizens on their heels. No one cares who is fighting whom. They all just want to survive the blast.

The three of us on the Administration Building balcony also forget one another as the horrific scene unfolds. I leverage my body against the balustrade for support and rise as an intense, high-pitched whistle screams overhead. Then the tower begins to crumble, and the cloud of dust picks up speed. All the screams from the crowd below are swallowed up by the thunderous noise of the collapsing tower. But only one thought consumes me.

The test subjects still in the Tower...

Thinking of those poor people trapped in the collapsing building turns my entire body cold.

But the cloud of dust continues its journey ever closer.

I sprint for the door on the heels of Seaduss and Forrest. The sound of shattering glass convinces me to dive behind a nearby desk, the solid wood backing to shield me from shattered glass and other debris blasting inward. I tuck my head between my legs and cover my face with the front of my shirt to block out the swirling dust.

Then the world plunges into darkness. The only sound is that of the receding whistle and barrage of debris.

My chest heaves as light finally returns. I raise my head to find the once rich, pristine office now covered in layers of dust, debris, and broken glass.

Forrest claws out from behind a sofa, his dark hair coated in dust. He coughs, but sucks in too much air and ends up swallowing more dust from the air.

I keep my shirt over my mouth, fighting the same urge to cough. My feet are unsteady as I try to pull myself up, and my knees buckle, forcing me to throw my weight against the desk to avoid falling.

In the middle of the room, Seaduss lies on the floor, a coffee table toppled over on him.

I stumble in his direction.

A shard of broken table pierces his gut, pinning him to the floor.

He kicks his legs out, holding the wooden spike. A distant look has already turned his wide, shocked eyes toward the ceiling.

More than anything, I want to defeat this man, but I don't want it to be like this. He deserves punishment for what he's done, not death.

I drop to my knees, grinding debris beneath me, and wrap my hands around his.

"Forrest…Forrest help." My voice sounds distant, unlike my own.

Forrest stumbles over, covering his mouth with the sleeve of his shirt. He drops to his knees on the other side of Seaduss and stares. Just stares.

Seaduss gurgles blood, coughing it up as his hands fall away from the wood.

"He's already dead," Forrest says, climbing to his feet. "No healing can help him now."

I shake my head. "He's not dead yet. He's still breathing. Ro— Rosie. Rosie can heal him…" I press my hands against the jagged wound around the spike. Blood pours out over my hands, reminding me of Bianca's death. The slickness makes it hard to apply pressure.

"They're both dead." Forrest shuffles stiffly toward the door in shock. "It's over."

Both? He can't mean Rosie. Maybe…maybe he means Dr. Cass. She did go to Paragon. Maybe Forrest thinks she died in the collapse.

He disappears into the hallway.

I sink back on my heels as Seaduss's chest stops moving, and I stare at the blood on my hands. Heaviness weighs down my shoulders, making it impossible to move. I blink slowly, my head spinning, trying to make sense of what just happened.

This wasn't my plan. I wanted Seaduss to survive. I wanted him to see reason and face the decisions he made. Now he's dead. *He's dead. And Dr. Cass may be dead, too.* I needed them alive. I wanted to give the people the chance to choose. It isn't my right to decide their fate.

Without realizing what I'm doing, I begin wiping my hands on Seaduss's body, trying to clean off the blood.

Cries and screams from the streets shatter the silence pulsing in my ears. I stagger to my feet and shuffle toward the balcony, leaving a trail of dragging footprints on the dust-covered floor. My legs shake, and I stumble forward, catching my weight against the balustrade, wrapping an arm around it to keep from collapsing.

Dead bodies litter the square. Not nearly as many as I expected. Only a few dozen versus hundreds. Some people struggle to get up or bow over a fallen loved one, wailing. The glass in all the buildings as far as I can see is shattered. Citizens stumble out of buildings, dazed. Then I gaze at the gaping hole in the skyline where Paragon Tower used to be.

The Protectorate did this.

Willow did this.

Shock ebbs away as white-hot rage burns in my veins. I grip the balustrade so tightly it hurts my fingertips.

So much for a peaceful ending.

I push away from the railing to head back toward the shattered doorway, then freeze in my tracks as I come face to face with Forrest again.

Forrest glares at me, his hands balled into fists at his sides. "You are the worst kind of rabid dog," he says, his voice empty, void of his humanity. "You've ruined everything."

Light warps around him and my jaw drops. I've never witnessed a Power like that before. It must be off-the-charts Divinic Manipulation.

Forrest's fist slowly rises, then he flattens out his hand, shaking with fury.

His Power slams against my already weakened body like a sledgehammer and a scream rips out of my throat, but my body won't move. I'm frozen in place, unable to do more than blink.

Forrest growls, "It's time to die."

Pure hate radiates from every part of him.

This isn't Forrest.

This is Super Forrest.

44

FORREST TURNS HIS HAND LIKE TURNING UP AN INVIS-
ible dial. As he does, the heat in my own body increases, burning
hotter and hotter. The intensity of it makes me tired, weak, but im-
mobilized, I simply stand there, unable to stop him. Sweat rolls down
my face and seeps out of every pore until I can't take it anymore. It's
too hot, like bathing in the heat of a volcano.

Something crashes against the tiled floor behind me.

"Forrest!" Bianca steps closer, scanning me before turning her
attention back to him. "Enough."

Forrest bares his teeth, not breaking focus from me. "Do you
understand what he's done?"

Bianca plants her feet beside me, cracking the tile as she digs in the
balls of her booted feet. She clenches her hands into fists, the muscles
in her body tightening and enlarging. It's more Power than I've ever
seen her hold. "What about what you've done? You lied to me, to our
parents. You killed me."

His gaze momentarily flicks to her and the heat lessens, but it only
lasts for a moment. "I didn't pull the trigger."

"You didn't stop the guards either," she says. "You were my
brother. Does that mean nothing to you?"

"It won't matter anymore if Elpis falls," Forrest says with a
conviction I would find unnerving if he weren't boiling me alive.

"Let him go." Bianca's hands ball into fists. "This is between us."

"No." Forrest turns up his imaginary dial and a groan escapes
through my already open mouth.

Bianca lunges at Forrest, twisting and grabbing his arm, then bending the arm around behind his back before placing several hard punches into his ribs.

His hold on me breaks, and I crumple to the floor, unable to catch myself before my head hits the ground. The tiles feel like ice through my clothes and I press against them, welcoming the cold.

Bianca sweeps her leg out in an impressive low spin that knocks Forrest off balance. His back hits the floor with a thump, but he recovers quickly. Too quickly.

I roll to my side, then push to my knees as my limbs all quiver. Forrest slaps a hand toward me and suddenly my body weighs too much, pulling me down, crushing me under my own weight. How can I possibly defeat someone with so much Power?

Beyond the shattered Administrative office, thunder and lightning rumble across the sky, striking against a translucent barrier around the building. Is the building under attack?

Bianca throws a punch at Forrest's jaw that makes a sickening crunch. As he works his jaw, I watch as stone retreats along his skin from the point of impact, as if he manipulated his own cells to turn into stone to protect his skin and bones from her punch. Her punch has little impact. *Except to infuriate him.*

"Why did you let them steal my memories?" Bianca asks, choking out the words.

Forrest turns to the side as he rises, keeping distance between himself and Bianca as best he can.

"I brought you back from the dead." Forrest raises his hands, indicating himself. "I did that, but you aren't thanking me for that, are you?"

The self-adulation makes my stomach twist.

Bianca moves so quickly I almost miss her lunging toward Forrest, wrapping an arm around his neck as she flips her body around behind him. The momentum slams them both to the floor hard enough to crack the tiles. I wince and move to help, but I can hardly move at all.

Forrest turns on his side and coughs up blood.

Bianca rolls across the floor, slamming her leg down against his chest with a half-scissor kick. More of Forrest's ribs crack.

I glance around on the floor for something to help. Anything. There's so much debris lying around that something must be useful in a fight.

Bianca kicks back onto her hands and springs forward for another attack as Forrest claws at the floor for leverage to get up, but his sister closes in on him quickly. Punch after punch connects with his jaw, skull, and ribs. Each time, he transforms his skin to stone, making her blows futile. Frustration twists Bianca's face into a snarl and she rises over Forrest.

"Why did you steal my memories?" Bianca raises a boot over his back.

The weight pressing down on me lightens, and I try to warn Bianca of the coming attack, but it's too late. Forrest flips over and grabs her ankle.

All the color drains from Bianca's skin. She stumbles to the right, grunting. Is she feeling the same effect as I am?

Forrest scrambles away as she rushes toward him, but her strides are slowed, and he easily evades her. Bianca pitches forward and thumps against the floor like an overturned statue.

I crawl toward Forrest, hoping to grab his leg, throw him off balance, put off his concentration, but weight once again crushes down on me, making my body feel five times heavier than it is. It flattens me to the marble tiles. I struggle to stay alert, let alone move, as more thunder and lightning hammer against the shield protecting the building. None of this will end well.

"Your loyalty to him was a weakness," Forrest says as he grabs Bianca's arm and twists her onto her back, releasing the arm swiftly— possibly out of dread that she would recover fast enough to get a hold of him. His hands move in a circle away from each other as he kneels over her. "I removed that weakness. To protect you. As I've always done."

Bianca turns her head to meet my gaze, and the haunting memory of her death returns...

...Bianca turns her head, meeting my gaze. Tears roll down her temple, and she shakes her head. Even from more than twenty feet away I can see her tensing her muscles, preparing for another strike. Then she screams, "Run!" A gunshot. Blood on the Paragon lobby floor...

Bianca screams, squirming on the tiles beneath Forrest. *He's torturing her.*

I muster all the strength I can summon and crawl toward them.

"I tried to help you," Forrest says.

I can't see his face, but his voice is thick with grief. Like she's already lost.

Bianca tries to buck him off, but Forrest snaps his hands closed into fists.

Her back arches off the tiles and her mouth opens in a silent scream. Blood trickles from her ears and the corner of her lips.

...Blood from inside Noah's body comes out of his pores, forming a swirling red cloud as Noah screams. The muscular Somatic body shrivels then withers...

Blood Power trumps a Super Somatic...especially being enhanced.

Tears blur the edge of my vision. He's killing her. He's killing his own sister. I claw closer. *Hold on. I'm trying to help...* The spike that killed Seaduss lies on the floor less than a foot from my fingertips. I redouble my efforts to reach it.

Bianca's back settles against the floor. Tears cleanse trails along her cheeks, dripping into her hair. Her voice is weak as she pleads with him. "Don't...don't make me...please..."

Forrest's shoulders slump, but he hasn't noticed my slow approach. Somehow, his Power continues to bear down on me without him even looking.

"It isn't supposed to be like this," he says, his voice thick with anguish.

"Fo-Forrest..." Bianca squeezes her eyes shut, taking a shuddering breath.

I won't let him kill her again. I can't. My fingertips brush the spike that killed Seaduss, and I bite my lip, then increase my efforts to grab it. Electricity from the lightning outside makes the hairs on my neck and arms rise.

Bianca notices just as my fingers manage to pull it closer and gives a small shake of her head. *Why doesn't she want my help?* Is it because this is her brother?

Bianca releases a ferocious howl, then kicks her legs out so hard her back rocks off the floor. Forrest soars through the air into the wall where his limp body embeds in the stone. The pressure from Forrest's Power vanishes and I collapse against the floor breathing a deep sigh of relief. Bianca rolls to her feet and stalks across the office.

"We need to go," I say, gasping and gulping down air. "The building is under attack."

"You go," she says, rolling her shoulders as she stops in front of Forrest. "I have unfinished business with my brother."

The coldness in her tone gives me chills.

I chew my lip. Should I leave her? It can't be safe with the Protectorate attacking.

"Why did you come back for me?" I ask, gazing down at her.

"I came back for answers," Bianca says. "You just happened to be there."

The statement is so matter-of-fact that my heart aches. The old Bianca would have been there to help me like she was during that final Survival test at Paragon. This girl is colder, more callous. Her fight isn't my fight. She has her own goals.

"Go." Bianca doesn't turn to me.

I hesitate. That's the same thing she said back in Paragon as she died. I left her then. I can't do it again. "Come with me."

Bianca spins around, glaring at me. "I need to do this. Please. Go."

Leaving her is a terrible idea, but I also know how stubborn Bianca is. She won't be swayed.

I pick my way to the balcony to assess the situation. My gaze sweeps over the chaos below.

Across the street, the courtyard in front of the Administration Building is a chaotic battleground. Men and women wearing DMA uniforms and street clothes launch Powers at each other on both fronts. A line of troopers struggles to stave off the flood of civilians attempting to break through their line and breach the front doors of the Administration Building. A handful of troopers in the back hold their hands toward the sky, perspiration beading on their brows as they work together to create a shimmering protective barrier around the building. I've never witnessed so much Power in one place.

Smaller groups of men and women usher people out of the courtyard to safety. The civilians attacking the building aren't just anyone. They're Protectorate mixed with the people who chose to fight back. Their anger toward the Directorate radiates from each strike as they throw everything they have at the Administration Building—concrete slabs roll off the translucent barrier; the ground quakes beneath DMA troopers; lightning spiderwebs outward along the shield. So many Powers. So much anger.

Amid the mass of warring bodies in the courtyard, I spot Enid fighting beside Miller and Jayme near the front lines. Their Powers batter in tandem against the shield blocking the building. A wave of earth and a funnel of wind followed by a barrage of lightning. I call out to them, but the roar of battle swallows my voice. *I need to get to them.*

Enid looks up—straight at me—and calls out, but I can't hear her any better than she can hear me. Someone in the crowd, or several someones, lifts an enormous chunk of the broken courtyard fountain high into the sky. My breath catches as it soars through the air toward the Administration Building. Miller and Jayme follow Enid's gaze.

The protective shield flickers as several DMA troopers are shot. In seconds, they bodies begin writhing on the ground. Only one kind of bullet has that effect. Their Powers are being removed.

I scramble for safety deeper in the office as the boulder races at the balcony, shattering the shimmering shield blocking the building. Thunder strikes and rocks the building, throwing me off my feet. The whole world lurches around me, tossing me to the floor. Walls and ceiling join the floor as marble tiles rise up to greet them. My ears ring.

A cloud of dust fills the air, and I cover my mouth and stagger to my feet. My head spins. Waving away the particles clouding the air, I call Bianca through the cloth of my shirt.

The air clears just enough to see the debris littering the floor and the gaping hole in the front of the building. I spin around in circles, limping from a gash in my leg, desperate to find signs of life.

"Bianca?"

What if that boulder crushed her?

"Bianca!"

She calls back to me, her voice muffled by a pile of debris. I climb toward the sound of her voice, over lumps of ceiling and steel rods. A steel support beam shifts and Bianca roars as she pushes the beam upward.

I rush to her aide, but my extra muscle is useless against the weight of the steel. "Are you hurt?" I ask, scanning her for signs of injury.

Blood mats her hair against her head where a gash flows. Dust covers her black tank top and leggings, with rips in the cloth here and there. Smaller cuts have already begun to cease bleeding. But the muscles in her body remain enhanced as she moves the beam an inch to the side where another mound of debris props it up.

"Broken ribs, and I think I dislocated my shoulder." She whimpers as she releases the beam against the mound of debris, then she sinks back against the body beneath her. Forrest's body. "I'll be fine. You go. Find your friends."

"I can reset your shoulder first," I say, remembering how I did it for Enid in the first Survival test at Paragon.

Bianca glances at Forrest before nodding and sitting upright. The two of them remain pinned beneath the debris, but if I reset Bianca's shoulder, I have no doubt she can get them out. I gently take her left arm and shift it into position. Bianca winces but doesn't complain.

"Ready?" I ask.

"Do it," she says, gritting her teeth.

I rotate the arm out swiftly, popping the shoulder back into place. Bianca grinds her teeth and tears water her eyes, but she doesn't make a sound.

I pull back and she begins rotating her arm, testing for motion. "I can help you out of here."

Bianca shakes her head. "Time is wasting. Find your friends. I'll deal with Forrest."

I hate the idea of leaving her here while the building is still under attack, but she's right. I need to find my friends. *I need to find Enid.*

I pick my way to the gaping hole at the front of the building to seek Enid out again.

Everything is eerily quiet. Bodies litter the ground, either rendered unconscious or killed by the removal of their Powers. Only a few people mill around, crouching beside bodies and using healing. But many of the injuries sustained can't simply be healed.

No sign of my friends.

The floor hums and vibrates beneath my feet, drawing my gaze downward.

The Protectorate has breached the Administration Building.

45

WITH HURRIED, THOUGH STAGGERED STEPS, I MAKE MY way out of the office to find an exit. If I can reach the lower floors, I should be able to find them. That's where Enid and Miller will be. I look up one last time, thinking of Bianca and how she yelled at me to leave. Still feels wrong, but I did as she asked.

The elevators are a poor choice with the building in such a state of destruction, so I head for the stairs, but the door barely budges. Something on the other side must be bracing it in place. I plant my feet against the floor and push with all my might, but it only moves an inch. Not nearly enough for me to slip through. But enough for me to see the rubble blocking the way. Destruction knocked free stone slabs and steel girders, which now prevent me from escaping.

Voices from the stairwell filter up to me.

"…check each floor."

Enid!

"I'll go to the top floor," she says.

"Enid!" I call out to her just as a thunderous rumble makes everything shake, swallowing my call.

Plaster shakes free from the ceiling and rains down on me.

"Enid," I call again, coughing.

"Ugene!" Her boots thump against the stairs as she ascends, climbing over collapsed bits of the ceiling. After a minute, her black hair bobs into view below. Her bright eyes shine as she looks up and sees me through the narrow gap in the door. "Oh, God. I thought you died."

Enid runs up the steps two at a time, leaping over fallen pieces of the building. She reaches the door and slips her fingers through the crack. I do the same and our fingers touch. It's such a small touch, but the gesture creates flutters in my stomach as relief washes over me.

"Where are the others?" I ask, my fingers gripping hers.

"Willow has some of them searching for remaining Directors," Enid says. "Jayme, Miller, and I broke off from the group to find you."

"What about Sho, Lily, and Rosie?"

"Sho and Lily are helping Willow," Enid says, clinging to me. "Rosie is helping organize healing for the injured with Doc."

That's good news. How does Doc feel about what Willow has done, destroying the Tower and killing all those people? Did he know it was part of her plan?

"Something is blocking the door," I say. "I can't move it."

Enid squeezes my fingers, then slips them back through the crack in the doorway to inspect whatever has me barricaded in. Just to be safe, I step away from the door.

Enid raises her hands toward the blockade, focusing all her intent on the problem. The blockade grinds against the floor. Her hands shake more violently with each second that passes. Enid whimpers then clenches her teeth and pushes harder. The shaking in her hands extends to her limbs and body, as if she is actually trying to physically push the blockade out of the way.

How much Power has she already used today? What if this is too much for her?

I brace my body against the door, gripping the handle for extra support, and push with all my might as she slowly grinds the rubble away. The gap sluggishly inches further open.

The moment the gap is wide enough, Enid releases her Power and rushes through, crashing into me as she throws her arms around my neck.

I pull her into a tight hug, afraid of letting go.

"I was so worried," Enid says against my neck.

I stroke her hair. "Me too."

"Willow was furious when you disappeared with Bianca," Enid says, pulling back just far enough to look me in the eyes. "She and Jayme had a full blowout with each other. And then we saw your broadcast and the videos people had recorded and sent into the station, and Willow convinced us we had to take action right away."

"She blew up the Tower, didn't she?"

Enid nods, nuzzling against my chest. "But we had no choice. If the Tower didn't come down, Paragon would have just picked up their research where they left off. The only way to get rid of the research was to bring the whole thing down."

"Did she clear the building?" I hold my breath, hoping, praying that no one was harmed when it came down.

"There wasn't time. We had to act quickly."

I recoil, a bitter taste in my mouth. The image of that dust cloud rushing toward the Administration Building rushes back. "You don't believe that."

"Wars are won through action, not inaction."

I flinch and pull away from Enid completely. Those are Willow's words. "She's manipulating you, Enid."

"You know what I suffered in that place," Enid says, planting her fists on her hips. "I couldn't allow Paragon a chance to restart and make another girl suffer like me."

This isn't Enid. This is Willow speaking through Enid. "No. The Enid I know wouldn't agree to destroy a building with thousands of people still inside. Willow is an Empath. I told you not to trust anything she says because she can Influence you to follow her."

Enid scowls. "I thought you would understand."

"Well, I don't, because this isn't you. It was *you* who insisted we shouldn't trust Willow back at The Shield. It was *you* who insisted we had to do something to save the people still in Paragon and under the Directorate's thumb." I step toward her, hoping, praying that I can get through to her. I slip my hand into hers. "Help me stop Willow."

Enid draws her hand back but doesn't pull it away. "You wanted to stop all of this."

"But I didn't want people to die." I dare to lean closer and place a kiss on her lips. Enid tenses, then relaxes against me. "We do this together," I say as our lips part. "Or not at all."

Enid blinks furiously, and her brows wrinkle together like they do when she's thinking really hard. Then her body shakes. "I helped her."

"It's not your fault."

"I thought...I believed..." Enid squeezes her eyes shut. "What did I do?"

"This was Willow's Influence. There's nothing you could do."

"Isn't this touching?" I hear a voice say behind me. I turn to see Terry step through the open stairwell door. His black hair is slicked back, though a few strands hang loose. Dirt covers his pale face.

Enid and I both jump back, but Terry seizes Enid's shirt and yanks her back, tossing her against the wall. Enid yelps. Before I have a chance to react, Terry raises a hand toward Enid's head.

Enid shrieks. "Don't. Please. Don't kill him. I'll do anything!"

What is she talking about?

Terry sneers. "The mind is such a fragile thing. Easy to plan hallucinations in one's mind."

My hands clench into fists so tight I can feel the tension all the way up my neck. I step toward Terry. "Stop."

"Ah!" Terry raises a finger at me. "Another step and I crush her mind into madness."

I freeze. Can he really do that? I can't allow this to go on. I have to stop him.

Enid's face contorts in terror, and she screeches and howls in agony in a way that makes my blood curdle. The sound bounces off the walls, echoing down the hallway, vibrating in my bones.

"What are you doing to her?" I ask, lurching a step closer. Furious with rage, sweat rolls down my temples.

"Forcing her to watch me torture you." Terry's tone is so blasé it turns my stomach. He chuckles and I want to punch him in the throat to stop the disgusting sound. "She can't handle much of this."

I bare my teeth, nostrils flaring. "What do you want?" Terry is a bully, and I've had enough of bullies.

"You." Terry inches closer. "Or that is, Dr. Cass wants you. She intends to restart her research, but she needs you to do it. I will receive a very generous stipend if I bring you to her."

"Forrest said she's dead," I say, my voice seething with the rage building in me, blocking all pathways to logic.

"She is very much alive," Terry says.

Enid's breaths are ragged as she cries, sinking down to the floor with her head in her hands, begging him to stop. Each of her pleas is a dagger in my heart. And with each dagger, my hatred toward him grows. I flex my hands out and back into fists as stiffness takes over my fingers.

"I can't get to her," Terry continues as if Enid isn't suffering abject misery at his feet. "But she is alive, somewhere beneath what remains of Paragon Tower."

Dr. Cass is alive? Some part of me knows I should manipulate this situation, outsmart Terry, convince him he's wrong and he's alone. Logic my way out of this. But the longer I watch Enid struggle, the less logic works in my favor and the more I want to destroy Terry, rip him apart, destroy him down to his very bones.

His Power is so much stronger than it was in Paragon. He never could have projected hallucinations in someone before. *And now he's torturing Enid.* I would do anything to stop him, and I can. I just have to be smarter. My muscles all coil tightly as my body turns rigid.

It's a struggle to keep my voice even with so much hatred burning on me. "Okay." I step toward him. "Let her go and I'll come with you."

A lie. He doesn't need to read my mind to know it. I won't go with him. I can't. I can't let him be rewarded for this. He needs to suffer like he's making Enid suffer.

"As you wish." Terry releases his hold on her, and Enid crumples to the floor in a heap.

"What did you do?" I growl, sneering.

"That sort of trauma takes a toll. Don't worry. She should be fine. But you…"

Terry's Telepathy slams against my mind like a jackhammer trying to break up concrete. He pounds at my skull with his Power again and again, pinching my head in a vice-like grip, squeezing tighter and tighter. Terry is trying to break the Wall Mom placed on my mind. *Maybe he can now.*

I hunch over on my knees, pressing my hands to my head as the cracks in the Wall spider outward. The world spins. Blood drips from my nose to the marble floor.

Terry hovers over me, shaking as all his Power focuses on breaking down the Wall.

Without the Wall, he can kill me. I can't let him win.

The thought is distant, as if it comes from someone else, a detached version of me watching from afar.

Every sound—the hum of the building, the grinding of stone against stone and steel, each booted foot moving over the ground in the floors below us—is like a hammer against my skull. Blood from my nose begins pooling on the floor.

"Stop…" The word is breathless, barely a whisper over the thunder in my head.

"I will break the Wall or kill you trying," Terry says, his voice strained from the effort. "Dr. Cass be cursed."

It requires every ounce of strength I can summon to put my hands against the ground and push myself upright. The muscles in my legs protest, wobbling as I suck in quick breaths to rise. I stumble, and my legs almost give out, but I reach out and grab Terry to keep from falling over.

"You never quit, do you?" Terry asks. His voice simmers with hate. "This is your fault. You left me to die in the desert. You left me in their hands while saving everyone else. I am what I am now because of you."

Trembling, I rise to my fullest height and do my best to stare at him, completely unintimidated. Blood trickles from my nose down across my lip. Every inch of me protests as his Power batters at my skull like a ram.

"Maybe, once I'm done with you, I'll make Enid forget who you were, too."

The implication of this statement takes a few seconds to sink in. *It was him. He stole Bianca's memories.*

My arms quiver violently as I clench my hands into fists. Logic is burned away by the fires of rage pumping through me. I'm not a great fighter, but Bianca taught me a thing or two during my time at Paragon. With my mind not working, and the rage dominating every cell in my body, fighting is the only answer.

My head weighs as much as a mountain, pressing down on my shoulders. I stiffen my spine. The world tilts again.

You won't touch Enid. He can't read the thought, but I feel it fiercely, burning through my body, giving me strength despite the drain his Power has on me. In a swift motion, I pull my head back, then ram it against his skull. The impact momentarily darkens my vision and my knees give out, but it worked. The contact is broken.

Terry stumbles away, and I grab his arm before I fall. Using him for leverage, I pull back my other fist and punch him in the kidneys. Terry doubles over, but I hold tight to his arm, thrusting an uppercut into his jaw. The impact tosses his head back and he twists his arm out of my grasp, retaliating with an ill-placed punch to the side of my jaw. I blink away stars as pain lances outward from the point of impact.

As he rights himself, working his jaw, I grasp either side of his head and yank his head down to meet my knee followed by a swift open-palm slap to each ear. Terry tries to stand up, but lurches to the side and falls over.

Adrenaline pumps through me, quickly dispersing the effects of his Power, though my nose still bleeds and my jaw throbs in pain. I can feel my lip puffing up at the corner of my mouth.

Finish him. I blink furiously to get the sweat out of my eyes, staggering a couple of steps as I seek out the owner of the voice before realizing it's my own.

Terry pushes to his hands and knees but tumbles onto his back. The slap to his ears must have affected his equilibrium.

I shuffle closer, then sink to a knee at his side. My speech is surprisingly slurred as I say, "You won't touch any of my friends again."

Terry laughs. A sound of madness.

The feeble fingers of his mental reach try to grab hold of my mind. I snarl, pulling back my fist, and jab him in the jaw once. Twice. Three times. Terry's body goes limp, and his eyes slip shut.

I sink to my knees and crawl to Enid's side, pulling her head into my lap as I lean against the wall. Laughter echoes in my ears.

My own laughter. The hallway darkens, and I close my eyes, welcoming sleep.

46

ALL IS DARK. I cAN'T BE SURE IF I'M FALLING OR STAND-
ing still. No sensation of motion makes my stomach tumble. No floor
presses against my shoes. No air brushes my skin. I'm in a void of
nothing. Experimentally, I move my feet, and find they shuffle as they
would over a floor, but nothing appears to be beneath me, and I can't
feel anything under my shoes.

This place isn't a dream or memory, as I've experienced in the
past. It's simply nothing.

Last I knew, I was fighting Terry in the hallway.

Am I dead? Panic captures me. Accepting death is one thing. Being
dead is another. Is Elpis free? What happened to my friends? I can
only hope their fates fare better than my own.

White lights blink to life around me. Hundreds of them.
Thousands. I move forward, reaching for one of the lights, but
it remains ever unreachable. Will the lights guide me like they did
through the streets of Elpis? I advance, my feet gliding over nothing.

A powerful female voice calls from the darkness. "Ugene."

I spin and gasp as a young woman with glowing green eyes steps
out of the darkness, her gown seemingly made of lights. Millions of
tiny lights pulse around her, casting a glowing aura surrounding her
slight frame. Black hair falls in ringlets over her shoulders. I'm unable
to look away from the woman in front of me. She is Celeste, yet she
isn't.

My head spins, and I press the heel of my palm to my temple,
trying to steady my thoughts. I step back. *What's going on?*

She cocks her head to the side much like a bird as she examines me. "Celeste...? Am I...dead? Where are we?"

"Death is not an absolute. Time is not linear," she says, and her voice carries both that youthful innocence I remember and a wizened understanding of things beyond my comprehension. She raises her hand, and the dots of light around us begin moving.

Stars. Those are stars, not lights.

None of this makes sense.

I watch the stars as they shift and swirl, then I glance again at Celeste. "That was you. Last night. The stars showed me the safest way to Bianca's house. That was you."

Celeste smiles, and it illuminates her smooth, youthful face. "I always knew you were special. I've walked this path countless times in countless ways to find this moment."

I watch the stars and notice they are making the same motion as those I saw in my dream. "How long have you been here?"

"A month. A century. A minute." Celeste raises her hand and pokes at the darkness with her finger twice, creating two stars. "As I said, time is not linear. There is no beginning. There is no end. Many believe their lives are a line from Point A to Point B." With her other hand, she makes a line between two stars.

"Others believe life isn't a straight line, but a zigzag from start to finish." She makes the motion, and the line shifts into a zigzag. "When really, our lives are more like a closed loop, and you can shift that loop, bend it, to connect at any point in time." She draws an infinity symbol between both stars, then flicks it with her finger and the stars begin shifting along the line of the symbol. A few times, they nearly touch at intersecting points, but never do. "This is the true path most people travel. But not you. Yours is different. It always has been and always will be." The stars come together along the loop, merging when the loop intersects. "Your path is malleable."

"Why?"

Celeste cocks her head curiously as if I should just comprehend. I wish I did.

"Because you make it so," she says simply, then plucks a single star from the merged point and holds it toward me in her palm. "To affect change, you must touch the true point."

"What is the true point?" I ask, reaching for the star. My fingers slip through it like it doesn't truly exist.

Celeste steps toward me, pressing the star into my chest. Afraid of being burned, a moment of panic surges through me, but I feel only the warm touch of her hand.

"Now," she says.

"What?"

"I've traveled this loop, searching for the true point. I've watched you die countless deaths seeking the path to the true point. It is now."

Pieces begin falling into place. I don't comprehend the full picture, but I understand well enough to get her meaning. Celeste has somehow lived forever and not long at all, and if the notes in her book are any indication, she has found a way to alter her place in time at the moment of her death. If she can do this, can I? Have I already, if I've walked this path so many times? The implications are enormous.

"You are talking about moving myself from one moment in time to another, right?" I ask, hoping I'm close to right. "Like time travel."

Celeste shakes her head. "Even the cosmos has limits. You cannot exist in two places at one time. To exist in one, you must not exist in it at the same time. It is not time travel."

If I can go to any other moment, I could save my father or my friends. I could prevent the collapse of Paragon Tower. "But I can do it."

"No."

The word hangs in the air, smothering the flame of hope blooming in my chest.

Celeste finally speaks, and her words make me bounce up on my toes. "*I* can."

"You can send me where I need to be, like at the Tower right before it falls," I say, stepping toward her. "I can stop Willow from destroying it."

"It comes at a cost."

"Anything."

Celeste's lower lip quivers and she turns her hands, examining them, then gazes at the stars, a distant look in her eyes. "If you go to the Tower and stop Willow, you will die, and your revolution dies with you. I have seen it before."

"But those people in the Tower will live." I don't want to die, but one death in exchange for the thousands in Paragon isn't a choice. It's a necessity. "I can't live with myself knowing I could save them."

"And what life will it be that they live?" Celeste asks. "If you save the people in the Tower, Seaduss survives and achieves his ambitions unopposed. Thousands more will perish under his direction. If you stay with him, his fate is fixed, as is Paragon's. The choice is yours."

My heart sinks. How many people were in Paragon Tower when it collapsed? Two thousand? Three? It doesn't compare to Seaduss' numbers.

When we were together at Paragon, Celeste read my aura and told me I would be faced with an impossible choice. So many choices crossed my path after her reading that I continually assumed the decision was made. Now I know better.

The choice was always ahead of me, a looming behemoth casting a shadow over everything I've done up to this point, waiting for me to come face to face with it. *At the true point.*

I either save thousands in the Tower and die...or save the city—and myself—and allow the Tower to claim its victims.

"The only path to true justice is through the fallout, or the battle begins anew," Celeste says, flicking the infinity loop so new stars begin traveling the path. "Restarting its course on the loop."

"Where do I go from here?" I ask, surprised at the tightness in my voice. Tears burn my eyes.

"Where you need to be." The sadness within me reflects in Celeste's brilliant green eyes.

I don't need to tell her what my choice is. Celeste already knows.

She probably always knew.

Wind caresses my skin, and I reach for her hand, afraid she will disappear. I never had a sibling, but I always saw Celeste as a little sister. I don't want to lose her again. "Wait, Celeste, will I see you again?"

"I am always exactly where I need to be." The stars that made up her dress scatter across the darkness, and her face fades.

"What do I do?" I ask quickly before she is truly gone.

"Exactly what you would always do." Her voice fades. "If given the right circumstances."

I rush toward where she stood, but the darkness recedes with each step, replaced by blinding light.

47

THE WEAKNESS IN MY LIMBS FROM TERRY AND FORREST abusing me with their Powers have vanished, in addition to the burning pain from gashes and bruises from battle and the collapsed building. For the first time since coming to Pax, I feel strong and clearheaded.

Time is not linear. I'm exactly where I need to be...

Thousands have already died at the Tower. Seaduss is dead, and if any members of the Directorate remained in the building, Willow will find them. What will she do once she discovers them? How many more need to die before Willow is satisfied?

This can't be what Doc wanted.

Enid's breaths come in short rasps as she lies with her head in my lap. A strand of dark hair curls over her eyes, and I brush it back from her face. What do I do with Enid to keep her safe? How long will she be like this? I scan the space around me and find we are no longer in the hallway. I'm sitting on a claw-foot sofa in an office with Enid's body draped across the length of the cushions.

Carefully repositioning her head, I slide myself out from beneath her and rise.

I'm exactly where I need to be. What does that mean?

The building no longer hums or vibrates. Whoever was using their Power on the structure has stopped. Willow probably had Naturalists creating a path through the wreckage to make the search easier.

With Enid safe for the moment, I search the desk drawers for something to restrain Terry. I can't do anything about him using his Power, but at least I can detain him for now. In one of the desk drawers, I find a package of zip-ties. It isn't perfect, but it will work. As I make my way to the hallway, I attach a few of them together so they make a long enough chain to connect his wrists together behind his back. Then I pull a strip of cloth from his own shirt and tie it around his eyes to blind him in case he wakes. His Telepathy won't be stopped by a blindfold, but it might be slowed.

I crouch over Terry, shifting him to his side and wrestling his arms into position, then securing his wrists together—but not too tight. He could break them easily if I pull them too tight. Standing over him, I chew my lip. I haven't felt so much hate for anyone since I attacked Forrest in the street. After considering his Power, I decide to wrap cloth around his head to block out sound from his ears. Another way to slow down his Power.

Bianca strolls down the hallway, Forrest's body tossed over her shoulder like a sack of flour. She walks as if he weighs nothing. What happened between them? What has she done to her brother?

"Did you find anyone?" she asks.

"Just Enid. The others are in the building somewhere." I grunt, trying to pull Terry up so I can get him into the office, but he's much heavier than I expect for someone so thin.

Bianca nudges me away with her toe and reaches down, grabbing Terry with one hand and easily hefting his body into the air.

"In there." I point at the office.

Terry is the one who altered Bianca's memories, but I wait until she starts fussing over Forrest in the office, restraining him, before speaking up. Terry now lies on the floor in the corner.

"Paragon used a Telepath to alter your memories," I say.

Bianca's back stiffens as she binds Forrest's ankles with multiple zip-ties. "How do you know?"

I glance at Terry. "Because he confessed."

Bianca spins around, following my gaze to Terry's prone form. In a few long strides, she crosses the room and I rush over to stop her. "Wait. I know you're angry, and I would love nothing as much as watching you beat him to a pulp, but if you hurt him, we may not get your memories back."

"Is that possible?" she asks, glaring at Terry.

I rub the back of my neck. "I don't know. But is it worth the risk?"

Bianca's hands clench and unclench as she contemplates how to deal with him. Ultimately, she huffs and returns to Forrest.

Electricity makes the hair on my neck and arms rise again, and flickering light from the hallway catches my attention. Then Miller's familiar voice echoes off the walls, "She hasn't reported, and she came up here. She must be up here."

I rush to the door and see Miller standing over Jayme. Lightning dances around Miller's body, controlled by his new rush of Power. He's prepared for a fight.

Jayme crouches beside the blood I left on the floor. "That can't be good."

"Miller!" I call out, realizing my mistake too late.

Miller spins, throwing a small ball of lightning through the doorway. I barely jump out of the way before the ball of lightning strikes the wooden frame right where I was standing.

"Ugene?" Miller steps through the door and a grin breaks across his face. "I told them you weren't that easy to kill."

The lightning momentarily winks out of existence as he claps me in a hug and steps back. Jayme joins us, scanning the room.

"You've been busy," Jayme says.

"Seaduss is dead, too," I say, just in case they didn't already know that. "I'm sorry guys, but I have to ask. Did you help Willow destroy the Tower?"

They exchange grim looks.

I heave a sigh. "Okay. I tried telling you before. Willow is an Empath. She can Influence people to do her bidding. If you helped, it isn't really your fault."

"We did what needed to be done," Jayme says, crossing his arms.

"No," I correct. "You did what she wanted you to do. We don't have time to debate about this right now, but all I ask is that you think for yourself. Would you really have killed thousands of people, many of them innocent victims, if she hadn't Influenced you to do it?"

Jayme opens his mouth, but I hold up a hand.

"No. Just think about it."

"I felt it," Bianca says from behind me. I spin around to face her. "Back at the safehouse, she tried to do it to me when we were alone, but I didn't fall for it. I let her think she did though."

"How?" I ask.

"Just acted like I was obeying her wishes when she tried to Influence me to stay put and not speak a word."

"No, I mean how did you resist?"

Bianca shrugs. "It just didn't work. Terry tried to read me once at training, and that failed, too."

They put a block on Bianca's mind. Why?

"Good." I can use this to my advantage. "I need you to do that again if she tries."

Bianca raises a brow. "It isn't something I consciously do. It just happens."

As if we'd summoned her by talking about her, Willow's voice emanates from the hallway. Jayme calls her in, and in moments the office is occupied by thirteen us. It makes the space cramped.

"You didn't tell me he was up here," Willow says to Sho over her shoulder as she meets my gaze. "You have some nerve, Ugene."

I sneer. "Don't start." I take note of everyone present—and the one person missing. "Where's Leo?"

Sho's eyes cast down at his feet. Jayme and Miller exchange uncomfortable glances. Lily bites her lip.

"He didn't make it out of the safehouse," Jayme says. "He died in the blast."

Momentary grief presses down on me. Leo was the last of my friends from high school, aside from Bianca who doesn't even remember me. We've lost so much…too much.

"Go find Seaduss," Willow says to Sho, pulling me out of my sorrow. "Bring him here."

"Seaduss is dead," I announce, freezing everyone in place.

"You're sure?" Willow asks, raising a brow.

"I saw it myself. So did he." I wave a hand at Forrest's unconscious body.

Willow stalks toward Forrest's unconscious body on the floor where Bianca bound him up. She crouches at his side and brushes a hand over his forehead. The gesture is almost compassionate.

"Do you know him?" I ask.

"A long time ago," Willow says, her voice distant as she gazes down at him. As if sensing we've noticed some momentary weakness, Willow's back stiffens and she stands up, testing his zip ties before nodding. Then she turns on me. "How did Seaduss die?"

"You killed him."

Willow smirks. "I think I would remember that."

"When you destroyed the Tower," I clarify, "he died in the fallout. If it matters, Terry says Dr. Cass is looking for me, so she must have survived your attack."

"Where is she?"

"I don't know. What would it matter?"

"We won," she breathes as if overwhelmed with relief.

"No. We didn't." I shake my head. How could she not understand what she's done? "There were innocent people in those buildings who died because of your actions today."

Other members of the Protectorate enter the office, dragging prisoners with them. *No, not prisoners. Directors.* Only two of them survived the attack. Two out of seven. Director Collins with her graying sandy hair in disarray around her wrinkled face, and Director Shielding with his eyes wide in apparent fear. Both are handcuffed with gags in their mouths. Willow waves for the Protectorate members to line up the prisoners against one of the walls. It strikes me that this is reminiscent of a firing squad.

"What are you doing with them?" I ask, stepping closer.

Chase's muscles tense and he shifts in my direction, making it clear that if I touch her, he will react. I don't know how I missed it before. Willow and Chase are no different than any other Psionic and Somatic. Just like the bullies in high school, or Terry and Derrek. Willow is the hunter, and Chase is her weapon. *That alone should have tipped me off.*

"Giving them a taste of their own medicine," Willow says with so much disgust dripping from her voice that my skin crawls. "Bring them over to the line." She waves at Terry and Forrest.

Chase and another Protectorate Strongarm I don't know grab the bodies and drag them toward the far wall.

Bianca steps between Willow and Forrest. "He is my brother. He is my problem."

"Move out of the way if you don't want to join them," Willow snaps.

It is a firing squad.

I rush up to Bianca's side. "Willow, stop. The fight is over. Seaduss is dead, the Directorate is finished. Let's find Dr. Cass and call this victory."

But it isn't a victory. Far from it.

"Enough people have died today," I say.

"Move or be moved," Willow commands, but I stubbornly refuse to move. "So be it."

Chase grabs my arm and yanks me out of the line of fire.

I snatch my arm away, but Chase clutches it even tighter the second time, pinching my arm in his strong grip.

"The Protectorate. The Directorate. Different name, same face," I say, throwing as much of my anger at Willow as I can. "I suspected as much from the start, which is why you didn't like me. Stop fighting. Use your Power for good."

"What do you think I'm doing?" Willow snaps.

"This isn't for good. You have the Power to make the battle stop. What more can you want?"

"You started this with your package and your broadcast. Now I'm forced to finish it before the Directorate has a chance to regather their strength and apply their final blow."

I don't struggle as Chase pulls me away. "This can't be what Doc wanted."

"He wanted this to end," Willow says, pulling out a gun and raising it at Forrest. The two Protectorate members who brought in the prisoners raise their guns as if she pointed them herself. I can't let her do this. I can't let her remove Powers, kill people, and make these helpless men responsible for her crimes. "He said as long as the Directorate or Paragon stand, we can never truly win." Sweat rolls down her face from the fatigue of using so much Power. She's using it, even now. "You forced my hand. And now they can no longer stand."

Tears roll down the desperate Directors' faces, leaving streaks in their dirty cheeks. Both shake their heads, trying to speak through their muzzles, eyes frantically pleading for me to stop Willow. I have no love for these people and what they allowed Seaduss and Dr. Cass to do, but that doesn't give us the right to shoot them.

Without warning, Willow fires at Forrest. Bianca bellows and throws herself at Willow, but too late. The bullet strikes Forrest in the shoulder, only slightly thrown off the mark by Bianca's sudden attack.

The other two fire as well. Miller sends a bolt of lightning at each of the Protectorate members, but too late. The two remaining Directors recoil against the wall and slide to the floor, writhing in pain.

Chase releases me to rush to Willow's aide. I fall to my knees beside the Directors, inspecting the wounds. One to the knee and one to the gut.

"Hold on, it's okay," I attempt reassurance as a fight breaks out behind me.

The gut-shot isn't too serious, and I hold on to hope that he will survive. *Director Shielding.* That's who this is. Director Shielding—the Director of Social Welfare—begins seizing and choking. *Power-removing bullets!* I rip the gag out of his mouth so he doesn't choke to death on the frothing foam bubbling through his lips.

Bianca slams her back into the wall beside us, attempting to dislodge Willow, who is strangling her as Chase punches her in the ribs.

I roll Shielding on his side so he won't choke on his own saliva. The woman beside him is Director Collins, the Director of Business Administration. She watches Shielding with wide, terrified eyes as she clutches her leg and cries through her gag. Neither of their Powers are useful in this fight, or in healing.

Bianca grabs Willow by the neck and flips Willow over her body, right into Chase.

I pull the gag from Director Collins's mouth.

"Do something," she commands in a shriek.

"I can't. There's no stopping it once it's started. The serum is already in your veins."

Collins whimpers and smacks her head against the wall. Then a bout of seizures rocks her body.

Chase flies past, his back skipping across the floor, and Bianca launches through the air, landing over the top of him and throwing fierce punches at his ribs. Chase kicks his legs to try and force Bianca off, but she has a hold on his vest, and all he does is make her buck. Bianca pulls back a fist and throws a bone-cracking hook into his jaw.

This is chaos. This isn't how we end the struggle.

Jayme rushes at Willow as she scrambles back to her feet. She grabs his leg, slamming him into the ground. I wince as she pounces on him, pinning his arms as she punches him in the kidney.

Miller's entire body pulses with lightning as he charges two Protectorate members. They scatter, but he throws lightning ropes at their legs and yanks them to the ground. As they wrestle against his Power, Miller strikes each of them with lightning darts in the chest. Both of them stiffen suddenly, then slump against the floor.

Enid startles awake and lets out a shriek, jumping to her feet and scanning the chaos around us. Her gaze falls on me and her shoulders sag. Tears shimmer in her eyes. *The hallucination!*

I rush to her side, but Enid is already recovering from the shock of seeing me up and well. Her eyes widen as she takes in the chaos around us.

Enid raises her palm, ready to strike out with her Power if need be. "What happened?"

"The Protectorate has fallen apart," I say.

"Stop!" Enid shrieks, and she throws a gust of wind outward at Bianca even as I grab her wrist and redirect it into Willow.

A gunshot bangs off the walls of the office. Willow's body is thrown across the floor by Enid's wind. Bianca holds a gun in her hands. At this moment in time, all is perfectly still.

"Bianca." I edge closer. "What did you do?"

"She's in charge, right? Without her Influence, this is over." Again, the coldness in Bianca's voice reminds me just how different she is now.

"No." Chase kneels beside Willow, stroking her hair and checking the wound.

Willow works her jaw, but her whole body has started shaking. The bullet grazed her leg as her body was thrust across the room with Enid's Power. Not a fatal shot, but clearly enough to remove her Power.

Chase lurches to his feet and charges at Bianca, but he only makes it one step before Miller rips lighting down into a cage around both Chase and Willow.

Willow clutches her leg, wincing at the pain. "I told you, we...we can't effect change without some nec-necessary losses."

"People aren't expendables," I say.

War had casualties, but they were soldiers who chose to fight, not civilians caught in the crossfire. What Willow did today was unforgivable.

"Bianca." I turn to her.

She holds the gun out to me. "I would do it again."

The words thump against my chest as I cautiously take the gun from her.

48

THE OFFICE BUILDING WHERE ROSIE SET UP A TEMPOrary hospital to help those injured in the fight is crowded with people, but she manages to find a secluded corner in the main lobby where Enid and I can have our injures tended to privately.

True to her intention, Bianca's shot sent Willow into a fit of seizures. She was rushed to this hospital where Doc and Rosie spent the better part of an hour trying to stop the serum from invading her body further. We still haven't heard official word yet, but those she was Influencing had their own wits about them now, so the prognosis isn't good.

Director Shielding died from blood loss and shock from the serum's reaction in his body before we could get him to the hospital. Director Collins nearly died as well, but Rosie was able to revive her at the last moment, though her Power was still removed.

I inspect my hands as if seeing the blood from all those lives on them. Everyone had blamed me. Seaduss. Cass. Terry. Willow. Was it my fault?

"What do you think happened to Cass?" Enid asks me.

I tear my gaze away from my hands. "I don't know. Maybe Terry was delusional."

Enid snorts. "He is certainly that."

No, he isn't. He's lost, like the rest of us.

I hop off the chair and head for the door. "I need air."

Enid frowns and starts to follow, but Rosie calls for her help. Grateful for a moment alone, I step outside the makeshift hospital and around the corner, scanning the destruction. The Administration Building—a formerly majestic capitol, with its front end ripped open like the mouth of a beast. Bodies still litter the courtyard. It will take some time to clear up the mess.

Footsteps shuffle along the sidewalk, and a moment later Doc sinks down onto a concrete ledge nearby with a sigh. He wipes his hands clean with a towel.

"Did you know about her plans to destroy Paragon Tower?" I ask, staring at the courtyard.

Doc hangs his head a moment, then raises his gaze to the horizon. "No. This isn't what I wanted either, Ugene."

"But you must have known it was a possibility." I cross my arms and face him.

Doc's eyes search mine as if looking for the correct answer. "Any time you start a revolution, even a peaceful one, you have to expect the possibility that the end result won't be so peaceful. That's the way of life. Nothing is ever as we suspect."

"Some would disagree," I say, thinking of Celeste. "Even when light breaks through darkness—"

"Darkness fights back." Doc's gaze is firmly fixed on me now. "She *did* find you."

Shock hammers against me. "You know Celeste?"

"An extraordinary young woman. A good thing Dr. Cass never truly understood her gifts." He tilts his head back, gazing at the clouds. "Replicating those gifts under these circumstances would have ensured our defeat swiftly."

"She's watching us right now," I say, wishing I could see the stars.

Doc huffs. "She's always watching." As he shifts his weight to stand, Doc groans, a clear sign of the toll this day has taken on him. Without another word, he heads back inside, leaving me blissfully alone. People shuffle past going to and from the hospital. Some tip their heads to me, but they all leave me in relative peace as I lean against the building and watch the sun slowly set.

"There you are." Mom steps up alongside me.

"Mom?" It's the first time since she pushed me out of her house that I've truly seen her, and it almost feels unreal, like she's an apparition from a previous life. "How did you find me?"

"Mother's intuition," Mom says, then grins. "Your mind was screaming for me."

It was?

I watch as a young man limps toward the hospital, cradling an arm that nearly hangs off his body, half his clothes burned off. But the DMA uniform is still unmistakable even in this condition.

Everything is a mess. Buildings destroyed. Lives lost. Downtown Elpis is a crater in a once stunning city. So much destruction and death. And for what?

"I don't think this is what Dad wanted," I say.

"He would have been proud of you, Ugene," Mom says, pulling me into a hug. The embrace is warm and reassuring. "Just as I am. Your words moved the entire city into action."

"To their doom," I mumble, clinging to her.

"Most of the people in this city will survive this day, and they will have you to thank for their freedom." Mom pulls back but I hesitate to let go. Her hands cup each side of my face. "You gave their fears voice and inspired them. It's exactly what your father would have wanted."

Tears shimmer in my eyes, and I blink furiously to reign them in, pulling away from her tender grasp before I fall apart. The fight is over, but it will take a long time to recover and rebuild.

Mom slides her arm around my shoulders, and we lean against each other, staring at the sunset as it paints brilliant hues of pink, purple, and orange across the sky.

And soon, the stars will come out again.

Part Four

"I'M NOT A HERO. I DIDN'T AIM TO START A revolution. I'm just a Powerless kid who wanted to be like everyone else. To be ordinary. I never asked for any of this, but once I understood what was happening, I couldn't stand by and do nothing. Everyone deserves an equal chance at a good life. Not because of their Power, but because of their character. That is how we rebuild."

~ *Ugene Powers*
One Day After Liberation Day

49

DR. CASS WAS FOUND AMONG THE LIVING, CLINGING to life beneath the remains of Paragon Tower. In her final moments, Hilde created a shield using her Power and her body to protect Dr. Cass. Doc and Rosie tended to Dr. Cass's wounds and locked her in a Power-dampening cell in The Shield where she remains under strict isolation.

I return to The Shield to gather my belongings—and Celeste's book—to move back to my house, and the temptation to speak to Dr. Cass is more than I can resist. Questions remain unanswered.

I pull up a chair outside her cell and gaze inside at the woman within.

She looks as fresh as if she just showered, and her clothes are immaculate despite being extra scrubs kept in the medical bay. Her sharp eyes flick to me.

"Well this is a switch," I say, unable to hold back a grin as I drape my jacket over my lap. Not so long ago, I was locked in a cell while she watched.

"They can't hold me here forever," she says confidently as if she knows something we don't.

But no one else remains in support of her. Forrest lost his Power and sits in his own prison cell downtown, right beside Director Collins. Most of the Paragon research department was at work the day the Tower fell. To our knowledge, Dr. Cass is on her own.

"Only until we know what to do with you."

"Self-importance is a dangerous thing, Ugene." She smirks.

I chuckle. "You would know." She certainly let her own self-importance lead to her downfall. "When I was at Paragon, you told me I would never have Powers. Why didn't you tell me the truth?"

"What truth is that?" She's toying with me.

"I know who I am, and about my mutation. Why did you hold the truth from me? What did you stand to gain by keeping me in the dark?"

She tilts her head, scrutinizing me. "You are a persistent and curious fellow. If I told you the truth, your requests for further research and potential solutions would have been endless. And it would have hindered my own research."

I nod. She's probably right about that.

"You know, I once believed this city needed Powers to survive," I say, leaning back in the chair. "And you had me believing I was both the problem and the cure. But you were wrong on all counts."

"What gifts of ignorance does adolescence bring," Dr. Cass says, rapping her nails on the door. "To truly believe such rubbish is folly."

"The very existence of The Shield proves you wrong," I say, waving a hand around us. "This entire base was built with little to no Powers. It's maintained just the same. The Protectorate may have done some things wrong, but this one thing they certainly did right."

"No, Ugene. This base was built before the Fall. Before the Purge, when the global economy was in full swing. Your friends simply inhabited it."

"True." I nod. "But the clean water and fresh food is all their doing. And they expanded, not just inhabited."

"In time, you will recognize that I was right all along, and you will look to me for guidance. When that day comes, I will simply smile at you and say no."

"Well," I say, smoothing out the wrinkles in my jeans as I rise. "Thanks to us, now that's a choice you have."

50

THE LEATHER HIGH-BACK CHAIR BENDS AROUND ME AS I sit at the desk, folded over my notebooks. Writing my thoughts has always helped, and I need to do justice to the day. Mom polished the desk with her lemon cleaner, and the smell is familiar, like home.

By the end of Liberation Day—as the media coined it—the Directorate was brought down. Doc and Sho organized search-and-rescue teams, and they worked tirelessly for two weeks just seeking survivors. More dead were found than living—a lot of people remained unaccounted for.

Rosie and Dr. Lydia worked together to gather as many healers as they could to help those injured in the chaos. Five buildings downtown were cleared out to act as temporary hospitals—in addition to the clinics around the city. The major hospital in Elpis had been in Paragon Tower, forcing Rosie and Dr. Lydia to creatively seek out and utilize resources. The two of them split the supervision of the locations: Rosie with two and Dr. Lydia with three. Clinicians maintained their own locations all over Elpis.

After Liberation Day, Doc held a press conference to announce the dissolution of the Directorate and the Protectorate and explained everything he knew about what Paragon and the Directorate had done. He also rounded up former Directorate aides—people who worked for sympathizers to the Protectorate's cause—to act as interim officials and help him establish a new government. I attended most of the meetings, offering insight whenever I could. It took weeks to hash out some of the details.

Willow's betrayal stung Doc deeply, and though he never mentioned just how much she hurt him, I could see the pain he tried to hide every time her name came up in conversation. Those under Willow's Influence were absolved and welcomed back into society. Some chose to stay at The Shield, and a few of the citizens chose to move there after learning of its existence. The blast doors that sealed it off from the rest of the world wouldn't be necessary anymore.

Former DMA tents all over the city became Missing Persons stations overnight. People poured in, seeking loved ones who went missing in the chaos. In some cases, people went missing before the fight, people the DMA scooped up under the guise of Proposition 8.5 or 9. Others were people who were known "volunteer" test subjects at Paragon. The list has grown insurmountable, but I review it every day. The current number approaches six thousand.

Forrest was placed under arrest and Rosie treated his wounds, though Willow's bullet had done its job, removing his Power. Mr. Pond visits him regularly. After the first visit, Mr. Pond hugged me—actually hugged me—and thanked me for saving his son. But Bianca is the one who saved him. While Mr. Pond agrees that Forrest needs to pay for what he did to those innocent test subjects and for his part in the entire Purification Project, Mr. Pond was thrilled that both of his children lived. For some reason, he believes I'm the one responsible for their survival when, in fact, the opposite is true.

The day after Liberation Day, Mr. Pond and I sat down in Mom's living room as she hovered in the doorway watching with Enid. The cameras made me uncomfortable, but Mr. Pond insisted that the people wanted to see me, to hear from me, so I agreed to the interview. My words were a simple message. We can never again allow ourselves to undertake such a lapse in humanity or allow the government to strip people of their basic human rights. Mr. Pond asked why I felt we allowed it to happen in the first place and my answer was simple. Fear. It's a powerful motivator. Fear can rob us of our common sense and make us blindly follow our leaders, trusting that they have our best intentions at heart.

One week after Liberation Day, the people voted for an Ambassador to help rebuild the government, someone to act as their voice and in their interest as a new government is established.

Enid moved into the spare bedroom in my parent's house, right across the hall from mine. She didn't have any family or friends, outside of those she'd made at Paragon. Though Mom insisted we have separate rooms, we spent more nights together than apart. The fighting was done, but the nightmares still plagued both of us. Somehow, when we are together, those nightmares diminish.

Bianca moved back in with her parents immediately following the events of Liberation Day, but it didn't take long before she moved out on her own. Her parents tried to set her up with memory therapy to see if she could regain anything Paragon stripped away from her. Bianca didn't like it. She feared it would resurface memories of what they did to her, and she enjoyed being blissfully ignorant of it. She told me she just couldn't live with the expectations her parents placed on her or the disappointment when she couldn't fulfill those expectations. "Maybe some things are best left in the past," she told me. "But right now, I just need to find myself."

I couldn't agree more. Maybe, along the way, she would find some pieces of our past together. I would love to have my old friend back.

Lily returned home, to her parents. Sho spends any second of free time he can find loitering around her place. When I asked Lily if she would like to help us rebuild, she politely declined. "I've seen enough, and I just want to get back the time I lost with my parents," she told me.

Miller and Jayme moved into a loft downtown, not far from the Administration Building where they spent hours each day rebuilding. Jayme's Power has dwindled. Dr. Lydia visited to check up on him after the dust settled, and she informed Miller that Jayme suffers from a rare nutritional deficiency that effects his bones. Using his Power has amplified the illness and the vitamin and mineral infusions she had been giving him no longer have the same effect. If he uses his Power, it will kill him much like it did my dad. And there are hundreds with Power-related illnesses in Elpis—perhaps even thousands. The search for a cure is in full swing, and I'm eager to step in and do my part.

Willow and Chase are awaiting trial tucked away in Power-dampening cells. The work to establish a system that will judge them fairly is still being thought out. At first, I had Willow helping with the Missing Persons reports, talking directly to people torn apart by their fear and grief, but too many of them wanted her head. For her own safety, it was better to hold Willow in a cell and leave her there for the time being.

I once believed there was no justice in this world. Now I know it's my job to ensure that there is.

A knock on the door interrupts my thoughts, and I try to scribble fiercely in the notebook to get everything written before it's gone. The door opens and shoes patter on the tiles a few steps in.

"It's time, Ambassador Powers," Bianca says, a smirk playing at the corner of her mouth.

With a sigh, I skim the page of the notebook, then snap it closed.

51

ENID AND I WALK FROM THE ADMINISTRATION BUILDING
to Tribute Park—the city block formerly occupied by Paragon Tower.
It took the crews months to clear out the rubble and build the
new monument out of the wreckage. Today, on the anniversary of
Liberation Day, Tribute Park officially opens, and half the city has
come to watch the ceremony.

The closer we draw to the steps leading to the massive infinity
symbol, the more my stomach twists into knots. My grip on Enid's
hand tightens.

The infinity symbol, inspired by Celeste's explanation of our lives,
fills the length of the city block and stands tall enough for people
to mingle under and around it. Along all edges, the names of every
person lost in the fight either on Liberation Day or leading up to it
are engraved in the sparkling, twisted metal. I watched with Mom and
Enid as they etched in Dad's name, along with all the friends I lost
along the way—Mo, Trina, Dave, Michael, Noah, Leo. The only name
I omitted was Celeste. Something tells me her name doesn't belong
on the monument. Where the symbol twists, the edges don't meet but
instead pass each other, never touching. And between those twisting
edges, an eternal torch waits to be lit.

Cameras point at the center of the memorial. I'll never get used
to the cameras. Enid nudges me, then kisses my cheek. Shaking, I pull
away and step in front of the cameras.

Miller, Jayme, Sho, Lily, Doc, and Mom all linger at the front of
the crowd. Having them present gives me courage.

Calming my anxious nerves, I take a deep breath, face the cameras, and recall the words I've been struggling with for months.

"A dear friend once told me that time is not linear. There is no beginning, no end, and our lives are a closed loop, connecting us to any point in time. I don't believe this means we don't die, or that we don't feel the loss. The memory of those we've lost always lives on, burning eternally inside of us. We can close our eyes and go back to any moment along that loop to revisit those memories and feel close to each other once more.

"Tribute Park represents that loop, not just to us, but for those who follow us. It serves as a reminder of what happens when we forget our humanity. Let the memory of what happened here burn eternal."

I step forward and my friends join me. Together, we light the eternal torch. As silence falls over Tribute Park, Enid slides her arm around my waist. I do the same and pull her closer to me.

We have lost so much, but we haven't lost each other.

I still find it hard to accept that we are all that remains of humanity. Maybe someday we can expand far enough to discover other pockets of people surviving. And then the world can truly rebuild.

Acknowledgements

I ALWAYS KNEW THAT SOMETHING ABOUT UGENE was special, but I didn't fully understand just what made him unique until I started writing this. It broke my heart to write the final words of this book. I grew so attached to him and all his friends.

Ugene's story began with a "what if" game between my husband, my stepson, and myself. What if there was a boy named Eugene who lived in a world where everyone has a superpower except for him, and the only job he could get was delivering flowers on a bicycle? The actual books have strayed quite a bit from that original "what if," but the ending feels completely appropriate for Ugene's journey.

I owe a huge thanks to my fellow writers of SPWG. Your candid advice helped me shape this into a much better novel. Your willingness to push through this book at a nearly neck break pace to help me publish it on schedule.

To my friends Amanda, Julia, and Melinda, your encouragement and enthusiasm for this project didn't go unnoticed. Special thanks to Amanda, who understood when I had to sacrifice an afternoon or evening out to meet deadlines. A writer cannot succeed without support.

Just like it takes a village to raise a child, it takes a tribe to create a book. I would be lost without my fantastic tribe and the communities of writers who have already walked in my shoes.

Once again, thanks to my editor, Maddy. Your eagerness and guidance gave me the courage to move forward with this project.

Thanks to all of you.

And of course, I am extremely grateful to my loyal readers. Everyone continues to tell me not to include you in my acknowledgements, that you wouldn't care or see it as sincere, but who cares what everyone else says, right? Rebel with me!

Show them they are wrong, and that you are a critical component in this book's success as much as anyone else by leaving a review on [Amazon](), [Goodreads](), [BookBub](), or your blog.

You can even email me. I LOVE hearing from my readers!

Read the Powers Series

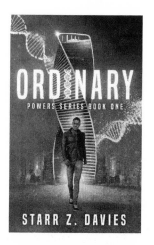

Ordinary (Powers Book 1)

Ugene only wanted a Power. What he got was something far more dangerous.

READING HOW IT ALL BEGAN.

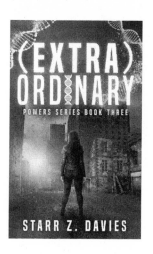

(extra)Ordinary (Powers Book 3)

Paragon wiped her memory. The DMA turned her into a weapon. But when a ghost comes back to haunt her, Bianca must choose ... justice or vengeance?

READ ON FOR AN EXCERPT.

(extra)ORDINARY

1

I OFTEN HAVE THIS REOCCURRING DREAM. I'M ATTACHED to a table with tungsten straps all over my body. A shriek echoes off the stark white walls of the room and rings in my ears. Every time, I wonder the same thing, What moron is making that racket?

And then I realize it's me.

I scream as the metal straps cut into my skin, bending against the force of my struggling body. I scream as the doctors work together holding me still enough to stab a needle in my arm and fire burns through my body. I scream as the straps break free and I rush the tungsten door, buckling it against the frame upon collision. I scream a name I can never hear over the shrill sound of my own voice and I pound bloody fists against the door as it continues to buckle but never breaks. I scream as they shoot me.

And then, I never scream again.

2

THE ROOM IS WHITE FROM THE TILED FLOORS TO THE
seamless ceiling. Along one wall, a bay of mirrors casts my reflection
back at me: a muscular girl in a black tank top and matching pants. I
stand from the metal chair—how did I get here?—and edge toward
the mirrors. The muscles along my shoulders cable down my bare
arms. The coppery eyes that gaze back at me are my own, but they
don't feel familiar. Anxious and confused, I pull my long hair over one
shoulder and begin braiding it loosely.

The room has no door. Only the single metal chair and the wall of
mirrors. Even the lights are recessed into the ceiling so deep I cannot
see where they are as if the ceiling itself glowed with light.

Anxiety presses against my chest and makes my vision swim.
Where am I? How do I get out? I ball my hands into fists at my sides
and watch as the muscles in my arms swell in size. Such power! It
pulses and hums in my muscles, intoxicating in its primal power. I pull
back a fist and slam it into the mirror.

The mirror vibrates and my reflection quakes as the mirror
absorbs the impact, singing a dull song of mourning.

"Do you remember where you are?" a male voice says from the
room around me.

I tilt my head back to gaze at the ceiling—not sure why though,
the voice isn't coming from this room—and turn in a slow circle.

"Do you remember where you are?" he asks again. His voice
carries the same inflection as before as if the question is a recording.

I close my eyes, dig in my mind for memories, but can only grasp flashes. A funeral. Two caskets. Someone beside me with his arm draped over my shoulders. He has the same coppery eyes as me. A squat, long government building with giant fluted columns and a balcony on the top floor. My finger pressed against a tablet.

I open my eyes slowly. "The Department of Military Affairs," I say.

"Why are you here?" he asks.

"To protect the city and the citizens from acts of terror," I say. The words don't register with my mind, but they feel right as they slip past my lips. "So that they don't lose their families to the terrorists like I did."

Silence.

I turn to face the mirror again. Someone must be on the other side. "Why am I here?"

"To protect the citizens of Elpis from terrorists," he says, spouting my answer back at me.

I shake my head. "No, I mean why am I here?" I wave toward the doorless room.

"You volunteered to be here."

Volunteered . . .

Again, the memory of pressing my finger to a tablet surface, but it feels foreign like it isn't my own memory. Despite the odd feel of the memory I do recall volunteering for a special DMA project. Terrorists killed my parents, and I was offered this chance by . . . someone. A man, whose face I cannot quite grasp, extended me the opportunity to join this secret project with the promise that it would help me avenge my parents. It would make me stronger, faster, better.

Anger burns in my chest as I step toward the mirror again, examining the way my deltoid muscles are so defined, the increased size of my biceps. Clenching my fists again, I watch as the cabling of each muscle in my arms becomes more distinct. With this kind of strength, I could punch a fist through the giant fluted columns I recall from outside the Administration Building. I could crush a man's skull with a single blow.

I could exact my revenge on the terrorist who killed my parents.

"I am ready," I say with confidence, and that simmering anger and hate burns in my voice.

Did you enjoy this book?
Don't forget to leave a review on Amazon and
Goodreads! It's like street cred for authors.

About the Author

STARR is a Midwesterner at heart. While pursuing her Creative Writing degree, Starr gained a reputation as the "Character Assassin" because she had a habit of utterly destroying her characters emotionally and physically -- a habit she steadfastly maintains. From a young age, she has been obsessed with superheroes like Batman and Spiderman, which continues to inspire her work.

Follow Starr:
Web: www.starrzdavies.com
Facebook: @SZDavies
Twitter: @SZDavies
Instagram: @S.Z.Davies

Get Dr. Joyce Cass's prequel short story FREE!
Visit: subscribepage.com/starrzdavies_webform